WANTON BEAUTY

"Your Grace, I have indeed done as you requested. I have dressed as befits your duchess and would now take my place at your table." With that, Georgina flung off the Kashmir shawl and dropped into a deep mockery of a curtsy.

For a moment absolute silence reigned. The low-cut gown she had chosen clung indecently to every curve.

Rathbourne's eyes shone with a peculiar gleam. "I am rendered speechless at such breathtaking beauty," he declared with uncommon warmth. He pulled her close to him.

"Y-you do not think the gown too daring, my lord?" queried Georgina. Drat the man! He was not reacting at all as he ought.

"On you it is everything that pleases," he rejoined smoothly.

"It is naturally my desire to—er—please," she stammered and only just managed to stifle an indignant gasp as she felt his touch trickle down the bare expanse of her arm.

"How thoroughly you duped me with that cool facade," he whispered huskily. Her senses reeled as his lips explored her neck.

"Release me, this instant!" she cried, pushing with both hands against his chest.

But it was too late. She had thrown down the gauntlet before the infamous Rathbourne. And he was never one to refuse a challenge . . .

THE BEST OF REGENCY ROMANCES

AN IMPROPER COMPANION (2691, $3.95)
by Karla Hocker
At the closing of Miss Venable's Seminary for Young Ladies school, mistress Kate Elliott welcomed the invitation to be Liza Ashcroft's chaperone for the Season at Bath. Little did she know that Miss Ashcroft's father, the handsome widower Damien Ashcroft would also enter her life. And not as a passive bystander or dutiful dad.

WAGER ON LOVE (2693, $2.95)
by Prudence Martin
Only a rogue like Nicholas Ruxart would choose a bride on the basis of a careless wager. And only a rakehell like Nicholas would then fall in love with his betrothed's grey-eyed sister! The cynical viscount had always thought one blushing miss would suit as well as another, but the unattainable Jane Sommers soon proved him wrong.

LOVE AND FOLLY (2715, $3.95)
by Sheila Simonson
To the dismay of her more sensible twin Margaret, Lady Jean proceeded to fall hopelessly in love with the silver-tongued, seditious poet, Owen Davies—and catapult her entire family into social ruin . . . Margaret was used to gentlemen falling in love with vivacious Jean rather than with her—even the handsome Johnny Dyott whom she secretly adored. And when Jean's foolishness led her into the arms of the notorious Owen Davies, Margaret knew she could count on Dyott to avert scandal. What she didn't know, however was that her sweet sensibility was exerting a charm all its own.

Available wherever paperbacks are sold, or order direct from the Publisher. Send cover price plus 50¢ per copy for mailing and handling to Zebra Books, Dept. 2851, 475 Park Avenue South, New York, N.Y. 10016. Residents of New York, New Jersey and Pennsylvania must include sales tax. DO NOT SEND CASH.

Duel of the Heart

BY SARA BLAYNE

ZEBRA BOOKS
KENSINGTON PUBLISHING CORP.

ZEBRA BOOKS

are published by

Kensington Publishing Corp.
475 Park Avenue South
New York, NY 10016

Second printing: December, 1989.

Printed in the United States of America

For Steven, my favorite romantical hero.
With special thanks to Bobbie Wolf, who has been so helpful in supplying me with technical information concerning equestrian and driving equipment and skills.
And to my sister-in-law Yvette Ann for suggesting I try writing a romance.

Also by Sara Blayne:
Passion's Lady

Chapter 1

"But Grandmama, this is Davey's home. Where else should we live but here?"

Lady Georgina Grey spoke calmly, as was her wont. Her slim hands were gripped lightly in her lap. The lovely face framed in soft curls the color of rich mahogany appeared sublimely tranquil. All in all, there was an arresting quiet about her. Aside from her striking beauty and her unusual height, that was the one thing which most forcefully struck anyone who came into her sphere. Lady Georgina Grey impressed all with an aura of unmovable calm. It made her grandmama, Lady Hortense Bellows, want to scream in exasperation.

"You could come to Exeter with me, Georgina," she said instead, controlling her frustration with tremendous effort. "You cannot remain here alone."

"But I am not alone. I have Nanny and Bolton and the other servants. Davey and I shall rub along well enough."

"Georgina, you are too young to live alone. Propriety alone demands that at the very least you have a female companion of your own station."

"Oh, Grandmama," Lady Georgina said with a hint of amusement in her well-modulated tones, "I am hardly a

9

green girl. After all, I have been married these past six years and widowed nearly one. I have a son six years of age. This is hardly the description of a woman in need of a chaperone."

"But how can you have a proper care for yourself, let alone Davey, when you are quite . . ." Here Lady Hortense faltered and bit her lip in consternation. The usually bright blue eyes dimmed behind a film of moisture.

"Oh, my dear!" she exclaimed, obviously greatly shaken at what she had been about to say. "I trust you will forgive a thoughtless old woman."

"It's all right, Grandmama," Lady Georgina returned, her lovely mouth curving in a rueful smile. "I know I am quite blind, or as near to it as makes no difference." One hand brushed across liquid brown eyes which remained remarkable for their warmth despite their sightlessness. "I can see shadows and lights. And sometimes I can almost make out the outlines of things." She heaved a sigh and dropped her hand to her lap.

"Oh, I know you are anxious for me. But you really mustn't worry. I shall do fine. It has been almost a year since it happened, and I have adjusted quite well."

"But you are so young—only four and twenty—and beautiful. It isn't right that you should be alone. You should marry again," the older lady insisted and dabbed impatiently at the corners of her eyes with a wisp of a lace hanky.

"Marry?" At last the seemingly boundless calm of the young woman was broken. The finely drawn eyebrows rose in startled disbelief. Yet almost immediately she recovered herself. When she spoke again, her rich contralto vibrated with compassion.

"Oh, Grandmama. You must not allow yourself to cling to false hopes. I know you mean well, but you must accept things as they are. As I have had to do. Grandmama, who would have me?"

Lady Hortense stared sadly at her granddaughter. She had detected no bitterness in the softly voiced question. Georgina merely spoke the truth as she saw it. And it was undeniable that there was much against her ever achieving a match. As the Countess of Emberly and the only off-spring of the deceased Viscount Edgecombe, she was possessed of a more than merely comfortable fortune. Financially she would be a fine catch. And there was no denying her beauty. She had been considered a diamond of the first water during the Season of her come-out some seven years before, and while she had lost the elfin slimness of youth, she had acquired the curvaceous slenderness of woman-hood. True, her near fatal illness and subsequent lengthy recuperation had left their marks. A certain haunting sadness seemed to pervade the sweet curve of her full lips. The large brown eyes dominated her face. And this utter calm which had once been a bubbling vivacity gave her an arresting air of maturity. Yes, thought her grandmama, Georgina was even more breathtakingly lovely than she had been as a green girl. Yet the young countess was right.

Who would have a woman with such a blatant deform-ity? The members of the *haut ton*, abhorring any aberra-tion or disfigurement, would either treat her with pity or would cut her altogether out of embarrassment. But they would hardly accept her. And even if by some miracle they did condescend to welcome her into their midst, how was she to go on at the fashionable gatherings where eligible bachelors were to be found? Was one to lead her about by the hand, thus drawing attention to her disability?

The formidable Lady Hortense visibly sagged at such a thought. Never could she wish her proud Georgina to be so humiliated. No. The gel was better off in seclusion at Greystone Manor. Yet it was still a shame that such a lovely creature should be so wasted. And despite her avowal that she should do quite well alone, the gel would need someone to help with Davey and with whom to pass the long, lonely days. Of the dreary nights, her grandmama refused to think. Georgina had loved David Lawrence George Grey, Earl of Emberly. The nights would be long indeed for his lovely young widow.

Lady Hortense eyed the calm young face with growing conviction. Georgina must be made to take a companion, and suddenly she thought she knew exactly the person for such a position.

"Very well, my dear," she said at last. "I shall say no more at present regarding your determination to shut yourself away from the world. No. I know you do not view it as I do. You have not given over grieving for David, nor do you wish to put to the touch your standing with the world. So be it. But you shall not live here alone. Since I cannot stay here with you, I am determined that I shall send someone suitable."

"No, Grandmama. I could not stand some addlebrained spinster with more hair than wit hovering about me. Smothering me with motherly concern, cutting up my peace with well-intentioned chatter. You know I could not. Nor do I wish for some quiet, mouse-like creature cringing at my every change of mood. Nanny is all the companion I need. And Davey."

"I shall keep these strictures in mind, my dear. But you shall have a companion of my choosing or your own. And do you persist in this foolishness, I shall simply be forced to lay the matter before your guardian. You shall not bamboozle him with such a faradiddle as you have handed me. No gel of four and twenty should be without a proper female companion."

Lady Hortense gazed with grim satisfaction at the sudden pallor of her granddaughter's cheeks. A sharp gasp had escaped the slightly parted lips. A look of horrified disbelief swept over the lovely features.

"Grandmama, you could not be so insensible to my feelings as to complain of me to Rathbourne. Hitherto he has been gracious enough to play least seen in our affairs. And though David thought the world of him, I prefer to raise Davey without his interference. No doubt," she added with what could have been a trace of pique, "he would not welcome being reminded of his obligations to the House of Grey. He has not deigned to so much as send his condolences for his cousin's passing. Besides, Grandmama, he is Davey's guardian. Not mine."

"As head of your late husband's family, Georgina dear, he is, in a sense, your guardian, too," Lady Hortense reminded her in a mild voice. "But I have no wish to bother His Grace with such mundane matters as a proper companion for his kinswoman. Merely tender me your word that you will give the female I choose for you a chance to prove her worth. It is not so much to ask an old woman who has shown you nothing but fondness. And it would greatly relieve my mind, child," she ended on a slightly pleading note.

Lady Georgina appeared momentarily nonplussed by the older woman's sly maneuverings. A slight frown marred the purity of her brow, and the lustrous brown eyes appeared thoughtful. Then a quiver of amusement touched the slightly pursed lips, and a gentle gurgle of laughter dispelled the tension which had arisen at mention of the young earl's guardian.

"Oh, you sly old thing," Lady Georgina scolded and shook a finger in the direction of her grandmama. "You know I should be sunk beneath reproach were I to refuse you on those terms. Oh, very well," she added on an exasperated note. "Send me this paragon, and I shall do my best to rub along with her. But should we not suit, dear Grandmama, that will be the end of it. You will accept my decision to remain at Greystone Manor alone. I have *your* word on that, have I not?"

Lady Hortense hesitated only the briefest moment. After all, she had achieved a great deal more than she had

13

anticipated.

"You have my word, Georgina," she replied firmly, then rose stiffly to her feet. "And now I must take my leave of you if I am to reach Plymouth before nightfall."

"Must you go so soon?" the younger woman queried a trifle wistfully. "You know Davey and I would love to have you for an extended visit. If not for a month or more, then another se'ennight at least."

The girl had risen as she spoke and turned to face her grandmother, one hand graciously extended as though in gentle supplication. She strolled unerringly to confront the older lady.

Lady Hortense marvelled at her granddaughter's ease of manner. In slightly less than a month, the girl had already learned her way around much of the sprawling house. And not only had she learned the names and personalities of the army of servants employed at Greystone, but she displayed an uncanny ability to identify them before they even spoke. Furthermore, she had taken into her capable hands the running of the young earl's estate and appeared to have won the admiration and loyalty of her manager, Mr. Connings, who had been with the old earl when Lord David Grey was a boy. In fact, it did seem that Georgina had adjusted very well to her new life, but Lady Hortense was not fooled by her granddaughter's courageous front. She had seen the haunting sadness in the lovely eyes when the gel had thought herself unobserved—standing in the garden alone, her face turned toward the sound of her young son's laughter coming from the lawns beyond the hedge—or had felt it in the evenings when sleep eluded the young countess so that she stole to the music room to play the pianoforte through the dark, lonely hours, the wistful notes drifting softly through the empty halls like the echoes of fond memories.

Oh, yes. Georgina had the courage and stubborn independence of a man, but she was still a woman, and a

14

woman who had loved passionately. She did not like to see so vibrant a soul atrophy into a recluse who lived only through and for her son. For despite her avowal that she should rub on well enough alone, Georgina never ventured further from the manor than the gardens or the brook which ran through the down along the bottom of the hill on which the house stood. Oh, she always had an excuse for not driving to the village or to the homes of the gentry in the county who had extended invitations. And she was ever the gracious hostess when anyone came to call, though few had done as of yet. No. In spite of everything—the calm exterior, the effortless way in which she had learned to move through her shadowed darkness—Georgina Grey was afraid. And that was very unlike the headstrong young woman who had left the safety and luxury of her girlhood to follow the drum. Something had occurred to change her, something which might account for the blindness which no doctor had ever been able satisfactorily to explain. But that something was lost in the darkness of the girl's mind. Lady Georgina Grey remembered nothing of the events leading up to her illness.

Lady Hortense, feeling suddenly very old, stifled a heavy sigh.

"No, no, my child," she said with a forced lightness and took the girl's proffered hand warmly in her own. "You cannot want a meddling old woman constantly beneath your feet. And I have matters to see to at home. I shall return in due time. Exeter is not so very far away, after all."

"No. Not so far," Georgina replied a little wistfully. "We shall look forward to having you with us often, Grandmama."

"No need to see me out, my dear," Lady Hortense added airily. "I do so hate good-byes."

Then she delivered a fond buss on her granddaughter's cheek and left the room with a firm step despite her three and sixty years.

Lady Georgina, feeling suddenly bereft, was left listening to her grandmother's retreating footsteps. When first she had arrived at the seat of the Earl of Emberly only a month earlier, there had been too much to occupy her to leave her time for much reflection on the course she had chosen. Nor had she been lonely. For the first time since she had awakened in Lisbon to discover herself widowed and blind, the sharp edge of grief had dulled to a persistent but bearable ache. Indeed, upon arriving at Greystone Manor, she had experienced a feeling of having come home at last.

It was exceedingly odd, she reflected, standing in the Blue Saloon, the peacock blue striped wall-hangings and pale blue caffoy-covered chairs and sofas but vague shadows around her. She had never been to Greystone Manor while her husband was alive. After her marriage to Major Lord David Grey, she had left England for India and then eventually for Portugal to follow her husband and the drum. And later, when the earl, David's father, had followed his son in death but a short month after Lord Grey fell at Talavera, she had not been well enough to return to England and Greystone. Yet that sublime feeling of having come home had still enveloped her as she stepped from the coach before the manor.

With a soft rustle of skirts she turned and crossed the room toward the source of sunlight slanting in through French doors. With only a slight fumbling, she found the latch and, releasing it, swung the doors open. Breathing in the cool sweetness of the morning breeze laden with the scent of honeysuckle, she stepped out onto the flagstones of the verandah and leaned against one of the cool stone pillars which supported the overhanging roof.

It was the scent of honeysuckle and freshly cut grass which had first greeted her arrival. She had listened to the clack of pruning shears among the hedges bordering the drive and to the muted murmurings of voices and guessed hurried refurbishing of the grounds was in full progress to welcome the new master. She smiled, remembering thinking how little the six-year-old Earl of Emberly would be impressed by such diligence. But she had been relieved by the evidence of his welcome among the retainers of Greystone. And, indeed, they had been welcomed royally.

The servants had lined the drive, with Bolton, the very proper but kindly natured butler stepping forward to hand them down and politely greet them. Lady Georgina had returned the appropriate phrases, then stood uncertainly in the gravel drive. It had been with a tremendous feeling of relief that she had felt her hand tucked neatly beneath the butler's arm to be led down the line of bobbing and curtsying servants. As she was introduced to each in turn, she had fought a sudden feeling of panic at the sheer number of retainers she would have at her command. How could she possibly learn them all and win their respect?

Yet Bolton had proven a veritable mainstay, as had Mrs. Porter, the housekeeper. They had been a happy household under the previous earl, a good lord who had cared for his estates and treated his dependents with justice and benevolence. And he had in return been served with loyalty and even affection. Lady Georgina and the young earl had fallen heir to their sustaining loyalty, and the entire staff had all taken to the bright-eyed boy and his gentle mother from the very first.

It had not been without its ups and downs, however, recalled the young countess, smiling a little to herself. With quiet but firm insistence, she had had repeatedly to send the hovering servants about their duties whenever she emerged from her chambers. Gradually they had come to accept that beneath the gentle, even fragile-appearing, exterior, there thrived an iron will and a fiercely independent spirit. The mistress would not be treated like a failing invalid or a fragile piece of porcelain.

Nevertheless, undetected, they watched her daily struggle to memorize the number of steps from her door to the

17

stairs, the number of stairs to the diningroom, the distance between table and chair and sofa, the doors which led to the various saloons and family rooms, the ballroom, the withdrawing room, and even the kitchens belowstairs.

She was unfailingly kind and infinitely patient with all those around her. And never once did they guess at the fear and uncertainty which lay beneath the surface. Had it not been for Davey and his need for a healthy, normal mother, she would long since have given in to despair.

As it was, their lives had gradually assumed a smooth pattern, and Georgina was far from feeling discontented with her lot. She was able, even, to conceive of once again enjoying a quiet happiness. Not the exhilaration of her former life with her beloved David perhaps, but not the aching emptiness of life without him, such as she had known until coming to Greystone Manor. It was as if he were somehow with her still in the sprawling house which had watched him grow to manhood.

"Oh, David," she whispered to the gentle breeze. "I *can* bear it. I must." Then, angry because she had allowed herself to fall perilously close to the doldrums, she deliberately turned her thoughts away from David to a wry consideration of her grandmother's most recent meddling.

The sly old puss had certainly slipped one in on her, she acknowledged with an amused quirk of her lips. She had been totally unprepared for so calculated a stratagem as to be threatened with Rathbourne's intervention in her affairs. Nor could she explain even to herself why the mere mention of his name should cause her heart to lurch with a sudden flutter of fear. She had never even met the man, though he had been David's cousin and most trusted friend. Yet it had ever been so since those long, lost days in Portugal when she had nearly succumbed to despair. It had taken all her courage to dictate the brief letter informing him of David's death, and in it she had mentioned nothing of her own illness or future plans beyond assuring him that

18

the young heir was safe and well. And it was just as well, for he had shown not the slightest inclination to concern himself in his ward's affairs beyond a brief acknowledgement that her letter had been received, and that had come from his secretary.

As for the duke himself, she knew little about him beyond the fact that he had been David's cousin, for Rathbourne's father and David's mother had been brother and sister. The elder by four or five years, Andrew Penwarren had assumed the status of surrogate elder brother and admired hero to the younger cousin, who was the only child of the Earl of Emberly. Rathbourne, the Penwarren's family estate, bordered the entailed lands which constituted the major holdings of the Earl of Emberly, and the two boys had been inseparable companions while growing to manhood.

David had spoken in glowing terms of the darkly handsome and impetuous youth. Apparently Andrew Penwarren had been possessed of a wild, unruly nature which led him into coil after coil, the loyal David eagerly following his elder cousin's lead. Georgina had envisioned a thoughtless, arrogant youth where David had seen only a daring adventuresome hero. No doubt much of the young duke's reckless disregard for the proud name he bore could be attributed to the fact that he had inherited the title at the tender age of fourteen, she thought, trying to be just. With neither a father nor a mother to guide him and possessed of enormous power and wealth, there had been no one to curb his propensity for self-indulgence. Yet even though she might understand the cause of the dissipations for which he was known on two continents, she could not like having him as guardian to her son. Davey would not be allowed to grow to manhood spoiled and indifferent to the responsibilities of his name and noble rank. Not as long as she had anything to say about it. And yet her own beloved David had chosen the arrogant duke to see to the welfare of his only son and

19

heir. Could she be wrong about Rathbourne? she wondered, not for the first time.

She had perhaps been predisposed to dislike the duke, Georgina admitted honestly to herself, for he had nearly caused an estrangement between her beloved and his father over several wild escapades among the Corinthian set of wild bloods to which the duke had belonged. Georgina did not like to think of her David gambling heedlessly at various gaming halls or racing his curricle neck for nothing across England. Such exploits as assuming the garb of a common coachman to drive a mail coach recklessly over the public thoroughfares or wagering exorbitant sums on the number of lords to be found on a certain evening in a particularly notorious bordello had finally caused the old earl to purchase a set of colors for his son and heir. This latter escapade had led to a duel with swords between an outraged marquess of dubious reputation and the hot-blooded young duke. Rathbourne had killed his man and had been forced to flee the country till the scandal should blow over.

Neither Georgina nor the rest of London had ever learned where Rathbourne had gone or what he did after that. He had not been in town during her come-out. Neither had he attended her wedding, though David had tried every avenue open to him to discover his cousin's whereabouts. The duke had not even acknowledged his guardianship over David's son after Talavera. She consequently thought him sadly remiss in his familial duties, which did not surprise her overmuch, for she knew him to be by reputation a hardened rakeshame.

"Oh, David," she murmured sadly. "How could you have been so mistaken in judgment? Why could you not see what he is?" And yet perhaps it was better that he had never known. Certainly she had never been able to convince him that Rathbourne was anything but the gallant hero he imagined him to be.

"I had not thought my hoydenish Georgina to be miss-ish," he had teased at her protest to his cousin's guardianship over Davey. But as he chucked her playfully under the chin and charmed her with his sweet smile, he had become suddenly quite serious. "You must not heed gossip, my darling Georgina. There's no better man in all of England than Drew, despite what the ignorant or the envious might say of him. When we are home again, the two of you will meet—my dearest, most lovely Georgina and the man whom, next to my father, I love best. 'Tis a moment I've long cherished. Then you will learn to love him as I do. There's not another to whom I should so willingly entrust my son's welfare or my beautiful Georgina. Trust me in this, my love. As you have trusted me in everything else."

"I want to, my darling," Georgina whispered brokenly. "But in this I must go my own way. Davey's future is too precious, and I cannot be weak. Not now. Not ever. I am all he has now."

The Duke of Rathbourne limped from his carriage, and, leaning heavily on his ebony stick, climbed the steps to Rathbourne House. A forbidding scowl darkened the unnaturally pale visage, denoting his black mood. A state of mind which was all too often upon His Grace of late, mused Hampstead, the duke's very proper London butler, as he opened the door to his employer.

With his habitually circumspect words of greeting, which the duke acknowledged with a deepening of his frown and a curt nod, Hampstead helped His Grace out of the many-caped greatcoat, saved the curly brimmed beaver from a precipitous fall to the parquetry tiled floor, and accepted the impatiently offered York tan kid gloves. He barely suppressed the sigh which rose to his lips as he watched the duke's broad back retreat across the spacious entry hall and up the wide, curved staircase, finally to disappear into the hallowed confines of his study. The butler winced as the door was firmly slammed shut. Moments later, he was balancing a laden silver grog tray on one hand as he stoically braved his master's presence.

The duke was sprawled in a heavy leather arm chair, his long legs immaculately clad in buff unmentionables and shining Hussars outstretched before him. The slender fingers of one hand monotonously drummed the arm rest. The high brow was furrowed in deep and apparently unpleasant thought. Hampstead was careful to keep his glance from resting on the livid scar which seemed to throb over the prominent cheekbone on the left side of the duke's face.

"I'll serve myself, Hampstead," Rathbourne said curtly without looking up. "Thank you."

"Your Grace," the butler intoned as he set the tray on a low table near the duke's side. Almost he asked if His Grace would be dining in this evening, then thought better of it as he hazarded a single glance at the firm jaw rigidly set, the muscle leaping along the jawline. 'Twas obvious the leg was paining him again. And no wonder, the way he kept driving himself. From the looks of it he had intentions of dipping rather deep—in which case he would not be thinking of Philippe's famous mushrooms stuffed with crab, his asparagus served *avec beurre noir*, or his *coquilles Saint-Jacques* which had made the French chef a much coveted prize among the fashionable elite. A pity really. Not only was the duke in very real danger of losing Philippe, but he was like to find himself flat on his back again did he not begin to have a proper care for himself. There was no dealing with His Grace, however, when the black mood was upon him. Hampstead spared his brooding master a covert look of pity, then quietly left the room, closing the door softly behind him.

Rathbourne sat a moment longer, reluctant to drag his weary body from the chair. He cursed himself for the pride which would allow no one to guess with what effort he disguised the pain of moving about on the injured leg. He should be grateful he could walk at all or that he even had two legs. He owed that miracle to a slip of a girl with a rare courage few men possessed.

"Damn her!" he ground out between gritted teeth and heaved himself from the chair. The sharp stab of pain made him stagger, and he cursed again. Gathering the decanter of brandy and a glass from the tray, he limped across the room and sank heavily into a seat behind an oversized oak desk. Impatiently he drew the stopper from the decanter and sloshed brandy into the glass. Tipping his head back, he tossed down the drink and leaned back in the chair, his eyes closed, as the fiery spirits explored his empty stomach.

With a sigh he poured a second glass, then stared broodingly at a slim packet of papers on the desk. After more than six months it was still all the information he had been able to gather about a tall, slender girl with hair the color of rich mahogany and brown eyes which had radiated warmth and compassion.

"Damn!" he said again and slammed his hand down on the desktop, nearly upsetting his drink.

How many females fitting her description could there have been nursing wounded soldiers in the hastily set up hospitals at Talavera? How many ladies of quality of any description? It was not the accepted thing for women of any station to nurse sick and wounded men, yet there had she been, a lovely creature whose quiet courage and strength had inspired hope. Despite the horrors of mutilated bodies and the endless hours of tending to the wounded, she had carried on with a quiet assurance which was balm to the suffering men. She was their "angel," and she was the phantom who haunted his dreams and tormented his every waking moment.

No matter how hard he tried, he could not banish her from his mind. In the darkness of the endless nights as the nagging pain kept sleep at bay, he saw her bending over him, the lovely contours of her face expressive of an enduring calm—and something more. A haunting sadness which never quite left her though her sweet lips might curve with that gentle, understanding humor which soothed his fears and made light of her own patent weariness. Nor could he forget the manner in which she had stood over him like an avenging fury as the much beleaguered doctors had insisted his leg must come off.

By God, she had been magnificent! Her usual composure quite vanished, her beautiful eyes flashing sparks of outraged passion, she had defied them.

"I am well aware that gangrene is a danger in such wounds," she had said, her voice vibrant with determination. "But I have seen no signs of corruption. You *cannot* amputate his leg simply because it is expedient! I shall tend his fever and his wounds. There is still time before such irrevocable measures need be taken."

Unbelievably, she had prevailed in her determination to keep the butchers from him. Somehow she had had him moved from the crude hospitals crowded with wounded to a small abandoned house. There she had stayed with him, sponging his face and body with tepid water to bring the fever down, changing the dressings on his wounded leg and face, tending to his intimate needs with a calm poise which had banished embarrassment or discomfiture. And when the army had been forced by the weakness of their numbers to withdraw, his fierce protectress had again proven indomitable. How she had managed to procure an aged horse and cart he would never know. Yet somehow she had, and they had made the retreat to Doughboy Hill, Campo Mayor, and finally to Elvas and the Convent of St. Paul.

He remembered little of the pain-wracked journey, for he had been lost in a tormented world of pain and delirium. He recalled the incessant jolting of the cart, the feel of a cool hand on his fevered brow, the sound of a low voice singing in Portuguese to the accompaniment of a guitar.

And her lovely face and sad voice as she told him about her handsome young lord for whom she had dared the perils of the battlefield hoping to find him alive.

Who was she? he wondered, as he had never ceased to wonder since first he had seen her in the hospital at Talavera. "I am Gina," she had said, "and I am your friend. I can tell you nothing more, m'lord. And when you are safe at last, 'twere better if you forgot me. It will serve neither of us if you were to learn who I am."

How long he lay at Elvas, he could not guess. At last the fever had broken and he had awakened to find his angel gone and Robbie bent over him, a crooked grin breaking across the anxious planes of his youthful face. But Robbie had known nothing of the girl except for a message which had found him searching the wounded for his brother.

Rathbourne leaned forward to pluck a creased and worn sheet of paper from the packet on the desk. The note was scrawled in a hurried hand and gave directions to the rooms where the duke had lain. Nothing more. Not even a signature. Good God, what had happened to her? he agonized, running a hand in a gesture of despair through his thick black hair touched with silver at the temples.

Elvas had been a nightmare. Nearly ten thousand men had been afflicted with Guadiana fever, and Rathbourne was plagued with fear for his angel. The dangers facing a young, unprotected female were staggering. Did she not succumb to the fever, she faced the depredations of the rough and uncouth soldiers and derelicts who roamed the streets of the town. Robbie had discovered no trace of her. Had her husband found her and carried her off to safety? He hoped so with all his being, yet a curious dream haunted him. The arrival of a courier, an urgent message, a cry of despair. Had they been figments of his delirium? Somehow he could not bring himself to believe they were.

He had not wanted to leave without her. She would come back, he insisted in a daze of pain. But Robbie had easily subdued him in his weakened state, and, dosed with laudanum throughout the torturous journey home to England, he had known nothing.

"Curse Robbie!" he muttered and leaned his forehead wearily against his arms folded on the desktop. Nearly five months wasted while he lay a prisoner in his bed, fighting the poison in his leg and the doctors who contemplated taking it off. Yet he had healed and finally left his sickroom to go in search of the girl who haunted his dreams, only to discover a cold trail and a doctor who remembered her but had never known her name.

The unexpected rap on the door brought his head up with a jerk.

"Go away!" he bellowed and reached for the forgotten brandy.

Hardly had he lifted the glass to his lips than the door was thrust open to reveal a tall, slender youth of about two and twenty years. Dark hair curled about his head in artful disarray. Blue eyes of a lighter hue than the duke's soberly studied the lean figure slumped in the chair. At last, ignoring the dark scowl with which he was greeted, the young man crossed to the desk to stand staring down at the older man, a slight frown creasing his youthful brow.

"Egad, Drew! You look terrible," he said baldly after a moment and dropped into a scroll-backed leather chair before the desk. "If you're trying to kill yourself, you're doing a bang-up job of it."

"Go away, Robbie," repeated the duke, then deliberately drained his glass. "I fear I am not fit company this evening." One slender hand reached for the decanter.

"Devil a bit," Robbie rejoined with a wry, quirk of his handsome lips and watched the brandy slosh against the sides of the crystal wine glass. "Oh, well," he added with a meaningful sigh. "I had news which I thought might be of some interest to you. But I suppose it can wait until later."

The young man rose easily from his chair and sauntered

towards the door.

"Robbie," came the duke's voice, ominously quiet.

The youth halted, a hand on the latch, and languidly turned, one eyebrow arched in innocent query.

"Do you value your quarterly allowance, you will cease to bedevil me with boyish pranks. Relate your news and pray it is worth your intrusion upon my present mood."

The young man seemed to consider for a moment before replying in a manner calculated to test his brother's uncertain temper.

"What I have to tell you can wait until after we have dined," he suggested blithely. "When was the last time you partook of anything more substantial than your admittedly excellent brandy? You look devilish sharp set, old man."

"You are sadly mistaken do you think to dictate to me, brat," the duke drawled repressively. "I cut my wisdoms when you were hardly out of leading strings, and I fail to see that my dining habits should be any of your concern."

"Oh, I am clearly motivated by self-interest," rejoined the youth gravely, though a gleam of mischief flickered in his blue eyes. "I have not the least desire to succeed to the title. And should you meet with an untimely demise—before your nursery has been set in order as it were—I should find myself in a devilish uncomfortable position."

Robbie Penwarren held his breath as his brother's aristocratic eyebrow shot upward. Then the duke's reluctant bark of laughter assailed his ears, and slowly the youth relaxed, his peculiarly sweet smile relieving the tension in his face.

"That's more like," he said cheerily and crossed the room to plop down in the chair once more, one long leg draped negligently over the arm.

Rathbourne rolled the brandy glass slowly between the palms of his hands as his glance rested speculatively on his brother's youthful countenance.

"You show a foolish disregard for your own well-being when you beard the lion in his den," he observed acerbically. "It is very likely your own early demise which you should take care to avert, bantling. I shall not be averse to throttling you should you persist in trying to meddle in my affairs."

Robbie Penwarren seemed not at all put out by his brother's dire threat to put a period to his existence. He settled himself more comfortably in his chair as if prepared for a lengthy visit.

"I suppose I shall simply have to risk it, old boy, since I do not intend leaving until you have fed me. I've spent the entire day in your service, with the result that I have missed both luncheon and tea. Perhaps you can exist on a liquid diet, but sadly I cannot. I am like to perish with hunger."

"Then by all means withdraw to the diningroom," responded the duke, a look of boredom settling over his handsome features. "I should find it most irksome did you suddenly succumb to a fainting spell from lack of sustenance. Do not, I pray, allow me to detain you further."

But the youth was not to be so easily outmaneuvered as he airily waved aside the duke's suggestion.

"You are in a devilish temper, I must say. Hampstead warned me, but I was sure you'd be glad to see me. Well, there's nothing for it but what you must put up with me now. You know I have never liked to dine alone. Devilish hard on the digestion, you know. No. I've taken the liberty of ordering a cold collation to be sent up. No doubt Hampstead shall be along with it directly. Excellent man, Hampstead."

"I am gratified to find you approve of my servants," Rathbourne said ironically. "No doubt Hampstead may depend upon your reference when I find it necessary to terminate his employment for disregarding my orders that I should not be disturbed."

The youth grinned at the masterful set-down, but refrained from rising to the bait. From beneath drooping eyelids he watched the duke withdraw once more into somber thought, the deep furrow returning again to the noble brow as he appeared to forget his brother's presence. Penwarren, observing the duke's tousled black hair usually fashionably arranged in the wind-swept look and the abnormally pallid visage just now tinged with grey, sighed quietly and shook his head. Rathbourne was obviously well to live, which was not an uncommon state for the duke of late.

The blue eyes softened with compassion as he studied the hard planes of his brother's face. There were some who said there was not a handsomer man in all of Britain, and despite the jagged scar, which in truth only added to the brooding mystique of the man, he was uncommonly blessed in appearance. Dark eyebrows arched arrogantly in a high, intelligent brow. High cheekbones made more prominent by his unwonted thinness, the result of the fearful battle against infection and later of the overpowering obsession which relentlessly drove him, gave Rathbourne an almost aesthetic cast which was further abetted by the long, thin nose, finely molded. The firm, sensuous lips were most often held in a controlled, stern line or allowed to curl slightly in a faint, sardonic smile. But it was the heavy-lidded eyes which dominated the face, the youth reflected wryly. Of a startlingly deep blue, they could chill the most insensitive boor with an icy intensity or dazzle the most elusive of women with their compelling magnetism.

How worn he appeared! Penwarren thought. The undeniable strength of an iron will had not lessened with the sufferings of the past year. Rather had it burned him to the socket. The shoulders were yet broad, and the muscles rippled beneath the fabric of his fashionably snug-fitting blue coat of Bath superfine. Yet the long frame was devoid of any surplus of flesh. The blue eyes were set in shadowed hollows edged with fine lines of pain and fatigue which had not been there a year earlier. Good God! He would drive himself into a relapse if he did not soon have a care for himself, thought Robbie, perilously close to despair.

A feeling of impotence touched the young man. He knew his brother's obstinate nature all too well. Rathbourne would never be persuaded to give up the search for his angel of mercy. Not till he had found the woman or ruined his health in the trying. It was the same intensity of purpose and fearless disregard for self which had made him invaluable to Wellington. And, indeed, Rathbourne had seemed to welcome danger as an outlet for a restless nature easily given over to ennui. For as long as Robbie could remember, his brother had seemed driven by something inside himself, and only one man had ever been able to exert any influence over him when he seemed determined on a course of self-destruction. But David Grey was dead, and now only Robbie Penwarren stood between the duke and his own volatile nature.

Mentally the young man shrugged. He could only hope the news he had to impart would alleviate his brother's black mood. He was determined at any rate to lure the duke away from London to Rathbourne Castle in the northeast of Cornwall. The duke had ever loved his ancestral home, and, indeed, the rugged cliffs overlooking the swelling sea had seemed in Rathbourne's youth well-suited to his stormy nature. Moreoever, once removed from the social sphere in which the duke had moved of late, the gaming hells and bagnios in which he sought surcease to whatever plagued his sleepless nights, he might begin to heal again, both in body and spirit.

The quiet rap at the door and the subsequent entrance of Hampstead with a cold collation of thinly sliced beef, roasted pigeon, lobster patties, fresh strawberries in thick cream, and squares of tangy cheese returned the youth's thoughts to his empty stomach.

Taking advantage of Rathbourne's abstracted air, he piled a plate high and placed it before his brother on the desk. Surreptitiously he removed the brandy decanter from the duke's reach and replaced it with a tankard of ale. This beverage had usually a salubrious effect on His Grace when he had been dipping rather deeply. Then, drawing in a deep breath, he leaped into the breach.

"Ah, but this is excellent," he said as he helped himself to a liberal portion of the repast. "You might as well set to. You look as if you haven't eaten anything solid in a week or more."

Rathbourne, made suddenly aware of his brother's persistent presence as well as his kindly intentions, glanced up sharply. Inwardly Robbie grimaced. The duke's grim smile was not the least bit reassuring.

"This new start of yours to play nursemaid ill becomes you, bantling," he remarked softly. "Allow me to determine my own life, an' you please. You shall begin by returning my brandy to me."

Robbie cocked an inquisitive brow at the older man. He was not fooled by the heavy-lidded look of ennui which masked the duke's countenance. He was in a dangerous mood, was the duke. But Robbie had played this game before and knew the bond of affection which lay between them was strong. He was determined to put it to the touch just this once.

"The way you're going, you have need of more than a nursemaid. A keeper would be more like," he scoffed. "Look at yourself! The Duke of Rathbourne wallowing in self-pity. I never thought to see you sink so low. Good God, Drew! Have you forgotten who and what you are? You're a Penwarren and a duke. Are you so lost to a sense of your own responsibilities that you would disregard those who depend on you, going even so far as to ruin your health? And for what? The lady is married. Do you plan to make her your paramour? Hardly an honorable way to repay your debt to her."

"Enough!" ground out the duke between clenched teeth. Involuntarily Robbie winced beneath the piercing flash of cold eyes. "You go too far. The lady saved my life. I'll thank you not to bandy her name about."

"Her name? You don't even know her name. Like as not she had reasons for remaining incognito. What makes you think she would welcome having her identity made known?"

It was a telling argument, one which the duke had considered often before. Damn the bantling! How could he explain to Robbie the compulsion which drove him near mad to find the girl, when he did not understand it himself?

In sudden rage over his own impotence the duke slammed one hand against the desktop and lurched to his feet. The pain in his thigh was merciless. He staggered and would have fallen but for Robbie's strong hand steadying him.

An anguished look swept across the youth's handsome face at sight of the turmoil in his brother's eyes.

"Drew," he said hoarsely. "For God's sake have a care for yourself." Then with a heavy sigh of defeat, he continued in an even voice. "I cannot understand what drives you, but I shall stand by you. I may have news of the lady."

"Speak on, Robbie," the duke said in a dangerously soft voice. "I am in no mood for a game of wits."

No, Penwarren thought somberly to himself, but how much darker shall be your mood if I am wrong in all this. Reluctantly he imparted his most recent findings to the duke.

"A lady bearing her description stayed for some time with Lady Fitzhugh in Lisbon. She was convalescing from some sort of illness. Upon recovering, she set sail for England. She and a small boy landed at Plymouth and took coach for an unknown destination in Cornwall."

"And her name?" interposed the duke in a taut voice. The youth could not meet his brother's glittering glance.

"I don't know," he answered and in frustration ran a

hand through his hair. "My source of information was an underfootman to Lady Fitzhugh's daughter. But the daughter has returned with her family to her husband's estate in Ireland. And Fitzhugh and his wife have sailed for India where he will assume an ambassadorial post."

"Then we have only to write the daughter in Ireland," observed the duke, his pale brow knit in thought as he limped around the desk to confront an uneasy Robbie Penwarren. Egad, the youth groaned inwardly. The fat was in the fire for certain now. And what if in the end it proved only another false lead?

"Yes," he admitted reluctantly. "Lady Ann Mallory. But an answer will not be forthcoming for weeks. Meantime, there is little we can do here." Suddenly he reached out to grasp his brother's arm. "Drew, come with me to Rathbourne. Wait there for word. Should the elusive lady be in Cornwall, you will already be on hand to search her out."

Rathbourne eyed the earnest young face thoughtfully, the aloof mask of the Corinthian descending over his own features so that Robbie could not read what he was thinking.

"At least consider it," he urged, fearing he had failed utterly to sway his brother.

"Perhaps," murmured the duke. Then, when he could no longer bear the pleading in his brother's eyes, he quietly added, "The plan has some merit." He let his voice trail off, and, feeling suddenly very weary, turned away from the youth.

His brother's obvious concern oddly touched him, and suddenly he was reminded of the boy's unflagging devotion as Robbie nursed him through the endless weeks of his illness and afterwards remained faithfully with him during his long recuperation. An unwonted feeling of shame for his own boorishness swept over him, and he was suddenly brought to a realization that he had indeed indulged his dark obsession with the past to the exclusion of all else. Robbie was right to remind him of his responsibilities. He had not visited his several estates since returning from Portugal. They would need his attention. And there was that other matter which his harassed secretary had only recently laid before him. Yes. He could attend to that matter as well while in Cornwall.

"Very well," he said at last, placing an arm across his brother's shoulders. And suddenly the smile which had the power to charm the hardest of hearts softened the austere planes of his face. "You win, bantling. We shall depart for Rathbourne on the morrow. Meantime, I suddenly find I am devilishly sharp set. And since I should not like to lose the very admirable Philippe, I suggest we must not send back this collation untouched."

Chapter 2

Lady Bellows, upon arriving in Exeter, entered her brick home in Bedford Circus with a billowing of her full skirts. Her portly figure draped in lavender sateen commanded immediate respect from the aged retainer who greeted her at the door with stolid dignity.

"Cheswick," she said to the butler as she swept by, "inform Cook I shall require only a tray sent up to my room. I am fatigued from my journey and desire a quiet repose. You will be pleased to say I am not at home to callers."

"Very well, m'lady," the butler intoned, bending staidly at the waist. "And may I say how glad we are to have you home again."

"Thank you, Cheswick," she replied as she passed through the receiving hall and headed directly for the stairs. "You can have no notion of how glad I am to have arrived at last. I fear I am far too old to be knocking about the countryside. But what else can one do when the young are in need of assistance? Oh, and, Cheswick," the lady added as she paused beside a cherry wood table upon which sat a silver tray laden with her unopened correspondence. "You will please inform Lady Grantham that I am returned and would speak with her at her convenience. I trust all is well with her?"

"Lady Grantham would appear to enjoy her usual state of health, m'lady," Cheswick returned noncommittally. He had served her ladyship with steadfast devotion for over forty years and had come to know exceedingly well every quirk of her forceful character, chief of which were a very generous heart and a propensity for taking it upon herself to solve the troubles of others in her own inimitable way. Indeed, those who did not know her as he did were wont to say she was a meddling old harridan, but Cheswick knew better. The mistress was as wise as she was good, and the latest object of her charitable manipulations was the proof of the pudding. For the poor wee lass had come to them in desperate need and had been readily granted a safe haven in which to recover her strength. She were better now, but hardly the vibrant, enchanting child she once had been. Ah, 'twere a sad thing, it were, he thought, though none of his inner musings showed through the façade of the proper English butler.

Nevertheless, Lady Hortense glanced up to scrutinze Cheswick with a shrewd glance.

"I see," she said, her voice suddenly grave. "Then nothing has changed." She sighed, a thoughtful frown puckering her brow, and proceeded to climb the stairs somewhat laboriously.

She was spry for one of her mature years and was outspokenly impatient with those matrons of her own generation who pampered themselves and retired ignominiously to their sofas or beds to await the inevitable culmination of advanced age. Yet her joints had begun to stiffen in recent years and she was dubiously aware that her three-day trek from the northeast of Cornwall to Exeter in Devon, though conducted in easy stages, had taken its toll on her. She entered her bedchamber with a weary sigh and was more than a little grateful to give herself over to the ministrations of her abigail. In due time she was comfortably ensconced in her bed, her iron grey hair which showed a lamentable tendency to grow unbecomingly thin tucked beneath a lace nightcap. Across her ample lap was perched a bed-tray which held her frugal repast of broth, tea, and toast.

Lady Hortense ate without relish the bland diet prescribed to her by her physician, to whom she was wont to refer as a quacksalver more interested in the condition of her pocketbook than in the state of her health, then turned to the pile of correspondence which had accumulated during the past se'ennight spent with her granddaughter. One letter in particular drew her frowning attention. The heavy scrawl denoted a bold, masculine hand. The all-too-familiar crest of the Earl of Vail elicited a short exclamation from the elderly dame. She hesitated only a fraction of a moment before breaking the seal and, with less than her usual good humor, perused the brief missive.

"The gall of the man!" she muttered as she came to the end of the message and resisted the temptation to crumple the paper and fling it from her in a fine fit of rage. Nobie had a right to know to what new lengths the insufferable earl was willing to go, she reminded herself. As if the gel were not tormented enough. It was fortuitous that she had decided upon a new course for her grandniece, one which suited very well her plans for Georgina Grey. A curious smile played about the wrinkled lips. She might have more years in her dish than she liked to admit, but she still had a trick or two up her sleeve. She fell into a rather pleasant daydream in which she pictured the odiously handsome earl at *point non plus*, until a light rap at the door broke her fanciful reveries.

With an unladylike snort at her own absurdities, Lady Bellows called out for her visitor to enter.

At her summons the door swung gently open to reveal a slim figure clad unbecomingly in an outmoded round gown of grey bombazine. Silvery blond hair, rather the color of moonlight, thought Lady Hortense whimsically, was pulled severely back from a small, oval face, delicately honed, with high cheekbones, a short, straight nose, and a firm little chin. The grey eyes beneath finely arched eyebrows were lovely, but they held an oddly frozen look not wholly dispelled by the welcoming light which had ignited in their depths at sight of Lady Hortense. The rather full lips, clearly designed for laughter, curved uncertainly upward, rather as if somehow they had forgotten how to smile. All in all, Lady Zenobia Grantham was a beautiful young woman, hardly more than a child. Yet the delicate contours of her face were marred by a strange brittleness which somehow robbed her of her youth. It was as if all the hopeful exuberance which might be expected in one of the tender age of nineteen had been suddenly shattered, leaving behind a bleeding, wounded creature who hid within a lovely shell.

"Nobie, my dear," Lady Hortense greeted the grand-daughter of her dearest sister Jessica with genuine warmth which overlay a deep feeling of pity for the girl and a slow-burning rage at the dissolute creature who had robbed the child of her innocence. She lifted a hand toward her grandniece, who quickly crossed the room to grasp it in her own small ones.

"Aunt," she murmured in a soft voice which expressed an affection oddly at variance with the cold planes of her face. "I am so glad you are returned. I had not wanted to go without saying my good-byes and thanking you for your many kindnesses."

"You are leaving Exeter, Zenobia?" Lady Hortense queried and bent a keen glance upon the girl.

"You know that I must. Please don't think me ungrateful, dearest aunt. But I have trespassed too long on your hospitality. And I do have a livelihood to pursue."

"Then you have found a position, my dear?" The matron watched with interest the slow tinge of color which crept over the girl's smooth cheeks. The little chin jutted finally under the older woman's intent scrutiny.

"Not precisely," she admitted in a tightly controlled little voice. "You see, I have not yet heard from the agency in London. Perhaps they have forgotten me. At any rate, I cannot wait longer here for them to acknowledge my application. Perhaps when I am in town, they will feel a greater obligation to place me in a position of employment."

"You are quite determined, then, to become another woman's drudge? A companion for some crotchety old woman like myself who will run you ragged with petty errands and humiliate you with condescension?" responded the old lady acerbically.

"Oh, Aunt!" At last a smile broke the severity of the frozen countenance, allowing a dimple to peep charmingly forth at the corner of the girl's mouth. "You know you are the dearest person. And your crotchets naught but a faradiddle to camouflage your generous nature. I should gladly stay by you and perform whatever service you might grant me to do. But I cannot remain here. You know that."

"Very well," was the brisk reply. "Then go you must. But not to London, my dear. I cannot turn you out on the world alone. I have found you a position."

The girl visibly started at this unexpected announcement. For a moment the grey eyes took on a vibrant light as Lady Grantham unconsciously pressed a hand to her small but shapely bosom.

"A position? But where? With whom?" she queried somewhat tremulously.

"As you know, I have spent this past se'ennight with my granddaughter, Lady Georgina Grey," Lady Bellows began judiciously. It behooved her to proceed with great care, for the gel was prodigiously proud. Zenobia, like her cousin Georgina, could not be pushed. Were she to believe it was charity being offered, she would bolt like an untamed filly. The older woman drew a deep breath and began to lay the bait, describing in some detail her welcome at Greystone Manor.

Slowly the light dimmed in the girl's eyes, as with an obvious effort she controlled the flurry of excitement and hope which had briefly animated her. She had come to know her great aunt rather better since coming to live with her some few weeks before. Patiently she resigned herself to allow Lady Bellows to tell the tale in her own characteristically circuitous manner.

"Georgina," Lady Hortense was saying, "has only recently returned to Cornwall with her son, the Earl of Emberly. But I told you that before I left and that she had been quite ill as well. But never did I suspect to what extent her illness had affected her."

The small catch in the elderly lady's voice was not feigned, nor was the suddenly suspicious brightness of her eyes. The girl, startled by such an unwonted display of the vapors in the indomitable Lady Hortense, clasped the older woman's trembling hand in her own strong young one.

"Oh, Aunt!" she cried in dismay. "Never say Georgina has succumbed to her illness?"

Zenobia Grantham had not known her second cousin well, for their families had not often come together. But she remembered a tall, gangling girl with laughing brown eyes and a daredevil disposition. Indeed, on the occasion of one of their rare visits to Georgina's family estate in Kent, Zenobia had been witness to her cousin's impetuosity. Despite the strictures of her parents, the thirteen-year-old girl had crept from the house, the much younger Zenobia tagging at her heels like an adoring puppy, and ridden a chestnut stallion reputed to be half-wild. What a glorious sight she had made clinging effortlessly to the back of the racing steed, her hair flying in the wind, her face flushed with the excitement of it all. She had impressed Zenobia then as an indomitable spirit more worthy of an intrepid boy than a slender girl who even then had shown promise of great beauty. It hurt her somehow to think so valiant a creature should be gone from the world.

"No, no, child," soothed the matron. "Georgina has for the most part recovered. Though I did find her sadly pulled. Like you, she is overly thin and refuses to have a proper care for herself. Nonetheless, her health is as good as can be expected after so harrowing an indisposition."

"Then why this sad face?" Zenobia probed gently. Never before had she seen her great aunt so obviously blue-devilled, and she was appalled further to note that the usually robust matron appeared suddenly quite old.

"She is blind, my dear," Lady Hortense said in a quiet voice all the more moving for its sudden calm.

"Blind?" repeated the girl with a small gasp. "Oh, not Georgina, who was ever so lively. How could this have happened?"

"Indeed," pronounced Lady Bellows with a somber shake of her head, "how could it? The cause is uncertain. She suffered a morbid fever for several weeks and there was evidence that she had been dealt a severe blow to the head. And yet none of these would seem to explain her present condition. The physician who attended her in Lisbon—apparently a reputable practitioner—held to the opinion that the eyes themselves are undamaged. He believes Georgina's blindness to be of the mind, though what he could possibly mean by that is beyond my understanding."

"But surely it must mean that she might see again," the girl said reasonably. "If it is true that her eyes are undamaged. But then why is she blind? It would seem to make little sense."

"It makes no sense at all. Yet the fact remains that my poor Georgina is indeed blind. And all alone now that David is gone. And her with a young child to care for. I cannot see how she shall bear up under it. It would wring your heart with pity if you were to see her, my dear. She puts up a brave front, but I who know her so well can see through it."

With a heavy sigh, Lady Hortense settled apparently wearily against the mound of pillows at her back and closed her eyes to hide their sudden gleam of triumph. She had not missed the play of emotions sweeping across Lady Grantham's normally guarded countenance. The gel's heart was malleable despite the wounds it had suffered, and she knew Zenobia was fairly caught. Yet she must take care nevertheless not to overplay her hand.

"You are tired, Aunt. I shall leave you to rest," came the soft, anxious tones of the girl.

"No, no. I would speak with you now. I shall rest better for having unburdened myself," Lady Hortense declared and valiantly opened her eyes.

Zenobia Grantham was leaning tenderly over her. Briefly the matron experienced a pin-prick of guilt for using the child so. Yet it was for her own good, she reminded herself. The gel would only come to grief if she were allowed to pursue her own madcap scheme to travel alone to London in the vague hopes of finding employment as companion to some stranger. Indeed, her chances of landing such a position were chancy in the extreme. She was far too young and very much too lovely.

A lady's companion in the norm was preferred to be a middle-aged spinster of unprepossessing appearance who would offer little in the way of temptation to any males of the household, for they would be like to view her as fair game. No. The gel must be saved from that disillusionment. Nor had Lady Bellows the least desire to see her grandniece succeed in landing such a position, since she could not wish for the dear child's spirit to be broken, as inevitably it must be, for a lady's companion was ever in the unenviable position of being something above the status of a mere servant and yet a great deal less than the exalted rank of those who employed her. Consequently, despised on the one hand for her gentility and condescended to on the other for her servility, she trod a precarious and lonely no-man's land.

Lady Hortense thus firmly quelled the small voice of her conscience and continued to weave her subtle web about the girl.

"Georgina is very like her father," she said with a sigh. "Sinjun was proud. Too proud to come to me when Georgina's mother passed on. I'd have taken him in hand and the gel, too. But he must have his way with her. And now she is as stubbornly independent as he was. Bless his soul. Neither did all those years roaming the heathenish wilds of India with Emberly do aught to soften the gel's spirit. When I told her she could not go on by herself, she'd have none of it. Oh, well. What would you? Young people care nothing for the wisdom of their elders."

She cocked a sapient eye at her grandniece and was gratified to see a sparkle of rebellion in the girl's grey eyes. At least resentment was better than the cold indifference Zenobia had displayed since coming to Lady Bellows. Mayhap the gel would yet heal her wounds given the right surroundings and someone to serve as an example of what the human spirit was capable of overcoming.

Before the girl could voice an objection to her great aunt's rather pointed remark, Lady Hortense had continued on a note of long-suffering.

"I might have spared my breath, of course. Georgina was vociferous in her refusal to admit she must have someone to live with her. Couldn't stand to have someone fawning on her or pitying her. And she as helpless as an infant and putting up so brave a front. You will be doing her a great service, my dear, when you go to her. Say for a visit at first. Then, when she has grown accustomed to your presence, she will be glad to have you stay."

"Oh, Aunt, I could not!" cried the girl, alarmed at her kinswoman's conniving. "She doesn't want me. I can hardly force myself on her. Surely you can see that."

"I see no such thing, Zenobia. Georgina needs you. Why, she can hardly care for herself," lied the matron glibly, "let alone a young boy full of mischief. And I should go on much better did I know Georgina had you to look out for her. You must not be selfish, child. After all, you want to earn your way, and you did say you wished to be of service to me. Well, I have shown you how you may. Surely you cannot deny me this small request."

"Small request?" Lady Zenobia eyed the wrinkled face of her elderly aunt with dismay. "It is hardly a *small* request you demand of me. My cousin has a right to her privacy. I should be sunk beneath reproach were I to force myself on her."

"Balderdash! Such a faradiddle of nonsense I had never thought to hear from you, Zenobia Grantham. Why, if you had seen the grief in that gel's face, you could not think it is *privacy* she requires. She used to be a vibrant, spirited chit. Reminded me of myself as I was in my salad days. Now she is only a pale ghost of the child I once knew. No. Privacy is the last thing she needs now. If you fail to go to her, Zenobia, you will only condemn her to lonely exile from all that she once knew and loved. I had not thought you could be so heartless. Such sentiments, or the lack thereof, are more suited to Vail. Indeed, I begin to wonder if the villain has not had his way with you after all."

The girl blanched alarmingly at the final words of condemnation, so unexpected as they were coming from the one person who had hitherto offered nothing but sympathetic support. She flinched visibly beneath their lash and dropped her head to hide the sudden hurt in her eyes.

Lady Hortense waited for the tears which she knew must come, but she was to be disappointed. For Zenobia Grantham suddenly straightened her slim back to lift accusing eyes to her great aunt. Once again the young face was a frozen mask, aged beyond its years, but within the marble-like rigidity, the grey eyes burned with bitter passion.

44

"Mayhap I am become heartless like Percival," she said in an unnaturally quiet voice. "Certainly he did all he could to wound that organ to death. I shall never love again. He has ended all that foolish sentiment for me. But I do care for Georgina. And should she consent to have me as a companion, under no false pretenses, I shall go to her gladly for as long as she needs me. But *she* must ask me, Aunt. Else I leave for London as I had planned."

Lady Hortense was stricken with the feeling of dreadful anguish as she stared into the hard young face. Had she gone too far? she wondered, then pulled herself sharply together. She had won a consent from the gel, and Zenobia would never go back on her given word. With a heavy sigh which was far from being feigned, she lay back against the pillows.

"Very well, my dear," she said and firmly grasped the girl's icy hand. "I did not wish to use you so hardly, but I had to make certain of you. For indeed you must leave Exeter very soon. I must tell you that Vail knows you are here." The small hand jerked convulsively. "I have received word from him. The conceited coxcomb! He generously grants you one week in which to return willingly to him. To resume your 'wifely duties.' Harumph! Slave is more like. I shall write to Georgina immediately. You need have no fear that she will not ask you to come to her once she knows how that blackguard has used you."

"No! You must not tell her! Not one word, Aunt," Lady Zenobia said in a fierce undertone. The hard gleam of desperation in the grey eyes wrenched at the older woman's heart. "Promise me, Aunt. Promise me, or I shall leave this house now."

The protest which had risen instantly to Lady Bellows' lips died at sight of the girl's reckless determination to throw all away in hasty flight. Her own plans had received a minor set-back, for the gel had trumped her ace, but she would still find a way to win Georgina's consent, she doubted not. Wisely deciding it was time to retrench, she slowly nodded her assent.

"I give you my word, Zenobia," she said, "to tell Georgina nothing of Vail. Though I cannot agree that it is wise for your cousin to be kept in the dark."

"Vail is a danger only to me, Aunt Hortense. And I could not bear for Georgina, or anyone, to know of my shame."

"This may be as may be, my dear. But how shall you explain to Georgina your separation from your husband?"

"I shall tell her nothing. Nor shall you. I doubt she even knows I was ever wed. Did you inform her? I did not."

Lady Bellows pondered this query for a time before shaking her head.

"No. I never did," she said at last. "For I disapproved, as you well know, your choice in husbands."

"Then who is left to tell her?" queried the girl in a flat voice, and the peculiarly hard brilliance of the grey eyes sent a shiver coursing down Lady Bellows' spine.

"Well," she said briskly and patted the girl's hand, "never mind all that now. What's done is done, and 'tis time it was forgotten. We shall come about, never you fear. You will be Zenobia Kingsley again. A more pleasing name than Grantham. Sweeter to my ears by far."

Thus it was that Lady Georgina Grey received a missive from her grandmama by courier some two days later.

Georgina, who had not yet overcome a certain feeling of helplessness which struck her when the unexpected occurred to upset her carefully established routine of things, stood uncertainly in the Blue Saloon, Lady Bellows' unopened letter in her hand. Her thoughts occupied with the particular difficulties inherent in receiving correspondence, she was hardly aware that Bolton still stood before her. Nor could she have guessed what a poignant picture she made, posed proudly before her wooden-faced butler, a rather lost expression upon her lovely face.

Bolton, who had come to know his mistress very well in the short time she had been at Greystone Manor, allowed his impassive features to relax somewhat as he perceived Lady Grey's dilemma. Suddenly he coughed gently and proceeded to deliver a modest speech, which, from any other member of the quality, would likely have earned him a severe set-down for unwarranted impertinence.

"If I may be so bold, m'lady," he began in carefully neutral tones which failed entirely to hide his kind intent from the acutely discerning ear of the young countess. "Perchance you are unaware that I was educated by my father's late master, the Earl of Lachlan. I both read and write with reasonable proficiency. It is not an accomplishment of which I wish to boast. It is only that the late earl found this a useful talent at times. And I have never been one to gossip among the lower orders."

Lady Georgina's brown eyes widened. She stepped forward to touch the butler's arm in a gesture of quiet affection.

"What ever should I do without you, my dear friend," she said with her gentle smile. "If you would be so kind as to read this message to me from Lady Bellows, I should be eternally grateful. It seems that I am in need of a companion after all. Or at least of a secretary," she added with a rueful grimace.

"I am ever at your service, m'lady," Bolton replied, bowing at the waist. Then straightening again, he paused for the briefest moment before daring to add, "I should not wish to be thought impertinent, m'lady. However, may I be so bold as to suggest that there is much in what Lady Bellows advises. Someone like yourself really should not be so much alone."

"But I am not alone, Bolton," replied the lady with an impish quirk of her lips. "I have you to take care of such matters as are beyond my limitations. And you do so

47

admirably."

A puzzled frown broke the impassivity of the butler's face, to give way almost immediately to the hint of a smile. The countess, he thought to himself, would never regret placing her trust in him. She was a rare one, indeed. And despite the half-mourning gown of pale lavender which was sadly out-moded, she appeared very much the great lady and with a heart to match.

Solemnly he took the missive from her ladyship's hand and broke the seal. With his usual impeccable dignity he related to his mistress Lady Bellows' message.

My dear Georgina,

I have not delayed in finding you the paragon of whom we spoke. She is neither old nor witless. Furthermore, she is our kinswoman. Miss Zenobia Kingsley, the granddaughter of my youngest sister, Jessica. Since the death of her parents in a coaching accident over a year ago, she has found herself in straitened circumstances. Presently she resides with me, but threatens to leave for London to seek a position as paid companion in order to earn her own way. Georgina, she has suffered such anguish! You will desire her to come to you, I know. She will not do so, however, unless you ask her and then only as a paid companion. For she is too stubbornly proud to accept anything which even remotely hints of charity. So very like someone else I know!

We await your reply most anxiously.

My love to you, my dear. And to Davey.

H.B.

"Well, of course she must come," Georgina said once Bolton had read to the end. Her heart went out to her young, orphaned cousin. "I must write to her at once. Bolton, where is my grandmama's courier?"

"I sent him to the kitchens, m'lady. He will be enjoying Mrs. Appleby's pigeon pie, I've no doubt."

"Good. The poor man must be exhausted. Please see that he has a place to sleep once he has finished replenishing himself and inform him that there will be an answer forthcoming to be delivered on the morrow."

"Very good, m'lady," responded the butler, obviously pleased with the proposed addition to the household.

"Oh, and, Bolton." Lady Georgina grinned a little ruefully. "I fear that I must make further use of your—er—talents. Is there any writing paper in the house? And would you mind penning an answer for me? I shall, of course, dictate the appropriate words."

"I should be honored, m'lady," Bolton replied quite truthfully.

The letter which Lady Georgina dictated sometime later was warmly inviting. She recalled the little dab of a girl with silvery curls and grey eyes which had shone gravely out of a tiny, round face. Five years Georgina's junior, Zenobia Kingsley had worshiped the elder girl who had treated her as an equal despite their age difference. Georgina, of a naturally sunny disposition, had sensed the child's shy reserve and spared nothing to draw the delightful gurgle of laughter from the younger girl. Patiently she had played at dolls with her though Georgina had never before shown the slightest interest in such seemingly idle pastimes. The older girl was a child of nature, her exuberant spirits demanding the more arduous pursuits of riding her beloved horses neck or nothing across the down, of rolling in hoydenish abandon in the grass with her favorite hound, or swimming with long, sure strokes in the ornamental lake on her father's estate.

But Zenobia, on the other hand, was a gentle creature who had seemed born for motherhood. She mothered her dolls, the kittens in the stables, the robin with a broken wing which Georgina had captured and given into her keeping, even Georgina herself when she had been severely punished for riding without permission her father's chestnut stallion.

Consequently, it seemed odd to Georgina that her cousin had not as yet married and begun her family. She must be eighteen or nineteen by now. And a beauty if she had fulfilled the promise of childhood. She supposed the tragic death of her parents must have prevented Zenobia's comeout. How sad life could be for some, she thought compassionately. Well, the child would make her home at Greystone for as long as she liked, and doubtless that would not be very long at all. For surely the young men of Tamar Valley would not be such slow-tops as to overlook a lovely young thing like Zenobia Kingsley.

Thinking such thoughts, Georgina made her way up the stairs with a firm step. Absently she ran her hand over the smooth bannister as she climbed and imagined with pleasure its polished sheen. The staircase curved upward to a wide hallway which ran the length of the east wing. Here was the picture gallery, she thought, as she trod lightly over the hardwood floor. She brushed one hand along the papered wall as she walked, her soft-soled slippers making only a whisper of sound. The scent of beeswax attested to the diligence of Mrs. Porter, who could not abide dust in her domain. Georgina touched the cool gilded frame of a large portrait. Randall, the First Earl of Emberly, undoubtedly stared haughtily down at her. He had the look of David, Mrs. Porter had informed her, and Georgina imagined hazel eyes with a glint of devil-may-care laughter in their depths, a hooked nose and wide, generous mouth, and in the firm chin a cleft which had given her delight and filled her with an unladylike compulsion to place a kiss just there.

She realized with a start that she was no longer walking and that an uncomfortable tightness had constricted her throat.

"This will never do, Lady Grey," she told herself firmly and forced herself to continue down the hall to the music room.

It was a warm spring's day in the middle of May, and the sash of the great bay window had been raised to let in a gentle draught. Georgina crossed to the open window and breathed deeply of the scent of a freshening breeze wafting in from the seacoast scant miles from the manor. On a day like today, she mused, a whimsical smile playing across her lips as she lifted her face to the delicious warmth of the sun's rays streaming through the window, if she were at home in Kent, she would be racing her favorite hunter Cassandra across the paddock. She pictured the first jump, a stone wall perhaps ten hands high, and the exhilaration of soaring as the grey mare made the leap.

"I wonder if Zenobia still rides," she murmured aloud. "Davey would like that. And perhaps she will take him to call on the families with children and they will return his visit. Indeed, perhaps Grandmama is wise to insist we have a companion after all."

She sighed, refusing to let her thoughts dwell on how she had looked forward to teaching her son to ride and to sharing with him the delight of coming to know his father's beloved Cornwall. They shared other things, after all, for she was not the type of mother to let others rear her child. Perhaps that was why she was so grateful Rathbourne had not chosen thus far to interfere. She knew she could not keep Davey forever to herself, nor would she want to. But while he was still so young, he was hers and hers alone, a part of David and herself which she could nourish and mold into someone fine and noble like his father.

Chiding herself for being so melancholy on such a glorious day, Georgina moved away from the window and crossed to the pianoforte. She ran her fingers lovingly over the keys, then seated herself on the bench. Melodies began to flow from her fingertips—light, lovely tunes she had shared with David, who had possessed a fine tenor—and, as always, her music evoked images of her husband and the love which had enveloped her like a warm cloak of security no matter how poor the quarters they had had to share. Then she had played the guitar, an instrument to which she had taken easily while in Portugal. It had gone everywhere with them, had even entertained the great Wellington himself on one occasion. It resided now in a wardrobe in her bedchamber. She had not had the heart to remove it from its battered case since Talavera and had turned instead to the piano, her first love.

Without thinking, she slipped into the haunting theme of Beethoven's *Pathetique* piano sonata which had been composed only shortly before her first and only Season in London some seven years before. She marveled that she remembered it still after so long, for she had not played at all since leaving England. This was her one gift from the delicate, fairy-like creature who had been her mother and who had created music with magic fingers and a talent which had made her a great favorite at musical soirees in her girlhood and later. Georgina, like her mother, could play by ear whatever she heard. With practice she might even have surpassed her mama's rare talent, but she had used her unusual gift merely to trick her music instructor into believing she had attained a competent rendition from hours of practice while in reality she had stolen from the house to ride freely over the countryside of Kent.

Now music sustained Georgina in the dreary world of shadows and near darkness in which she lived. Her talent had deepened as the pianoforte had come to fill the lonely hours when Davey was occupied with Nanny or when sleep eluded her in the seemingly endless nights. Secure in her music, she forgot the loneliness, came to terms with her grief.

The haunting notes of the sonata died away in the suddenly still room. Georgina sighed contentedly, then covered the keys and rose to make her way from the music room and down the long gallery toward the nursery.

They would take a lunch to the bourne which ran through the grounds within easy walking distance of the house, she decided. Nanny would go with them to keep an eye on Davey. She would revel in the feel of sunlight against her face. No matter if her nose freckled or her skin turned brown. Nanny would notice and scold her for it, but she did not care. David had adored her freckles, and it would be so good to be out for awhile.

Chapter 3

Lady Georgina sat at the great desk in the library savoring the smell of leather-bound volumes. With difficulty she attended to the report being made to her by Connings, her estate agent. A slight frown marred the purity of her brow as she sought to concentrate on roofs which needed repair, the sheep dog which must be replaced, and the problems of drainage in some of the outlying farms.

Indeed, the entire morning had been fraught with one demand after another. She had spent better than an hour in consultation with Mrs. Porter about menus and the rooms to be prepared for Miss Kingsley, whom they expected any day now. The linens had required sorting and some set aside for mending, then the accounts must be gone over with Bolton's help, and now Connings had come to her with the never-ending decisions regarding the smooth running of a great estate. Thus the morning had flown, and still she had not found time to deal with the startling news which had reached her by post as she rose from the breakfast table to begin her day's routine.

Rathbourne was coming, indeed, was very likely already in residence at Rathbourne Castle, which lay but an hour's journey by horseback from Greystone Manor. His estate bordered Emberly, and she should have known that eventually he would come. But why did it have to be now when she herself had hardly settled in at Greystone? Was it only coincidence that he should suddenly make his appearance so soon after her arrival here when he had ignored her for nearly a year since she had written to inform him of David's death? Or had he some deeper motive?

Perhaps he was dissatisfied with her management of his ward's extensive holdings, she worried. Certainly she had found it difficult at first, though she had helped her father with similar matters more than most had known in the lonely years following her mother's death.

Georgina had been fourteen then, a hoyden despite her mother's patient tutelage in such things considered necessary to a daughter of the aristocracy, and she had taken to farming with a love for horses and the outdoors which matched her father's. She had gone everywhere with him, and the tenants had soon learned she had a level head and a quick eye for needed improvements. Thus her father, who had never quite recovered from the loss of his wife, came to depend more and more on her young strength. She shared in the decisions with him regarding the estate and handled the troublesome accounts. But she had not been dependent then on another to be both her eyes and her ears. Though she trusted in Connings' loyalty, she suffered qualms over judgments she was forced to make solely on his reports. Had her decisions been ill-conceived? Why had he come, His Grace of Rathbourne?

With an effort she brought her attention back to Connings, a man past middle-age who had clinging to him the fresh scent of the outdoors. She smelled, too, the faint aroma of tobacco and pictured this quiet man who spoke with the soft burr of the Cornishman drawing contentedly on his pipe as he waited for a mare to foal or as he watched the sheep grazing in the paddocks. Then with a slight start, she realized he had ceased to speak and was waiting for her to say something. Quickly she marshaled her scattered thoughts.

"I am not personally acquainted with Mr. Parsons," she said, trying to recall just what her agent had been saying. "But I have heard his sheep dogs are well thought of in the valley. If you feel the pup will serve as a replacement for Jasper, then I shall commission you to purchase him from Mr. Parsons. As to the Dicksons, I have heard nothing but good. And if Mrs. Dickson is indeed expecting another addition to the family, we should perhaps consider moving them to the old Pickering farm. The lease on lives is ended with none other at present to take it over, and the cottage is larger. You indicated previously that with a little work it could be made quite livable, I believe?"

"*Ais*, m'lady," Connings answered stolidly. "Belike it won't take much more'n a new thatched roof."

"Very well. You may make the necessary arrangements with Dickson. Oh, and, Connings. I should be pleased if you would see to the purchase of a good milch cow for the Dicksons. Jonas, one of the stablehands, is of that family, I believe. And Denby has informed me that the boy is looking sadly pulled of late. It seems the cow has gone dry and poor Mrs. Dickson is hard put to keep her brood fed. Perhaps a few chickens as well, and a rooster. Children need milk and eggs if they are to be healthy."

"*Ais*, m'lady," Connings said with his customary reticence, but Georgina detected a sudden warmth in his voice. Connings, she judged, was a good overseer who understood that an estate tended to prosper when its tenants did. Silently she blessed the old earl, David's father, for having employed and earned the loyalty of such competent servants. It made her tasks easier. She stifled a sigh. Even so, there was a great deal for her to do, and maintaining her son's inheritance until such time as he should reach his majority was becoming a sad drain on her energies.

A sudden commotion in the hall arrested her thoughts, and she turned her face toward the library door. It was not long before an eager rap heralded the arrival of the young Earl of Emberly just arrived from his riding lesson under the patient tutelage of Denby, the head groom.

"Come in, Davey," the countess called in her rich contralto, then smiled as the resulting rush of eager young feet paused just within the room and a small voice gravely remarked, "I beg your pardon, Mama. I didn't know Mr. Connings was here with you."

"It's all right, darling. Mr. Connings and I have just finished. Make your bow, then come tell me about your riding lesson."

"Mr. Connings," the young voice said politely, and Georgina knew that he bowed as a young gentleman should to his elders. "How are you, sir?"

"Right as rain, your lordship," Connings replied with a smile in his voice. "I trust your ride were enjoyable, milord?"

"Oh, yes, Mr. Connings. It was glor-r-ious." The boy's voice lingering over the final word brought a smile to his mama's lips. "Denby let us take a jump today. Mrs. Dobbins went at it like a trooper, and Denby says I have a seat like Papa's. My papa was the best horseman in the cavalry, Mr. Connings. Wasn't he, Mama?"

Georgina swallowed a sudden lump in her throat. "He was a superb horseman, Davey," she said quietly. "I never saw anyone look grander on a horse."

"Nor did I, m'lady," added Connings warmly. "I recollect when Lord Grey were a young lad, not much older than you be now, milord. Unbeknownst to his papa, Master David slipped out of the nursery and joined the hunt on one of his papa's hunters. Did right well for a halfling, 'cepting only he come t'grief. A fall of timber atop a low ridge tripped 'im up. He broke his arm, milord, but he held to th' reins like a veteran and brung his mount home, he did. His papa's heart weren't in th' scolding he gave th' young scamp, methinks."

"My papa did that?" exclaimed the child, his voice vibrant with awe.

Georgina suffered a tremor of fear for the impressionable young boy and wished the trusted retainer had held his peace. Davey was quite capable of attempting to imitate his papa's youthful exploits. But Connings had gone on to affirm the veracity of his tale.

"Indeed, he did, your lordship," he said and thought as how the lad were the very picture of his papa with his bright eyes and eager smile. *Ais*. And he had already his papa's determined jaw with a suggestion of the telling cleft in the chin. The Greys bred true, they did, and proud, he thought. But neither had he missed the young countess's small, anxious frown, and he was quick to take up the threads of the tale.

"But Master David had learnt his lesson, he had. And never again did he take out his papa's cattle, lest he were granted leave to have done. For his papa's hunter were lamed by his mischance, and your papa were proper sorry for it. Helped to care for the horse himself, he did, despite his hurt arm, till the animal were right as a trivet again. A proper gennleman your papa was even then," the agent ended, his telling encomium having been gently delivered.

"Thank you, Connings," Georgina said a trifle mistily. "It is obvious you were very fond of his lordship. The earl is fortunate to be able to learn of his papa from such a loyal friend."

There was an embarrassed shuffling of booted feet as Connings coughed slightly and shifted his weight.

"It be naught but th' truth, m'lady," he said gruffly. Then, "If you'll not be needin' me further, I'll be takin' myself off to Parsons', your ladyship. An' I'll see Dickson gets the milch cow. Never you fear."

"Indeed, Connings. I know I may depend on you. Good-bye."

She listened to the firm footsteps retreat across the

carpeted floor. The door had opened and softly closed again before Georgina opened her arms to the small boy who slipped comfortably into them. She bent to fondly kiss his forehead and noted with a small pang how tall he had grown. She breathed in the scent of fresh air tinged pleasantly with the aroma of horses which lingered about him and hugged him close for a moment. But soon he wiggled restlessly in her arms, and reluctantly she let him pull free from her embrace. Sternly she quashed the fleeting thought that he was growing all too swiftly away from her.

"Darling, I have some news which I believe you will find pleasing," she said lightly. "Come, let us stroll in the garden for awhile before tea."

"What news, Mama?" the child asked and obediently took his mother's hand.

Together they left the library and descended the stairs. Georgina gently turned the boy's query aside and led him into a more detailed account of his afternoon's ride. The child complied eagerly, and Georgina listened, content to put off for a few moments the troubling contemplation of Rathbourne's pending visit.

By unspoken consent, they retreated into the Blue Saloon and made their way through the French doors and across the flagstone verandah to their favorite retreat, an enclosed rose-garden in the center of which gurgled a small fountain. The boy led his mother to a marble bench situated near the fountain and shaded by a leafy grape arbor. Dutifully he sat beside her.

Fondly Georgina listened to the thud of small, booted feet against the marble wall of the pool and to the splash of a hand trailing through the water. He was full of youthful energy and, though happy to be in his mama's company, was yet impatient with so tame a pursuit as sitting quietly in the garden. Reluctantly she broached the subject uppermost in her mind.

"Darling, we are to have a visitor soon. A very dear

friend of Papa's. The Duke of Rathbourne, who is also your guardian."

"His Grace is coming here?" the boy exclaimed, a note of awed excitement in his childish voice. "But I shall like that above all things, Mama. Denby says he is as famous a horseman as Papa. And a better swordsman. Denby says there's none to equal His Grace with pistols or his fives. Do you think he shall teach me how to box, Mama? Do you?"

Georgina bit back the sharp retort which sprang to her lips at the boy's unexpected outburst. Davey's obvious admiration for the *Non Pareil* had taken her off guard. That he could so easily accept the rakish duke as his papa's superior in anything hurt her. Had he so quickly forgotten David, the tall, gentle soldier who had hitherto been his only hero? Almost she lashed out against the overloquacious groom who had fired the boy's imagination with tales of the duke's infamous exploits and thus created an idol to supplant the boy's father in Davey's affections. But her tongue was stilled by the child's subsequent innocent observation.

"But no one could beat Papa. Could they, Mama. Why, he was the best officer in the whole regiment. The Iron Duke himself said so when he came to tell us about Papa being killed. I miss Papa awfully. Don't you?" he finished in a gruff little voice.

"Yes, darling. Awfully," Georgina managed despite a tightening in her throat. "But he will always be with us in our memories."

"I suppose so," Davey said doubtfully, and Georgina's heart gave a little lurch. "Only when I try to remember what he looked like, I can't see his face anymore. Why did he have to go and die? Didn't he love us anymore?"

"Of course he loved us, Davey," Georgina hurried to assure him and subdued the impulse to snatch the small body desperately close. Why had she never realized the child might blame himself for his father's death? He had seemed to understand about soldiers and the dangers they faced in times of war. Vainly she searched for the words to ease his misplaced guilt.

"Your father had no wish to leave us, Davey," she said after a time. "But he was a soldier, and many soldiers died. You know that. You mustn't blame yourself. It is not unusual to forget what someone looks like once they are gone. That doesn't mean you don't love them anymore."

The child seemed to consider her words as the silence stretched between them. Georgina waited with her heart in her throat for him to speak.

"I do love Papa," he said gravely after a time. "Someday I shall be a soldier just like him. Shan't I, Mama?"

Georgina laughed softly and hugged the child close.

"Yes, darling. Just like your papa if that's what you wish. But you are also the Earl of Emberly. And that means you have responsibilities here at home. That is why His Grace, the Duke of Rathbourne, is coming here. To see that you learn what you must know to be a good earl."

"Indeed, Madam?" commented a deep, masculine voice drily. "I wonder if His Grace is aware of the treat in store for him."

Georgina was startled into uttering a low gasp. Unconsciously she pulled her son close to her side in an instinctive attempt to protect him from the unknown. With an effort she stilled the sudden pounding of her heart and told herself she was acting like an utter peagoose. A stranger in her private garden was nothing to become vaporish over, after all. No doubt Bolton was within shouting distance if she needed him. She forced herself to take a deep breath and rose gracefully from the marble bench that she might meet her visitor with greater presence.

"I fear you have taken us by surprise, sir," she said with calm dignity. "We are not accustomed to receiving callers unannounced. No doubt Bolton was away from his post on some household matter or another. I shall have to speak to him about leaving the door unattended, I fear."

There. That should give the impertinent man pause for thought. How dare a perfect stranger intrude where he had not been invited. But the response to Lady Grey's artful set-down was couched in unruffled tones distinctly colored with amusement.

"That's given me some of my own, no doubt. Bolton, however, is not to blame. I was used to run tame in this house as a boy, and I fear neither of us thought to defer to your probable wishes in the matter. I do humbly beg your pardon, ma'am."

Indeed, thought the lady, fighting a sudden urge to giggle. It occurred to her that she had never heard anyone sound less humble. Who was this arrogant intruder? Obviously one accustomed to having his own way. The birth of a sudden suspicion caused her to turn and face him full on. She felt the sunlight warm against her face as her movement carried her from beneath the shadowed shelter of the arbor. She was startled to hear a sudden low gasp issue from the direction in which her visitor's voice had come.

"Who are you then?" she asked, suddenly a trifle breathless. "That you are so familiar with this house and the servants employed here?"

For an endless moment silence reigned over the enclosed garden. Georgina became acutely aware of the low drone of a honeybee somewhere in the blossoms nearby and of the sudden heady perfume of roses and honeysuckle cloying in the still air. Why did the man not answer? she fretted unreasonably and felt Davey stir uneasily beside her. She wished she could stop the steady rush of the fountain as she strained to hear above its seeming roar.

"Sir," she said, goaded at last to break the unbearable tension. "I do not wish to seem uncivil, but if you do not identify yourself, I shall be forced to call for Bolton."

Still he did not answer, and she began to wonder if he had slipped away. Then she was surprised to hear him draw in a long, shuddering breath, as if he, too, were discomposed. Yet when he spoke, his deep voice showed little sign of it. Indeed, only one who depended upon her hearing as Georgina did, would detect the rigidly controlled emotion beneath the level tones.

"Again I must ask your pardon, ma'am," he said, and this time the apology had a taut irony about it which Georgina found singularly odd. "As I had sent word of my imminent arrival, I naturally assumed I should be expected." He paused and instinctively Georgina knew he had made his gesture of respectful obeisance, bowing gracefully, no doubt, from the waist. "I am Rathbourne," he announced.

This time Georgina could not stop the bubble of laughter which rose unwittingly to her throat. In the sudden release of tension, her delicious gurgle burst forth, and she stretched out her hand in welcome to His Grace, the Duke of Rathbourne.

"Your Grace," she said, her voice still vibrant with laughter. "Please accept my apologies if I have seemed uncivil. I should have guessed your identity immediately. Indeed, I did suspect. But since I have never before heard your voice, I fear I could not be sure. You are most welcome at Greystone Manor, my lord duke, and I pray you will continue to treat my son's house as your own."

Georgina experienced a sudden start as she felt her hand lightly clasped and lips brushed in a feather-light caress against her knuckles.

His touch was gentle, but she sensed strength in the long, slender fingers and was surprised to detect calluses on the palm. An outdoorsman, she thought and recalled his reputation as a formidable Corinthian. There was about him the pleasing aroma of clean linen mingled with tobacco and shaving soap, a masculine blend of scents which triggered memories of David. She felt his shadow fall across her face as he straightened, and when he spoke, his deep voice sounded above her head. He was quite tall, she thought, to tower so above her own generous inches. She lifted her eyes toward the sound of his voice and wished suddenly that she could see his face. David had said he was quite the handsomest man he had ever seen.

"You are very kind, ma'am," he was saying in a lazy drawl which was meant to hide his thoughts behind a worldly cynicism or ennui. He would have that sleepy, heavy-lidded look of the man about town, she mused, and smiled at the vision of a tall form clad in fancy puce satin with rings and fobs to shout the tulip. But, no, she quickly amended. The voice was far too self-assuredly masculine to belong to the simpering dandy. He would have more the subdued elegance of the town smarts who adhered to Beau Brummel's precept that the clothes of a well-dressed man never called attention to themselves. "But I shall not so impose on your hospitality," he continued. "In future I shall have myself announced."

"Be that as it may, Your Grace," she said and gently released her hand. "I fear I have been sadly remiss. Allow me to present to you your ward, the Earl of Emberly. Davey, make your bow to the Duke of Rathbourne."

"I am pleased to meet Your Grace," the young earl said obediently and bowed as a proper gentleman was expected to do. But then his eager young voice betrayed his boyish excitement at meeting the Nonesuch. "Is it true, Your Grace, that you floored Gentleman Jackson himself?"

"Davey!" Georgina interjected in dismay.

"But he did, Mama. Denby said he did. Oh, how I should like to've seen you draw his cork, sir. Denby says you're top-of-the-trees. I should like above all things to see a mill one day. Denby saw Mendoza fight Jackson once. I guess Denby's seen and done just about everything. Won't you show me how you did it? How you landed Gentleman Jim a facer?"

"This Denby would appear to be amazingly well-informed," commented the duke in his lazy drawl. "However, in this instance I fear he may have exaggerated somewhat. I did not floor the gentleman in question. I merely slipped a lucky punch in under his guard."

"You mean you landed him a facer. Denby said you did."

"Davey. I believe we have heard enough of Denby," observed Georgina quietly, but there was no mistaking that she meant business. "I see I shall have to speak to him. Apparently he had been entirely too free with his speech."

"But, Mama! You mustn't scold Denby. I shan't forgive you if you do. He's not like you and Nanny. He doesn't molly-coddle or forever tell me to mind my manners. I like Denby. He's my friend."

The young voice had grown noticeably sulky at the end of this diatribe, and Georgina was swept with guilty dismay. Had she indeed kept him too close? Yet it was her place to see he learned the behavior proper to a gentleman, and a gentleman did not comport himself like a stablehand in polite company. She drew breath to call the child to account, but the duke was before her.

"We must be gratified, no doubt," Rathbourne remarked conversationally, "by such loyalty to one who stands your friend. However, it does occur to me that Denby is perhaps not best served by your making a corker of yourself. Odd as it may seem to experienced men of the world like Denby and ourselves, using boxing cant in the presence of ladies is frowned upon. Such behavior shows a boorish disregard for their more delicate sensibilities. A gentleman thus reserves discussion of the manly arts exclusively for other gentlemen." If the duke heard the lady's low gasp of indignation, he pretended to be patently unaware of it as he continued to instruct the errant young earl in the niceties of polite behavior. "Nor does a gentleman talk back to his elders. You, my young friend, are in grave danger of making a complete cake of yourself. I suggest, therefore, that you owe your mother an apology."

There was a moment of silence as the boy digested his guardian's words and Georgina grew rigid with indignation at the duke's calm assumption of command. Sternly she reminded herself that he had every right as the boy's guardian to correct her son. But to tell him such a faradiddle of nonsense in her very presence was the outside of enough. And yet she could not deny that what he had said was commonly accepted by the society to which they belonged and that she had often found herself on the verge of disrepute for her headstrong insistence that a woman was not a shrinking violet which might thrive only in the environs of a glasshouse.

Thus Georgina bit her tongue to keep from delivering the duke a sharp set-down in front of the boy. No matter what her own feelings might be on the subject of the duke's guardianship, Davey must not be made to suffer for them. And he would if he became a bone of contention between Rathbourne and herself. With an effort she maintained the unruffled front with which she had learned to deal with adversity. After all, she had no wish to give the troublesome duke the satisfaction of knowing he could upset her equilibrium. But his next words brought a slow warmth to her cheeks. Evidently the odious man had the faculty for reading her mind.

"Make your apology, bantling, and take yourself off that I may make my peace with your mama. It appears that I, too, have managed to get off on the wrong foot with the lady and must make amends."

The lady's chin rose a fraction of an inch. There was no mistaking the sardonic amusement couched in the deep voice. Clearly the insufferable duke was laughing at her. Then Davey was tugging at her skirts.

"I do beg your pardon, Mama," the young earl said earnestly. "I know I should not talk so in front of you. Denby said as much. So you really shouldn't be mad at him, should you?"

"No, darling. Nor am I. So long as you know it is not proper behavior for a gentleman. Go to Nanny now. I feel sure your tea is waiting for you."

"Yes, Mama," the boy said, his usual bright spirits revived at the mention of tea and the biscuits which always went with it. "I'm pleased to have met Your Grace. And you will come back again, won't you? I really should like to hear how you slipped one in on Gentleman Jim. Perhaps sometime when it's just us men?" he ended ingenuously.

"Quite so," Rathbourne drawled, properly grave. "I've no doubt we shall be seeing a great deal of one another. Especially if my ward is to acquire the proper science of fisticuffs."

The child's breath, sharply indrawn, whistled in the momentary stillness.

"Do you mean it, sir? Shall I truly learn to box?" he queried, afraid to believe his ears.

"It would seem so, bantling," observed the duke drily. "Since it is, as your mama has already pointed out, the duty of your guardian to instruct you in those things an earl should know. And now you shall remove yourself in order that Lady Grey may inform me of my further duties. Somehow I feel sure she has a great deal to say to the subject."

"Indeed, Your Grace?" Georgina retorted sweetly. "And yet 'twould seem there is very little I should be able to tell you. I am, after all, but a female of delicate sensibilities. What should I know to the point? Davey, you may leave us now. No doubt Nanny will wish to hear about your promised treat."

"Indeed, yes! And Denby, too!" cried the boy in alt as he sped away. "He said I should find His Grace a right 'un."

Georgina, listening to the child's boisterous retreat, felt suddenly unaccountably flustered at finding herself alone with His Grace, the Duke of Rathbourne. She was acutely aware of his towering presence in the close confines of the garden and had to struggle to keep from fidgeting like a nervous schoolgirl at her first grown-up party. This will never do, my girl, she told herself, and forced the semblance of a serene smile to her lips as she turned toward the duke.

"Perhaps you would care for tea, Your Grace," she began politely, only to be cut short by an explosive utterance from the gentleman.

"Have done, Lady Grey!" he said harshly. "The boy is gone now and we may lay our cards on the table."

"I beg your pardon?" gasped the lady, her brown eyes widening in startled indignation.

"You needn't pretend innocence with me, Madam. I don't know what game you are playing, but I most certainly intend to find it out. Since coming into your presence, I have been 'Your Graced' into an acute state of discomfort. David and I were very close, and regrettably he is gone now. But after all that you and I have been through together, such formality is patently absurd. You will call me Drew, or Rathbourne at the very least. And you will kindly explain to me why you never told me you were David's wife."

"Obviously I am in the presence of a Bedlamite," was the lady's astounded rejoinder. "The banns were read seven years ago as is proper prior to the joining of two persons in wedlock. I fail to see how you could claim ignorance of David's resulting marriage to me."

"Don't play the fool! Of course I knew David had married. But why did you not tell me *you* were his wife? Or were you convinced I should hold it against you?"

"Indeed, why should I?" Georgina queried in a state of utter befuddlement.

"That is what I am trying to find out," countered the duke in a dangerous voice. "The least you could have done was write to let me know you were safe. Have you any notion of the anxiety I have suffered thinking you might have succumbed to the fever or worse? And all the time I was searching the Continent for you, you were here. I believe you owe me some explanation for such blatant irresponsibility."

"Oh! You, sir, are abominable!" Georgina said furiously, unable to believe what she was hearing. "I did write to inform you of my whereabouts and that the Earl of Emberly was quite safe. But you showed a remarkable lack of interest in the affairs of your ward. Nor did you see fit to extend the smallest condolence for the passing of your cousin. Oh, how I wish I might be able to see your face, for I cannot credit my ears with what I have just heard. How could David have been so mistaken in your character? For you must know he accounted you his dearest friend."

She was not prepared for the taut silence which greeted her outburst. She stood rigidly straight, her bosom heaving with indignation, and waited for Rathbourne to answer to her heated accusations. But he did not speak, and the silence between them was broken only by the harsh expulsion of his breath. As though he had suffered a physical blow, she thought in sudden wonderment. Why did he not say something? she fretted, unconsciously tilting her head to one side in an attitude of listening. Then she felt him draw near, sensed the feather-like touch of his hand against her cheek, and she drew sharply back, her heart pounding with sudden unreasoning panic. She wheeled as though to flee from him, and a low cry escaped her lips as she came up hard against the marble bench, a rending pain shooting through her knee.

Strong hands grasped her arms to steady her.

"Softly, child," the duke said and eased her down on the bench. Then, "You've hurt yourself!"

"N-no. It's nothing," she gasped, struggling to calm the turmoil which left her lost and reeling in her world of darkness. And all the while she was acutely aware of the man standing over her in concern. "How very clumsy of me," she managed a trifle breathlessly. "You must not think I am in the habit of stumbling into things. Usually I am quite adept at finding my way about."

"No doubt," he said in an odd voice. There was a telling pause. "Forgive me. I didn't know . . ."

"No. Please," Georgina began in a rush, then, appalled at the shrill pitch of her voice, broke off what she had been about to say.

"It would seem we have been talking at cross-purposes," he said after a moment. "Perhaps we should begin again."

"Yes. Perhaps we should," she managed more calmly and grasped her hands in her lap to still their trembling. Really, the man had a most unsettling effect on her which promised to make their acquaintanceship anything but smooth if she did not soon learn to control it. Suddenly her keen appreciation of the absurd brought a reluctant smile to her lips. She had certainly made a memorable first impression on the Duke of Rathbourne.

"I do beg pardon for ripping up at you," she said ruefully. "I hardly know what came over me just now. Normally I am not like to fly into the boughs. What a ninnyhammer you must think me."

"Quite so," replied the duke harshly.

Georgina could not stifle a gasp at such gross incivility, but before she could make a suitable response, he had continued in a voice hard with barely suppressed anger.

"You not only did not see fit to make known to me your whereabouts, but neither, Lady Grey, did you inform me of your—er—disability. And, furthermore, if Bolton is to be believed, you have taken upon yourself the running of this estate. And without benefit even of a suitable companion who might have at least facilitated your role as chatelaine of this very sizeable establishment. You, ma'am, are foolish beyond permission."

"I beg your pardon," pronounced Georgina in awful

tones. "By what right do you speak so to me? May I remind you that you are not *my* guardian."

"That, Madam, is nothing to the point."

"It is everything to the point! I do not recognize your assumed authority over me and will thank you to play least seen in my affairs."

"Believe me I should like nothing better," rejoined the duke in acid tones. "But unfortunately my cousin has made that an utter impossibility. I am his son's guardian, and as such it is my duty to point out to you that young females of quality do not live unchaperoned. Have you no regard for your own reputation, you might at least think of your son and the name he bears."

It was in her mind to bring him down a peg by informing him of her cousin's pending arrival, but Georgina's usually dormant temper was loosed at long last. She would not give him the satisfaction of knowing his accusations had some merit. For to acknowledge that she had agreed to accept a paid companion in her home was to do just that. Instead, she ripped up at him, flinging in his face the one thing she held most against him.

"Duty, Your Grace?" she said icily. "How dare you speak of duty now, when my husband has lain dead these many months. You could not even be bothered to send condolences on the death of a man who loved you like a brother. No doubt your engagements in town were too pressing for such common courtesy."

"No, ma'am," the duke replied in cutting tones. "I was, I fear, recovering from wounds received at Talavera. Or have you so conveniently forgotten that little episode?"

Georgina's anguished gasp was harsh in the sudden stillness. Terrible remorse robbed her of speech. Nor did the duke's final words register in her stunned consciousness. Her hands flew to her heated face. Oh, God, she thought. He had been there, too. Like all those other poor souls. Like David. And she had flown at him like the veriest fishwife. No wonder she had not heard from him. He must have been gravely wounded.

"Forgive me," she said in a voice hardly above a whisper. "I did not know."

"Did not know?" he returned in astounded accents.

"No. How should I? I myself was—ill—for a long time after David . . . Well, no matter. I do most sincerely beg your forgiveness for my thoughtless words. My memory of the Peninsula is—clouded. But I do know you must have suffered dreadfully. I have *not* forgotten the agonies of those poor men."

"I see," he said in an odd voice. She could feel him staring down at her and found herself plucking at the folds of her skirt nervously. "Just what do you remember?"

"Please," she evaded, twisting her head sharply away from him that he might not see the uncertainty, indeed, the fear which must be plain in her face. "I would rather not dwell on the past."

She flinched at the cool touch of his hand against her cheek. Inexorably he turned her face toward him. What was happening to her? she wondered as she tried in vain to still the sudden trembling in her limbs.

"Forgive me," he said, more gently than she had yet heard him speak. "But I must know how you came to be . . ."

"Blind?" she finished for him when his voice suddenly faltered. "Oh, you need not fear for my sensibilities. Grandmama says I have none. And it would hardly do to be missish about something I cannot help. But however that may be, I fear I can actually tell you very little about how I came to be as I am." She grew silent for a moment, and when she finally spoke again, her voice was oddly colorless. "I can remember nothing of the events which preceded the onset of my affliction. Indeed, several weeks of my life are apparently irretrievably lost."

"Lost? You remember nothing of . . . of what hap-

72

pened?" he amended in a curiously strangled tone.

"I know only that I left Lisbon to search for my husband, and I think probably nothing could ever wipe out the memory of that dreadful march to Talavera. But after that, everything is a blank."

"Good God!" exclaimed the duke in horrified accents. "How came you to make the march to Talavera? Surely David would never have allowed anything so patently foolhardy."

"Very true, Your Grace," Georgina replied ironically. "And considering your recent lecture on the proprieties surrounding females of quality, I fear you will not like to hear how I managed it."

"No doubt," he said grimly. "Yet you will tell me nevertheless, an' you please."

"Actually I do not please, but I suppose you will learn of it anyway," she rejoined a trifle bitterly. "You see, after Obidos and Roliça, David insisted I return to Lisbon with Davey and await him there. And so I did, while he went on to fight at Vimeiro. But then I could stand being apart from him no longer, and I determined to leave Davey with the Fitzhughs in Lisbon and rejoin David's regiment, which was even then reported making for Talavera. By means which I shall not reveal to you, I obtained a lieutenant's uniform of the 52d regiment of Light Infantry and joined the march to Talavera."

"You did what?" Rathbourne exclaimed fiercely.

"I said you would not like it," replied Georgina calmly. Then, with a slightly furrowed brow, she added, "Actually, I suppose it *was* foolhardy, considering the conditions which prevailed upon that march. I was fortunate, however, to have been taken as aide to Colonel Beckwith and thus was provided with a horse. The dear colonel never guessed the stripling he had taken under his wing out of compassion for my apparent youth was a woman."

"Had he done, you no doubt would have met an ignominious end, my girl," Rathbourne observed darkly.

"No doubt. Yet what I witnessed of the sufferings of those men was surely punishment enough for my small deception. Just imagine! The 52d marched over sixty-two miles in twenty-six hours. And in the intense heat of July! And this after already having come from Santarem to Malpartida de Placencia! I saw men kill themselves rather than take another step, and I do not know how many fell to brain fever."

"Close to ten thousand by the time we had retreated from Talavera. Good God! I cannot believe you could be so henwitted!"

"Perhaps," she said, her eyes huge and suddenly haunted. "But I had to go after David. It was something I felt. You see, I knew somehow that if I did not reach Talavera in time, I would never see him again. Rather like those soldiers who inexplicably know before they go into battle that they are going to die." Her voice broke then, and she suddenly averted her face. "David knew," she whispered as if to herself. "That's why he left me behind."

After a time she continued to speak in a dull, lifeless voice. "But I was too late. Talavera was already a British victory and David was gone forever. I searched the wounded for him, helped those I could to escape the grassfires started by the cannonfire. My God! I believe more died in that burning inferno than succumbed to wounds. And then afterwards, the fever. I never found David and can only surmise his body was burned with the thousands of other corpses by Crauford's men during the clean-up. As for myself, I must have gone a little mad or succumbed to the fever myself, for I remember nothing of what happened thereafter and know only that I was discovered two months later wandering the streets of Elvas."

"Elvas!" ejaculated Rathbourne in a strangled voice. "But how came you there? Surely you must remember something!"

"No. Nothing. I was delirious, out of my senses. Somehow, moreover, I had suffered a severe concussion to the head."

"And the blindness?"

She sighed wearily, wishing he would go. Her head had begun to ache abominably, as it always did when she tried to remember those lost weeks, and she pressed her fingertips hard against her temples.

"I don't know," she said, dropping her hands again to her lap and clutching them tightly together. "The physician in Lisbon could find no reason for it."

"But he must have had some explanation!"

"No," she answered, her smile ironic. "It would seem the problem is not physical so far as he could tell. Apparently I simply do not wish to see." Then suddenly impatient to have done with it, she waved one hand dismissively. "Oh, what does it matter? Whatever the reason, the fact remains that I am quite without sight. And now that I am come to the end of my tale, I feel your curiosity must be satisfied, Your Grace. Surely we can talk of something else."

"Not yet," he said, and she felt his eyes intent upon her. They were blue, she thought irrelevantly. David had said he had the look of the black Celt with raven hair and eyes the color of the Cornish sea on a still, clear day. "There's just one thing more. I should like to know how you made your way back to Lisbon, then I shall trouble you no more."

"Indeed?" she queried silkily. "And I had thought to have you constantly about to see that I conformed to the proprieties of my exalted station."

"Hornet," he said feelingly. "No doubt that, too, can be arranged. Now you will tell me how you found yourself once more in Lisbon, my girl."

"Well, if you must know, two officers from the Bomb Proof Barracks discovered me. The men of the Barracks were responsible, you see, for removing the dead from the hospital at the Convent of St. Paul in Elvas. One of them had seen me there some time before tending the wounded. It seems I was raving something about needing to reach the Fitzhughs and Davey in Lisbon. Lord Fitzhugh himself fetched me from Elvas to his home and kept me there till I was recovered enough to return to England. And that, my lord duke, is everything.

"Not quite, madam," Rathbourne observed ominously. "You sent word of my cousin's demise. That much I recall despite my own indisposition at the time. I remember nothing as regards *your* circumstances. Why was I not informed?"

"And what were my circumstances to you, my lord duke?" Georgina countered impatiently. "Was I to cry to my son's guardian that I was blind? I am not so craven, sir. I felt I must learn to manage on my own if ever I was to be more than a helpless invalid. Don't you see? I had my son to think of. He had need of a whole and healthy parent. And, indeed, we have rubbed along quite well up till now."

The countess lifted her head proudly and dared him to gainsay her, but happily the duke was spared a retort by the arrival of Bolton on the scene.

"Begging your pardon, milady," intoned the butler from the French doors which opened on to the garden. "I am sent to inform you Miss Kingsley has arrived."

Georgina breathed a sigh of relief. How fortuitous was her cousin's arrival! She had no wish to hear Rathbourne's judgment of her past actions. She knew well enough by now that it would hardly be favorable. His arrogant assumption of command over her life and Davey's was not enough, but he must lecture her on the proprieties as well. She thought she had rarely encountered a ruder, more overbearing man. Nor was it likely that he would consider her efforts at overseeing Emberly at all adequate. She doubted that he approved of managing females. Well, she would just have to show him how wrong he was to ill-judge her. She was neither an invalid to be pitied nor some witless female in need of someone to manage her affairs.

With that thought firmly in mind, Georgina rose gracefully from her seat on the marble bench and inclined her head tranquilly toward the butler.

"Thank you, Bolton. Where have you put Miss Kingsley?"

"In the Blue Saloon, milady."

"Very well. Please have a tea tray brought to us there. I feel sure His Grace must be thirsty after our lengthy discussion."

Then, turning to Rathbourne, she arched one delicate eyebrow. "My Lord Duke?" she invited graciously. "If you would care to accompany me to the house, I believe you will find Miss Kingsley of particular interest."

"As you wish, Lady Grey," he answered after a moment. "But do not think this discussion is at an end."

"I should never be so foolish, my lord duke," she murmured sweetly and turned to stroll casually toward the house.

Almost absently her hand brushed along the yew hedge which flanked the short walk to the point where it ended at the flagstone terrace. Without pausing, she stepped up the few inches from the gravel walk onto the flagstones and walked unerringly to the French doors. She heard the duke following behind her and for the first time became aware that he walked with a decided limp, the uneven gait accompanied by the hollow tap of a walking stick against the flagstones.

Rathbourne stepped in front of her, and she heard the soft click of the latch followed by the faint creak of the doors opening.

"Madam?" he said, and she smiled demurely as she walked gracefully past him into the house.

Once inside the Blue Saloon, she paused, her head unconsciously cocked to one side. The soft rustle of skirts from across the room drew her attention. She turned to face the Adams fireplace before which she surmised Miss Kingsley was standing, probably absently admiring the Sévres figurines ranged on the mantelpiece while she waited perhaps a trifle uncertainly for her cousin's arrival.

"Gina?" came a rather strained voice which was quite unfamiliar to the countess.

Instantly Georgina stepped forward with one hand extended in welcome, while the other trailed surreptitiously along the back of the settee, guiding her flawlessly around it.

"Zenobia," she said, her rich contralto expressive of sincere welcome. "How good of you to come to me in my time of need. I was grieved to hear of your own sorrow. But we shall both come about now that you are here."

Lady Grey's fingers curled around the soft hand placed uncertainly in her own. She was startled to feel how cold was that small member and instinctively she drew her cousin near that she might embrace her.

The child was of dainty proportions, Georgina discovered, as her cousin's curls tickled her chin. The countess breathed in the sweet perfume of lavender water and talcum. Impulsively she placed a hand gently on either side of the cool cheeks.

"Nobie," she said softly. "It has been so long, and I have so looked forward to having you here. I wish to 'see' you. Do you mind?"

"N-no, Gina," the girl answered hesitantly. Then she stood stiffly as Georgina's sensitive fingers explored the contours of her face.

The child was too thin, Georgina thought, as she felt the prominent cheekbones beneath the soft, smooth skin. The nose was small and straight, the chin delightfully pointed and probably stubborn. There was a pensive frown between the delicately arched eyebrows, and the full lips were unsmiling. Poor Nobie, she though. She has not yet got over her grief. The girl's hair was soft and pulled back

78

behind small shapely ears in the lobes of which were tiny earrings—her mother's pearl droplets, no doubt. The high, wide forehead presented an image of sensitivity and intelligence. There was a tautness about the slender neck in which Georgina could feel the pulse throb almost painfully fast. Why, the child seemed frightened of her!

Mischievously Georgina pressed a finger lightly at the corner of her cousin's mouth.

"It was here, I believe," she said mysteriously.

Immediately she felt the soft lips curve tentatively upwards.

"Yes, most definitely. The most beguiling dimple I have ever seen. Do tell me, my dear lord duke, that it is yet there."

"Indeed," drawled a bemused Rathbourne. "And as lovely as you have described it."

Georgina's delightful laughter gurgled forth as she felt the girl draw slightly away from her. The head dropped as though to hide a blush, and the countess hugged Miss Kingsley bracingly about the shoulders.

"Never mind, sweet Nobie," she murmured in the girl's ear. "I am so glad to have found you again. Come, let me make you known to His Grace, the Duke of Rathbourne. My lord duke, this is Miss Zenobia Kingsley, my cousin. She has come to lend me countenance and to make brighter my shadowed existence."

Chapter 4

His Grace, the Duke of Rathbourne, mounted his mettlesome roan stallion and began the return ride to Rathbourne Castle lost to everything but the memory of Georgina Grey and the appalling realization that in finding her, he had lost himself. The rolling green parks dotted with sheep and the brisk scent of the sea failed to rouse him as it had done on his earlier ride to the manor. Indeed, he rode like one weighted down by a terrible burden, his broad shoulders bowed as though he had sustained a mortal blow.

With bitter clarity he recalled the fateful stroll down the short gravel walk toward the figures of a slender woman and a small boy seated beneath a grape arbor. He had been intent upon dispatching as quickly as possible a duty he little relished, for he had not looked forward to reliving the sharp agony of grief which his cousin's death had occasioned him and which would undoubtedly be rendered even more poignant in the memory-laden hallows of Greystone Manor.

Rathbourne's cousin had enjoyed a special intimacy with the duke which had never been granted to any other, not even to Robbie, who was thirteen years his junior and who had ever looked upon him as the infallible, heroic elder brother. For David Grey had known and understood what bitter uncertainties plagued the youthful Andrew Penwarren, who had experienced little of happiness and nothing of love.

His mother, considered upon her come-out to be a diamond of the first water, had proven a diffident creature intimidated by life in general and by her husband most in particular. Having provided the duke with an heir early-on in the marriage, she had retired with obvious relief from an active participation in anything more strenuous than lying abed and consuming sweetmeats and novels of a romantic vein. Until one night her lord and master, unaccountably recalling her existence, had chosen to exercise his husbandly rights, which had resulted nine months later in the birth of Robert Geoffrey Charles Penwarren, an event followed soon after by her own untimely demise. Andrew Penwarren, having by this time already achieved his thirteenth birthday under the auspices of a host of nannies and tutors, was little affected by the loss of his mother with whom he had had little or no discourse before her death. Unfortunately the same could not be said of his father, for whom, unaccountably, the boy had entertained an awed affection.

The previous duke, a nobleman of brilliant intellect and manly physique, had been a noted *Non Pareil* in his youth and something of a statesman in his maturity, but for all his accomplishments, he knew nothing of the human heart. Of a naturally cold disposition, he had shown little affection and no patience for the proud, sensitive youth who had had the misfortune to inherit his mother's startling beauty. For the duke had mistakenly associated his son's childish vulnerability with the weakness of character which had long alienated whatever affections he might once have had for his duchess. Finding little in his son to applaud and much with which to find fault, he had sought to mold the boy into a man worthy, in his own narrow view, to wield the wealth and power of a great dukedom. He had succeeded only in driving a wedge between himself and his son, and in the end had died a hard and bitter man who in his disillusion had refused to allow the heir into the presence of his dying father.

David Grey alone had been allowed to witness his cousin's grief, and only he had understood the hard cynicism which had led Rathbourne to every sort of wild excess and self-indulgence. Indeed, only at Greystone Manor had the young duke known any peace from his own, particular hell, for there he had enjoyed not only the friendship of his cousin, but the quiet understanding and affection of the Earl of Emberly as well—until his wild exploits had finally tried even the patience of that kindly man and Rathbourne had been banned from ever crossing Emberly's threshold so long as the old earl lived.

Thus the Duke of Rathbourne had come reluctantly to the rambling old house to meet his cousin's widow and the young heir who was his ward. Preoccupied with his own haunting recollections of David Grey and Greystone Manor, he had not been prepared for the tender scene upon which he had unintentionally intruded.

At first he had noticed nothing odd in the woman's demeanor other than a convulsive gesture of protection toward the child when he startled them with his unheralded arrival. The arbor was thickly covered with leafy foliage, and he had still been somewhat blinded by the brilliance of the sun after the shadowed interior of the house. Consequently he had not recognized her until she had stepped from beneath the arbor into the sunlight.

The world had seemed to blur and fade away so that only he and the girl had remained. But even as he had reeled from the unexpected shock of finding his angel in the garden at Greystone, he had been struck by her own marked failure to recognize him. He had stood quite still, drinking in the features which had never ceased to haunt him. The dark eyes so lustrous against the pale translucence of her skin had seemed larger and even more hauntingly lovely than he remembered them. With a pang he noted the fine-boned face, thinner now than before, more mature, yet unbelievably beautiful. There was the same quiet self-possession about the enticing mouth and firm chin. How well he remembered that aura of calm. Communicated in her infinitely tender touch, it had soothed his feverish ramblings, eased his tormented dreams. Her hair the color of rich mahogany was gathered in a loose knot at the nape of her neck. At Talavera she had worn it boyishly short so that it had clustered in beguiling curls about her face.

Enthralled, he watched one hand flutter nervously to her bosom. What had she said? He forced himself to concentrate on the words. She seemed oddly fearful, her head cocked to one side as though listening for something, and suddenly he had realized that she was frightened of him. Incredibly she was demanding his name. And he had reacted true to form, he thought bitterly as he recalled the sudden cynical birth of suspicion that she was playing him for a fool. What was she after, his elusive angel? Well, she should have it and more as soon as he had her to himself.

Intrigued and more than a little piqued by her refusal to recognize him, he had made some reply and been momentarily disarmed by her ripple of enchanting laughter. She was superb in her role of the innocent, he mused sardonically as he dutifully turned to acknowledge her introduction of the child. Then he had looked at the boy for the first time and beheld a childish replica of David Grey, and suddenly he had gone cold with rage as the full impact of his discovery hit him at last. Good God! No wonder she had taken such care to hide her identity from him, the scheming little wretch. All the time she had been David's wife!

In the agonizing months during which he had searched for her, tormented with the fear that she was dead, he had imagined a multitude of reasons for her secrecy. But nothing could have prepared him for this. He could have forgiven her anything, he had foolishly thought, anything except that knowing who he was, she had given herself to him.

Had it not been for the boy, no doubt he would have called her to account then for her deceit. But he had had to bide his time till he could be rid of the child's presence. In a quake of impatience he had watched the young earl retreat to the house. Now he would have the truth, he vowed darkly.

Rathbourne writhed in the saddle as he recalled his harsh accusations and her indignant fury. "Oh, how I wish I might be able to see your face," she had said and in that single utterance had shattered his façade of anger. What a fool he had been not to realize before! Yet the brown eyes, so wide upon his face, had not the look associated with the blind. He had seen the sparks of anger slowly receding from their lustrous depths to be replaced by puzzlement.

Fearfully, as though afraid she might crumble beneath his touch, he raised shaking hands to touch her face. Disbelief had vied with anguish as helplessly he watched her turn away from him. Her cry of pain as she struck the marble bench had jolted him to his senses. But even as he reached out to keep her from falling and eased her down on the bench, he had been filled with a bewildering agony. How could she have been so false, so removed from all sense of decency as to face him with the knowledge of her guilt? Oh, God! *His* guilt. And yet something kept him from condemning her out of hand, the memory, perhaps, of the sweet passion they had shared that last night in Elvas before she had vanished from his life as mysteriously as she had entered it.

He had been shivering with icy waves of fever, tormented by the pain which never left him, and yet everything, the minutest of details, had been etched in his memory, but disjointedly, like some strange mosaic whose pieces had been jumbled. He recalled fretting at the detestable scent of daisy-like flowers in an earthenware pot near his bed and and being gently chided by the voice of his angel saying they were *matricaria* and that their presence would help relieve his pain and ward off infection. No less revolting had been the stench of sulfur mingled with the odor of a tallow candle whose faint, flickering flame cast weird shadows against the whitewashed stucco walls and the vaulted ceiling of carved wood the Portugese called *alfarge*. The images of birds and flowers fluttered through his memory, the patterns woven into the counterpane draped over him and on the faded cotton curtains billowing gently in the small breath of an evening breeze stealing in through the ogival window from the inner patio to be found at the center of every Portugese house. There had been flowers, too, in pots on the window sill and from somewhere beyond the window the incessant chirrup of a *grilo*, a cricket ensconced in a tiny wicker cage to inspire someone's caged linnet or goldfinch to enraptured song. And always an awareness of the slender girl moving quietly about as she tended to his needs or sitting quietly on the *arca*, the carved wooden chest which, along with the bed and a brass washbasin set on a plank supported by trestles, made up the sparse furnishings of the small room.

He moved restlessly on the bed, his head turning incessantly on the pillow, his teeth chattering with cold despite the heat of the wretched Plain of Alentejo in late August and the woolen *cobertores* heaped on top of him. Lost in a dream of the remembered horrors of Talavera, he cried out and bolted upright in the bed, the pain ripping through his thigh to leave him reeling and gasping for air. Strong young hands forced him firmly back against the pillows, even as his angel's voice broke through the threatening curtain of darkness.

"My lord, you must remain still. You will break open the wound."

Obediently he lay back, staring at her as if seeing her for the first time—the lovely oval of her face pale in the candlelight, the huge eyes like pools of translucent darkness anxious upon him. He licked dry lips, tried to say her name.

"Gina—I . . ."

"Sh-h," she whispered, smiling gravely as she pressed the back of her hand gently against his cheek and then his forehead.

She was so beautiful, his angel, his mysterious Gina. Suddenly there was so much he wanted to say to her, but the words would not come to him. A chill shuddered down his long length—the fever which seemed to ebb and flow like the tides of an icy sea washing over him, robbing him of coherent thought so that he knew only that he was so very cold and that he wanted her dreadfully, needed her as he had never needed anyone before. His hand closed around her wrist, and he felt her go very still. A quiver rippled through her slim form as he slipped the wrapper off her shoulders, but she made no move to stop him, and with trembling fingers he undid the ribbon at the front of her nightdress, his tormented gaze never leaving hers. His breath whistled in his throat at sight of her supple beauty, the high well-formed breasts and slender torso tapering to a tiny waist. He held her with his eyes, willing her to understand without words. For a long moment she searched his face, her own filled with a haunting sorrow. Then with a long shuddering sigh, she uttered a small moan and lowered her head to kiss him.

She had made love to him with tenderness and a quiet urgency—a desperation almost—which haunted him. The desperation of grief and loneliness, he thought as, oblivious to the sounds of the river and the wind sighing through the trees, he looked over his shoulder at the steep wooded hills of the Tamar Valley. And in unexpected bitterness he knew she had been making love not to him but to a memory of

David.

Rathbourne's lips curled in a hard, cynical smile at his own hypocrisy. How unlike the dissolute duke to play the role of outraged sensibilities! He, who had been branded a dangerous rakeshame by the time he was two and twenty. Yet despite his disgust at himself and his disillusion with the mysterious lady of Greystone Manor, he had been moved to reluctant admiration for her undeniable courage. How many women of his acquaintance, or men for that matter, would have dared to do all that she had done? And not just on the Peninsula, but here at Emberly as well, for the estate continued to prosper under her capable management, and it appeared she had won the respect and loyalty of the retainers, for he could not have mistaken the faint glow of warmth which had peeked through Bolton's normally impassive countenance as he spoke of the young countess. She was an enigma, was Lady Georgina Grey, and suddenly he had found himself lecturing her on the improprieties of living without benefit of a female companion. And all along his real objection had been that she had taken on more than should be expected of a woman alone. But then he had known from the beginning that his angel was dauntless. If she had not been, he would no doubt be in his grave.

Then had come the final blow. For she was not the consummate actress he had thought her to be. Good God, she remembered none of it! His blood had run cold to hear her tell of the march from Santarem to Talavera, and suddenly he had been grateful she had not the other horrors of the retreat to Campo Mayor and Elvas to haunt her. He had experienced an unexpected desire to spare her any further pain, something he had never felt for any woman.

"Damn her!" he muttered aloud. She was everything he had ever dreamt of in a woman. Sensitive, beautiful, caring, and possessed of an outrageous independence, a quick intelligence, and a lively sense of the ridiculous which set her apart from the other women he had known. And she was proud. He recalled the way she had carried herself, her back straight, her head held high, as she strolled with easy grace toward the house, and he saw again her triumphant smile as she walked unerringly past him and across the Blue Saloon to greet her cousin. He had known a sharp stab of envy as he watched her explore with sensitive fingers the young woman's face. If only she had touched him so, he thought, then wondered if the thin line of the scar on his cheek might have triggered some vestige of memory in her.

And then the idea had come to him. If she remembered nothing of those weeks of pain and hardship, if, indeed, she remembered nothing of him and their single night of shared passion, then was it not as if it had never been? Only he knew she had come to him in tenderness and compassion and unquestionably out of grief for her own loss, for he could not doubt that she had truly loved his cousin. Indeed, it had been love which had led her to assume male garb and follow her husband into the battlefield and thus love which had exacted such a heavy price as the forfeiture of her sight. She was not at fault, nor would David have held her to blame. And he could not. For suddenly he understood his strange obsession to find her. From the very beginning he had wanted her for his own.

In the grips of sudden realization, Rathbourne straightened his powerful shoulders and looked out across the green barrows. In the distance the twin towers of Rathbourne Castle perched on the rocky cliffs above the sea glinted in the waning sunlight. Of all his several holdings, this one dating back to the first Earl of Rathbourne, who had been so named by William the Conqueror, the title having been changed to Duke in 1692 by William III after the battle of La Hogue, called to something deep within him. His roots, no doubt, he used to speculate cynically. Since reaching his majority, he had by choice lived away from Cornwall, for his memories of Rathbourne were not pleasant and he had preferred the rather more dissolute pursuits to be found in London and abroad. Yet despite the years spent in fleeing from his haunted memories, he could not deny a stubborn pride in the ancient pile, nor even an irrevocable bond with the long line of Penwarrens who had held it and preserved it as it was.

His sweeping glance encompassed the battlemented walls atop which his flag furling in the breeze formed a crimson stream against a grey bulge of gathering clouds. Rising above the castle's rocky promontory the hills were rugged with steep ravines bristling with cork-trees, live-oaks, and heath—the deer park through which he had roamed as a boy—and tumbling down its side from one rocky terrace to another, Glangorn Gill spilled over the edge of the cliff known as Llan Penrhyn or Promontory Chapel, to the grottoed coves below. Ancient oaks, beech, ash, and sycamore crowded the steep slopes rising to a terrace on which perched a gothic alcove overlooking Whitsand Bay to the south and east, the long sandy beaches awash with the rising tide and the sea swelling in restless anticipation of the building storm. He had a sudden yearning to board his ketch, *The Swallow*, moored in one of the numerous narrow inlets known as "the zawns" which lay below the castle, and ride out the gale. Instead, he lifted the reins and sent his restless mount at a gallop across the wold and along the narrow trail which led through the deer park to the castle. But neither the storm nor his wild, heedless pace could still the tumult which Lady Georgina Grey had aroused within his breast. Indeed, not until she was chatelaine at Rathbourne Castle would he know any peace again.

Wearily the duke cantered through the gateway into the castle grounds and relinquished the stallion to a groom. The heavy oak door to the main house, which once had been the circular keep but which had long since been expanded and modernized by succeeding generations to afford a greater comfort than that to which their ancient ancestors had been accustomed, swung open at Rathbourne's approach, revealing the slightly stooped form of Fergus, the aged butler who had served the family through two generations of Penwarrens.

Replying somewhat absently to the old retainer's greeting, Rathbourne relinquished his curly brimmed beaver and chamois gloves.

"Is my brother within?" he asked, shrugging off the light spencer worn over his riding jacket of bottle green superfine.

"*Ais*, Yer Grace. Lord Robert *es* in the library."

Rathbourne nodded and strode briskly across the huge entry hall, his bootheels tapping hollowly against the black and white tiled floor. Despite the warm spring weather, a fire crackled in the open grate of the huge Gothic fireplace in an attempt to ward off the chill dampness of the sea trapped within by the thick stone walls of the castle. Colorful tapestries draped the walls, the legacy of generations of Penwarren women who had preserved history with nimble fingers. Rathbourne experienced the familiar sensation of having stepped through a portal into history as he walked past suits of armor standing like silent sentinels along the winding staircase to the second story. The feeling left him as he opened the door to the library and stepped into the more cheerful environs of the bookroom.

His glance embraced the book-lined walls and hardwood floors graced with rich oriental rugs. The room smelled pleasantly of leather—leatherbound books, leather-upholstered chairs and sofas. It was a masculine room with heavy, sturdy furniture and rich, dark woods.

Rathbourne took in with a humorous quirk of his lips the long form of his brother slumped in a chair before the Adams fireplace. A pile of books littered the floor about his outstretched legs. The long, slender fingers turned the page of a scholarly treatise on the cultural and religious significance of the dolmen to the Druidic Celt. A furrow of concentration creased the high brow above gold-rimmed reading spectacles. Too absorbed in his reading, he had not noted the duke's entrance, and Rathbourne studied the sensitive features of his young brother with an uncomfortable feeling of guilt.

Of a scholarly bent, Robbie was at peace among his beloved books, and Rathbourne was well aware that his own lengthy illness followed by his obsession to find the girl who had saved his life on the Peninsula had kept the boy far too long from his studies. Robbie had distinguished himself at Oxford and was well on his way to becoming a noted authority on Cornish history. He spent hours immersed in his books or touring sites of prehistoric hill-forts, the numerous coits or dolmen located in the granite hills of Cornwall, or the remains of isolated stone cottages inhabited by the Celtic tribesmen and was saved from becoming a total recluse only by an equally compelling interest in the living culture around him. Robbie Penwarren liked people. He liked talking to them and enjoyed listening to them even more. Already he had amassed a sizeable collection of Cornish folk tales and superstitions painstakingly documented and recorded. Blessed with a naturally athletic physique, he was tall and slender with wide shoulders and long-muscled limbs and, though of slighter build than his Corinthian brother, moved with the same effortless grace. And if he lacked the sense of leashed power and strong magnetism of his elder brother's dominant personality, he was nonetheless possessed of a compelling sweetness of disposition and a highly developed intellect which drew others to him.

The duke had never fully understood this younger brother who seemed of a higher plane of existence, but nor had he ever underestimated his worth. The boy was a rare being of profound compassion and understanding, and the duke had watched over him with a fierce protectiveness since first he had laid eyes on the helpless infant left motherless at birth.

"I perceive," drawled the duke at last, "that you are well lost to the world and shall wish me to perdition. Yet I do not hesitate to beguile you with my presence. I have news."

Robert Penwarren blinked and looked up at the pale visage of his brother. Behind the thick lenses of the reading glasses, his blue eyes appeared abnormally large. Absently he reached up to remove the spectacles, then eyed his brother appreciatively.

"You've received word from Ireland," he guessed at sight of the duke's studied impassivity. The Corinthian's thoughts were veiled beneath heavily drooping eyelids, yet Robbie sensed his brother's emotions held tightly in check.

Rathbourne strode deliberately across the room to a grog tray and poured two brandies before satisfying the youth's keenly aroused curiosity.

"No, bantling," he said as he turned, glasses in hand. "I have *found* my elusive angel."

"Found her? But where? How?" Robbie straightened suddenly in his chair. The book allowed to slide heedlessly from his lap to the floor was perhaps the measure of his surprise.

Rathbourne's thin lips curled in a sardonic smile as he handed Robbie a brandy.

"At Greystone Manor. Ironically it appears that the woman I have sought fruitlessly all these months is our kinswoman. Lady Georgina Grey as it were."

"Good God!" Robbie ejaculated. "Not David's widow?"

"Even so," uttered the duke, his expression unreadable behind the bored mask of the Corinthian, and dropped into a leather armchair across from his brother. Pensively he sipped the brandy while Robbie eyed him speculatively.

"You seem uncommonly subdued for having achieved your goal," the youth observed sapiently, then quietly added, "Do you want to talk about it?"

Rathbourne allowed a heavy sigh to escape his lips and ran a hand wearily over his scarred cheek. When at last he looked up, Robbie was shocked to see the careful mask drop away. The lean features looked aged and drawn, the marvelous eyes haunted. Robbie winced at his brother's sudden ironic bark of laughter.

"She is blind," the duke said baldly and, lifting his glass in a brief toast, tossed off the drink in a single bitter gesture. "A marvelous twist of fate, would you not agree? After all these months to find her, David's grieving widow. And blind because of me. For it would seem she contracted the fever in Elvas and somehow suffered a blow to the head. She remembers none of it or of me. I find that a capital jest indeed."

An uncomfortable silence broken only by the cheerfully crackling fire fell over the room. Robbie searched for words to ease his brother's bitter pain and could find none. He was startled by the duke's fist violently striking the arm of the chair.

"My God! I have never before encountered such a singular female. To think she not only experienced the march to Talavera but survived it as well. Damn her! No woman of gentle birth should have witnessed that, let alone done it. And she remembers none of what came after. She has absolutely no recollection of having dragged the Duke of Rathbourne halfway across Spain to Elvas."

"But you told her?" Robbie demanded, watching his brother heave himself from the chair and limp heavily toward the grog tray.

"No! And nor will you," Rathbourne answered, turning to impale the youth with a piercing glance. "It is better that she remembers nothing of those weeks. There is enough of horror in her memory. I will not add to it." Nor remind her of our single night of passion, he added grimly to himself and, taking up the decanter in one hand, returned to his seat and poured another brandy.

Robbie took one look at his brother's taut face and bit back the objection which rose to his lips, asking instead that the duke in some measure satisfy his curiosity about the lady. Whereupon he listened enthralled at the incredible tale of Georgina Grey's dauntless courage and stubborn determination.

"Never has there been such a march," the duke said somberly. "You cannot imagine the Peninsula in July. The heat was abominable. Men shot themselves rather than suffer it longer. Even on horseback it is a miracle that she made it. And when they reached Talavera, to be met by the sight of thousands of wounded. The plain was covered with grass belly-high to a horse. During the battle the grass caught fire. The wounded were burned or made worse by their attempts to drag themselves to safety. I myself was pulled out by the sargent-major. And *she* was part of that."

Robbie was appalled at the image of the young woman seeking among the wounded and dying for her dead husband. He could not fully imagine the horror of the battlefield, but he had seen the frightful conditions which had prevailed at the Convent of St. Paul. Overrun with wounded and victims of Guadiana fever, it had been a scene from hell. The only treatment for the victims of the fever had been to douse them with tepid water in the hopes of bringing down the fever, and the wounded, infested with flies and filth, had suffered mass amputations to counteract gangrene. The stench alone had sickened him. The naked bodies of the dead stacked like cords of wood in ox carts to be hauled off to a common grave would forever haunt him. Summoned by a message from one of Rathbourne's fellow officers, he had determined to remove the duke with all speed from Elvas, attributing his brother's violent ravings about his ministering angel to the vagaries of a fevered brain. Even now he did not regret his actions. Rathbourne would most certainly be dead now had he remained in Elvas.

But now this. Had he been at fault? he wondered. If he had searched for the girl then, could he have prevented the tragic consequences of her impetuosity in having stayed amidst the charnel of Elvas to nurse the wounded Rathbourne? He did not know. He knew only that his brother was alive and the girl was blind, perhaps inadvertently because of him.

The duke's low voice jolted him from his uneasy thoughts.

"You must not blame yourself, bantling. No, I know how your mind works. At least in matters of conscience. You did what you had to do. What I should have done had our roles been reversed. Let it rest there."

Slowly Robbie nodded, unconvinced.

"What will you do now?" he asked quietly.

The duke sighed and tossed off the remainder of his brandy. For a long moment he stared into the bottom of the glass, but when he glanced up at last, the familiar sardonic grin curled his lips.

"I am the Earl of Emberly's guardian. It is time, I think, that I took up my responsibilities. Tomorrow I am promised to young Davey. Tonight I rather fancy I shall become thoroughly foxed. Do you join me?"

"Only should we dine first. I am devilish sharp set, old man. All this country air, you know."

"Quite so," responded the duke drily but agreed to an early supper and retired to his rooms to relieve himself of all his dirt.

Robbie followed more slowly. He little relished one of Rathbourne's drinking bouts. The duke was possessed of a hard head and was normally a four-bottle man, whereas Robbie was the exception to the hard-drinking rule of his day. Not that he was a Methodist. He merely preferred a clear head and a good book to the accepted frivolities of his set. A good brandy before bed, a little wine with his meal, an occasional bout with friends were the usual extent of his indentures. But this night promised to be a rare one, and he fully intended to begin it well-fortified with victuals.

His thoughts turned again to Rathbourne and the girl. Never had he seen his brother so affected by a woman. There had been many women in the duke's life—all of them beauties of the first water. But none had touched that well-armored heart, until now. He could not picture the woman capable of assuming male garb to seek her husband on the battlefield. An Amazon, no doubt, he mused fancifully. A large mannish woman with an iron constitution. And yet he could not imagine Rathbourne attracted to such a creature.

Robbie shrugged. Perhaps it was merely pity or a feeling of honor which moved the duke. Yet she had captured Emberly's heart as well, and David had had his choice of the eligible females on the marriage mart. None of it made sense. Suddenly he looked forward with unusual eagerness to meeting this paragon among women. He would make it a point to accompany the duke to Greystone Manor on the morrow. Only briefly did he think with regret of his books lying abandoned about the floor of the library. This promised to be a rare event worthy of the sacrifice of a few hours.

His step was suddenly much lighter as he traversed the long hallway toward his rooms. The sound of a tuneless whistle drifted in his wake, but the Duke of Rathbourne in his own chambers did not hear it. He stood in the center of his dressing room clad only in breeches and boots. His gaze was distant and somber, the high brow furrowed in thought. He was oblivious to the careful ministrations of his valet, who moved quietly about the room as he laid out evening clothes and prepared the duke's bath. Occasionally his gaze rested briefly on his master's face, wondering, perhaps, what dark thoughts occupied His Grace.

Pringle had been with Rathbourne since the nobleman's

youth and knew well his many moods. It would not have surprised him overmuch had he known Rathbourne was thinking of Talavera, for he had tended the duke during the months of his illness and had learned to associate Rathbourne's rather vacant stare with recollections of the Peninsula. He knew a great deal as well about the mysterious woman who had saved his master's life, having listened to the duke call out to her repeatedly in his delirium. Once again he blessed the lady, as he had often done in the past months, for her courageous heart.

Rathbourne was indeed lost in memories of the past. He was thinking of Georgina as she had looked when first he had regained consciousness in the hastily contrived hospital at Talavera to find her bent over him, a cool hand pressed against his brow.

"You are awake," she said with a gentle smile and, lifting his head, placed a tin cup to his lips.

He drank the tepid water gratefully then stared in disbelief into the bewitching young face regarding him with compassion. He thought he had never before seen anyone so lovely though she had been dressed in a well-worn peasant dress which was too large for her. It hung on her slender frame and was inches too short for her generous height. A wide leather belt was cinched snugly about her narrow waist and on her feet she wore high-top leather *gambadoes*, Spanish riding boots, which reached above her knees. She appeared weary and perhaps a little remote, until she smiled.

"Who are you?" he whispered, thinking that had it not been for the agony of his wounds and the sufferings of the men around him he might have believed he had died and gone to heaven. For she was like an angel of mercy.

She seemed to hesitate.

"I'm Gina, Your Grace," she said, then smiled apologetically. "Forgive me. But I must change your dressings. The doctors are overwhelmed with wounded, you know, and have condescended to allow me to help wherever I can. You are not the first I have tended. I beg you will trust me."

He had hardly been in a position to protest, he remembered with a grim smile. Watching her calm assurance as she removed the bandages from his face, he had wondered how she came to be there. She had the look of quality about her and her speech was refined. Yet though she grew a trifle pale at sight of the ugly saber cut on his cheek, she had not flinched. He winced as she cleansed the wound, and her lovely eyes flew to his in compassion.

"I'm sorry. Are you in great pain?"

He could not answer such an absurd question. One dark eyebrow arched in arrogant dismissal, but her smile melted away his irritation.

"That was stupid," she said. "My husband says I'm an utter peagoose." Then the smile abruptly faded to be replaced by an oddly lost look. In sudden alarm he raised a hand to grasp her wrist. Slowly the dark eyes refocused and he went limp with relief. For the first time he noticed the fine lines of strain at the corners of her mouth and in her eyes the lingering shadows of remembered horror and guessed she was not so unmoved as she sought to appear. She is married then, he recalled thinking and had experienced an odd lurch in the region of his heart.

He thought he would swoon as she turned her attention to his leg. Yet her touch was gentle, and he was grateful it was she who removed the bandages and deftly cleaned the wound. He was bathed in sweat when she had finished and was only vaguely aware of the shadow which loomed suddenly over him. Then he heard his angel say something and looked blankly up at a dirty, bewhiskered face and the epaulets and uniform of a major in the medical corps. The officer appeared harassed and bone-weary. The grimy, blood-stained hands probed the wound until Rathbourne thought he must scream. He *had* fainted then.

The rest was like a dream which made little sense. He

heard voices—the doctor's raspy croak and the girl's rich contralto, impatient and sharp with anger.

"You cannot do it!" she was saying, her voice low and taut. "The wound shows no sign of putrefaction. You cannot take his leg simply because it would be expedient."

He had never known such fear as took him then, not even in the press of battle with men screaming and falling all around him. He would rather face a hundred French soldiers single-handedly than the surgeon's bloody saw. He struggled against the waves of panic, tried to steel himself to meet the inevitable with a semblance of manhood. But it had been the girl who knelt beside him in the end, her touch a trifle unsteady as she swathed his leg in fresh bandages.

He could not understand what had happened. Not then. Nor later when the disgruntled privates had come to bear him away to a deserted cottage and to a cot with clean linen. Indeed, it was not until days afterward that he had been able to piece the whole together and had known that his angel had fought for him and prevailed.

Bitterly he cursed himself as he stood in his chamber at Rathbourne, oblivious to everything but his own tormenting thoughts, for Georgina Gray had demonstrated the same dauntless courage through all the succeeding weeks of hurried retreat from Talavera and the subsequent seige against infection and fever in the teeming confines of Elvas. And he had repaid her by dishonoring her. Yet even as he reeled beneath the agony of remorse, he could not subdue his growing elation at having found her again. Incredibly, providence had granted him the chance to in some measure make it up to her.

Rathbourne stirred and appeared to shake himself free of his dark brooding. With a start he realized Pringle had spoken to him.

"Well, what is it, man?" he snapped irritably.

"Your bath, Your Grace. The water is growing cold."

"Oh, yes. Very well, then," he muttered and allowed himself to be helped from his clothes. Then, sinking down into the steaming water, he felt his muscles go lax and the throb of pain in his thigh ease to a dull ache. With a sigh he rested his head against the high back of the tub and closed his eyes.

"Will there be anything else, Your Grace?" Pringle inquired tonelessly.

Rathbourne glanced up into the valet's carefully impassive features and smiled wryly.

"I fear I've been a sad trial to you, Pringle. I wonder that you don't accept Lord Harvey's numerous bribes to remove yourself to his employ."

"Oh, no, Your Grace," responded the valet with a slight shudder. "I hardly think Lord Harvey and I should suit. I fear his lordship demonstrates a lamentable preference for the extreme, and no doubt I should spend all my time attempting to dissuade him from donning lavender waistcoats or puce unmentionables."

The duke arched an imperious eyebrow.

"And I feared you must suffer ennui from my unexceptional mode of dress," he drawled repressively. "I am no doubt gratified that you apparently consider my taste impeccable."

"As to that, Your Grace," rejoined the valet, assuming a guileless expression. "You are more fortunate than Lord Harvey, for you have had me to instruct you in the fashions proper for a gentleman since you were hardly out of short coats. I must say that thanks to my ministrations you have not turned out too badly."

"You are impertinent, Pringle," the duke observed with an appreciative gleam in the heavy-lidded eyes. "I wonder why I put up with you."

"I have no idea, Your Grace. Perhaps it is my unparalleled ability to turn out an impeccably dressed gentleman."

"No doubt that is it," the duke agreed and with closed

eyes laid his head back against the edge of the tub.

Pringle allowed a faint smile to warm his gaunt features. And well you know, Your Grace, he thought to himself, that I should never leave your service. Noiselessly he turned and crossed to the fireplace to check the towels warming before the low-burning fire. His gaze passed over the dozen immaculately pressed white neck cloths draped in readiness over the back of a chair and the dark blue coat, white waistcoat, and grey knit unmentionables laid out neatly on the bed.

As he went quietly about his tasks, the same faint smile quirked his lips. At long last he had witnessed the first sign of a lessening of his master's black mood.

Chapter 5

Georgina forced herself to sit quietly as Gilda, the scullery maid recently recruited to serve as abigail, brushed her thick curls. The maid's strokes had rather the finesse of a groom currying a plough horse, she thought ruefully and had to restrain herself from snapping at the girl. After all, Gilda, one of a family of twelve, was just turned sixteen and lacked the proper training for a lady's maid, she firmly reminded herself. The girl was understandably nervous at her sudden and unlooked-for promotion to the coveted position of abigail to the mistress of the house. Doubtless she would improve given enough time, Georgina reflected, but could she risk in the meantime the likelihood of being snatched bald? On the verge of falling into a fit of the vapors, Georgina wondered how she could dispense with the child's services without hurting her feelings, when the brush caught on a particularly obstinate tangle.

"That will do, Gilda," Georgina said a trifle sharply, her eyes watering as the girl attacked the tangle with singular determination. "Perhaps you should see to that rip in the rose sarcenet gown now."

"*Iss*, m'lady," the girl answered in a low voice but did not immediately move from her mistress's side.

"Yes, Gilda?" Georgina prodded after a moment. "Is there something wrong?"

"Oh, yes, milady. Nothin' edn't right, for I know I bean't no good at tendin' proper ter thy needs. I do try, only I always seem to be all thumbs. Truly, milady. I never thought to be a lady's maid. Me hands are rough from gaird and growder what be used for cleanin' the crock and kettle. I'm more used to sweepin' and tendin' the cloam and bakin' ire than to combin' thy lovely hair. 'Twere better did 'ee send me back below stairs afore I shames meself all the more."

"Is that truly what you want, Gilda?" Georgina queried gently, touched by the child's sincerity, for she little doubted that when it came to wielding a broom and to scrubbing and preparing the earthenware oven and the flat sheet of iron known respectively in Cornish as the 'cloam' and the 'baking ire,' Gilda was quite at home. "I had no wish to cause you any unhappiness when I removed you from your former duties."

"Oh, nay!" the girl cried miserably and sank to her knees, one hand reaching out to timidly touch her mistress's arm. "I would gladly serve 'ee, milady. And count meself luckier than what I deserve. For I must tell 'ee that meself and Bromley Wilkins have come to an understanding. We would wed when there be enough put aside fer the taking of a small house with a bit of land fer the milch cow and a few pigs besides. And 'twere like a miracle sent from heaven when ye summoned me to be thy maid. Ye've the heart of an angel, milady. But it edn't right that 'ee should have to suffer me clumsy ways."

"I see," murmured Georgina, dismayed by this new turn of events, and found herself suddenly longing for the simplicity of her former life following the drum when she had had only David and their son to worry about. She simply could not bring herself to dismiss the child out of hand. "For the present we shall leave things as they are," she temporized instead. "And in a few weeks' time, if you still feel that you wish to return to the kitchens, I shan't keep you here. Now dry your tears and see to the sarcenet gown, if you will. After all, it wouldn't do for Wilkins to see you with red eyes, now would it?"

The girl uttered a watery giggle at Georgina's small attempt at humor.

"Thank 'ee, m'lady," she answered with a small sniff and, curtsying, left to do her mistress's bidding.

Georgina shuddered to think what the girl's awkward fingers would do to the fine fabric of the dress but preferred the sacrifice of an insensate gown to the further torture of her own person. Wistfully she thought of Nanny's gentle touch and unerring candor when it came to the dressing of her former nursling, especially as Georgina herself was no longer able to assess her own appearance. But Nanny had enough to do to keep up with the energetic young Earl of Emberly, and Georgina was acutely aware that her former nurse was not growing any younger. It had been at Georgina's own insistence that a girl be found to tend her personal needs so that Nanny might be relieved of caring for her as well as Davey. Thus she had only herself to blame for her present predicament.

With a sigh, she waited for the sound of the door closing behind the exiting abigail before taking up the brush and running it luxuriously through her hair. With each stroke she experienced a measure of satisfaction at the knowledge that the heavy tresses had grown so that they reached to her shoulders now. She grimaced, remembering the pang she had suffered as she snipped off her lovely hair to a length more befitting her masculine disguise. David had loved her hair, had loved to run his fingers through the silky mass falling to below her waist. She remembered thinking he would probably throttle her when he saw what she had done.

How long ago it now seemed. How young they had been! Sometimes she felt incredibly old when she remembered back to the days in Portugal. She no longer knew how she had ever found the nerve to join the regiment and make that horrid trek to Talavera. And it had all been for nothing, she reflected bitterly, for she had been too late to see her love one last time. Damn him! Why had he been so adamant in his refusal to let her accompany him? It should have been her choice, not his.

"Oh, David," she whispered to the empty room. "How could you be so selfish? We had so little time."

Georgina caught her soft underlip between her teeth. No, no, she told herself sternly, appalled at the turn her thoughts had taken. This would never do. Their time *had* been short, but it had all been good. Few people were fortunate to share in a whole lifetime as much as they had done in six short years, she reminded herself. And she still had Davey and Greystone after all.

"Now quit being such a gudgeon, Georgina Grey," she scolded and quickly fastened her hair in a knot at the nape of her neck. Then resolutely she stood and made her way from her chamber and down the stairs to the breakfast room.

The mingled aroma of ham and fresh coffee greeted her entrance. She paused momentarily in the doorway. A soft scuffling of feet alerted her to another's presence. She caught the scent of pomade and shaving soap and suppressed a small, mischievous smile.

"Wilkins," she said calmly, "would you be so kind as to fetch me a plate of ham and eggs. Toast, too, I think, and coffee. Has Cook sent up her gooseberry jam? I find I have a particular craving for it this morning."

"*Ais*, m'lady," replied the footman, grateful Bolton was not there to witness the unwitting grin which had come to his lips. Wilkins, as understudy to the formidable butler, was diligently cultivating the stonefaced dignity which marked the superior servant. But Lady Grey were a right 'un, she were. Had she not taken his darling Gilda to be lady's maid? And he guessed with keen perspicacity that her ladyship enjoyed this daily game of discerning the presence and identities of her servants. Now how had she known it was himself serving in the breakfast room today? he wondered. It was not his usual duty. Needlewitted was the countess, he thought proudly and moved quickly to serve his mistress her breakfast.

No sooner had Georgina seated herself at the table and dismissed Wilkins to pursue his other, various duties than the soft swish of skirts and the sweet scent of lilacs alerted her to the arrival of another member of the household. The countess turned with a welcoming smile to greet her cousin.

"Nobie. You're up early. I thought perhaps you would lie in today. You must be worn to the nub after your journey. Did you sleep well? Is your room everything to your liking?"

Startled, Zenobia Kingsley halted just inside the door and regarded the countess gravely. Georgina, she thought, had not the aspect of one who was blind. Where she had expected the blank look of the sightless, Georgina's large brown eyes fixed unerringly on her cousin's face held a warm light of welcome. And the previous afternoon and evening the young countess had moved freely about the house with calm assurance. There had been no hint of helplessness, no awkward groping or embarrassing stumbling over things. Certainly Lady Grey evinced none of the manifestations of the invalid Zenobia had expected from Aunt Hortense's description of Georgina.

"My room is both spacious and lovely, my lady," she said tonelessly. "I have no complaints."

Georgina cocked her head in an oddly touching manner, a questioning look in the brown eyes. A hint of a frown marred the purity of her brow as she sought to make sense of her cousin's unexpected aloofness.

"Nobie," she said quietly. "We are cousins, you and I. I am not 'milady' to you. Never that, my dear. Did you not sneak the sweetmeats and pastries up to my room when my father banished me there for stealing a ride on his stallion? Was it not you who mothered and comforted me during the week of my disgrace? Dear sweet, gentle Nobie. Am I not your own Gina?"

A blush tinged the girl's pale cheeks becomingly even as the lovely grey eyes dropped self-consciously to the floor. Georgina could not see her cousin's discomfiture, yet she sensed it in the slight sound of a sharply indrawn breath. Now what was this? she wondered, pity in her heart. The girl had ever been of a quiet nature, but her heart had always been open and true. She could not be mistaken in her memories of the child's ready affection for her elder cousin, surely? What had changed her cousin so?

"Nobie?" she prodded gently when still the girl did not answer.

Zenobia drew in a long, shuddering breath and raised her head in a gesture of firm resolve.

"Those days are long past, my lady," she said, her voice deliberately flat to camouflage her vulnerable emotions. "I come to you now as a paid companion. I have no wish to abuse my position because of our kinship. Indeed, I see now that I should never have come."

"What nonsense is this, Nobie? Tell me why we cannot be friends and equals despite the irrelevancy of a salary paid and received? I cannot understand how such a nodcock notion should have entered your head."

"Oh, don't you see?" retorted the girl in a hard voice. "Lady Hortense deceived me. She said you had need of me. But I see no evidence of it. I shall not stay here out of charity."

"Charity? Good God, Zenobia!" Georgina exclaimed in sudden, swift anger as a full comprehension of her cousin's manner became abruptly clear to her. "What would you have me to be? A piteous creature fumbling about that you might lead around by the hand and administer to as to some mindless child?"

"No! Oh, no, Georgina," the girl cried and took a pleading step toward her cousin. "Oh, I praise God you have no such needs. You are magnificent. As you were those many years ago. Fearless and indomitable as I have always longed to be. And, as in those days, you have no real need of me. You would humor me as you did then and would no doubt assign me some small tasks to do to salve my conscience. But still it would be charity which I cannot accept."

Georgina paused before answering in order to collect her thoughts. She could sense the tumult in her cousin's breast, indeed, had heard the anguish in her voice, and she felt her own hurt and anger ebb. She had not expected that her cousin might have come to her out of pity, though perhaps she should have done, and the sudden suspicion that that had indeed been Zenobia's motive had put her out of all countenance with the girl. Yet suddenly she thought she detected her grandmama's subtle hand in all this.

Oh, it was just like her grandmama, the sly old thing, to portray her granddaughter as a helpless invalid in order to enlist the sympathies of this difficult child. But how dared she! Georgina fumed. Whereupon her ever ready sense of the ridiculous came suddenly to the fore. Poor Nobie. It must have been rather daunting to arrive at Greystone expecting to find a morose, possibly bedridden wraith of a woman only to discover Georgina, hale and hearty and proudly displaying her hard-won independence. No. She could not in all conscience blame the child for what must seem a conspiracy between Georgina and Lady Hortense to provide her with a home among her own kin. It was all an unfortunate misunderstanding.

"Oh, Nobie," she said on a note of exasperation. "Such a tempest in a teacup as you have made of this. Of course I have need of you. I need your eyes, you gudgeon. Through you I shall see again. You shall describe to me all those things I cannot see. My son's glowing face. The sky on a summer's day. The parks and fields of Greystone. You shall read to me and write for me. I have worn mourning clothes far too long. You shall help me to choose a new wardrobe. And, Nobie."

"Y-yes?"

"Do you think you might do something with my hair? I can do nothing but bind it in this loathsome knot, and my—er—abigail is untrained, to say the least. I know I must look a fright, and it is most disconcerting, I assure you."

"Oh, Gina!" the girl cried, a gurgle of laughter surprised out of her. "You haven't changed a bit. I'm so glad. I had all sorts of appalling images of you. Aunt Hortense said you were only a shadow of the girl I once knew. How wrong she was! But you *are* sure, really and truly sure, that you have need of a paid companion?"

"Shall I tell you a secret?" Georgina, gladdened by the first normal tones from her cousin, queried conspiratorially. Warmly she extended a hand toward the girl who promptly took it in her own small clasp. "I fought Grandmama most stubbornly on that very thing. I was sure Davey and I should rub along quite well on our own. You see, I had dreaded to have some poor old spinster forever hovering about. You know the type. But I have come to see that Grandmama was quite right. I do need someone. And I warn you I shall work you most shamefully. Oh, Nobie. I am so glad you are come to stay with me."

"A-and I, Cousin. I know I could be happy here. That's why it seemed somehow wrong for me to stay. Please say you will forgive me."

Georgina could not help but wonder at such an odd statement. Why shouldn't the child be happy? Was she still so afflicted with grief that she should somehow blame herself for her parents' tragic death? But not wishing to press her cousin for fear of driving her once more into her shell, she said nothing but merely squeezed the girl's hand warmly before releasing it and turning back to her breakfast, which, she doubted not, was grown quite cold by now.

"Help yourself at the sideboard, Nobie. And I shall see if I can do justice to Cook's culinary genius. I confess I am quite famished."

The girl crossed obediently to the buffet and helped herself to toast and coffee, then seated herself across from Georgina.

"Only toast, Nobie?" Georgina queried gently. "You cannot be anxious about putting on a little flesh? You are already much too thin. But never mind. Your appetite will grow now that you are in the country, I promise you. And you will need your strength to keep up with Davey. I did not mention, I believe, that part of your duties will be to take Davey about the county. He needs to meet children of his own age if he is to be truly at home here."

"But how did you know . . .?" the girl began and then giggled enchantingly. "Gina, you are a complete hand. How could you know I took nothing but toast? I am never hungry in the morning, but you surely could not recall that from our brief visit to your home so long ago. And what makes you think I am thin? I warn you that you are beginning to sound very like Aunt Hortense."

Georgina grinned mischievously at her cousin.

"I shan't tell you all my secrets. It would take all the fun away. I am accounted something of a wizard, you see, and I shouldn't wish to spoil my image. Wilkins, the footman, believes I am uncanny simply because I always know he is here from the scent of his pomade and shaving soap. You, on the other hand, I shall recognize whenever lilacs pervade the air. As for your breakfast, it was simply guesswork. You were not long enough to have taken much on to your plate. And I heard no sound of the covers being removed from the serving dishes. Or the scrape of a spoon for that matter. Hence, it had to be toast."

"And my too-slender figure?" the girl queried archly.

110

"You forget. You let me 'see' you yesterday afternoon. I could feel the fine bones of your face were too prominent."

"I see. And what of the duke? What were your impressions of him?" Zenobia asked, enthralled by her cousin's perspicacity.

"Ah, the duke," Georgina replied reflectively. Indeed, what had she thought of His Grace? She recalled with a slight heightening of her color the odd sensation of having been touched by fire when he kissed her hand. And the way he had of upsetting her equilibrium with his insufferably acerbic tongue. But she would tell none of this to her young cousin.

"The duke," she said instead, assuming the air of a great seer, "is uncommonly tall. He walks with a decided limp, but is nevertheless athletic. A sportsman. He assumes an air of ennui. Indubitably his eyelids droop. He dresses elegantly in coats by Weston. His Hessians are indecently shiny. He wears a single fob and displays nothing of the dandy. He is, I should judge, a noted Corinthian. His neck cloth is exquisitely tied but is not so high as to impair the flexibility of his neck. His hands are strong, long and slender. I should think he is an excellent horseman, for his touch is firm but gentle."

"Excellent, my dear," applauded a deep voice. "But how do you know my eyelids droop?"

A startled exclamation escaped Georgina's lips. Mortified to have been caught apparently gossiping about the insufferable duke, she was further appalled to feel the blood rushing to her face. Why was it that she must forever be on the wrong foot when the man appeared? she wondered fatalistically, even as she turned with a charming smile toward the door of the breakfast room.

"Your Grace," she said sweetly. "I fear I did not hear you announced."

"That is hardly surprising since I saw fit to forego that formality," he drawled at his laziest. "You did say, I believe, that I was to run tame in your house?"

"Odious man," Georgina rejoined and favored him with her most quelling frown from which she could not quite banish the slight twitch of amusement at his polished brass. "Then it is only what you deserve, hearing what was not meant for your ears."

"I am decidedly *de trop*, ma'am. And can only most humbly beg your pardon."

"I am quite sure I have never heard anyone less humble, Your Grace," she rejoined with an appreciative gurgle of laughter. "But to show I am not of a grudging nature, I accept your apology. Perhaps you would care to join us for breakfast. *After* you have introduced us to your companion?"

A low chuckle greeted her sally, and Georgina was hard put not to reveal the sudden leap of her heart as she realized he had drawn quite near her without her being aware of his approach. Instinctively she proffered her hand and felt again that odd tingling of nerves course up her arm as he took the shapely member in his own and lightly brushed his lips against her knuckles. All too aware of the disturbing effect of his proximity, she sought gently to extricate her hand, only to suffer further confusion as he tightened his grip.

"I have brought my brother, Robert Penwarren, to pay his respects, ma'am," he said easily. "And to meet his young cousin, the earl."

Georgina was aware of firm, light steps even as Rathbourne released her and stepped back to allow his brother to approach her. Again Georgina extended her hand, wondering a trifle hysterically as she did so if she had succumbed to some rare malady which had rendered her pervious to the touch of a gentleman's handclasp. But Robbie's light grip failed to produce similar unnerving results and she was able to respond easily to the young man's polite greeting.

"Lady Grey," he was saying in a pleasant baritone which possessed qualities similar to the deep tones of his elder brother, though nothing of the ennui, "I am pleased to meet David's lady wife at long last. And I, too, must apologize for having barged in on you unannounced. I lay the blame entirely at my brother's feet."

"My lord. You stand pardoned. And now I should be pleased to present my cousin, Miss Zenobia Kingsley."

There was a decided pause before Robert Penwarren made his bow to the girl whose back had been turned toward the door. Georgina was suddenly bewilderingly aware of a charged atmosphere in the room and sought vainly for its source. She nearly jumped at the light touch of a hand against her shoulder and Rathbourne's low drawl close to her ear.

"A facer, ma'am," he observed with a definite smile in his voice. "My young brother has indubitably succumbed to the vision of loveliness."

Again Georgina was forced to choke back a low gurgle of laughter. The man was irrepressible. Yet she experienced as well a feeling of gratitude that he had so accurately assessed her momentary confusion and seen fit to alleviate it. She sensed a kindness in him which she had not expected of the infamous Rathbourne and realized with a twinge of guilt that it was indeed very possible that, due to his much vaunted reputation, she had prejudged him.

Thus she awarded him a grimace of distaste alleviated by the gleam of humor in her eyes and wished she could see the scene being enacted between the two young people.

She would not have been disappointed, for Miss Kingsley's lovely features were suffused with a becoming blush, and the young man's obvious admiration shone in the stricken look with which he regarded her. Robbie Penwarren had indeed been given a leveller.

Breakfast that morning at Greystone Manor was an unusually merry affair. The two gentlemen, though they admitted to having broken their fasts earlier, agreed they could eat any time and made a hearty meal of it. Georgina fairly sparkled as she bandied words with Rathbourne, whom she found to be as dangerously charming as his reputation had accounted him. However, she soon discovered he was far from the society fribble she had been led to expect. He spoke with ease and knowledge on any number of topics encompassing politics, the war, literature, and humorous *on dits* concerning the *Beau Monde*. His humor was dry, his comments characteristically acerbic, but he was never cruel. She was impressed with his practical knowledge of farming and an obvious interest in his vast estates and the welfare of his dependents. Thus it was that she found herself relating with a total ease of manner the many difficulties she had encountered at Emberly and only later did she realize how skillfully he had drawn her out.

"Connings believes the drainage of the lower farms can be improved, but it will entail a rather large expenditure. Still, it would increase production of land which has been little better than barren up to now. And if successful, would pay for itself many times over," she said, a pensive frown creasing her lovely brow.

"Then why do you hesitate?" queried the duke. "From the reports I have received it would not appear that the funds are lacking."

"No," Georgina admitted, then sighed. How could she confess to her reluctance to commit her son's revenues to such an extensive project based purely on her agent's reports? Were she able to visit the outlying farms and see for herself what was needed, she knew she would know what course to take. No sooner was that thought formulated than she was startled anew by Rathbourne's seeming uncanny ability to read her mind.

"Perhaps we should ride out and view for ourselves the

advisability of Connings' proposals," remarked the duke casually.

"No!" she said rather too emphatically, then bit her lip in consternation at her sudden outburst. With an effort she stilled the sudden sweep of panic the duke's suggestion had aroused. Surely the man must realize she could not possibly ride. "No," she repeated more calmly. "I'm afraid that is quite out of the question, Your Grace."

"But you do ride, do you not, ma'am?" the duke persisted.

"I used to," she said and for the life of her could not keep a wistful note from her voice. "But that was a very long time ago. I no longer ride."

"But, Gina, I have never seen your equal on horseback," Zenobia interjected impulsively, then gasped as sudden realization of her cousin's dilemma hit her. "I-I beg your pardon. I should not have spoken," she ended miserably and, hands clasped tightly in her lap and her head lowered to hide her consternation, lapsed into an uneasy silence.

Georgina could not miss the contrition in her cousin's low-voiced utterance and was instantly stung with remorse for having precipitated the whole affair.

"No, no, my dearest Nobie," she gently chided. "Why should you not speak? Indeed, I am flattered that you remember my prowess. But that was a long time ago, and I fear I am sadly out of practice. I simply have other things to occupy my time now. But I should be grateful for your advice, Your Grace. It is true that heretofore I have had to rely solely on Connings' judgment pertaining to the running of Emberly."

"Indeed," said the duke oddly. "And it has no doubt been a heavy burden for one in your—er—circumstances," he added.

"I have only done what had to be done," Georgina answered stiffly, her eyes sparkling with resentment at what she viewed as his condescension. "I have not done too badly, I think."

"No, no. Do not fly up in the boughs. I was not impugning your accomplishments, but merely observing that it must be difficult for a woman alone to run such a large estate. But, of course, now that I am here, I shall relieve you of such onerous tasks."

"Relieve me of . . . !" Georgina began in offended tones. But immediately she caught herself. Careful, my girl, she mentally cautioned herself. After all, Rathbourne had every legal right to take over the management of his ward's holdings. Forcing herself to take a deep breath, she clasped her hands tightly in her lap and began more calmly. "I beg your pardon," she managed rather more reasonably, though she still seethed inside. "But surely you could wait to peruse the books before judging me incompetent. This is not the first sizeable estate I have had a hand in running."

"Indeed, Drew," Robbie interjected in a misguided attempt to ease the situation. "You've hardly given our cousin a fair chance to prove herself."

"You misjudge me, Robbie," Rathbourne countered smoothly, and Georgina could just picture the arrogant lift of an aristocratic eyebrow. The lazy drawl deepened as the duke continued. "I do not doubt Lady Grey has overseen her son's inheritance admirably. However, that has little to say in the matter. I am Davey's guardian, and as such it is obviously my responsibility to see to his best interests. It was your wish, was it not, ma'am, that I should take more seriously my familial duties?"

Georgina choked back an involuntary bubble of laughter at Rathbourne's subtle maneuverings. How dared he throw her words back in her face! The man was impossible, but he had scored a palpable hit. And it was true that she found it more and more draining to maintain Emberly as well as the manor. But nor was she certain she wished for his interference. How easy it would be to grow to depend upon someone like Rathbourne, who she felt instinctively was well able to deal with any adversities which might come in his way. But she had fought hard for her independence, had done so, despite all odds, for the sake of her son. No, it would not do to give in now. She was not sure she could win the battle a second time.

"If I have led you to believe I wished you to relieve me of my responsibilities at Emberly, Your Grace, I beg you will disregard it," she said, striving for her usual calm. "It is *my* duty to see to Davey's best interests. Who better than his mother? Nor should we expect you to add the burden of Emberly to your own vast interests. I should gratefully accept your advice on such matters as concern the running of my son's estate, but more than that would be to ask too much of familial duty," Georgina ended and steeled herself to do battle royal to defend her bastions.

"As you wish," he agreed affably, spiking her guns with a velvet drawl, dripping ennui. "No doubt Emberly were better left to your own capable hands." Georgina clenched her teeth to prevent her lower jaw from dropping in a most unladylike gape. Was that a yawn she had heard, suppressed, no doubt, by an indolent hand? "I shall satisfy myself for the moment with a perusal of your books and a ride to the outlying farms. I believe the first matter may be attended to this morning after I have seen my ward. We may save the latter for the morrow. Shall we make it an early ride? Say ten or so? We can pack along a picnic lunch. No doubt Robbie and Miss Kingsley would enjoy the outing as well."

"I say, Drew. That's an admirable notion," Penwarren agreed with obvious enthusiasm.

Georgina hastily altered her previously favorable impressions of the youth. Obviously he was hat in hand with the conniving duke, who had so cleverly put her at *point-non-plus*. For to refuse to accompany him to the outlying farms would be tantamount to admitting she was unequal to the task of running Emberly, and to agree to his demands was to agree to go on horseback, since, due to the rough terrain, carriages and other wheeled conveyances were virtually unheard of in Cornwall. True, David's father had kept a landau the last year or so before his death, a completely enclosed vehicle with glass windows to keep out the inclement weather and, indeed, the very conveyance which had carried her and Davey from Plymouth to Greystone Manor and Lady Hortense to the ferryboat in Torpoint, but the journey over the nearly nonexistent roads had been harrowing at best, and the carriage was totally impracticable for a mere country outing. In the near absence of wheeled conveyances, either mules, which the Cornish called "moyles," or horses with their cargo hung on great hooks slung on either side of the animals were the usual methods of transporting nonhuman loads in these isolated wilds. Of course, there was the occasional ox cart, but she had little wish to resort to the ignominy of being hauled about like so much freight. Blast the man! What was she to do?

She was saved from immediate reply, however, by her cousin's sudden unexpected intervention.

"Obviously it is anything but an 'admirable notion'," Miss Kingsley uttered scathingly. "How can you be so insensible to my cousin's wishes, my lord? Lady Grey has said she does not ride. And I—I could not." The girl's voice quivered and died away into an embarrassing silence.

Good lord, thought Georgina, feeling as if she had entered Bedlam. What now? There had been a definite note of panic in her cousin's voice. Was the child afraid of horses? But no. Zenobia used to ride with her cousin. Surely that was not it. But then what had overset her so? She did not need to see the girl's face to know she was indeed agitated.

"I beg your indulgence, Miss Kingsley," Rathbourne calmly intervened. "Of course, we shall abandon the idea should it be so utterly impracticable. You must forgive me. Somehow I has not thought Lady Grey to be of an invalidish persuasion. She had not the look of frailty. However, I naturally have no wish either to endanger her health or to offend your delicate sensibilities."

"Oh!" Georgina gasped, not sure whether to laugh or to deliver the duke a stinging set-down. "I am not in the least bit frail or vaporish, I assure you. My cousin and I shall be ready at your convenience."

Now, why had she said that? she wondered, when she had fully intended to second her cousin's refusal? Immediately she wished she might take back her words as she experienced the familiar dread at venturing beyond the known boundaries of her shadowed world. She told herself that it was not really fear which had kept her confined to the house and the familiar grounds all these weeks, but only a dislike of appearing foolish before strangers. What a charming picture she should make being taken around her son's estate on a leading string. Thinking to retrench without loss of pride, she grasped at the first plausible excuse for reversing her hasty decision which came to mind.

"But then perhaps I have not considered properly," she said, as if having just been visited with an afterthought. "I doubt there are suitable mounts at Greystone for my cousin and myself."

But apparently the duke was not to be so easily put off. "Nonsense," he said, and Georgina was quite sure she detected a quiver of amusement in his voice. "Lord Emberly used to keep a fine stable. Robbie can look over your cattle before we leave, and should there be none suitable, I shall furnish mounts from my own."

Georgina's smile was perhaps a trifle stiff, but she nodded graciously and murmured, "You are too kind, Your Grace."

"Not at all, ma'am," he rejoined instantly.

The day passed quickly enough despite Georgina's growing uneasiness concerning the proposed outing on the morrow. The duke's meeting with his ward was not at all what she had anticipated. Obviously the young earl found much to admire in his guardian, who proved surprisingly at ease with his ward. He was neither condescending nor forgetful of his own position as guardian to the boy. Rather he treated Davey with the tolerance due an equal, albeit a youthful one, who yet must comport himself within certain bounds in order to win his guardian's approval. And the young earl, quickly judging Rathbourne to be up to every rig, showed an eagerness to please the *Non Pareil*. Indeed, Davey was on his best behavior, for he had almost immediately won what he patently considered a major concession. The boy was to be allowed to leave the nursery as soon as a suitable tutor could be found to begin his formal education.

Georgina, upon being informed of the proposed alteration of the established order, anticipated a stormy clash of wills between the arrogant duke and the ruling force behind the nursery. But obviously she had misjudged her man. Nanny Slade proved to be putty in his hands.

"You have done admirably with the boy, Mrs. Slade," he remarked after granting permission for the child to withdraw with his cousins on the proposed tour of the earl's stables. "But it must be obvious to a woman of your unquestionable experience that Lord Emberly is ready to leave the nursery and begin his instruction under the auspices of a tutor."

"Indeed, Your Grace," Nanny said without hesitation. "An' about time, too. I've done all I can for 'is lordship, I'm sure. And now there's others wot 'ave greater need o' me. Though they be grown hoity-toity o' late. Wishin' for a proper abigail an' all. An' wot 'as come o' it? Freckles! An' gowns wot were better burned than worn by a lady o' quality. Well, if it be a proper lady's maid they wants, then that's wot they shall 'ave. It'll take some doin' I doubt not. But I'll whip that lazy Gilda into line. Jest see if I don't."

Thus Georgina, upon leaving the nursery, found herself beset with a multitude of self-doubts. How could she have been so remiss in judging the needs and wishes of her loved ones? Was she indeed so self-centered that she had failed utterly to see her son's longing for masculine guidance? Had she remained deaf as well as blind to his new maturity, keeping him in the nursery out of her own need to have him a child and dependent upon his mother? And Nanny. Dearest Nanny. Had she truly been so insensitive as to overlook the possibility that her old nurse might prefer to continue in Georgina's service, indeed, that Nanny Slade would be deeply hurt by such an arbitrary arrangement as to confine her to the nursery and solely the duties entailed therein?

"You must not blame yourself, you know," Rathbourne said quietly as he opened the door to the library and allowed Georgina to precede him into the room.

"I-I beg your pardon?" Georgina stammered and cocked her head to one side as was her wont when listening for nuances of tone.

"Nanny Slade is not as young as she was used to be. Obviously your primary concern was for her welfare and Davey's. It must have been difficult for you to ban her from her accustomed position of ruling the roost. In her mind you are still her nursling."

"And how I have missed her!" Georgina confided with a rueful smile. "Gilda is a sweet and biddable girl better suited as kitchen maid than a lady's dresser. But she was the one most easily spared from her normal duties. And by the time I had discovered my error, she had already let slip how much her new position meant to her. She and Wilkins have an understanding and are waiting only till they have accumulated a small nest egg before tying the knot. You must see that I could not send her back to the kitchens after that."

"No, I don't suppose *you* could," he said oddly. "But that is easily gotten around. You need only grant the newlyweds a 'lease on lives' to a vacated cottage along with

121

a bonus in the way of a wedding gift."

"Oh, dear. *Must* it be a lease on lives? I know it is the custom in Cornwall, but I confess I cannot like it. To be given the use of a house only till the death of the longest-lived of three chosen people seems both heartless and barbaric. I have heard of elderly widows turned out of their homes simply because they have been unfortunate enough to outlive the last 'lease-life.' Could I not simply grant them the use of the house for so long as they shall need it?"

"You could," Rathbourne admitted after a moment's hesitation. "If you are willing to incure the censure of most of your neighbors. It's a system designed to benefit the landowner, since the cottage and all improvements on the land revert to him upon forfeiture of the lease. And it is true that hundreds of acres which might otherwise have remained waste have instead been rendered productive in this way."

"But at what expense to those who spend their lives working land which might at any moment be taken away from them! No. There must be a better way."

"Can the distinction truly be so important to you?" queried the duke curiously after a moment. "After all, I was merely suggesting a politic way to dispense with an unsatisfactory servant."

"But of course it's important," Georgina answered steadily. "I feel a certain responsibility for Gilda and Wilkins. Surely you must see that if I am to deny them the rather substantial income which Gilda earns as my abigail, I must make certain that in the end they do not suffer for it."

"Oh, indubitably, ma'am," responded the duke drily. "Indeed, I begin to see that I am in danger of developing a social conscience. If I had any sense at all, I should no doubt leave you to your dilemma and return straightaway to the depravities of London. However, since my familial obligations necessitate my continued presence, I am moved to offer an alternative solution to your problem. It is the

122

custom to grant permanent ownership to anyone capable of raising a house on a given site in the space of a single night."

"But that's not possible! Is it?" queried the astonished countess.

"There is precedence for it. Actually no one cavils over a measure of cheating. The materials, for instance, might be gathered ahead of time. Or the window and doors constructed before the actual house-raising. The young groom's friends are allowed to help as well. And then, too, the cottage need not be more than four walls and a roof which can either be added to later or replaced by a more substantial structure. The important thing is that the builder must inhabit the cottage immediately upon its completion."

"But then that is the very thing!" Georgina exclaimed. "No doubt Emberly could provide something in the way of furnishings and other household items to help the newly-weds start out in some comfort. How fortunate that Nobie has arrived in time to help me pick out just a few things which might be of use." It shall give her something to take her mind off whatever is troubling her, she added to herself and frowned, remembering her cousin's earlier odd behavior. Then turning toward the duke with a warm smile touched with a hint of uncertainty, she held out her hand in a gracious gesture of gratitude.

"I am indebted to you, Your Grace," she said and felt a blush tinge her cheeks as his slender fingers closed lightly over hers. "It was kind in you to so easily solve one of my difficulties. Perhaps I begin to see why David was so insistent that our son should be entrusted to your care."

"Am I then to assume that you did not so trust me, ma'am?" he queried with a slight tightening of his clasp about her hand.

"I confess to having entertained certain doubts," she admitted with simple candor, and, gently withdrawing her hand, turned and walked a few steps away, her fingers trailing seemingly absently along the back of a velvet plush sofa. "You must know that your reputation is not exactly one to inspire confidence in the bosom of an apparently overprotective mama. I fear I have been used to think of you as an unsavory influence. Indeed, the man who so nearly caused an estrangement between David and his father. But David's affection never suffered a moment's doubt. He was used to say of you that no man was so greatly misunderstood or so unjustly impugned. Perhaps you can find it in your power to forgive me for being among those who believed the worst of you."

Rathbourne's sudden bark of laughter rang harshly in the room.

"Do not be too quick to invest me with virtuous attributes, ma'am," he drawled cynically. "Whatever you have heard is very likely true. I have hardly led an exemplary life."

"No," Georgina agreed with a demure smile. "I did not suppose you had. But I suspect you may not be so black as you would have others to believe. I discern in you a certain kindness, my lord duke, which you are at great pains to conceal behind a veneer of cynicism. And a keen intellect which belies your reputation of reckless indifference. Indeed, it occurs to me that you, sir, have been more sinned against than sinned."

"Then you should be operating under false assumptions, my dear," he answered in a voice made hard with self-derision. "I have been at great pains to earn my notoriety, I assure you."

"Indeed you have, if I am to believe all the tales which David had to tell of you," she replied with a mischievous assumption of innocence which quite disarmed him. "Yet you were ever the hero to him, as you are fast becoming to his son as well. And it is no mean feat to pull the wool over Nanny Slade's eyes. So you see, I have little choice but to

124

reassess my previous opinion of you. You, my lord duke, stand condemned of being a friend in need."

"And you, my dear, are a green girl if you believe any such thing. In the end I shall only disillusion you."

"Shall you?" she queried, suddenly grave. A slight furrow marred the purity of her brow as she tilted her head toward the sound of his voice. "I wonder. For I must tell you that at times I have had the oddest feeling that I might trust you with my very life."

He was saved from having to reply to that unnerving admission by the sudden commotion of youthful voices outside the door followed by the entrance of Miss Kingsley and Robbie Penwarren bearing with them the scent of violets and fresh air.

Georgina, pleasantly surprised at the sound of her cousin's gurgle of laughter, marveled that Penwarren had somehow managed to penetrate the girl's reserve as with a warm smile she turned to greet the two young people. Her pleasure in her cousin's unexpected transformation was, however, to suffer a sudden check as Lord Robert blithely informed her that Emberly's stables were complete to a shade.

"I have chosen a lively little mare with a sweet disposition and unimpeachable manners for Miss Kingsley," he added, failing to see the brief flicker of fear in Georgina's eyes as he glanced down at the blushing girl at his side. "And for you, ma'am, a long-legged chestnut which promises to be a great goer."

"Excellent, Robbie," interjected Rathbourne, who, keenly attuned to the minutest alteration of Georgina's mood, had not been so remiss. "Now if Lady Grey would be so good as to tell me where I might find Emberly's books, I shall undertake to look them over this evening."

"Oh, indeed I had forgotten," Georgina said and crossed to the heavy oak desk to retrieve a leather-bound ledger from one of the drawers. "Bolton was kind enough to enter the numbers for me," she added, proffering the book to Rathbourne. "However, I balanced the figures, and should there be any errors, they are mine."

The duke made no comment, as accepting the book, he bowed over her hand and bade her a farewell.

In a moment they were gone, leaving Georgina strangely restless and filled with trepidation for the morrow's outing. Perhaps it will rain, she thought bleakly as she prepared for bed later that evening and, crawling between the sheets, fell at last into a fitful sleep disturbed by haunting dreams of Portugal and a faceless stranger and of David, strangely accusing.

Chapter 6

At the sound of a soft scratching at her door, Georgina started from an uneasy slumber and bolted upright in bed, one hand pressed to her breast.

"Who is it?" she called out a trifle breathlessly, her voice unwontedly strained in the lingering aftermath of her nightmare.

"'Tis awnley Gilda, m'lady," came the timid reply. "I've brung 'ee thy morning cup o' chocolate."

With a soft groan, Georgina sank limply back against the rumpled pillows and closed her eyes tightly for a moment as she willed her heart to still its wild pace. Made ruefully aware of the dull throb of a headache, she schooled her features to a semblance of her usual calm before bidding the abigail to enter. Nevertheless she suspected she must appear wan and pale, her eyes woefully heavy-lidded, for she felt dull and weary, as if she had slept little through the night, and for once she was grateful that it was Gilda and not Nanny Slade who waited on her. She little doubted Nanny, who never missed a thing, would have guessed immediately upon laying eyes on her that inexplicably the nightmares had come once again to cut up the young countess's rest. Inevitably she would have hovered over her former nursling like a hen with one chick, a circumstance with which Georgina felt not at all prepared to cope.

Why had the tormenting dreams returned? she wondered and tried to recall the haunting images which had plagued her through the night. Everything seemed clothed in mist, the figures which crept in and out of her unconscious mind all the more sinister for their indistinctness. It was odd, the way she always dreamt in pictures. She had never given the matter much thought before the onset of her own affliction, but had she done, she no doubt would have supposed the blind were not visited with dreams, or at least that their unconscious fantasies would be as shadowed as their waking reality. Yet in the realm of sleep she was not blind.

Oh, how she wished that she were! For the visions which had come to haunt her as she lay in her sickbed in Lisbon had driven her to the brink of madness, until at last, preferring the oblivion of wakefulness to the tortured reality of her nightmares, she had refused to sleep. In the end, she had had to be dosed with laudanum to induce a dreamless stupor into which she had gratefully fled. And even after emerging from the slow weeks of recuperation to begin the long struggle for mastery of her altered existence, she had still been visited night after night with dreams of David, dreams from which she had awakened in a cold sweat, the sharp edge of her grief made more unbearable by the persistent visitations of her lost love. For always he seemed to accuse her, and always just as she reached out to enfold him in her arms, he would turn away from her to vanish before the forbidding aspect of a stranger. But then she had come to Greystone Manor and that strange feeling that at last she had arrived home. And miraculously the nightmares had ceased, leaving her at peace—till now.

The sudden chime of the marquetry bracket clock on the mantelpiece startled her out of her reverie. Nine o'clock! She had overslept and must now make haste to dress if Rathbourne were not to arrive before she was ready. Almost she succumbed to the temptation to make her excuses and remain abed. But that would have been to cry craven, something she could not do without jeopardizing her ability and, indeed, her right to command her own life as well as to oversee her son's. Somehow she could not bear to appear vulnerable before the Duke of Rathbourne. She must just make the best of a bad bargain and get through the coming ordeal with as much grace as was possible, she told herself wryly.

Yet such wise counsel brought her little comfort as reluctantly she threw aside the bedcovers and, calling to the abigail to lay out her riding habit, slid out of the high four-poster bed to the floor. Without waiting for Gilda, she poured water from the porcelain pitcher into the washbasin and quickly washed. She had just slipped into her worn velvet riding habit of military green and her high-top Spanish riding boots when Zenobia made her appearance in her cousin's chambers.

"You are going then?" the girl said without preamble as she halted just inside the door.

"Oh, Zenobia. Thank goodness," said the countess turning with an overbright smile to greet her cousin. "You are just in time to adjust my hat. You may go now, Gilda. Miss Kingsley will finish up."

Neither woman spoke as they waited for the girl to make her curtsy and exit, closing the door carefully behind her. Then Georgina quickly made her way to the dressing table.

"Quick, Nobie. I need your hands and eyes," she said, retrieving a worn leather travel case from the bottom drawer of the vanity. "A little rouge, I think, and perhaps just a dab of powder. I know I must look a fright."

Miss Kingsley, noting her cousin's unusual pallor and the shadows beneath her eyes, was made instantly anxious for Georgina.

"Gina, you have been ill. Tell me what is wrong."

"It's nothing," Georgina said, attempting to maintain a cheerful front. "My rest was a trifle disturbed is all. But I'm depending on you to make me presentable."

"But if you are indisposed, perhaps we should cry off," persisted the girl. "Indeed, I should rather. Doubtless I could be better employed here seeing to your correspondence or any of a number of other matters."

"But surely you would not wish to disappoint Lord Robert?" Georgina gently teased. "For I'm quite sure he would be. He was obviously taken with you, Nobie."

"Then, indeed, I must not go," the girl answered in suddenly frozen tones. "For he can have nothing to do with a paid companion. Nor I with him."

"And why should you not?" Georgina queried, trying not to lose patience with her cousin. Obviously something was troubling the child, and indeed she was not unsympathetic, but she could have wished for a more propitious time in which to delve into the nature of Zenobia's extremely odd behavior since coming to Greystone. Stifling a sigh, she resigned herself to playing devil's advocate. "Your birth is as good as his, after all. And if you have no fortune, he shall not miss it. He stands to inherit a deal of money from his maternal grandmama and no doubt Rathbourne will settle a sizeable amount on him when the boy decides to set up his nursery."

"That is all the more reason I should not be seen with him," said Miss Kingsley in stubborn tones. "I should be thought mercenary and quite forward. Gina, when I agreed to come to you, it was in the expectation of escaping the difficulties of an—an *unattached* woman. Nothing good could come of setting aside the proprieties of my position. Surely you see that."

"Are you not being just a trifle oversensitive about your straitened circumstances, Nobie? For indeed it is not something of which you need feel ashamed. You are not the first to find herself suddenly in the lurch, and you must not view it as if your life had come suddenly to an end. After all, you are young and beautiful. There is no reason why you should not one day wed."

"No!" Zenobia cried, greatly distraught, and began to pace distractedly. "You don't understand. How could you? You know nothing about me."

For a time Georgina, listening to the angry swish of her

cousin's skirts as Zenobia continued to prowl restlessly about the room, struggled to contain her impatience while she waited for the girl to unburden herself. However, when this appeared to be some time in the coming, she finally held up a restraining hand.

"Nobie. You are giving me a headache with all this pacing, and I hardly relish the thought of having a path worn permanently in David's oriental rug. I confess to a certain sentimental attachment to it. Please be seated and tell me what has sent you into the boughs."

Miss Kingsley came immediately to a halt before Georgina's chair and with a quivering sigh sank to the floor at her cousin's feet.

"Oh, Gina," she said in a tremulous voice which augured ill for Georgina's peace of mind. "You must release me from my promise to remain at Greystone. You must be made to see that I shall bring you nothing but grief if I stay."

"I see that something has disturbed you," Georgina corrected in a reasonable voice. "And unless *you* see fit to enlighten me directly, I shall most assuredly develop a megrim."

However, as this speech failed to elicit the desired response, or indeed any discernible response at all, Georgina was hard put to contain her mounting frustration, for the lengthening silence put her very much at a disadvantage.

"Nobie?" she prodded at last and, reaching out to probe the darkness before her, brushed her hand against her cousin's bowed head. "Nobie, I beg you will tell me what is troubling you," she said and cradled the girl's face between her hands. Whereupon Miss Kingsley uttered a stifled sob and, and dropping her head in Georgina's lap, burst immediately into tears.

Mystified and no little alarmed at this unexpected display of the vapors, the young countess stroked her cousin's hair and waited for the weeping to subside to a convulsive

131

sniffle, upon which she placed a lace hankie in Zenobia's hand and bade her blow her nose.

"Now," she said firmly when it seemed the younger woman had achieved a measure of composure. "You will please tell me why you are set upon leaving me before you have even given yourself an opportunity to discover whether we should not suit one another quite admirably—as I little doubt we shall, once you have gotten over this nodcock notion that you are somehow sunk beneath contempt merely because you are gainfully employed. Nobie, why are you so afraid to accept as your due the admiration of a quite unexceptional young man? I confess that I am greatly surprised at your apparent reluctance to one day marry, for I used to think what an admirable wife and mother you should make some fortunate man. Or is it simply that you cannot like Robbie Penwarren?"

"Oh, it is not that at all!" exclaimed the girl, pulling away to gaze earnestly into her cousin's face. "Indeed, L-Lord Robert is everything one could admire in a gentleman. But I can never marry him or any other man. And if I remained here, I should never again know any peace. Please, Georgina. Do not try to make me say any more, for, indeed, I should only refuse."

"I see," the countess temporized, though she did not, in fact, understand at all. She knew only that she must somehow persuade the child to give up the foolish notion of fleeing the protection of her family. "Very well," she said after a time, "I shall not press you for an explanation. But nor will I release you from your promise to remain as my companion. You will continue in your present situation for an agreed term of trial—say two months. After all, it will take me at least that long to find someone suitable to take your place. And indeed I must tell you that Rathbourne has made it quite plain he will not allow me to go on without a proper companion. However, be that as it may, if at the expiration of two months, you are still of the same mind, I shall release you with the promise of securing you a position wheresoever you shall choose. Now, have we a bargain?"

Her cousin was quiet for so long that Georgina feared she had failed quite utterly to persuade her, but at last the girl drew herself up to her full height and took in a deep breath.

"Two months, Gina," she said tonelessly. "But only that you may find someone to replace me."

"And you will accompany me on this morning's outing, Nobie. No, I must insist just this once. Lord Robert cannot be allowed to come all this way only to be given some last minute excuse. After today you need not accept any further invitations if you do not wish to. Are we agreed?"

"No good can come of it, but I suppose I must be civil," Miss Kingsley acceded grudgingly.

"Good," Georgina rejoined in no little relief at having won a temporary reprieve. "Then since we have settled that, I beg you will finish repairing the devastation wrought on my face by a nearly sleepless night. I should prefer not to keep the gentlemen waiting when they arrive."

Georgina could not quite suppress the flutter of apprehension in her stomach at the sound of the knocker echoing hollowly through the foyer. Nor was she aware that her hand closed convulsively about the handle of her riding crop as she continued down the curving staircase to the Great Hall into which Bolton had just admitted Robert Penwarren and the Duke of Rathbourne. This will never do, my girl, she told herself wryly and strove for at least an appearance of her usual calm. And, indeed, it would have taken a most discerning eye to detect anything at all out of the ordinary in Lady Grey's demeanor as she stepped easily across the parquetry tiled floor, one hand graciously extended and a composed smile on her lips, to greet her guests.

However, it soon proved apparent that the duke was not

one to be easily fooled.

"If the prospect of a simple outing is enough to rob you of your sleep, why did you not simply tell us to go to blazes?" he said in a harsh undertone as he took her arm and led her beneath the arched portal out into the gravel drive in the wake of the two younger people who had quickly outdistanced Rathbourne and Georgina's more sedate pace. Surprisingly Robbie had managed after a great deal of persuasion to induce the exceedingly reluctant Miss Kingsley to accompany him on a side tour of the cherry orchards and a Norman ruin in the upper reaches of the valley. Georgina, who had been preoccupied with issuing final orders to the servants regarding a late supper upon their return, had remained in ignorance of the telling point in Robbie's argument, which had been the gentleman's low-voiced suggestion that perhaps Lady Grey's future happiness might be best served by allowing her some time alone with the duke. Consequently, much to Georgina's surprise Miss Kingsley had in the end accepted Penwarren's invitation, and it had been agreed that they should catch up to the duke and Lady Grey in time for nuncheon.

Thus Georgina, who had not wanted to interfere with what she hoped would be her cousin's pleasure, found herself quite alone with the unsettling Rathbourne.

"I do beg your pardon," Georgina instantly rejoined, no little astounded at the duke's uncivil manner. "However, I believe I did on more than one occasion express a reluctance to ride."

"Oh, did you," he commented acerbically. "And yet I seem to recall that you accepted my invitation over the rather vociferous protest of your vaporish cousin. You must pardon me if I find it difficult to believe a mere 'reluctance to ride' could have precipitated such an unsettling effect. You are, after all, the female who dared the deprivations of the march to Talavera without the batting of an eyelash.

And now, my girl, without further roundaboutation, you will tell me exactly what has sent you into a quake and cut up your peace."

"I am not in a quake, my lord," Georgina protested indignantly and wondered if she were indeed too transparent. "And I fail utterly to see why you should think I am in any way unsettled."

"Never mind how I know. I do not fully understand it myself. But though you conceal it admirably, my dear, I was aware the moment I set eyes on you that something had discomposed your usual unruffled composure. And I warn you, I shall not give over until you have told me the whole of it."

"Oh, very well, Your Grace," she submitted with a reluctant laugh. "I do confess to some trepidation. Indeed, I was very near to crying off. Perhaps I am being rather idiotish, but I have not been on a horse for a very long time, and I used to take great pride in my horsemanship. Consequently, I have not liked to think I should be a veritable gazingstock before all the world."

"But that is an utter absurdity," he said roughly, halting her in her tracks as he firmly turned her to face him. "You, madam, could never be anything but admired."

"And you, sir, are being kind, which is not at all what I should have expected from you," she replied, not knowing whether to feel flattered by his exorbitant praise or amused at his uncivil manner of expressing it. Her smile gently upbraided him. "My friend and adviser should on the contrary deal only in plain pounds."

"Meaning that I have offered you Spanish coin," he observed wryly. "But you are wide of the mark, my girl, for I am neither kind nor in the habit of toadying to impertinent females with more bottom than brains. And even if you cannot see yourself in a mirror, you must know you are a diamond of the first water."

"I know nothing of the kind, Your Grace. Actually I

consider myself possessed of only passable looks, for I am hardly in the accepted mode, being much too tall and brunette besides," she retorted lightly and, turning, began to stroll once more along the flower-bordered drive, her senses suddenly inexplicably alive to the splendor of the summer's day. The scent of sweet-williams and lilacs perfumed the air, and she doubted not that the yellow blossoms of the laburnums hugging the front of the house were in glorious bloom. A gentle breeze kissed her cheek as she turned her face toward the sun and tried to visualize the well-trimmed lawns sloping eastwardly to the bourne. Feeling rather more contented with the world than she had upon awakening that morning, she turned her head to smile serenely at the duke as he came up beside her once more.

"For my part I find the prevailing fashion of petite blond beauties insipid," he remarked, a peculiar warmth in his deep voice. "But no doubt you are in the right of it and should be considered a positive antidote."

"Now you are being absurd, Your Grace," she gurgled and was surprised to discover that she had so far forgotten herself in the quick exchange as to have come suddenly upon the waiting mounts with her previous qualms quite in abeyance, which, upon later reflection, she doubted not had been the duke's intent all along.

A low nicker followed by the warm softness of an inquisitive muzzle against her neck startled a low exclamation from her.

"Ho, my beauty," she cried softly and without conscious thought reached up to catch the bridle above the bit. In the purely instinctive gesture of one born to love horses, she laid her cheek against the silky softness of the animal's and rubbed a hand along the opposite side of its face and down the proudly arched neck.

"Oh, but you're a dainty prancer, I've no doubt," she crooned and, never ceasing her soft murmurings, knelt to run sensitive hands down each foreleg then, rising, explored the sleek lines of the back to the well-muscled haunches.

"What is your name, my lovely?" she queried softly, coming back to stroke the wide forehead tapering to a dainty nose.

"He be called Ahmar for his chestnut coat, me lady."

Georgina's head lifted in startled surprise.

"Denby? Is it indeed you?" she said, turning her face in the direction from which the voice had seemed to emanate.

"Aye, me lady. The very same," he answered, and Georgina had scant difficulty in picturing the little bandy-legged groom, a disreputable jockey cap crushed between his hands and a shock of red hair atumble over his forehead, the same irrepressible Denby who had served as Major Lord David Grey's batman, first, in India and, later, on the Peninsula until a wound received at Obidos had seen him mustered out of the regiment and safely ensconced at Emberly as the old earl's head groom.

"It's a fine name and no doubt suits him," observed the countess in an effort to hide the sudden leap of her heart at this unexpected encounter with David's long-time servant and comrade from the old Bengal and Peninsular days. What a nodcock she was to be sure, she ruefully chided herself, for she should have known Denby would be in attendance on his mistress today. "He has the scooped face and the eyes of the Godolphin Arabian, low and wide apart," she added, turning once more to stroke the handsome creature. "And the daintiness of size, for he cannot stand more than fourteen hands."

"Aye, an' there be the mark o' speed on 'is off-hind leg as well—the onliest mark on 'im. He's a prime 'un, me lady," said Denby proudly, coming to stand at the young stallion's head. "An' not a mean bone in 'is body. The old earl meant 'im for th' major, but I expect things bein' what they was 'twixt you an' himself, this laddie woulda come to you in the nat'ral course of events. If you knows what I mean."

"I know, Denby," the countess answered a trifle mistily,

for indeed she little doubted that upon first sight of this prancing beauty, she would not have rested till she had charmed him from David. "And thank you."

She hugged Ahmar's lovely, arched neck once more, and thought that perhaps she had been wrong to avoid the loyal-hearted Denby no matter how painfully he reminded her of the past. How well he knew her! But then he had been an inseparable part of those harrowing times. It had been Denby who calmed her fears with an unshakable stoicism when she first set foot in the exotic wilds of India, a green girl of seventeen, newly wed. And Denby who had guided her through the perilous shoals of military etiquette and the rigid hierarchy of the officers' wives in Calcutta. And Denby as well who had helped her nurse David through the fever amidst the humid heat of the Bengal in July.

Oh, God! The memories seemed suddenly to press upon her so. She touched the fingertips of either hand against throbbing temples. If only she could escape for a time to the music room, to be alone and to lose herself in the soothing refrains of a sonata till her head should cease to pound and she could think calmly once again.

Rathbourne's hand upon her arm brought her to the present with a start.

"I-I beg your pardon?" she gasped, made suddenly aware that he had spoken.

"If you are ready, ma'am, it's time we were on our way," he drawled, apparently oblivious to the look of lost bewilderment in the white face turned up to his.

Her lips parted to say that she was taken suddenly ill and must cry off until another time when suddenly strong hands closed firmly on her waist and lifted her, protesting, in the air.

"Oh!" she cried in mingled fear and outrage and clutched frantically at the duke's broad shoulders as he thrust her unceremoniously into the saddle. But her right leg had found and curled instinctively about the horn and she instantly righted herself as Rathbourne withdrew his hold to set her left foot in the stirrup. For a moment Georgina's mind went blank as she hovered on the brink of panic. Then the familiar feel of the reins placed in her hands and the horse standing patiently beneath her steadied her somewhat. Slowly she relaxed.

"Miss Kingsley was very much in the right of it," came Rathbourne's voice out of the dark mists which clouded her vision.

"I-I beg your pardon?" Georgina replied, stiffly turning her head as she sought to locate the duke.

"You do have a fine seat and display to distinct advantage on a horse. Tell me, ma'am, were you used to ride astride before you joined the Fifty-second?"

A sudden burble of laughter was startled from her at this offhandedly uttered remark.

"Indeed, Your Grace," she admitted, her rich contralto noticeably less strained. "I was not unfamiliar with breeches and a man's saddle when I was a child growing up on our estate in Kent. If it had been otherwise, I doubt that I should have managed to pull the wool over the colonel's eyes."

"I suspect, Lady Grey," he reflected drily as he mounted and came abreast of her, "that you were a sad trial to your mama."

"I did try to be a dutiful daughter while she was alive," Georgina mused, automatically lifting the reins and turning her mount to follow the sound of Rathbourne's hack moving out slightly ahead of her. "Though I would consort with the stablehands and did spend more time with my horses and hounds than at the pianoforte. But it was not until she passed on that I quite joyfully became a complete and unruly hoyden. Which did nothing to lower me in my father's eyes. For he had always wished for a son and was more than willing to allow me to perform the duties which would have fallen to the male heir had there been one. In the end he entrusted much of the running of the estate into my hands."

"Which I feel sure you performed most admirably. Indeed, I wonder that you were ever induced to abandon a lifestyle of comparative independence to make your come-out in town," he commented whimsically.

"Oh, that was Grandmama's doing," she replied with a wry grimace, recalling the row which had been precipitated between her maternal grandmother and her father over what Lady Hortense had viewed as the necessity of Georgina's eventual marriage. "You see, had I never married, I should have been at the mercy of my father's cousin who inherited both the title and the entailed lands at my father's death. So though I could not like the idea at the time, I soon learned that she was in the right of it. For you must know that Papa succumbed to a fatal inflammation of the lungs shortly after I left with David for India."

She paused for a long moment, remembering the brick house on Curzon Street which had been leased by her grandfather from the Earl of Wichester for the season of her coming out. Lord Bellows, related in any number of ways to many of the great houses of England but who for many years had preferred the lifestyle of a squire on his country estate in the wilds of southeast Devon, had celebrated his granddaughter's come-out with a lavish ball in the great ballroom in which nearly four hundred of Society's elite had duly presented themselves at Lady Bellows' invitation. Georgina, fresh from the country and imbued with a natural vivacity and beauty few of her contemporaries could match, had enjoyed an instant success. She had liked it well enough but it had meant little until Lord David Grey had loomed suddenly out of the crowd, a tall, slender young man with laughing hazel eyes and a smile which turned her knees to water. From that moment on, she had been fairly caught, and it soon transpired that the lovely young heiress and the handsome young officer from Cornwall were an accepted thing.

Nothing could have been more perfect than the courtship followed by the June wedding, thought Georgina with a whimsical smile, except for the continued absence of the one man with whom David had longed to share his happiness.

"Where were you," Georgina asked suddenly, "when David and I married? You must know that he tried everything to find you. But while we had heard rumors of you in Rome and later in Greece, no one seemed to know anything for sure."

"No, I don't suppose they did," he replied in such a way that Georgina could almost visualize the cold, sardonic curl of his lips. "After I was enjoined by—er—circumstance to remove myself from England, I knocked about for a time aboard *The Swallow*. I never stayed in any one port for longer than it took to tire of the local entertainments available to a man of a more than modest fortune and possessed of appetites long-since jaded. My correspondence seldom caught up with me before I was gone again, pursuing a new will-o'-the-wisp."

"And you never once returned home in all those years?" Georgina exclaimed softly, wondering at the loneliness of so lengthy an exile.

."I did not say so," he returned in some amusement. "I visited Cornwall and Devon several times to ascertain the well-being of my brother and my various holdings. Did you fancy me a tragic figure worthy of your pity? I wasn't, I assure you. Actually I knew perhaps more of happiness living the life of a vagabond sailor than I have ever known before or since."

"Did you," Georgina said. "I am glad. I have often thought I should have liked to try the life of a mariner. Though I should have missed my horses. But on my few sea-voyages I was never ill, and I confess to having enjoyed the sea immensely. Why did you fight that duel?" she added, as though it were really an incident of no little account. Whereupon she felt a blush stain her cheeks. "Oh, I do beg your pardon," she gasped. "I know it is none of my business. But I have wondered about it ever so long. And David refused absolutely to discuss it except to say that had he been allowed to tell his father the truth of the matter, the earl would not have so easily banned you from his threshold. Which, I confess, served only to inflame my curiosity."

"David always was one to put a kinder light on the paltry escapades of my misspent youth," Rathbourne observed with an odd inflection in his tone. "The truth, however, is hardly less inglorious than the tale which we took pains to circulate. I was, you see, enamored of a married lady at the time, something which in my previous illustrious career as a rakeshame and a bounder I had avoided as being liable to rather tedious complications."

"Then there *was* a woman involved!" Georgina exclaimed ingenuously. "I was quite sure that had to be the case since I could think of no other mitigating circumstances which might have excused you. She must have been something quite exceptional to have captivated one of your reputed experience."

"Indeed," agreed the duke, who was deriving no little enjoyment from his companion's astute observations. "I should hardly otherwise have succumbed to the belief that I had at long last found my love. Unfortunately, I was not the only one she had convinced of her obvious attributes—an aspect of captivating innocence enhanced by as lovely a face and figure as it has been my misfortune to behold."

"One of those blonde beauties, I should think," Georgina interjected with a thoughtful air. "With cornflower eyes and a pleasing plumpness which deceives one into supposing they are as helpless as a child and just as innocuous. Oh, I understand perfectly how even you might have been taken in, for men invariably feel moved to protect

142

such visions of delectable vulnerability. You should not refine overmuch on your own lack of perspicuity in this instance, Your Grace. Very often it takes another woman to see through the façade to the scheming adventuress beneath."

"No doubt you are in the right of it," His Grace conceded, his voice quivering with mirth. "For you have described the lady to perfection."

Whereupon Rathbourne was treated to a delightful grin which made Georgina appear no older than a precocious schoolroom miss.

"Now you are laughing at me," she scolded in rueful amusement. "But I assure you I know what I am talking about. I have encountered any number of such paragons since my come-out. And always I have observed they have the same effect on men. It is a practice I have often deplored in my own sex, since it does little to improve the already lowering opinion males entertain for females. That we are deceitful creatures bent on entrapping hapless males into matrimony or less virtuous ends. Or, worse, that we are indeed helpless and incapable of ruling our own lives."

"Something, ma'am, for which *you* could never be faulted," he observed rather pointedly. "But to return to the sordid tale, the lady in question contrived to encounter me one afternoon during the daily promenade in Hyde Park, upon which she enacted a singularly convincing Cheltenham tragedy, informing me, though I was at some pains to extract the pertinent information from amidst her disjointed utterances, that she had previous to her marriage committed a youthful indiscretion with a certain notorious marquess. An indiscretion, moreover, for which that very same gentleman had been milking her dry. She confessed to having already pawned several pieces of jewelry and was faced with either confessing all to her husband or seeking the services of a cent-per-cent."

"She sounds a remarkably silly female. I should have

143

thought by this time she might have begun to pall on you. Hitherto you have certainly not struck me as one to tolerate a vaporish inamorata, no matter how otherwise enticing she might be."

"How very well you appear to know me," said the gentleman, apparently much struck. "For indeed, I was by then wishing myself well out of it. However, there is no accounting for the vagaries of youth. I determined for my own reasons to put a period to the marquess, whom, I judged, would not be greatly missed. To this end, David and I concocted the infamous wager, knowing, I might add, that the villain regularly frequented a certain bagnio."

"You seem to have gone to a great deal of trouble, Your Grace," Georgina mused, a slight frown marring the purity of her brow. "Could you not simply challenge the rogue to a duel without all the pretensions of a wager?"

"Not without bringing scandal down upon the lady, something which would have defeated my whole purpose and spoiled the farce. For that, in the end was all it was," he concluded with a chilling laugh. "No sooner had I dispatched the gentlemen and made good my escape from England than the lady for whom I had imagined a virtue possessed by few of her sex eloped with an American nabob."

"Did she?" Georgina queried in accents of astonishment. "How very enterprising of her to snatch the bird at hand! I should not have expected her to be so astute. It must be assumed she did everyone a favor by so precipitously removing herself from the scene of infamy," she concluded, thinking that the heartless jade deserved to have been horsewhipped for having caused so much grief.

"I can only bow to your judgment on the matter, ma'am," Rathbourne commented with an easy laugh and urged his long-legged bay to a brisker pace.

After that they rode on in silence for a time, and Georgina came gradually to an awareness of birdsong and the drone of honeybees in the air. The scents and sounds of the forest were for the most part unfamiliar to her, though she readily identified the peculiar two-noted cry of the chiffchaff and the distinct rap of a woodpecker in a tree nearby. The smell of the rich, moist earth, of ferns still damp from a heavy dew, and of blackthorn bushes which in another month would be thick with the dark, globular sloe-plums filled her with a sense of the effulgence of the Cornish woods. Simultaneously the whisper of trees made restless by a breeze flowing inland from the sea and the cool touch of the shadows cast by the thick branches and interspersed with the fleeting warmth of sunbeams filtering through the leaves made her tinglingly aware of its nearly impenetrable wildness. The sudden sound of a large body crashing through the brush off to her right startled a low exclamation from her even as her mount precipitously reared in fright and come down running.

She was vaguely aware of Rathbourne calling to her to hang on, advice which seemed wholly unnecessary in the circumstances. There was little else she could do; the animal had got the bit between its teeth and was fleeing wildly. To avoid being knocked from her bolting mount by a low-hanging bough, she kept her head down and leaned as far forward in the saddle as the horn would allow—and suddenly she was glorying in the swift flight, the old familiar thrill of racing on the brink of danger filling her with a sort of wild elation.

She heard Rathbourne drawing up behind her and experienced a sense of disappointment that soon it would all be over. It was then that she felt the animal's long stride shorten ever so slightly and the powerful hind quarters gather for the leap.

"A wall!" Rathbourne shouted from behind her. "Nine hands high!"

Then Ahmar was in the air and Georgina, concentrating solely on the feel of the animal in flight, sensed the split second when horse and rider seem to hover at the apex before beginning the descent. Instinctively she braced herself for the jarring impact of the landing, her heart in her throat. She knew with bitter certainty that if the little stallion should stumble, they were both in for a nasty fall. Then they were over, and Rathbourne was beside them, one strong hand reaching for the bridle. In seconds he had pulled the heaving stallion to a halt and had turned grimly to appraise the damsel in distress.

"Oh, but that was glorious!" Georgina gasped. Her pulse was still throbbing with lingering excitement as she leaned forward to run a soothing hand along Ahmar's sweat-dampened neck. "What I shouldn't give to see what you can really do, my little beauty," she crooned, then straightening, turned a glowing face toward Rathbourne. "What frightened him?" she asked, laughing a little with the sheer enjoyment of her unlooked-for adventure. "I heard something in the underbrush, and then we were off, just like that."

"It was only a deer," he answered, an odd tautness in the deep voice. "Are you all right?"

"Why yes. Why shouldn't I be?" she answered steadily, her lovely head cocked at an inquisitive angle. "I may not be able to see, but I am not entirely unaccustomed to the sudden starts of a spirited animal."

His low-muttered oath brought a quizzical grin to her lips.

"You needn't be so concerned, Your Grace," she said quite calmly. "I am not made of porcelain. And you were right to induce me from the house. I had nearly forgotten the marvelous feel of a horse beneath one on so glorious a day. But should we not be getting on our way? I am persuaded the hour is growing late, and we have still to reach the headland."

He did not immediately answer, and she was hard-put to guess his thoughts as she felt his gaze intent upon her.

When at last he spoke, he caught her off guard.

"You, my little nodcock, are quite possibly the most exasperating female I have yet encountered," he informed her in a voice of tempered steel. "No doubt you are a bruising rider, and as I have been privileged to witness how amazingly adept you are with cattle, I can only hope you will forgive me if I seem a trifle perturbed at what appeared to me a near mishap. I was operating under an apparently erroneous supposition based on your previous lack of confidence. I see now that I was mistaken. No doubt you shall next inform me that you are quite capable of finding your way alone. As to the lateness of the hour, you need not concern yourself. We are even now on the boundaries of the land in question."

"Oh, dear, I have upset your equanimity, haven't I?" she said, striving to keep the laughter from her voice. "And without a doubt I do owe you my heartfelt gratitude for having sayed my life."

"That, my girl, is fustion. And well you know it," he returned in sardonic amusement at her rather tardy assumption of demure femininity. "I begin to marvel that my cousin did not throttle you years ago, as I shall certainly be moved to do if ever again you cause me to live through such a moment."

Georgina, sensing the depth of feeling contained in this blighting speech, immediately sobered. In the excitement of the moment she had not stopped to consider with what trepidation Rathbourne must have viewed her headlong flight on the bolting stallion. No doubt he had been gripped with a sense of impotent horror as he beheld her flinging straight for the stone wall and visualized the probable outcome. And it was quite true that David had abhorred her propensity for getting herself into a coil and for what he considered her total lack of sensibility when the thing was safely over and done. Poor Rathbourne. She had proven a sad trial for him.

Thus it was that she turned upon the unfortunate nobleman a breathtakingly sweet smile and held out a conciliatory hand.

"I am sorry to have given you such a fright," she said, upon which a mischievous gleam irrepressibly replaced the gravity in her lovely eyes. "However, I cannot deny that I enjoyed my little adventure immensely and do not in the least regret it. Perhaps you will not judge me too harshly when I tell you that even so, I have no wish to repeat it and will endeavor most earnestly to avoid any further mishaps. Am I forgiven, Your Grace?"

His rueful bark of laughter caused her heart most unaccountably to give a leap.

"You, Lady Grey, are unmitigated baggage," he said, his voice vibrant with lingering humor, and enclosed her slender fingers in a warm clasp. "And while I can find it in my heart to forgive you, it shall doubtless be some time before I forgive myself. And now, shall we proceed to the business at hand?"

Georgina was more than glad to comply, as she had begun to experience a heady disturbance of her senses at his touch which threatened to leave her quite disoriented. With a vague sense of unreality she heard him dismount and felt him draw near.

"I think perhaps you might obtain a greater impression of your surroundings if we continue on foot," he suggested, apparently unaware of the sudden warmth of her cheeks as he fitted his hands to her small waist and lifted her down from the saddle.

For a moment she swayed against him as her limbs threatened to give way beneath her, due, no doubt, to their being stiff after the unaccustomed ride on horseback, she told herself. The masculine scents of shaving soap and tobacco teased her senses even as his strong hands, closing about her arms to steady her, unsettled her already precarious equilibrium, and suddenly she was most acutely aware that she was miles from anywhere and quite alone with this most disturbing Duke of Rathbourne.

"Oh," she uttered a trifle giddily and tried to back a step, only to have her ankle twist nearly out from under her.

"Easy," he warned. "The footing can be treacherous. Take my hand and step carefully."

Suiting action to the words, he grasped her hand in a firm grip and led her across the headland to the remnants of shallow furrows left from former attempts to cultivate the boggy land. Georgina, listening to the river in the distance, tried to picture the valley in her mind as Connings had described it to her.

They were south of the Tamar where the steep, wooded declivities gentled to broad fertile slopes hugging the river. Further up and down the valley cherry and apple orchards interspersed with small farms bordered by hedgerows followed the winding contours of the waterway, but here where the valley curled and converged with a wide combe seemingly scooped from the hills, the grade was shallow and the arable land gave way to marshy bottoms. Connings had suggested that the underlying rocks, which had in any case to be removed before the land could be properly worked, should be used to construct across the mouth of the combe a 'Cornish hedge' supplied at periodic intervals with drains. The bottoms could then be filled in and graded with sand brought in from the beach along Whitsand. She had heard of similar feats accomplished by the indomitable Cornish and with less help than Emberly could provide should she decide to undertake the task.

"Connings' plan has merit," Rathbourne observed when they had walked off the proposed field. The duke had described in detail the lay of the land, even insisting that Georgina test the texture of the soil with her bare hands, so that she had actually begun to see everything in her mind's eye. "But it would require a deal of men and labor, and there would still be the danger that everything might be washed out when the river flooded," he added reflectively.

"Perhaps not if we kept well above the course and supplemented the floodwall with a thick hedge of blackthorn," Georgina suggested, reluctant somehow to give up the scheme.

Thus the morning passed swiftly with Lady Grey and the Duke of Rathbourne immersed in the discussion of practicable methods of drainage, erosion control, and economic feasibility. And if occasionally Georgina discovered herself listening more to the deep resonance of her companion's voice than to the actual content of the words and if at times that mesmerizing voice faded away in the middle of a sentence to be suddenly taken up again at the inquisitive lift of one of the lady's exquisite eyebrows, still neither would have claimed the morning had been wasted. Indeed, it was in startled surprise that Georgina heard her cousin hail them from beyond the stone wall which had nearly been her undoing earlier that morning and realized the time had quite flown.

"Georgina!" cried Miss Knigsley in open astonishment as she drew near enough to see her cousin quite clearly. "Are you all right? Good heavens, do not say you have suffered a fall."

"Indeed I shan't," Georgina laughed, and suddenly Zenobia was reminded of that slender young daredevil who once had stolen a ride on a half-wild chestnut stallion so many years ago. "For I just managed to avoid such a calamity. Can you have so little confidence in my equestrian skills, Nobie? Why only yesterday you were bragging on me."

"N-no, of course not, Gina. It's just that you are splattered from head to foot with mud, and I thought—"

"Oh, dear, I'm afraid I quite forgot myself," Georgina grimaced and turned accusingly toward the duke. "This, sir, is all your doing," she added ruefully. "I must look a fright. Why did you not tell me?"

"On the contrary," came the deep, drawling tones tinged with humor. "You present a charmingly earthy appearance. I believe I like you very well as you are."

"Oh, indeed," Georgina retorted, screwing her face up at the gentleman. "No doubt rustic maidens with dirty faces are quite all the fashion these days."

"Not so you'd notice," admitted the duke. "But then you must ever be accounted something of an original wherever you go."

Unaccountably she blushed at a subtle nuance in his voice which she could not quite define, and, calling to Nobie to come help set her to rights again, she turned away to hide her confusion. Oh, botheration! she fumed inwardly. Why had he the power to make her feel like the veriest simpering schoolroom miss? There really was no explaining her exceedingly idiotish behavior since she had made Rathbourne's acquaintance. Well, she must simply take greater care to guard herself against whatever it was about His Grace which seemed somehow to threaten her hard-won tranquillity and peace of mind, she told herself sternly, then immediately became lost in contemplation of the way his voice seemed to vibrate just so when he was teasing her or the way he had of making her forget herself for hours on end and of putting her at her ease so that suddenly she would find herself confiding to him things she would never dream of telling an almost total stranger. It was all utter nonsense, she chided herself, but at times she had the oddest feeling that she had known Rathbourne for a very long time.

Chapter 7

In the days and weeks following Georgina's first excursion beyond the confines of Greystone, Rathbourne and Robbie Penwarren became frequent visitors to Emberly, with the result that Greystone and its inhabitants witnessed a distinct alteration in the quiet, orderly existence which had earlier prevailed. The old halls had seemed to quicken with new life and were wont to reverberate with the sounds of merry laughter the likes of which, Bolton was reported to have remarked, had not been heard since the days when His Grace and Master David were scampish young scapegraces cutting up wild. And, indeed, what with the young earl's newly begun lessons in the manly art of fisticuffs, the additions to the household of two lop-eared hound puppies, innumerable snails, frogs, and garter snakes, and a squealing, pink-skinned shoat which threatened to wreak havoc on the meticulous Mrs. Porter's housekeeping, plus the impromptu tiffins of tea and saffron buns often followed by riotous sessions of jackstraws or "fore-and-aft," the Manor enjoyed seldom a dull moment.

Even the servants went about their daily tasks with a buoyancy which was clearly reflective of the satisfaction they took in beholding their mistress's growing happiness. For her ladyship appeared suddenly to blossom. Her aura of sweet-tempered calm which was yet touched with an underlying sorrow had been supplanted by a seemingly irrepressible light-heartedness manifested in a decided propensity to hum as she gathered flowers from the garden or to fall suddenly into dreamy silences, her lovely lips curved in a fanciful smile.

Georgina herself seemed unaware that she was behaving in any way out of the ordinary, nor did she once stop to consider that her attitude toward the Duke of Rathbourne had undergone a distinct change. For, where previously she had resisted the very thought of becoming in any way dependent upon anyone, and most in particular upon her son's guardian, she had gradually come to turn more and more to the duke for advice in regard to the sundry worrisome matters involved in running Emberly, with the result that she had imperceptibly come to discover that she was feeling far less drained at the end of the day and that she suddenly had more time to devote to herself and to Davey. But perhaps even more importantly, along with her deepening contentment, which she attributed to the lessening of the nagging worries inherent in having sole responsibility for the overseeing of her son's inheritance, had come a cessation of her nightmares. Indeed, they had ceased as abruptly and as mysteriously as they had begun. Upon which, to Bolton's quiet delight and Nanny Slade's vociferous approval, Georgina had unaccountably begun to evince a sudden interest in refurbishing her wardrobe. For the first time since David Grey's death, those closest to Georgina began to hope that at last she had begun to give over her grieving, a circumstance for which they suspected they were greatly indebted to His Grace, the Duke of Rathbourne, for his unobtrusive intervention in her ladyship's affairs.

And, indeed, Rathbourne, with a thoughtfulness and tact which would have surprised his acquaintances, had undertaken the task of removing as many of the obstacles to Lady Grey's contentment as her stubborn pride would allow. Had he dared, he would have exercised his legal prerogatives as the earl's guardian to relieve her of the onerous responsibilities of Emberly in their entirety. As it was, he was ruefully aware that he must proceed with great caution lest he undermine Georgina's growing trust and thus endanger all that he hoped to accomplish. For no matter how he might wish to be in the position to grant her a totally care-free existence and regardless of the fact that he chafed under the restrictions imposed on him by her fiercely independent nature, he would not have had her any other way. He knew of few who could have borne with such fortitude what she had been made to bear.

Thus, while Rathbourne was grateful he had not discovered his angel a hopeless invalid, her spirit broken by sorrow and grief, he was yet troubled by something he sensed in her but could not quite define. When first he had suggested they ride out to see the outlying farms, he had not been insensitive to her very real reluctance to comply with his proposal. On the contrary, he had considered her reaction natural under the circumstances. He had maneuvered her into the position of having to accept his invitation only because he had felt sure in the end she would discover her fears to be unfounded. Nor had he been disappointed, for she had handled herself and her mount with characteristic hardihood, even going so far as to astonish him with her total lack of feminine sensibilities over her perilous mishap. He would never forget if he lived to be a hundred the terror he had experienced as the mettlesome stallion took that blasted wall. Nor his profound relief that she had come through unscathed. And while he had expected her to be near to a swoon after her harrowing experience, he had found her radiating keen pleasure in her un-looked for adventure, her eyes sparkling and her lovely face aglow with excitement. Never had he known such a woman.

She was an enigma, was his mysterious Lady Grey. For despite her seeming independence and the courageous manner in which she met every obstacle in her path, he had glimpsed her very real vulnerability. It had not been a reluctance to trust herself on a horse which had caused her to blanch at the thought of visiting the bottoms, or a dread of being made an object of pity before others which had robbed her of her sleep. Nor did he believe for a moment that it was the circumstance of her blindness which filled her with an irrational dread of venturing beyond the boundaries of Greystone. It was something else, something much more deep-seated, and somehow the little bandy-legged groom was a part of it. For why else should his angel reel at the sound of Denby's voice, her features swept with sudden anguish, so that in spite of her earlier appearance of firm resolve to go through with it, Rathbourne had been instantly aware of her intention to cry off and retreat once more to the safety of the manor? And, when later he had made it a point to become better acquainted with Emberly's head groom and had learned Denby had been David's batman, he had no longer doubted that whatever troubled Georgina was inextricably tied to her past and to David. And suddenly he had truly begun to wonder at the underlying cause of her blindness and for the first time to doubt the wisdom of his decision to keep her ignorant of those lost weeks in Portugal.

More and more he was persuaded that the mysteries surrounding Georgina would only be resolved by discovering what had happened to her after she left him in Elvas. Nor was Georgina the only one to cause Rathbourne concern in those first weeks in Cornwall. It had become increasingly obvious that Robbie had developed a decided tendre for the lovely Miss Kingsley. The matter would have afforded Rathbourne no little amusement had he not become instinctively aware that all was not as it should be with the young woman.

His first impressions of Lady Grey's cousin had understandably been rather vague, since he had still been reeling from the shock of encountering his angel in the garden at

155

Greystone. Thus he had noted her obvious youth and beauty and an apparent attempt to hide both behind an overly severe and decidedly unbecoming hair-do and bonnet and a shapeless traveling dress of grey bombazine. Her expression had been rigidly guarded, her demeanor something less than charming, until at last Georgina had beguiled a grin from the girl with her teasing. He had been struck then by a sense that Miss Kingsley was in some sort of trouble, a feeling which had gained in strength the more he saw of her. For though she continued to be unfailingly polite to all those around her and was ever solicitous of her cousin's needs, she had yet seemed to erect a barrier around herself which not even Georgina could penetrate, let alone Robbie, for whom she maintained an icy reserve calculated to keep him at a distance.

Robbie, however, reflected the duke wryly as he stood in the library at Rathbourne, his elbow propped on the mantelpiece and a glass of brandy held lightly in one lean hand, was apparently made of sterner stuff than Miss Kingsley had calculated. Thus far the young whelp had demonstrated a stoic patience and an unshakable optimism that eventually he would break through the girl's stubborn reserve.

"Damn the chit!" he muttered to himself and wondered what it was about Zenobia Kingsley which had bewitched the boy. She certainly had not cast any lures in Robbie's way. He had to grant her that. Indeed, if anything, she was exerting an honest effort to put off her determined suitor at every turn. And while there was no denying she was a diamond of the first water, Robbie was not totally without town bronze and had experienced his share of fair-haired beauties. No, he mused cynically, 'twas more likely the miserable young cockerel had been captivated by that aura of wounded innocence which fairly exuded from the girl.

Yet despite the fact that all his instincts warned him Miss Kingsley was trouble, Rathbourne had thus far been content to sit back and let things run their natural course. After all, he was well acquainted with the streak of obduracy which lay beneath his brother's sweet-tempered exterior and knew as well that to come out openly against Miss Kingsley would only serve to stiffen Robbie's resolve, something which at all costs he wished to avoid. Thus far the girl had shown no inclination to give in, and so long as she continued in her present manner, he need not interfere. Still, since he had already decided to go up to London within the week, it would do no harm to make some discreet inquiries while in town, he thought, though he little liked the notion of snooping into the chit's past. After all, he was hardly one to hold himself up as any sort of moral judge, he mused with a wry twist of the lips. Nor was it likely his brother would easily forgive him for anything so underhanded; never mind what Lady Grey's probable reaction would be.

"Damn!" he muttered again and downed the remainder of his brandy. What a confounded coil. And yet there was one bright ray in all of this, he reflected, recalling his visit to Greystone earlier that day.

He had hardly been prepared upon arriving at the manor to discover the whole household in a dither of excitement. Even Bolton, the old stonefaced butler, had greeted him with a decided twinkle in his eye, and for once Miss Kingsley, who quietly wished him a good-day as she whisked upstairs on an errand with Robbie in tow behind her, had seemed positively to glow with hardly suppressed good humor, which not even Robbie's rapt look of admiration could wholly dispel. With a feeling of having stepped into Bedlam he allowed himself to be ushered into the Blue Saloon to discover Georgina Grey perched on a low stool in the center of the room and Nanny Slade hovering about with various and assorted tapes and measures, pins and paper patterns.

"Rathbourne," gurgled Georgina, turning a laughing

face in the duke's direction as Bolton announced her noble visitor with proper aplomb. "I'm afraid you have arrived at an inauspicious time. I have been positively coerced into discarding my 'wholly disreputable gowns what no proper lady'd be seen dead in,' as Nanny has so charmingly described them. And have been sentenced to stand still as a stone statue till such time as I have been thoroughly poked, prodded, and measured for a new wardrobe. Not the sort of thing, I am convinced, which can possibly interest a gentleman."

"On the contrary, ma'am," drawled the duke, drinking in Georgina's sparkling beauty. She was dressed in a faded lavender round gown which she used to wear when working about the garden but which did nothing to detract from her tall, slender gracefulness. Her lovely hair shining like polished mahogany had been released from the confines of the habitual knot at the nape of her neck to fall in a silken mass down to her shoulders. He had difficulty believing the magnificent brown eyes dancing gloriously with laughter could possibly be sightless as he seemed to lose himself in their glimmering depths. Never had he seen her so bewitchingly lovely. "I have been considered something of an arbiter of ladies' fashions," he continued, allowing just a hint of provocative irony to color his voice. "You will find I am well versed in both style and price, having footed the bill for not a few such folderols on various and sundry occasions."

"No, have you?" Georgina exclaimed in an excellent show of astounded innocence as delightfully she arched her eyebrows at him. The little minx, he thought, wondering suddenly how much longer he could bring himself to wait before he dared claim her once and for all as his own. "Then you are the very one we need for a matter of some delicacy."

"I am, as ever, yours to command," he returned with elaborate gallantry and inclined his head in gracious acceptance of whatever fate she might mete out to him.

"You, sir, are a complete hand," she chuckled. "But I shall take you at your word, for I confess to being in something of a bind. You see, I have been persuaded that I have been a positive frump for far too long. It is time I did something to spruce up my image. However, I've been informed that that presents something of a problem since there is very little available amidst the Cornish wilds in the way of fashionable modistes or suitable fabrics. You see, I had thought to send Zenobia as far as Plymouth to search out what she could of what we shall require. But as Robbie has informed us that you are very soon to make your way to London on business, it has occurred to me that—"

"You need say no more, ma'am," interjected Rathbourne. "I shall doubtless derive no little pleasure in renewing my acquaintance with Bond Street, Asprey's, and any number of the fashionable modistes who once enjoyed my patronage."

A distinct snort was heard to emanate from Nanny Slade's censoriously pursed lips.

"Oh, dear," Georgina soulfully mused, a suspicious twinkle in her brown eyes. "I had forgotten your lamentable reputation, Your Grace. But since you have seen fit to remind me, perhaps we should reconsider. After all, do you condescend to perform this small commission for me, I shall very likely be awarded the unlooked-for distinction of being thought the latest in Rathbourne's incomparable line of inamoratas, shall I not? A prominence for which I fear I am woefully unsuited. Why, think how lowering it would be to your otherwise illustrious career!"

"On the contrary, madam," Rathbourne gently demurred, his lips curving in an appreciative smile which Georgina did not have to see to apprehend. "In the unlikely event that your name should be linked with mine, you, my little baggage, could only lend elegance to a reputation which has hitherto been woefully lacking in discrimination.

159

But since the occasion shall not arise, it does not signify. I have no intention of compromising your reputation. My cousin, Lady Kathryn Ingram, will undertake to see to everything."

"Katey Ingram?" Georgina queried in surprise. "But that is marvelous. I've often thought of her and wondered how she went on. For you must know we used to be quite familiar."

"She goes on at her usual frenetic pace, despite the frequent additions to her already prodigious brood," offered the duke, observing with interest a certain aura of wistfulness in Georgina's expression. "But then you may discover all these things for yourself when she arrives at Rathbourne to serve as my hostess during the off-season. By the way, you have thought to include a ballgown in your proposed wardrobe, have you not?"

It soon transpired that not only had she not for an instant considered the purchase of a ballgown but that she perceived no necessity to rectify the omission, since it was quite obvious the need for one would not arise.

"That, my girl, is where you are wrong," Rathbourne calmly interjected when it seemed she had finished, at which time Robbie Penwarren and Miss Kingsley saw fit to make their entrance. "You will most certainly attend the festivities to be held at Rathbourne, of which the ball is to be only one of the several planned events, since they will be in honor of the new Earl of Emberly and his gracious *maman*. I'm afraid it would be considered exceedingly odd if you did not make an appearance," he ended in a bored voice and pointedly ignored his brother's expression of amazement and Nanny Slade's worried glance as he stepped forward in apparent nonchalance to take Georgina's fluttering hand in his own and helped her down from the stool.

Zenobia Kingsley, too, had not failed to note that her cousin's face had gone suddenly white or that she had appeared to sway slightly atop the stool. Going instantly to Georgina's side, she awarded the duke a cold stare. The man was overbearing and utterly heartless, she thought with bitter resentment. Could he not see what his arrogance had done? Did he not understand that Georgina was not ready yet to put her newfound peace of mind to the test? But Rathbourne only returned her look with a slight arch of an imperious eyebrow, his blue eyes beneath heavily drooping lids unreadable.

"Gina, you are gone suddenly quite pale," Zenobia said, turning solicitously to her cousin. "Come. Sit down for a moment. I shall ring Bolton to bring the tea tray."

"No, no. I'm quite all right. Really," Georgina demurred, having quickly recovered her equanimity. "His Grace merely took me by surprise. But I have not changed my mind," she added, turning toward Rathbourne, her expression faintly quizzical. "No doubt you mean to be kind, sir. But do you not think Davey is a trifle young to be honored with a ball? Perhaps a children's party would better serve."

"No doubt," he answered with double-edged meaning which brought a slow flush to the lady's pale cheeks. "But I thought I made it quite clear the ball was to be only one of several planned events. There will be entertainments more suited to the younger set. You cannot cut yourself off from the world forever, Georgina," he added in a soft aside. "No matter how much you might like to. It is time you assumed the responsibilities of your position as the Countess of Emberly."

"And you think she has not, Your Grace?" suddenly queried Miss Kingsley in outraged disbelief. "I fail to see how she could have done more."

"Do you, Miss Kingsley?" the duke murmured coldly and allowed his gaze to linger speculatively on the girl, until at last, as if recalled to a realization that she had spoken out of line, she bit her lip and lowered her eyes to hide their glitter of rebellious resentment. Immediately Penwarren, who had been thoughtfully observing the suddenly charged scene, was moved to intercede on Miss Kingsley's behalf.

"Georgina has done remarkably, Miss Kingsley," he said easily. "Drew would be the last one to deny that. No doubt he is referring to Emberly's position as a very old and prominent house in the county. The countess will be expected to continue the old earl's tradition of being something of a leader among the local gentry. I'm afraid there has already been some comment on Lady Grey's failure to call on the prominent families in the area."

"But it could not be helped," Georgina declared flatly, her previous ebullience quite vanished. "I-I have been in mourning."

"And now that you are not," observed Rathbourne maddeningly, "it is time you were presented to your neighbors. They will not eat you, you know."

"Will they not?" Georgina queried heatedly, her lovely eyes flashing in resentment at his high-handed meddling in her ordered life. Then suddenly she seemed to catch herself. Turning sharply away, she strode with studied familiarity the few steps to the French doors opened to the afternoon sun. For a long moment she stood with her back to the others, her face tilted toward the sunlight falling warmly on her face. Rathbourne, watching her from beneath drooping eyelids, saw the slender hands clench and unclench at her sides. A faint smile played about his lips at the thought that he had at last breached her formidable defenses, for in that moment before she had turned away, he had glimpsed the Gina of old, his fiercely protective angel who had enthralled him so long ago.

Thus it was with no little surprise that he saw her take a deep breath and, expelling it, turn to face them with an assumption of her usual quiet composure.

"You are right, of course," she said calmly, and a wry glint of admiration flickered briefly in Rathbourne's eyes.

"I have been remiss in the social amenities. For myself, what anyone thinks of my preference to live in comparative seclusion is unimportant. But for Davey it is different. He must not be made to suffer for his mother's inadequacies. Therefore, though I have no wish to embark on the social rounds now or anytime in the near future, I will give the matter my due consideration. More than that, I cannot promise. Meantime," she added with a glimmer of a smile, "though I refuse unconditionally to purchase a ball gown, since I shall not be attending any such functions, perhaps it would be advisable, Nobie, to include one or two evening dresses in our order. Though I don't doubt for a moment they shall only constitute a shockingly wasteful extravagance and shall in the end gather dust from disuse."

Georgina firmly turned the discussion into different channels after that, and Rathbourne had had to be content for the time being with the lady's concession to at least think about the matter. As for her refusal to attend any balls or to order an appropriate gown for such an event, he was not overly concerned. It would be a small matter to add an item or two to her list of necessaries once she had turned it over to him. Nor did he doubt for a moment that she would eventually come around. Lady Georgina Grey would go through an ordeal of fire if she believed she did it for her son's sake, he judged with a wry twist of his lips, but then he had been counting heavily on that aspect of her character when he fabricated the tale of the planned festivities. It now remained only to convince his cousin to remove herself, her beloved husband, and their noisome brood of young hopefuls from the lap of luxury in Brighton to the obscurity and relative discomfort of his remote Cornish castle.

In retrospect he rather thought he must have been visited with a momentary lapse of sanity to have even for an instant contemplated anything so patently absurd. Kathryn Ingram would doubtless sooner embark on a trek to the West Indies than come to Rathbourne. But at any rate he had jolted Robbie out of any false sense of complacency, His Grace reflected in sardonic amusement. For Robbie was well aware that their mettlesome cousin had never given over the hope that one day a match might be made between the duke's heir apparent and her eldest daughter, a chit of some sixteen or seventeen years. At least the besotted young whelp would have something other than Miss Kingsley to contemplate in the days to come, concluded Rathbourne, who strongly suspected Lady Grey's paid companion would be unable to resist indefinitely Robbie's determined campaign, based as it was on tact, patient understanding, and a sincere-hearted regard.

Nor was the duke wide of the mark by far, as was soon evidenced by the scene being enacted in the rose garden at Greystone Manor even then.

Zenobia Kingsley, fleeing the haunting melody of a Portuguese love song drifting from the music room, slipped noiselessly through the Blue Saloon and out the French doors into the seclusion of her cousin's private garden. Grateful to be alone at last after an afternoon which had been both bittersweet and trying in the extreme, she let drop the careful mask with which she faced the world and wandered aimlessly among the roses, her thoughts far from the budding beauty around her.

Lord Robert had come again as he had come almost every day since foolishly she had ridden with him to the old Norman shrine and allowed herself to become enamored of the sweet scent of apple blossoms, of the loveliness of the morning touched with golden shafts of sunlight glancing through the trees, and, most particularly, of Robert Geoffrey Charles Penwarren himself, whose sweet smile was like intoxicating wine, robbing her of all caution, indeed, of her very reason.

Oh, God! She could not bear to think of him, for to do so

was to taste bitter gall. He was everything she had ever dreamt of in a man—strong but gentle, and possessed of a rare understanding. But she had no right to dreams, she reminded herself. Oh, why had she found her love only when love was forbidden? She had believed her heart was dead and had thus found a sort of respite from the pain of living. Why did it quicken now with new life, putting to the lie her belief that she had paid for her disobedience?

Curse him! Curse his eyes which looked at her with a kind and gentle warmth and day by day melted the hard core of her resolve. He was worse by far than the man who had destroyed her innocence in a single moment of unguarded passion and sent her fleeing from her bridal bed before she had been made a wife in truth as well as in fact. The Earl of Vail had only slain her heart. Robert Penwarren would destroy her soul.

And what if he did? whispered a small, insidious voice. Was it so important? Would it be so wrong to be loved even for a little while?

"No! I won't listen!" she cried out loud and pressed her hands to her ears as if she might indeed shut out the deceitful whisperings of her own awakening heart. At last, as if her limbs could no longer bear her, she sank heavily onto a marble bench and wearily laid her head in the crook of one arm propped along the back.

How long she rested there, lost in the sweet lament of her cousin's song which had pursued her to the garden, she did not know. She was not aware of the sun retreating behind the wall of cedars or that dusk was nearly upon her. Nor did she hear the soft crunch of footsteps along the garden path or hear them when suddenly they ceased.

Robbie Penwarren's voice obtruding on her solitude startled her into awful awareness.

"Miss Kingsley. Forgive my intrusion, but is something troubling you?"

Zenobia uttered a small gasp and, blushing furiously,

rose hastily to her feet.

"What are *you* doing here?" she blurted before she thought. Instantly recalling herself, she stifled a small gasp of consternation and, dropping her head, said in a low, wooden voice, "Forgive me, my lord. I-I thought you had gone."

"Poor Zenobia. I didn't mean to startle you," he said and wondered why she was trembling. "I promised to take Davey fishing this afternoon and have only just got back. I saw you from the nursery window up there and wanted to say good-bye."

It was on her tongue to rebuke him for speaking so familiarly when she had not given him leave to do so, but she seemed suddenly to have lost all powers of speech as she committed the supreme folly of glancing up into his eyes. Oh, why must he look at her that way?

"You know you shouldn't linger so long," he scolded, then grinned slightly as he added with a twinkle in his eye, "like some 'sweet bird, that shunn'st the noise of folly/ most musical, most melancholy.' " But then suddenly he sobered. "Did you need to be alone so much that you would risk taking a chill?"

"I'm not cold, and I'm never ill," she retorted, turning sharply away. "I—I wish you would leave me alone."

He was silent for a time, though he did not gratify her wish by retreating. After a moment he caught her gently by the arm and turned her that he might see her face. Startled, she looked up to see him smiling gravely, his eyes gently quizzing her.

" 'In solitude,' " he quoted irrepressibly, " 'What happiness? who can enjoy alone,/ Or, all enjoying, what contentment find?' "

"I do not look for happiness, my lord," she said bitterly and pulled her arm away. "And what small measure of contentment is permitted me, can be found only in solitude. You are prodigiously fond of Milton this evening," she added waspishly and retreated a few paces, wishing he would go and leave her to her own unquiet thoughts.

Instead, however, she was surprised by his sudden rueful laughter.

"I am prodigiously fond of Milton most all of the time, Miss Kingsley," he assured her in amused tolerance. "A vice which has done little to endear me to most of my set. Actually I'm far too bookish to be good *ton*, but fortunately Rathbourne's credit is good enough to carry both of us. Are you fond of poetry?"

"Perhaps," she shrugged, suddenly nervous again, and tried to turn the subject to a less disturbing vein. "I was listening to Georgina and quite forgot the time. Did you hear her singing? She has a rare gift with the pianoforte, but I did not know her voice was so lovely, too."

"It must have been a melancholy song to have made you so pensive," he observed sapiently, watching her nervously pluck the petals from a magnificent yellow tea rose.

She bit her tongue but could not stop herself from replying, nor could she quite subdue a small, oddly mischievous hint of a smile.

" 'I am never merry when I hear sweet music,' " she quoted, challenging him with a single, fleeting look.

" 'The reason is, your spirits are attentive,' " he answered instantly, and burst into easy laughter. "Even Milton must pay homage to England's greatest bard."

The garden was steeped in muted shadows cast by the gloaming light of dusk. Robbie sighed, thinking how beautiful Miss Kingsley looked and wishing he could tease the sadness from her eyes.

"You know," he said suddenly, "we're taking a chance staying out after dark like this."

Zenobia flashed suddenly doubtful eyes in his direction, wondering what new tack he had taken.

"What can you mean by that, my lord?" she queried suspiciously.

"Why, this is the time the Cornish piskies begin to wake up for the night's revelries. No. Really," he laughed, seeing her frown of disapproval at what she must have considered his foolishness. "A Cornishman takes care never to offend one of the little people. Why, ask any farmer's wife and she shall tell you how every night she sweeps the hearthstone and leaves a basin of fresh spring water before it so the piskies can bathe and spruce up a bit before they form the circles in the green. Upon which, she quite devoutly says her prayers and goes to bed."

"Don't you think that's rather odd in her?" queried Miss Kingsley, suppressing a helpless smile at his light-hearted teasing.

"Why, not at all," he solemnly assured her, but even in the faint light of the newly rising moon, she detected the gleam of humor in his eye. "We Cornishmen are not so single-minded as you uplanders. We know there's a deal more to a man's soul than the vicar teaches. There's song and poetry. A Cornishman eats and breathes music. God knows there's little enough else to sustain him more often than not. The piskies are real enough to people who work all their lives for barely enough to stay alive. Magic, Miss Kingsley, is as much a part of Cornwall as Wesley and Methodism."

He had sounded so very serious at the last that she was for a moment fairly caught.

"But surely *you* don't believe in magic!" she exclaimed, then blushed as she realized how he had led her so cleverly into the trap.

"Well, it all depends on what you mean by magic," he returned, drawing near enough that she saw quite distinctly a sudden gleam in his eyes which she very greatly mistrusted. "I look at you, for instance," he said, smiling dangerously, "with the moonlight glinting in your hair and your eyes, your huge, sad eyes full of secrets, and I find myself wondering just exactly who and what you are."

"Stop!" she whispered harshly and turned as if to escape, but Penwarren caught her wrist and held her.

"What is it, Zenobia?" he said softly. "What are you hiding from?"

"N-nothing. This is all utter nonsense," she insisted, twisting her wrist until it hurt as she tried to make him let her go. But suddenly he no longer seemed the gentle youth who had charmed her moments earlier with absurdities about piskies and magic and the like, but a man who somehow frightened her.

For a long moment he held her with eyes that glittered in the moonlight with an odd sort of intensity, then just as swiftly he seemed to change back again, as if the laughing eyes and gentle smile were a mask he wore to keep from scaring her away.

"Very well," he said, lightly teasing once again, "if you won't tell me your dark secret, Miss Kingsley, I suppose I shall just have to guess."

She gasped as suddenly he drew her to his chest and held her a helpless prisoner in his arms.

"Now let me see. What are you then?" he murmured tantalizingly and gazed deeply into her troubled eyes. "But it is all there for any true Cornishman to see," he said suddenly, making her jump in nervousness. "Tell me the truth. Your father was the seventh son of a seventh son, was he not. And he chose you as the one to receive his gift of magic. No? Then you must have rescued a mermaid lured to the rocks by moonlight. Yes, that must be it. You helped her back into the sea and in exchange were granted the power of a Cornish pellar, one of those strange beings who can command Cornish charms and commune with the piskies."

"I am nothing of the kind," she retorted and in her desperation resorted to Shakespeare once again. " 'Do you not know I am a woman?' " she said, pleading with her eyes to make him stop though her heart was saying some-

169

thing quite different. " 'When I think, I must speak.' "

Suddenly the smile faded from his lips.

"Yes, you are a woman," he said huskily and bent his head to kiss her with sudden, undisguised passion.

Zenobia groaned softly when at last he drew away. Never had she dreamed a kiss could be like this. Suddenly she was swept by bitter despair. Heaven help her, she thought, for she did not see how she could ever go back to the way she had been before Lord Robert had shown her what it might be to be truly loved by him. Then she heard him whisper her name and felt his lips against her hair, and suddenly she forgot everything but the man who held her and the overwhelming tenderness which filled her with such terrible, sweet passion.

Georgina, wearied at last, allowed her fingers to go still on the piano keys and wondered how much time had elapsed since, driven by a turmoil of conflicting emotions, she had retreated to the comfort of her music. Vaguely she was aware that the dinner gong had sounded some time past. It must be late, she thought and experienced a twinge of guilt for having indulged herself at the expense of those who served her so loyally. No doubt Cook was in a pother at having her oxtail soup, stuffed Cornish hens, herb pie, and Loundes pudding returned not only untouched but unattended as well. And probably Bolton was in a latent stew of anxiety over her absence. And who could blame them? They did their best to see to her comfort and the smooth running of the household. She at least owed them the civility of adhering to the schedule she herself had established upon arriving at the manor.

Little did she know with what real disquiet Bolton had hovered outside the door to the music room, the tiniest suggestion of an anxious frown forming the veriest hint of a crease between his eyebrows. Early on he had learned to gauge his mistress's state of mind from the temper of the music emanating from the music room. Of late her ladyship had been prone to abandon the more ponderous pieces for Haydn's scherzi, but this new predilection for ballads signaled a change in mood which was not only peculiar but singularly disturbing. Indeed, tonight he had been sorely tempted to brave the jealously guarded province of the nursery and Nanny Slade in the hopes that she might be able to offer insight. He had, however, been saved from so improvident a venture by the unexpected appearance of Nanny Slade herself upon the landing.

The old nurse spared the aging butler a single discerning glance over the tops of rimless spectacles before clucking her tongue and shaking her head in apparent disapprobation.

"She's in a fine fit o' th' doldrums. Oh, 'tis plain as a pikestaff. An' jest when things was lookin' up, too. But like as not His Grace is in th' right of it so far as he went. Don't do her no good t' shut herself away. What she needs is fer someone t' rile her good and proper. She used t' have a rare fine temper afore all this come about, an' it 'ppeared fer a time the lad'd be th' one t' jar her outa whatever's ailin' her. Till he took to 'andlin' her wi' kid gloves like all th' rest. I've took care o' th' lass since she were a squallin' babe, an' she weren't nivver one t' take things layin' down. 'Tain't natural the way she goes about like nothin' couldn't touch her. 'Tain't like 'erself atall."

"I shouldn't wish to seem impertinent, Mrs. Slade," Bolton interjected in his ponderous way. "I don't hold with the staff gossiping about their betters. But if there should be anything we could do to help her ladyship, I should be gratified were you to inform me."

"Pshaw. 'Tain't likely anyone kin help Miss Georgina, savin' for 'erself. Or 'Is Grace, God willin'. But ye've a heart 'neath all that starch, I'll say that fer ye. Now you go on and tend to whatever needs tendin'. I'll keep an eye on

171

her ladyship, nivver you fear."

"Very well, madam," Bolton, who was little used to being ordered about as if he were a scruffy lad in shortcoats, intoned a trifle stiffly. "But bear in mind if you would that Lady Grey has naught but friends at Emberly."

Georgina, who little guessed how closely her retainers looked to her welfare, emerged from the music room and made her way down the long gallery to her chambers at the west end of the great hall. Finding the latch, she let herself in.

"So ye've come at last, 'ave ye?" came Nanny Slade's brusque observation. "An' about time too. 'Tis a cold tray wot was a hot meal, missy. But 'twill 'ave t' serve."

"Nanny! What are you doing here?" Georgina queried in startled surprise. "Where is Gilda?"

"I've sent th' girl t' watch over 'is lordship till I 'ave ye settled. Now jest stand still an' let me get these buttons. An' no backtalk. Nanny's 'ere now an' ye'll do as she says."

"Oh, Nanny," Georgina laughed. "I have missed you so very much."

Georgina soon found herself comfortably arrayed in a cotton nightdress and seated docilely before her dressing-table while Nanny Slade brushed her hair with long sure strokes.

"I'd almost forgotten the magic of your touch," Georgina murmured, feeling her muscles go deliciously lax. "Dear Nanny, you have always known exactly what I needed. But I am convinced it is going on quite late, and, knowing you as I do, I am well aware that you have done enough for a Trojan already today. So please, don't worry yourself further about me. It's time you looked to yourself."

"Humph," Nanny grumbled. "An' 'tis more than wot kin be said for you, mistress. 'Tain't as if ye've flesh to spare that ye should skip meals an' set the 'ouse all higgledy-piggledy wi' your sudden starts. I'd come t' expect better o' ye. But what's done's done. An' now if you ain't keen t' 'ave

172

Cook as well as Bolton all worriet to a frazzle, ye'd best set yourself to cleanin' th' platter, so's t' speak." And still scolding, she saw her charge settled in bed with a bed tray across her lap before at last she stumped from the room.

No sooner had the door closed behind the redoubtable nanny than Georgina set the tray aside untouched. Slipping down from the high-poster bed, she wandered restlessly to the great oriel window overlooking the front of the house. Shivering a little in the slight breeze flowing in through the open casement, she curled up in the window seat, her knees folded to her chest, and breathed in deeply of the mingled scents of roses, freshly mown grass, and the freshening promise of a morning shower.

In time her thoughts inevitably turned again to Rathbourne's unexpected announcement and his provoking insistence that she assume the neglected duties of chatelaine to the House of Emberly. In retrospect, she supposed she should never have expected people to understand her reluctance to go about again. But she had thought Rathbourne, who had seemed to apprehend her position very well, would be more sensitive to her desire to be left alone.

A ball indeed, she thought in dismay. She would have a fine time of it ensconced along the sidelines with the matrons and the chaperones. And the whole time to have to listen to the music and the sounds of laughter, her toe no doubt tapping to the rhythm of the dance while she contrived to evince an interest in the effusions of some overly vociferous mama concerning the eminent eligibility of her darling unwed daughter. Really, it was just too absurd. And once it was known she had laid aside her black gloves, there would be no end to her mounting obligations, not the least of which would be making and receiving calls and attending and giving soirées, musicales, and alfresco luncheons—everything, in short, which she had hoped to avoid in these Cornish wilds. Good heavens, she was blind!

Surely no one seriously expected or even desired her presence at the sociable events in the county. She would only be an embarrassment to them and to herself as well.

Why was he doing this to her? she wondered with mounting resentment. He was Rathbourne, after all. A rakeshame and a rogue. When had he ever cared a whit for the social niceties? And who was he to dictate to her as to how she should go on? In a few weeks' time he would weary of the rustic simplicity of Cornwall and return to his proper milieu in town, leaving her to the bumblebroth into which he had tossed her.

She told herself she would be glad when he had gone that everything might return to the way it had been before he had chosen to obtrude himself into her life. But immediately she knew it was a lie. She would miss him exceedingly when at last he took his leave of her and Greystone Manor. He had inexplicably become a fixture in all their lives. Perhaps Davey's most of all.

Indeed, she worried at times that the boy was become too attached to the Duke of Rathbourne, who almost from the first had seemed to fill an aching void left by the death of the young earl's father. Davey had idolized David Grey, and he was fast coming to look upon the duke, possessed both of a commanding presence and a surprising tolerance for the foibles of the very young and backed by an awesome reputation as a nonesuch and a Corinthian, as some sort of a demi-god. In the end would not her son, who had already sustained the death of his father, be hurt again?

Rathbourne, after all, had his own life to lead, and one day, no doubt when he had fully recovered from his harrowing wound, he must return to it. Indeed, because he was a duke, he must even one day marry and set up his own nursery to insure the perpetuity of the title. And well he should, she told herself firmly, for he would make a wonderful father. But since this previously unconsidered prospect accorded her neither pleasure nor comfort and of a sudden perceiving where her errant thoughts had led her, Georgina determined to banish the troublesome Rathbourne from her mind. To this end, she rose at last from her cozy niche and found her way back to the great empty bed.

Earlier Nanny had passed a warming pan between the sheets before allowing her mistress to climb into their delicious warmth, but Georgina had lingered in the windowseat, and the sheets were grown cold again. Curling up into a ball, she tucked her feet into the warm folds of her gown and hugged a pillow close. Suddenly she felt very cold indeed, and very much alone.

Chapter 8

His Grace of Rathbourne, impeccably attired in a double-breasted cutaway coat of blue superfine, an immaculate marcella waistcoat, a neckcloth graced with a single amethyst pin and tied in the quietly elegant style known as the "ballroom," white kerseymere breeches, silk stockings, shoes resplendent with diamond buckles, and the requisite chapeau bras, stepped down from the barouche before the Castle Inn in Brighton at precisely ten o'clock. The drizzle which had attended his arrival some two hours earlier at the house he kept in the fashionable district along Steyne Street had long-since ceased. The morrow gave promise of being a fair day, he thought fleetingly as he passed through the arched portal into the foyer and checked his cloak and hat. With any luck he would be on the road to Cuckfield by morning and in London by evening. The playful strains of a country dance just then commencing greeted him as he paused at the threshold to sweep the crowd with a bored glance before sauntering into its midst.

The unexpected appearance of the tall, languid form in the teeming assembly rooms created no little stir among those gathered there. A sudden fluttering of fans quickly followed by a low buzz were ample evidence of the excitement generated by so unprecedented an event. Rathbourne in Brighton was enough to cause comment, but Rathbourne at anything so innocuous as an assembly was sufficient to set tongues to wagging for a month. Many a feminine pulse quickened at sight of the sternly handsome

FREE

BOOK CERTIFICATE

ZEBRA HOME SUBSCRIPTION SERVICE, INC.

YES! Please start my subscription to Zebra Historical Romances and send me my free Zebra Novel along with my first month's Romances. I understand that I may preview these four new Zebra Historical Romances Free for 10 days. If I'm not satisfied with them I may return the four books within 10 days and owe nothing. Otherwise I will pay just $3.50 each, a total of $14.00 (a $15.80 value—I save $1.80). Then each month I will receive the 4 newest titles as soon as they come off the press for the same 10 day Free preview and low price. I may return any shipment and I may cancel this arrangement at any time. There is no minimum number of books to buy and there are no shipping, handling or postage charges. Regardless of what I do, the **FREE** book is mine to keep.

Name _____

(Please Print)

Address _____ Apt. # _____

City _____ State _____ Zip _____

Telephone (___) _____

Signature _____

(if under 18, parent or guardian must sign)

Terms and offer subject to change without notice.

12-89

MAIL IN THE COUPON BELOW TODAY

GET FREE GIFT

To get your Free **ZEBRA HISTORICAL ROMANCE** fill out the coupon below and send it in today. As soon as we receive the coupon, we'll send your first month's books to preview Free for 10 days along with your **FREE NOVEL**.

ACCEPT YOUR **FREE GIFT** AND EXPERIENCE MORE OF THE PASSION AND ADVENTURE YOU LIKE IN A HISTORICAL ROMANCE

Zebra Romances are the finest novels of their kind and are written with the adult woman in mind. All of our books are written by authors who really know how to weave tales of romantic adventure in the historical settings you love.

Because our readers tell us these books sell out very fast in the stores, Zebra has made arrangements for you to receive at home the four newest titles published each month. You'll never miss a title and home delivery is so convenient. With your first shipment we'll even send you a FREE Zebra Historical Romance as our gift just for trying our home subscription service. No obligation.

BIG SAVINGS AND **FREE** HOME DELIVERY

Each month, the Zebra Home Subscription Service will send you the four newest titles as soon as they are published. (We ship these books to our subscribers even before we send them to the stores.) You may preview them *Free* for 10 days. If you like them as much as we think you will, you'll pay just $3.50 each and *save $1.80 each month* off the cover price. *AND you'll also get FREE HOME DELIVERY.* (There is never a charge for shipping, handling or postage and there is no minimum you must buy. If you decide not to keep any shipment, simply return it within 10 days, no questions asked, and owe nothing.

features made more romantic by the thin line of the scar running along the prominent cheek bone, and few of the ladies present, young or matronly, unwed or otherwise, failed to yearn for at least a glance from the intriguingly cool blue eyes. Thus it was that Lady Kathryn Ingram, her delightfully plump figure enchantingly arrayed in a rose jaconet ball gown gathered beneath an ample bosom and falling from a V in the back to a graceful train, her blond hair caught in loose coils at the crown and her heart-shaped face framed in soft tendrils about the forehead and temples, glided forward to greet her cousin with a mischievous grin on her lovely lips and a quizzical warmth in her hazel eyes.

"Drew! How good to see you looking so well," she said with sincere affection as she slipped her arm through his and led him firmly from the crowded floor and the ogling sea of faces into an unoccupied foyer, that she might have the fascinating Rathbourne for a few moments to herself. "And how shocking that you need only to appear to create a turmoil in every woman's heart," she added teasingly. "Whatever are you doing here? Don't tell me you have finally realized it is time you took a wife and have come to look over the latest crop of simpering young misses, for I shan't believe you. A green girl would bore you ere ten minutes had elapsed from the time of introduction."

"How well you know me, Cousin," drawled the duke, his thin lips curving in the slow, sensuous smile which had mesmerized not a few unsuspecting hearts. "I should most certainly tire of a simpering miss. Fortunately I have not come in search of a green girl to make my bride, but solely to see you, my dearest Kate."

"Have you?" Lady Ingram queried, favoring her tall kinsman with a dubious glance. "And Ferdie and the children, too, I shouldn't wonder."

"Exactly so," Rathbourne agreed without a flicker of an eyelash. "How is your sizeable brood?"

"With Ferdie's mother in Hempstead. All seven of them.

So you are quite safe," she answered with a distinct twinkle in her eye. "Though, knowing you as I do, I cannot doubt that you made sure of that before making your presence known to me."

"What an odd notion you must have of my character, Kate. I had, quite to the contrary, looked forward to making their acquaintance," the duke demurred with only the slightest twitch of the lips. "It was recently brought to my attention that I have been derelict in my familial duties. Consequently, I had hoped to make reparation by extending to you and your prodigious family an invitation to visit Rathbourne. An invitation which still stands, I might add, for you and the incomparable Ferdie."

"Enough, Drew Penwarren," Lady Ingram warned, choking on a helpless gurgle of laughter. "Remember me? I'm the one who witnessed your loosing a toad in Mrs. Crinkston's parlor. And the one who lived on bread and water for a week because she wouldn't tell who turned Squire Rutherford's prize bull in with Rollow Sprague's brindle cow. You can't pull the wool over my eyes, my best loved and most provoking cousin. You want something. And had I a lick of sense, I'd walk away before you talked me into something I'm bound to regret."

"Poor Kate. For a whole week?" quizzed the duke gently, his gaze oddly shuttered. "I was sure you had been granted a pardon after I confessed all to my father. I never knew he had made you pay as well for that absurd schoolboy prank."

"No, how could you when you were already on your way back to school the very next morning," she said, dismayed at where her wayward tongue had led her. "After David told me how severely His Grace had punished you for it, I made him promise not to tell you. You mustn't blame yourself. In spite of my loathing for your father, it was the most glorious summer of my girlhood. And when Papa came to take me home again—after you had been sent away

178

to school—and he found out what had happened, he was furious. Oh, Papa was marvelous, Drew. How I wish you could have seen him. He went to my uncle and demanded an apology. It was worth having lost a pound or two of excess flesh to see Papa stand up to his brother, the duke, just once in his life. And besides, he made it up to me. He bought me two new dresses. Can you imagine that? The clergyman's daughter with so much finery? Poor Papa. He could never understand my hunger for pretty things or why I jumped at the chance to get away from his beloved parish to live in London with my aunt. Only you and David ever really understood. Until I met Ferdie, of course."

"Ah, yes, the inestimable Ferdie," Rathbourne mused, drawing forth an exquisite enameled snuff box from the pocket of his coat and helping himself to a pinch of his favorite blend. "How does he go on?"

"How he *does* go on is what you really mean," laughed Lady Kathryn. "Oh, I know you and David never approved of him. You have always considered him rather silly. But he has been good to me. And he loves me, foolish as that may sound. In spite of the fact that you and David believed I was making a mull of my life, Ferdie and I rub on quite well together. We both like to enjoy life, you see."

"It has been some time since I thought otherwise, you foolish little peagoose," observed the duke with a sudden gleam of amusement in the sleepy eyes. "After all, it would be the height of absurdity to suppose you and Ferdie were anything but consummate lovers when you produce with such awesome regularity one new bundle of joy after another."

"Drew Penwarren, that is quite outside of enough," Lady Kathryn admonished, blushing rosily. "I daresay you haven't changed a whit despite the image of distinguished maturity which you now wear," she said, reaching up to brush her fingertips through the silver locks at his temple.

For a long moment their glances locked with warm

affection, then suddenly Kathryn Ingram grew unwontedly grave.

"What has happened to you, dearest Drew?" she queried softly. "I can see you have suffered. Was it the war? I heard you had been wounded—"

She let her voice trail off as the old familiar mask of the Corinthian descended like a shutter over Rathbourne's handsome face. He turned away to gaze thoughtfully at the whirl of dancers beyond the alcove, and when he looked at her again, he was the infuriatingly inscrutable Rathbourne whom none could really know or touch.

"It would be a mistake to suppose I'm some sort of romantic hero, my darling Kate," he said, with a sardonic curl of the lips. "If I have suffered, it has doubtless been from a surfeit of boredom from which my brief fling as a soldier offered a fleeting escape. I enjoyed it exceedingly until I was unfortunate enough to catch a musket ball in the leg. However, not only have I managed to survive, and intact—aside from a limp, which, I have been told, is all the rage, thanks to our friend Lord Byron—but no sooner have I risen from my bed of pain that I am granted a singularly unique cure for the onset of ennui. Indeed, I find myself the guardian of a small boy who is possessed of a lamentable likeness to his father at that age and a fiercely independent mama who is both blind and devastatingly beautiful."

"Georgina Grey, by all that's marvelous!" exclaimed Lady Kathryn. "It has to be." She paused in her outburst, a shadow flickering briefly across her eyes. "I was so terribly sorry about David," she said after a time in a low, vibrant voice. "You know how I loved him."

"Yes. Poor David," murmured the duke tonelessly. "Odd, isn't it, that he should have bought it over there in that mess when really all he ever wanted was to raise pigs and cattle in Cornwall. But that's the way of it, isn't it. And now I'm left to see to the proper rearing of his son and to

180

the welfare of his lovely widow. No doubt even Father would have appreciated the irony in that."

Lady Kathryn was silent for a moment as she watched the scar leap along the duke's lean jawline, his gaze distant and singularly hard. Poor Drew, she thought pityingly. How little he really understood any of them. David, who had always looked with his heart, had as ever seen clearly in this instance too. He, of all people, must have known how greatly Rathbourne would need a conduit to the community of men and women if ever David were gone from the world. David Grey's motives were as clear to Kathryn Ingram as they were obscure to Rathbourne, yet she knew it would be useless to try to make her cousin understand that David had undoubtedly died easier knowing he had made certain that the three people he had cared for most in this world would be inevitably brought together.

"So, Georgina has come home at last," she said instead, wondering how two such strong-willed individuals could possibly keep from being constantly at loggerheads. "As I recall, she made her come-out during the Season following Rupert's advent into the world—he's my third, you know. It was just after the Peace of Amiens, and everyone was so gay. I remember Ferdie trying to ease my mind about David's becoming a soldier. He said that if Emberly must purchase a set of colors for David, that at least we could be grateful he would not have to fight Boney. Ah well. Who could have known the peace would be of such short duration?" she reflected sadly and shook her head. "Anyway, David brought her to meet me at Fanny Elmhurst's soiree. A dreadful squeeze, and all because it had been rumored Maria Edgeworth would be there to read from *Belinda*, her newest romantic novel at that time, you remember. Georgina was such a lovely girl. So fresh and full of life. And so obviously in love with David. We hit it off from the very first. It must be nearly a year now since David's death. I cannot help but wonder how she is bearing up. Is she here with you? Is that why you've come to Brighton, Drew? To bring Georgina here in order that she might take up her life again where she left it?"

"Lady Grey is firmly ensconced at Emberly," replied the duke, an odd glint in his eye. "And she has no intention of ever leaving. In fact, I should think 'taking up her life where she left it' is what she most heartily wishes to avoid."

"But why? Surely she is not set on wearing the willow for David forever? That is not at all the Georgina Grey whom I once knew."

"Not having been acquainted with her in those halcyon days, I cannot speculate as to her state before David's death," observed the duke drily. "But from all that I have heard and seen of her, I should say you will find her greatly altered. Whether it is her lack of sight or her grief which binds her to that damnable mansion—or something else— remains to be discovered. Which is why I need you to come to Rathbourne as soon ever as you can. And why I shall be on my way to London with the morning light."

"But, Drew!" exclaimed Lady Kathryn in sudden awful comprehension. "You cannot mean Georgina is actually blind!"

"I believe that is what I said," he returned with some impatience but immediately softened as he realized his cousin's very real distress.

"But I thought you were only speaking figuratively before," she uttered abruptly, her hands fluttering in a gesture of abstraction. But just as suddenly, she had regained a semblance of calm. Giving the duke a level look, she demanded that he tell her everything.

Lady Kathryn listened enthralled as Rathbourne retold the tale of Georgina's daring charade and her desperate attempt to find David Grey on the battlefield. He told her everything as Georgina herself had related it to him, leaving out only what he knew of those missing weeks in Georgina's memory.

182

"She had been managing Emberly with only the servants to help her," he said as he came to the end of the tale. "It would seem that she has won the loyalty of everyone from the stablehands to Mrs. Porter, the housekeeper, who has been there through two generations. And you would not believe the change in Bolton, who absolutely dotes on her and who had been serving both as butler and some sort of quasi-amanuensis until Miss Kingsley arrived. I actually caught him out in what can only be described as a perfectly mawkish grin. *Bolton*, mind you. And all because his mistress had decided to refurbish her wardrobe."

"It all sounds perfectly fantastic," Lady Kathryn agreed, observing her cousin with keen interest. An odd, rather baffled smile played about the duke's stern lips, and the normally cool eyes had begun to burn with a quiet intensity as he described the peculiar effect Lady Grey wrought on all those with whom she came in contact. And suddenly she knew nothing could keep her away from Rathbourne despite the very real antipathy she felt for the castle perched on the Cornish cliffs overlooking the sea.

"What about this Miss Kingsley you have mentioned more than once?" she queried abruptly. "The name rings a bell, though I cannot presently recall the family. Who is she?"

"Miss Zenobia Kingsley. Lady Grey's kinswoman on the distaff side of the family," replied Rathbourne, suddenly thoughtful. "Georgina introduced her as her cousin, but I believe she is once or twice removed."

"Ah, but then she must be Harriet Townsend's daughter. Harriet was Lady Bellows' niece, and she married Arthur Kingsley, Viscount Lynton, of Hertfordshire," Lady Kathryn said, pleased with herself. "A sizeable estate with a respectable fortune, I believe. Indeed, as I recall it, the daughter was considered something of an heiress, as there were no other children. Lynton's younger brother was heir to the title and the entailed estates, but it was the accepted on dit that the girl had a more than respectable marriage portion."

"Then am I to suppose the girl was brought out?" queried Rathbourne in some surprise.

"Well, naturally. She was in a fair way to becoming one of the town's reigning beauties not two years past," Lady Kathryn returned, mystified by the nobleman's sudden intense interest. "Why should that surprise you?"

"It surprises me that such a paragon should never have married. Indeed, it surprises me a great deal," the duke said strangely.

"It is odd, now that you mention it, for there were at least two quite eligible *parties* who had demonstrated a marked tendre for the girl. And not a few gazetted fortune-hunters, among them the infamous Earl of Vail. However, the poor child's Season was cut short by the tragic demise of both her parents. A carriage accident, as I recall. But even so, I cannot at all understand why she should find herself in suddenly straitened circumstances. Are you quite sure she is not simply Georgina's guest? I should have thought she would be quite well to rub. Indeed, I—"

Lady Kathryn's further observations were abruptly cut short by Rathbourne's low-muttered curse.

"Drew! What is it?" she cried, startled by the duke's sudden lunge for the doorway leading to the assembly rooms.

Rathbourne vouchsafed no immediate reply as he swept the crowd with a searching glance.

"*Drew?*" Lady Kathryn prodded, when she could no longer contain either her curiosity or her impatience. "Whatever are you about?"

"Softly," he cautioned, drawing her back into the alcove. "There was someone listening at the door."

"Listening? But why? Who—" sputtered the lady in no little confusion, then, pausing, fixed the duke with a darkling glance. "Drew Penwarren, if you are up to one of your old tricks, I shall not find it one whit amusing. Why should anyone wish to eavesdrop on us? And why should you take such exception to it if they were?"

"My poor Kate," Rathbourne rejoined, laughing as he flicked her nose with a teasing finger. "I fear I have behaved rather badly. But there was something deuced odd about the gentleman. Did you perchance catch a glimpse of him?"

"I did not," she stated flatly, continuing to eye the Corinthian with unallayed suspicion.

"Never mind. Doubtless it was nothing," he said then and smoothly turned the subject back to the proposed visit to Rathbourne, upon which it was soon agreed that she and Ferdie would arrive in Cornwall at the end of the fortnight.

"Oh, and one other thing," the duke added, apparently as an afterthought. "Now that Lady Grey had laid aside her black gloves, she has commissioned me to see to the ordering of a new wardrobe in town."

"Has she," commented his cousin, quizzing him with raised eyebrows. "And you, I take it, have agreed?"

"Actually I have, for reasons of delicacy, delegated that task to you, Cousin," Rathbourne drawled irrepressively. "I know you will not mind indulging your passion for shopping even if it should entail a brief trip to town. And should you happen to come across a few things for yourself, I should naturally expect to stand the blunt. I shall leave the catalogue of Lady Grey's needs with my secretary, who will on request see that it is delivered to you," he ended, apparently having taken her unvoiced consent quite for granted. Nor did she gainsay him, though she might like to have done merely to bring him down a peg, for he was odiously in the right of it. She liked nothing better than to be given an excuse to do some shopping, nor would she hesitate to acquire a few exorbitantly priced folderols for herself at his expense. He could well afford it, and it would give her a sort of perverse pleasure in giving him back some of his own. It was, after all, the game they had played since they were children.

To Lady Kathryn's disappointment but hardly to her surprise, Rathbourne did not linger long. Upon kissing her lightly on the forehead and wishing her godspeed, he strode languorously through the press, pausing here and there to return the greetings of various acquaintances as he made his way to the door.

It occurred to Lady Kathryn, who was watching the duke's leisurely progress with a certain amusement, that not only was Rathbourne exciting a great deal of attention from the female contingent but that he was carefully perusing everyone around him.

"*Now* what the devil is he up to?" she murmured aloud.

"I beg your pardon, my dear? Were you speaking to me?" a voice made distinctive by a soft, affected lisp queried at her shoulder.

"No, Ferdie," she said without turning. "Only to myself."

"Ah," he nodded. Then following her gaze, Lord Ingram suddenly raised his quizzing glass to one eye. "I say. Isn't that Rathbourne just leaving?"

"Mm-hmm," she affirmed absently, absorbed in her own thoughts.

"But then it must have been he about whom Vail was inquiring."

"Vail?" asked Lady Kathryn, turning at last to look at her husband who lounged at her side. He was gloriously attired in a periwinkle cutaway coat, the tails of which descended nearly to the trim ankles encased in canary silk stockings, and an apricot flowered waistcoat and dyed-to-match neckcloth tied in the 'Trone a Amour'. These were exceeded in splendor only by the exquisitely ruffled silk shirt, the collar points of which appeared to embrace the powdered and rouged cheekbones, and by the skin-tight satin small-clothes which were of a particularly brilliant shade of *eau de Nil*.

"Why yes, my sweet," lisped the exquisite, his pale blue eyes guileless behind heavily drooping eyelids. "Just moments ago. His lordship wished to ascertain whether I was acquainted with the 'overblown Beau Brummel whom all the ladies were ogling.' When I replied that I had not seen such a personage, he saw fit to inform me that the 'old gent' had absconded with my lady wife. I must say I am relieved to discover it was only your cousin. I had every expectation of having to challenge the man to a duel, something which I should have found extremely vexatious. So fatiguing, you know, rising at dawn."

Lady Kathryn, recalling to mind an image of her cousin's magnificent, broad-shouldered physique clothed with a tasteful elegance which was clearly the envy of every young blood in attendance there, smothered a convulsive giggle behind her fan at Rathbourne's probable reaction to having been described as an aging smart and awarded her dandified spouse a loving glance which was yet brimful of mirth.

"Oh, yes, my dearest Ferdie. So very fatiguing indeed," she gurgled and, taking his arm, led him into the quadrille which was only just then forming.

True to his word Rathbourne was on the London road with the first light of dawn. Before leaving Cornwall, he had made arrangements to have his curricle and team of matched bays at hand upon his arrival in Steyne Street that he might cover the last leg of the journey up to town with greater dispatch than was possible in the travel carriage. Having instructed Pringle to follow in the barouche with the trunks, the duke covered the dozen or so miles to Cuckfield well within the hour and set down at the King's Inn to breathe the horses.

The weather was clear and the road sound despite the previous day's wetting. The sun climbing in the east was already warm on Rathbourne's face as he stood in the inn yard, a tankard of ale in hand, and watched the ostlers change the team of the north-bound stagecoach while the passengers—a stout matron in the company of a fubsy-faced schoolboy in shortcoats, a town smart who appeared pockets to let, a merchant, a taciturn farmer in homespun, and a particularly rough-looking lout who had the appearance of one more at home footing a pad in Hounslow Heath than riding a coach to London—stretched their legs. Traffic had been light for the most part thus far, consisting of a farm cart or two, a freight carrier, and the London mail-coach. Consequently, the duke, stepping back into the shade of the ivy-covered stoop before the entrance to the inn, observed with idle interest the approach from the south of a post chaise drawn by a team of four-in-hand.

The postilion sounded the horn to signal a change of teams as the post-chaise swept into the yard and came to a halt scant feet from the duke. It soon became apparent that its single occupant, a gentleman who, except for a particularly soft, white hand resting on the gilt head of a walking stick, remained indistinguishable in the shadowy interior, intended to forego the comforts of the King's Head, as no attempt was made to let down the steps that he might disembark.

Rathbourne was about to turn inside the inn to pay his shot when his attention was caught by the exceedingly odd behavior of the lout, who, strolling apparently aimlessly to the far side of the chaise, paused to accost the gentleman within.

" 'Tis a fine morning, wouldn't ye say, milord?" he queried in an oddly sinister voice though the words and manner in which they were spoken smacked of obsequiousness.

Rathbourne's gaze narrowed with sudden keen interest on the dirty, bearded face shaded beneath a battered broad-brimmed hat. Pale blue eyes squinted up at the unseen gentleman with an unmistakable craftiness which left little doubt that the rogue was up to no good. Whereupon it occurred to him that he had seen that face before, the prominent nose of prodigious proportions, long and hooked like a great beak, the thin, cruel lips quirked in a mirthless smile, and the fleshy jowls which had used to be clean-shaven when he had seen him before—where? He could not quite place the fellow, though he felt instinctively the man was not what he presently appeared to be.

Then the villain lifted his hand to remove his disreputable headgear, and at sight of the soiled but shapely member, a thread of memory was recalled of hands which had moved with quick cleverness and eyes which had stared palely at him across a card table with hard dislike. The duke's gaze narrowed for a long moment on the whiskered face, and suddenly a cold gleam of a smile flickered briefly across the thin lips.

"Belike ye doesn't ken who I be," the ruffian had gone on to muse. "But I knows ye, I does. Ye be Vail, an' if'n ye was to take a close peep, like as not ye'd see some'un ye'd thought nivver to lay eyes on again in this world. Course we run athwart one another oncet before, so to speak, since the old days when we was honest thieves together. Not that ye seen me exactly, since I were forced more or less to lay ye out cold afore ye'd had yer way with the new bride. And as it turned out I be right sorry to have ruined your wedding night, for Lynton and his lady wife was killed coming after their girl and I nivver got a bloody ha'pence fer all I done fer 'em. Still I spose there was some satisfaction in paying ye back in a small way fer that doublecross three years ago."

Rathbourne saw the gentleman's hand clench on the gilt head of the walking stick.

"You!" he breathed, the brief exclamation expressing venomous dislike.

"Ah, I knew it'd come to ye," grinned the villain maliciously. "I wouldn't pull that toad-sticker of yours, mate. I knows ye from old, remember. And I knows ye doesn't carry that stick for ornament."

"What do you want, you old fool?" queried the gentleman in a hard voice. "Keep in mind that I could kill you, and no one would hold me responsible once it was known who you were. So don't try to push me too far."

"Ye could try, but I've me doubts as to who'd end up dead, my young cockerel," the villain reflected with a chilling grin. "But be that as it may, at present I'm here to offer you a chance to make good on what you owe me, Vail. A small nest egg as it were to tide me over for a spell. In return, I might be willing to tell ye where yer little bride has got to. I've kept me eyes on her for ye, I have, milord. I knows where she is."

Vail's mirthless chuckle brought a hard gleam to the rogue's pale eyes.

"You *are* an old fool," taunted the arrogant voice. "I am already well aware of my wife's whereabouts, you see. And now if you do not remove yourself immediately from my sight, I shall be forced to forget that we were once business associates and shall reveal your identity to all these good people."

With that, the gentleman leaned imperiously out the other window and shouted impatiently at the driver to make haste.

The duke caught a fleeting glimpse of a dissolute countenance remarkable for its peculiarly sallow complexion and for black, glittering eyes, which alighted briefly on Rathbourne's tall form then away again as the coach lurched and rumbled out of the inn yard.

Rathbourne, having instantly identified in the single passenger of the post-chaise the eavesdropper from the Castle Inn the night before, straightened suddenly to his full height to stare fixedly after the receding chaise. Then, observing that the lout was making for the coach to which the passengers had been called to re-embark, he called out in a soft, steely voice.

"Not so fast, my man. I should like a word with you."

The villain turned with cat-like quickness to warily probe the shadowy stoop.

"And who might ye be that ye should hide in shadows and call Anson Fenton yer man?" he answered dangerously, his hand stealing to the handle of a pistol protruding from a wide leather belt about his waist.

"I shouldn't were I you, m'lord," drawled the duke in bored tones and with a single, leisurely stride, stepped free of the ivy-covered portico. "It has been a number of years since I was regrettably forced to instruct you in the improprieties of cheating at cards. And yet I feel certain you cannot have forgotten the distasteful episode."

The villain's face paled beneath the grime and whiskers.

"Rathbourne!" he uttered on a sudden, explosive breath.

"Even so," observed His Grace with the imperious lift of an eyebrow. "And you, my dear Viscount, appear surprisingly hale for a man who has been dead for the past three years. And now, my Lord Cheseldine, you will tell me what interest you and the Earl of Vail have in Miss Zenobia Kingsley."

Rathbourne kept to a steady pace, covering the remaining distance to London in an impressive three and a half hours. Even so, he had failed to overtake the postchaise. By the time he had reached Horley, he was forced to the conclusion that his highly profitable sojourn at the King's Head had allowed Vail too great a start on him. Yet he doubted not that he would yet be granted the privilege of meeting the earl—in Cornwall.

Drat! How could the chit have been such a fool as to fall for a man of Vail's repute? And then what must she do but seek to hide herself away at Greystone! he thought with scant charity for the girl who had in her stupidity placed his angel in jeopardy along with herself. He was tempted to wring the miserable female's neck upon his return and thus save everyone a deal of trouble. A fine coil she had got them all into what with Robbie behaving like a mooncalf over her, little suspecting his dearest Miss Kingsley was actually Lady Grantham, the estranged wife of the Earl of Vail, and Georgina having welcomed her without a suspicion that the wench was not what she had presented herself to be. Nor dared he enlighten her, for presently she would have enough with which to cope if all that he had begun to suspect about her blindness and loss of memory proved to be true. He would not allow this other business to interfere, no matter to what lengths he might be forced to go to protect her from it. And one thing was certain. Either Vail or Cheseldine was capable of anything, and though he had done his best to neutralize the latter for the time being—even going so far as to enlist his aid in safeguarding Georgina and Miss Kingsley in exchange for Rathbourne's silence and the promise of a sufficient amount to see Cheseldine out of the country when all this was finished—he was well aware he would be an utter fool to trust the blackguard for a moment. He would much prefer to turn the rogue over to Bow Street now and be done with him, but to do so would be not only to insure that Vail should have the proof he needed that he was indeed wed to the heiress, thus making inevitable the scandal which would follow and Miss Kingsley's utter ruination, but would distract Georgina Grey as well from the more vital process of regaining her memory.

Rathbourne was still pondering the singular occurrences of the past few hours when he pulled up before his town house on Grosvenor Square. Relinquishing the bays to a groom, he strode up the shallow steps and through the open doorway tended by the wooden-faced Hampstead.

"May I say that you appear much improved in health,

Your Grace," offered the butler, inclining his head respectfully, after the initial greetings had been made. "Cornwall would seem to have had a salutary effect."

"I am gratified that you think so, Hampstead," Rathbourne replied drily. "I shall be going out again directly. Have the phaeton brought around an' you please. And inform Philippe that I shall have a guest for dinner this evening. The usual time."

"Very well, Your Grace. Oh, Your Grace. I have been instructed to personally see that you receive a certain missive delivered only this morning. It is there on the salver with your other correspondence. Mr. Forbes, having only just returned himself, has not had the opportunity to forward your mail as of yet."

The duke paused only long enough to flip in a cursory manner through the not inconsiderable stack of calling cards, already outdated invitations, and miscellaneous correspondence which had accumulated in his absence, before taking up a plain, sealed missive lacking any identifying insignia. Breaking the seal, he quickly perused the brief message within. When he had finished reading, he refolded the missive and for a moment appeared to lose himself in thought as absently he tapped the carefully creased letter-paper against his fingertips. Then suddenly he seemed to have reached some sort of decision as he glanced peremptorily over his shoulder at the butler who waited to be dismissed.

"You say Forbes is within?" Rathbourne inquired brusquely. Upon being informed that Mr. Forbes had, immediately upon arriving, repaired to the study, the duke proceeded directly up the stairs to a relatively spacious closet adjacent to the library which was reserved exclusively for his secretary's use.

Oliver Forbes, a man of some eight and twenty years, had come into the Duke of Rathbourne's service straight from Oxford and had remained for the six succeeding years to the

193

present with apparent contentment. He was possessed of an average build, a not unpleasing countenance, and an astute intelligence and penetrating wit which had made him of invaluable assistance to His Grace on innumerable occasions.

"Your Grace," he said, a little surprised at his employer's unexpected presence in his sanctum when he had thought the duke still in residence at Rathbourne.

"No need to stand, Oliver," drawled the duke, waving a languid hand negligently in the air. "I am sorry to intrude on your privacy so soon after your arrival. However, I confess to a certain interest in what you may have been able to discover on my behalf."

"Very little, I'm afraid, Your Grace," Forbes answered, settling once again into his seat behind the mahogany desk and drawing forth from a side-drawer a slender packet. "Apparently Dr. Delgada, the physician who attended Lady Grey in Lisbon, could add little more to what we already know. He could find no physiological explanation for his patient's blindness. She had suffered a severe blow to the head and had contracted a morbid fever, as a result of which she was delirious for some time. Delgada could make little of Lady Grey's ravings, though she talked about Major Grey for the most part and seemed to blame herself for his death. In addition, she seemed to have experienced some sort of trauma, the cause of which, whether physical or emotional, he was not able to determine. Though due to the sudden onset of her blindness and her loss of memory concerning the time preceding her discovery in Elvas, he apparently suspected the latter. I'm afraid that's about it, sir, except that from all that I was able to learn, Dr. Delgada is highly thought-of in Lisbon. I myself found him to be gracious and learned, as well as sincerely concerned for Lady Grey's well-being. Is this of any help to you?"

"I'm not sure," mused the duke, frowning. Recalling himself to his secretary's presence, he smiled slightly and was once again the imperturbable Corinthian, his thoughts hidden behind an indolent mask. "You've done well, Oliver. Thank you. And because I know how much you must enjoy these little intrigues of mine, I have come up with a new assignment for you."

"I'm all ears, Your Grace," the young man returned with something less than enthusiasm. Not that he objected to having risked a sea voyage through enemy waters to Portugal on behalf of his employer or minded being kept in the dark as to the duke's motives in all of this. After all, he had seen the assignment as a welcome diversion from the daily round of sifting through and answering the duke's considerable correspondence, screening all who wished appointments with His Grace for one reason or another, or any of the other innumerable details for which he alone was responsible. However, he had looked forward to a day or two in which to catch up on the work which had been neglected for the se'ennight of his absence.

"Yes, I see that you are all eagerness," observed the duke with a slight twitch of the lips, "and who can blame you? However, I trust you will not find these new tasks excessively demanding. First you will locate a tutor suitable for my ward and see that he departs directly for Emberly. After which, you will discover as much as you are able about a Miss Zenobia Kingsley, the only child of the deceased Viscount Lynton. And, Oliver, I know you will be discreet. However, I do wish you will bear in mind that the young woman is Lady Grey's kinswoman. I prefer that neither she nor Lord Robert learns that I have made any inquiries."

"I understand, Your Grace," Oliver Forbes replied without any discernible emotion despite the fact that his mind teemed with speculation as he watched His Grace turn with something less of his usual languor and exit through the door.

A short time later, Rathbourne, having rid himself of all his travel stains and having managed without the aid of his valet to make himself presentable in a bottle-green jacket and buff unmentionables, was tooling his high-perched phaeton east from Grosvenor Square along Brook Street. Turning south on Bond Street, west on Grafton, and south again on Albermarle, he came at last to the Royal Institution, which had been founded a decade earlier "for the promotion of science and the diffusion and extension of useful knowledge." Instructing his groom to walk the matched pair of greys, he climbed down from the driver's seat and entered the august halls of scientific and literary research.

Sometime later he was conducted by a clerk to a laboratory which smelled distinctly of formaldehyde and was notable for its peculiar collection of skeletal remains. Its single living occupant other than the duke was an inordinately tall, thin man in his middle thirties who was bent over an examination table totally absorbed in ascertaining the exact dimensions of a human skull, one of several similar specimens which gaped vacantly at their noble visitor.

When several moments had passed without his host having become aware of his intrusion, Rathbourne coughed gently.

"I am ruefully aware that I cannot possibly offer so much in the way of inducement," he drawled with sardonic humor, "as these, your honored subjects. However, I fear I must insist, Julian, that you at least acknowledge my presence."

At Rathbourne's initial words, the tall figure jerked erect and swiveled to reveal a homely face made attractive by a broad grin and a glad expression of surprised welcome.

"Drew! Whatever are you doing here?" he ejaculated, fairly wringing the duke's hand.

"I have come to invite you to dinner, and from the looks

of you, I am just in time to save you from death by starvation."

"No, no. Thanks to your generosity, I eat regularly these days," Julian laughed.

"Which means whenever you happen to think of it and furthermore can tear yourself away from your scintillating skeletons long enough for a cup of tea and a biscuit or two," rejoined His Grace. "However, I warn you in this instance that I shall not accept no for an answer. And to insure against your less than reliable memory, my coach will come for you at eight." The duke paused briefly before continuing in a quiet voice. "I need your advice, Julian, on a matter which is of the utmost delicacy. I'm depending on you, old friend. No one else will do."

Upon having made this rather odd remark, Rathbourne quickly turned the topic of conversation to Julian Bradford and his peculiar scientific endeavors. A short time later he had made his departure.

At precisely twenty minutes after eight, a somewhat mystified Julian Bradford was ushered into Rathbourne's private study at Number Six Grosvenor Square. He had changed his rather less than immaculate laboratory smock and nondescript unmentionables for a somewhat creased and poorly cut brown cutaway coat and green nankin breeches which had seen better days. Thinning blond hair worn unfashionably long had been brushed carelessly back from a noticeably receding hair-line.

"Julian," Rathbourne drawled, turning from an apparent contemplation of an austere likeness of the previous duke which stared down in cold hauteur from its place above the Adams fireplace. "I am truly sorry to have to drag you from your work. Please sit down. Would you care for some sherry before dinner? I was fortunate to have procured an excellent *amontillado* before the war made it difficult to come by."

"Perhaps a small libation to celebrate the coming together of old friends," Julian said, holding up a thumb and index finger to indicate the amount of spirits he deemed advisable in the circumstances. "I try to keep a clear head these days. So much to do, and I am so close to finalizing my evidence disproving the theory that insanity can be predicted from the external manifestations of the skull."

"Ah yes," murmured the duke, turning away to pour two fingers of sparkling sherry into an exquisite Jacobite-baluster wine glass. "And shall your theory that some forms of mental aberration are a result purely of outside forces and events with which the mind cannot cope thus be vindicated, do you think?"

"It is my sincere hope," Julian answered fervently. "Then, perhaps, victims of insanity will no longer be chained, beaten, or starved like wild animals, and institutions on the order of Bedlam will become merely stark reminders of man's ignorance." His impassioned outburst was interrupted by a sudden spasmodic fit of coughing which severely racked the thin body.

"Easy, man," Rathbourne said, his brow furrowed in unwonted concern, when the fit had passed. "Here, drink this."

"Beg your forgiveness," Julian wheezed, struggling for breath. "Blasted cough comes and goes." Then taking the wineglass from Rathbourne, he sipped gratefully before settling back once more, his pallor receding somewhat with the effect of the sherry in his system. "There, you see, I'm fine now."

"Somehow I doubt that very much," Rathbourne said, narrowly eyeing his friend. "How long have you had that cough?"

"So long that I have ceased to concern myself with it," Julian laughed. "And so should you."

The duke was not given opportunity to reply, as Hampstead appeared after a polite knock to inform His Grace that dinner was served.

Conversation over Philippe's *poisson Veronique*, followed by *salade Niçoise, coq au vin rouge*, Florendine of veal, glazed carrots, and ending with a strawberry trifle, was kept to generalities. Indeed, it was not until the duke and his dinner guest had retired once more to Rathbourne's study for brandy and cigars that Julian at last broached the purpose behind his friend's invitation.

"I am very nearly certain that you have not gone to all this trouble to entice me from my laboratory simply to reminisce over our days together at Eton," he remarked casually as he studied the duke over the rim of his brandy snifter. "What's troubling you, Drew?"

Rathbourne's short bark of laughter sounded oddly harsh in the peaceful environs of the bookroom.

"You have always been one to go straight to the heart of the matter, have you not?" he mused sardonically. "And why should we not. I have asked you here because you were once the finest physician of my acquaintance and because you are one of the few people I know I can trust implicitly. The matter, you see, involves a lady's honor, which I have impugned."

Dr. Julian Bradford offered little in the way of comment as Rathbourne's low voice rose and fell amidst the quiet of the evening, revealing for the second time in less than twenty-four hours the story surrounding Lady Georgina Grey's incipient blindness. This time, however, the duke left nothing out of the telling.

"I know of Delgada by reputation," he said at last, when the duke came to the Portuguese physician's description of Georgina's symptoms. "A good man, I believe. And you say he could find nothing physiologically wrong with her eyes?"

At Rathbourne's confirmation, he nodded slightly and mumbled something to himself before once again addressing his host.

"And he theorized the patient was suffering from emotional trauma. Yes, everything would seem to tally. Actually, such cases are not all that uncommon. The patient is faced with something which lies beyond his ability to cope, and he reacts by attempting to shut it out altogether. In this case, I would surmise the lady in question saw something so dreadful or so distressing that her mind responded by blocking out not only all memory of it but the sight of it as well. The fact that she does not remember you or her valiant efforts to save not only your leg but your life would seem to me to indicate that whatever is troubling her is connected somehow with you."

For a moment he paused then and, removing his thick-lensed spectacles, began to polish them with a suddenly conscious air.

"After you made love to her," he said at last, his gaze remaining fixed on his eyeglasses as though they were a subject of extreme interest, "how would you describe her state of mind?"

"She wept in my arms," Rathbourne uttered harshly and rose with sudden violence to pace angrily before his carefully impassive friend. "And cried out her husband's name. But she displayed no signs of trauma. Good God, man. Whatever may be my reputation, I did not rape her!"

"No, of course you didn't," Bradford said quietly. "I never supposed that you did."

"Then what *do* you suppose, Julian?" demanded the duke and, coming suddenly to a halt before his friend, transfixed him with tortured eyes. "That it is my fault she is blind? By God, it is what I have told myself since first I began to understand it was not her blindness which cripples her. Keeps her bound to that blasted manor and living in dread of anything which might make her forget she belongs to David."

"I never meant to imply any such thing, Drew!" Julian

broke in, alarmed at the depth of his friend's suffering. "It occurred to me that Lady Grey might be experiencing acute remorse, not because she made love to you, but because she discovered that she was *in* love with you. Don't you see. It is quite possible that she had never really dealt with the fact of her husband's death, let alone with the possibility that she could ever love a man other than her husband. But even that should not be enough to incur such an extreme reaction. No. I believe something else happened in the immediate wake of these two discoveries. Something which, in her already exhausted and troubled state, was too much for her to cope with. It is imperative to learn what happened to Lady Grey after she vanished from your rooms in Elvas."

"But I have learned what happened, Julian," replied His Grace with deadly calm and extracted from his inner coat pocket the plain, unmarked missive which had reached him only that morning. "And now I can say with utter certainty that Georgina Grey is indeed blind because of me!"

Chapter 9

Georgina, hearing the sounds of laughter issuing from the schoolroom, paused on her way down the long gallery. For a moment a whimsical smile replaced the sober line of her lips as she listened to her son's childish treble gurgling above the deeper chuckle of Mr. Fairfax, the tutor newly engaged to instruct the young earl. The two were evidently enjoying an early breakfast together, she guessed, hearing the rattle of china.

Emmet Fairfax, some two and twenty years of age and second to the eldest of seven sons of a clergyman of modest means, was newly graduated from Oxford and had been in need of immediate employment. Georgina had been impressed with the soft-spoken young man from their initial meeting, sensing in him a shy good-humor and a gentle wit. More importantly, however, the earl had taken to him wholeheartedly. After only the first day, Davey had come to his mama with an enthusiastic account of the tutor's vast knowledge of rocks and the creepy-crawly things which lived beneath them, of games and stories which the young man had been used to share with his younger siblings, and of all the wonderful things Davey would be able to discover in books just as soon as the child had learned how to read them. Georgina had from that moment ceased to worry about her son's leaving the nursery and Nanny Slade. Undoubtedly his new tutor was well able to take him in hand.

Musing that the addition of Emmet Fairfax to her growing household was something else which she owed to Rathbourne's unflagging devotion to Emberly's affairs, Georgina turned and continued on her way to the study. It seemed that even when he was away from her, she still was surrounded by constant reminders of his pervasive influence in all that concerned her. First the arrival of the tutor engaged in London by His Grace, and now this morning's audience with Wilkins. A troubled frown touched her brow.

It was Nanny Slade who had first alerted her to the "strange goings on" about the manor. Complaining that Gilda had apparently traded what few wits she possessed for moonbeams in her head and that everyone from the butler to the kitchen maid was playing a game of mum's chance whenever the old nurse was within earshot, Nanny had been of the strong opinion that something havey-cavey was afoot. "Belike, th' whole kit 'n caboodle had taken to the Free Trade," was her honest opinion. But Georgina, skeptical that her household would be involved in smuggling despite Cornwall's reputation for it, had entertained rather different suspicions. Cornering Bolton in the breakfast room one morning shortly after Nanny Slade's dour warnings, she was able to worm enough out of the unwontedly close-mouthed butler to suspect Rathbourne's hand in all that was surreptitiously going forth. Indeed, she was able to piece together from little snatches of hastily hushed conversations among the staff that the duke had commissioned Bolton to suggest in a subtle manner to Wilkins that there was a prime piece of land within walking distance of the manor which would be just the thing for an industrious young couple desirous of setting up housekeeping on their own.

In addition to Bolton's contrivance, she suspected that Denby, too, had been made part of the scheme, as she had heard Davey telling his tutor that the stablehands and several of the underfootmen were in on a great secret about which his mama was not to be allowed even an inkling. From all of this, Georgina had come to the strong conclusion that plans had been set into motion to marry her abigail off to the butler's understudy by installing them in a "one-night" cottage of their own. Doubtless all was in readiness for the raising—the clay for the walls, the straw for the thatched roof, a ready-built window and door—else Wilkins would not have requested this interview, hinting shyly that it was to ask permission of the mistress of the manor to marry that he did so.

That she had subsequently learned from Connings that the land in question was part of a freehold which had recently reverted back to Rathbourne had clinched the matter of the duke's complicity and had also put her out of all countenance with his high-handed methods. Suggesting a solution to the problem of her inept abigail had been one thing, but to donate a parcel of land to the scheme, no matter how small, was quite another. It placed her in the uncomfortable position of being in his debt, something which she could not like for reasons she could not fully explain even to herself. Consequently, she had ordered Connings to search out an equally suitable property which fell within the unentailed holdings of Emberly's domain. Unfortunately none having the added advantage of a close proximity to Greystone was to be found, which had left her fuming at *point-non-plus* and determined to call His Grace to account for his excessive manipulations on her behalf.

How very like Rathbourne to take it upon himself to see to the ordering of her affairs, she thought irritably as she came at last to the study and, letting herself in, shut the door with what smacked very much of a childish petulance. Oh, for pity's sake! Whatever was the matter with her? she fretted in sudden realization of the absurdity of her behavior. After all, remembering how only this morning she had snapped at Gilda for nothing at all, an occurrence which had sent the girl fleeing from her on the verge of tears, she could not help but question the stability of her own state of mind. It was not at all like her to use a servant so. Nor was it her usual practice to lose all patience with her cousin, going so far as to accuse her of moping about the house and neglecting her duties, which had been the case only the previous evening. No matter that the girl had been absent that afternoon for better than an hour, when Georgina had most particularly needed her help in sorting out some figures of expenditure contained in Connings' bi-monthly report, or that later, as they had sat down to the evening meal, Nobie had been distractingly inattentive, displaying a marked tendency toward the doldrums when only a half hour earlier she had been brimming over with uncharacteristic high spirits. At least the child was displaying *some* emotion, which, if it did seem to vary from one extreme to the other with bewildering rapidity, was yet a vast improvement over the guarded dispassion which had characterized her upon arriving at Greystone. No, Georgina told herself firmly, there was no excuse for venting her own ill-humor on others. She must simply learn to guard against this newfound propensity for flying into the boughs at a moment's notice. Perhaps it was merely a fleeting aberration in temperament, she mused wryly, which would in time pass after having run its natural course.

Whereupon it suddenly occurred to her that she had been uncommonly out of sorts for some time now, in fact, ever since the vexatious Duke of Rathbourne had departed Cornwall for London. The realization struck her with such unexpected significance that she sank rather weakly into one of the leather-upholstered George I red walnut arm-chairs fronting the oakwood desk. Good heavens! Her bizarre behavior since the advent of Rathbourne into her ordered existence displayed all the earmarks of a pubescent girl's first crush.

"Oh, botheration!" she uttered out loud, very much put out with herself. "This will not do at all, Georgina Grey. You are not some green girl to be swept off your feet by the first man who comes along. Or by any man ever," she added firmly. She had loved once. She had no wish to love again. But the sentiment, even voiced aloud, was not all that reassuring when one considered the matter quite soberly.

She had never before fully realized the extent to which she had come to depend upon Rathbourne's unobtrusive mantle of protection until it had in part been removed by his absence. In some surprise and a great deal of dismay she realized she missed his almost daily visits, the way he had of seeming to pop up out of nowhere when she least expected it, like the day in the garden when she had stupidly mislaid her garden spade and had been reduced to groping in a less than dignified manner in the dirt for it, only to have it placed suddenly in her hand. It had, of course, been Rathbourne, startling her with his undetected presence so that she had wondered how long he had been there without her knowing it. It was positively uncanny the way he had of stealing up on her unaware, especially in the light of the utterly disturbing effect he had on her senses whenever he was near. With a blush she recalled a particu-larly unsettling experience which had occurred in this very room not many days after their ride to the bottoms.

Rathbourne had called on her one afternoon when, except for the servants, she was alone in the house, Zenobia having gone at Georgina's insistence for a ride with Davey and Robbie Penwarren. There was some question, the duke informed her, concerning a recent sale of a bull to a neighboring farmer, and he had wished to check the tally sheets which were kept in a pocket at the back of the ledger.

"But of course," she had replied, going immediately to the desk and kneeling down to run her hand over the smooth wood till she found the ormolu handle to the bottom drawer. "They should be in here."

The leather-bound tome was rather large and unwieldy, and she was having no little trouble in trying to remove it.

"Here. Let me help you," Rathbourne said upon perceiving her difficulty and had bent over her to reach for the book just as she had turned her head to make some absurd remark about being blind, not helpless. Oh, how great had been her mortification at having her lips brush unwittingly against his clean-shaven cheek! Nor was she prepared for the sudden leap of her pulse at the unexpected contact and for the bewildering rush of never-forgotten sensations through her body. For a single, dreadful moment she seemed to have lost all ability to move, as he turned with a sharply indrawn breath and pressed his lips to hers.

Oh, God, how natural it had been to return that kiss! For she had. She could no longer deny it, not even to herself. But then he had pulled away, and suddenly she had come at last to her senses.

"How dare you!" she had blurted, angry at him for taking advantage of the situation, furious with herself for having responded.

"Georgina," he said oddly and, grasping her shoulders between his hands, pulled her to her feet. "Georgina, I—"

"No!" she uttered in a voice she hardly recognized and backed hastily away. Almost immediately she recalled herself enough to come to an uncertain halt, her hands pressed convulsively to hot cheeks as she struggled to regain her composure. "No," she repeated more calmly. "Please, don't say anything. Oh, it is so dreadfully absurd. I know you did not mean anything by it. No doubt you are quite used to kissing any number of females with even less provocation."

"Oh, indeed. Any number," he replied with a sudden quiver of amusement in his voice, "with hardly any provocation at all."

"To be sure," she rejoined, uncertain whether to laugh or scream at the impossible coil she had gotten herself in. "But I, on the other hand, do not make it a practice to—to—well, to accept the advances, no matter how unintentional they might be, of—of—"

"Practiced rakes?" he offered helpfully.

"I beg your pardon. That is not what I meant at all," she said, awarding him a censorious frown.

"Oh, then you do accept the advances of practiced rakes," he rejoined instantly, apparently much struck at the notion.

"Of course I do not!" she nearly choked. The beast to tease her so, she thought and suddenly could not contain her laughter any longer. "You, sir, are abominable," she observed ruefully, when she had got her breath again. "How dare you roast me when I was only trying to explain why I behaved so idiotishly."

"Gudgeon. There was no need for you to explain anything. I understood perfectly why you reacted as you did. But to try to excuse me by saying it meant nothing to me to kiss you was idiotish in the extreme. I apologize, ma'am, for so far forgetting myself as to take advantage of you. But I cannot regret it, since, quite the contrary, I enjoyed it immensely."

That had not been at all what she wished to hear from him. Indeed, he had only managed to complicate matters further. Up till now he had been her dear and trusted friend. Why could he not be content to leave it that way? she fretted and would have left him then, except that in all the turmoil of the past few moments she had quite managed to lose herself. Indeed, she was hopelessly disoriented. Without a single landmark—one of the chairs, the desk, the settee, something to set things all to rights again—her world was quite deprived of boundary and direction, and she was at its mercy.

Rathbourne's voice speaking with unruffled calm cut through her sudden sense of confusion.

"It would be a shame to waste so lovely a day by remaining indoors, don't you think?" he was saying, and she jumped a little as he smoothly took her hand and tucked it in the crook of his arm.

"I—I beg your pardon?" she stammered, startled at the sudden change of subject.

"There's the scent of lilacs on the breeze coming in the window. Do you smell it? And surely you cannot resist the warmth of the sunlight against your face. I am convinced we should do much better in the garden."

"Y-yes, of course," she answered, made suddenly aware—just as he had intended—that the sun did indeed caress her cheek. For now she knew she faced the bay window set in the west wall of the library and that, furthermore, the door must be to her right. What an odd man he was to be sure, she thought. With only a few well-chosen words he had given her world of darkness back its familiar shape and dimension.

It was this sort of thing which kept her constantly off balance where Rathbourne was concerned. He could be so devastatingly kind one moment and so infuriatingly arrogant the next. She had thought she would be glad to be free for a time from his unsettling presence, but truth to tell, she had come quickly to miss their often witty, but always scintillating, verbal exchanges and the constant delight she experienced at the extent of his familiarity with any number of wide-ranging subjects. And if she were to be entirely truthful with herself, she must admit that she had grown quite accustomed to having the duke intervene on her behalf as regarded so many of the details of running her son's estate.

But in this matter of her abigail, he had gone too far.

Indeed, he had trespassed in her private concerns, for while everything he had done up to now had concerned some aspect of Emberly and was thus well within the proper bounds of a guardian overseeing his ward's best interests, the running of the household was not. She was the Countess of Emberly till such time as her son should reach his majority and take himself a wife. Until that day, Greystone was her proper province and hers alone.

The soft scratching at the door alerted her to Wilkins' arrival. With a sigh she relegated all thoughts of Rathbourne to the back of her mind and bade the prospective bridegroom to enter.

"Milady?" Wilkins queried nervously, the tell-tale scent of pomade accompanying him into the countess's presence.

"Yes, Wilkins. Come in, please." She had risen as she spoke and now turned to face him, her slim hands folded together at her waist. "You wished to see me?"

"*Ais*, milady, I did at that, though now that I'm here, I'm fair at a loss for words."

"Then perhaps I can help you. You have come to request permission to be married, have you not? And since I know you to be of a loyal disposition, it must be Gilda who is your intended. How am I doing so far?"

"Right on the peg, milady," responded the footman, a grin in his voice.

"Thank you, Wilkins. But I'm afraid I cannot take credit. You all but told me everything yesterday when you asked to see me. And I've known for ever so long that you and Gilda were unofficially promised to one another. So when is the happy event to be?"

"Well, as to that," hedged Wilkins, "I had word that a praicher, one o' the travelin' Methodists, had set up his parish at Saltash. And I—," he faltered in such a manner that Georgina had little difficulty imagining the embarrassed wash of color which did indeed stain his cheeks. "Well, I thought to have the banns read there two Sundays past. This bein' Saturday, tomorrow's reading should make all proper and legal-like. And since next week's the Vigil of St. John, we thought to have the wedding day after tomorrow, milady," he finished in a rush.

"Did you indeed?" Georgina laughed. "But if that is the case, is not this interview somewhat behind the times?"

" 'Twould seem so, milady. And I'm beggin' your pardon for it," he said, greatly relieved, or so it seemed to Georgina, who was listening with keen enjoyment to his every nuance of expression. "But the real heart of the matter is that Gilda has asked me to speak to you on her behalf. She's not much more than a child when all's said and done, milady. And bein' as how you were so good to make her your abigail and all, she just didn't see how she could ask you to let her go. So I'm asking for her. You see, we're of a mind to set up housekeeping on our own. And what with my increase in wages—for which I thank you, milady—and what little we've set by, there's no need for Gilda to work outside the home. At least for the time being."

"I see," Georgina mused, experiencing a small twinge of conscience before such unaffected earnestness. "Then I suppose I must let Gilda go and wish you both the best, mustn't I."

"Thank you, milady," Wilkins fairly beamed. "I told Gilda she shouldn't be afraid to talk with you. Why, you're cut of the same cloth as his lordship, the old earl, and the Major. And so I told her."

"Why thank you, Wilkins, that is high praise indeed," smiled Georgina.

" 'Tis naught but the truth. And begging your pardon, milady," he added shyly before turning to leave, "but you will come to the weddin'? We should be that pleased if you did. It's to be in the chapel with the Reverend Goodwin presiding."

"Then of course I shall be there," Georgina promised,

wondering whether the night of the house-raising was to be before or after the ceremony.

She had little time, however, to ponder the matter, for no sooner had Wilkins departed than a commotion in the great hall below lured her from the study. Drawn to the head of the stairs by a tumult of frantic voices all apparently intent upon being heard at once, she could make out only enough of what was transpiring to cause her considerable alarm, for it seemed someone had suffered some sort of riding accident. Terrified that Davey had been the victim, Georgina made her way swiftly down the stairs.

"Bolton!" she called, trying to make herself heard above the uproar, with the result that she was immediately bombarded with any number of persons demanding her immediate attention. "*Quiet!* Everyone!" she shouted at last, her patience quite at an end. A startled silence descended precipitously. Georgina took a deep breath and folded her hands calmly before her. "Now," she said quietly, "Bolton will please tell me what has happened."

"It's Denby, milady," replied the butler gravely. "He has suffered some sort of mishap and is badly injured, it would seem."

"Denby?" Georgina repeated, experiencing an odd weakness in her knees.

"It were an accident, yer laidyship," spoke up a new voice, one which affected Georgina oddly, rather as the nerve-prickling wail of the Indian jackal which senses a stricken animal had done. Not that the man actually sounded like that wretched beast, she reflected sardonically. It was just the way he made her feel, as if he were sizing her up for an easy prey.

"It's Fenton, isn't it?" she inquired, trying not to let her involuntary revulsion show in her voice.

"*Ais*, yer laidyship," wheedled the voice, and the odor of garlic and onions assailed her senses as the creature sidled up to her. "An' I seen the colt bolt an' Denby drop th' reins. 'Twere a green colt what Denby were but newly breakin' to the bit. I yelled for 'im to jump, but belike he never heard. The next thing he were on the ground an' all still-like. I were afeared t'try t'move 'im by meself, but then some o' the lads happened along an' I come on t'home t' warn 'ee that th' poor bloke be in a bad way. Belike he won't last th' night, your ladyship."

"Where is he then?" Georgina demanded, her voice suddenly harsh with fear for the ever-loyal Denby. "You will take me to him at once."

"I believe they are bringing him up to the house now, milady," Bolton interjected kindly.

"I expected thee would wish t' make ready fer him," Fenton hurried to add.

As if he expected a reprimand, Georgina thought, dissatisfied somehow with the man's account of his actions. However, having nothing tangible for which to fault him, she could do naught but accept his word for the time being.

"Yes, I see. Thank you, Fenton. I feel sure you have done all that could be expected," she said as graciously as she could. Then, suddenly aware that everyone was looking to her to tell them what to do, she drew a deep breath and willed herself to think calmly.

"Very well," she managed with every appearance of composed self-assurance. "Have Denby carried upstairs immediately. To the Rose Room. Mrs. Porter, see that one of the girls prepares the bed for him, then fetch me anything suitable for bandages. Bolton, you will see that someone rides immediately for the doctor in Saltash and then inform Cook that we shall need hot water. Oh, and, Bolton. Have you seen Miss Kingsley this morning?"

"She said that since it was Mr. Fairfax's day off, milady, that she was taking Lord Emberly berry-picking. They went out right after breakfast, I believe."

"I see," said the countess tonelessly, hard-put to conceal her sudden and no doubt unreasonable irritation at learning that once again Miss Kingsley was absent from the house without her knowledge. "Then ask Nanny Slade to come to the Rose Room, if you please. The rest of you, return to your usual duties at once."

The hall was soon cleared of all but a footman delegated to attend the door, and it was not long before Denby had been installed in the hastily prepared Rose Room.

"He's a nasty blow to the side of his head," Nanny Slade pronounced as she finished her examination of the injured groom. "And belike his left leg is broke. Looks t've been a nasty fall."

Upon which Denby suddenly stirred and uttered a faint groan.

"Not—a—fall," he whispered feebly but quite distinctly nonetheless.

"Denby. You mustn't try to talk," said Georgina, coming to the side of the bed. "We've sent for the doctor, and Nanny and I shall try to make you as comfortable as possible till he arrives."

"He can't hear you, Missy," Nanny interjected gruffly. "He's drifted off again. Which be a blessin'. Now 'twere best for you t' leave everythin' to me. I'll do what's needin' t' be done, nivver you fear. The boot's got t'be cut off and likely his clothes as well. An' the sickroom bain't no proper place for a lady."

"You forget, Nanny," Georgina returned calmly. "I have tended sick and wounded men before. You will need someone to hold him when you remove the boot, and then the leg must be splinted to keep it immobile till the doctor arrives."

"Quite so, ma'am," observed a new voice drily from the doorway. "However, may I suggest that Mrs. Slade is quite right when she says this is no place for you."

"Rathbourne!" Georgina exclaimed in sudden, over-whelming relief. Her lips parted in a glad smile as she whirled toward the sound of his voice. "You are back!"

"As you see," he drawled in his inimitable way, and Georgina had no difficulty envisioning his slight, ironic bow. "And apparently in good time. Now if you will kindly remove yourself that Mrs. Slade and I may properly attend to the unfortunate Denby's needs . . . ?"

"But I have no intention of leaving, Your Grace," Georgina informed him, her smile quickly altering to an expression of set determination. "Nor do I intend to indulge in a pointless discussion of a lady's proper place. Nanny, you and I shall hold Denby while His Grace tends to the matter of the boot."

Georgina straightened to her full height, her head lifted in proud defiance, as she steeled herself to resist the duke's unnerving ability to impose his will on others. However, she might have known Rathbourne would do the unexpected.

"Very well. Since it is hardly to Denby's benefit to debate the matter, I suggest we get on with it," he drawled, his tone of incipient boredom bringing a flush to her cheeks. She did not have to see to perceive the sardonic twist of his aristrocratic lips or to apprehend that he viewed her stance in the light of a childish fit which must in this instance be tolerated. Oh, how typical of the man! she mused in rueful amusement. But this time he should not get the best of her.

"Exactly so, Your Grace," she returned in dulcet tones and awarded him a bracing smile. "I am gratified that you perceive the wisdom of immediate action. I believe we are ready if you are."

His reluctant bark of laughter brought an answering grin to her lips.

"On the contrary, ma'am," he returned oddly after a moment. "You are not at all gratified by my wisdom. However, be that as it may, you will in time be made to profit by it. That I promise you."

"I'm grateful for what you did for Denby," Georgina said

215

wearily as she joined the Duke of Rathbourne some time later in the withdrawing room. "Dr. Poynsby is confident the leg will mend properly, and he commends you on the job you did of splinting it. I left our patient resting comfortably with Nobie to watch over him."

"I am no doubt relieved to know Dr. Poynsby approved my clumsy efforts," murmured the duke as he led Georgina unresisting to the sofa and firmly bade her to be seated. "Here, drink this. It will put some color back in your cheeks," he added, taking her hand and placing a glass in it.

"What is it?" she said doubtfully, holding the glass to her nose and taking a whiff of its contents. "Ugh, brandy! No thank you, Your Grace. I'm afraid I quite prefer sallow cheeks."

"You will do as you are told, my girl," observed the duke sternly, "else I shall most certainly pour it down you."

"Shall you?" she queried, cocking her head with great interest to one side. "Tell me. Is that how you normally charm your women into complying with your wishes? I know you will pardon me for asking. You see, I've not been acquainted with a notorious rake before, and I'm afraid I'm quite ignorant of what to expect from you."

"You, my impertinent little baggage, shall expect to be throttled do you not cease to play little miss innocent. Now drink."

"Oh, very well," she acquiesced, wrinkling her nose at him. "But only because you were so obliging as to help Denby. I am not usually so easily coerced."

"Ah, yes. The unfortunate Denby," Rathbourne murmured when Georgina, after managing to choke down a swallow or two of the noxious brew, had lowered the glass. "Tell me. How did he come to be in such dire straits? I shouldn't have thought from the looks of him that he would be one to let a horse get the better of him."

"Nor should I," agreed Georgina when she had got her

breath again. "There's no one better with cattle than Denby."

For a long moment Rathbourne said nothing, but Georgina was too absorbed in her own thoughts to notice. She was hardly aware when the duke reached down and gently took the brandy glass from her hand.

"What troubles you, my girl?" he said quietly, touching a fingertip to the furrow between Georgina's eyebrows.

"It's the oddest thing," she rejoined, turning earnestly to face him. "Denby regained consciousness just for a moment right before you came in. He managed only a few words before he swooned again, but he pronounced them quite clearly. He said that it was not a fall. That's all. I didn't pay much attention to it then. There wasn't time. But now I cannot help but wonder what he meant."

"I doubt there is any need to trouble yourself over it," drawled the duke negligently. "The man was clearly out of his head. It's probable he won't even recall what he said when he regains consciousness."

"Perhaps," murmured Georgina in a troubled voice, wanting to believe that was the case. The little groom *had* been in a bad way.

But Georgina was not to be so easily convinced. She had known Denby far too long to believe he could be caught unaware on a green colt. And even if the young stallion had bolted, the seasoned groom was not likely to have so lost his head as to drop the reins. No, Fenton's account simply did not ring true. And, what, after all, did she really know of Anson Fenton? Though he had been born and reared near Saltash, he himself had admitted to having been pressed into the navy as a young man, hardly more than a boy, from which time he had been away from his home till a French musket ball had nicked his lungs and made him unfit for further service. It had been this which had won Georgina's sympathy when the wheedling Fenton, apparently down on his luck and willing to perform any sort of labor, had approached her one afternoon little more than a se'ennight past as she strolled near the bourne with Davey and Miss Kingsley.

"No. I believe Denby was quite lucid at the time," Georgina stated flatly. "Lord knows what it must have cost him to rouse himself even long enough for those three words. He meant it as a warning, I'm sure of it. Indeed, it would be quite like him to think of me before himself," she added, bitterly ashamed of how she had continued to hold the little groom at arm's length merely because she was too craven to face the memories he evoked.

"Are you indeed," remarked the duke, rather repressively, she thought with a quizzical quirk of an eyebrow. "Very well, if you are so certain it was not an accident, can you suggest any reason why someone should want Denby out of the way?"

"That is just what I've been asking myself," she answered reluctantly, "and I cannot think of any plausible explanation for it. I simply cannot see that anyone would gain by Denby's death. He has nothing of any material value beyond his wages and what little savings he might have managed to accrue. He has no family and, so far as I know, lives a comparatively quiet life. I believe he spends most of his time at the stables even on his days off. And except for Fenton, he seems to rub well enough along with everyone."

"Fenton?"

"The man who witnessed what happened to Denby and brought him home," Georgina said with an involuntary grimace. "He's a new man I hired only a week or so ago to work in the stables. For some reason Denby seemed to take an instant dislike to him. Nor can I blame him. There's something I cannot like about him myself, though I can never quite put my finger on what it is."

"Another of your unfortunate foundlings, ma'am?" queried Rathbourne drily, leaving no doubt in Georgina's mind that the insufferable man was experiencing a renewed onset of ennui as she caught the tell-tale sounds of his flicking open a snuff box and languidly inhaling a pinch of the stuff. "I should have thought the inept abigail a sufficient lesson for you."

"How perfectly odious that you seem always to be right, Your Grace," she said with a rueful laugh. "Indeed, I *should* have known better, but he seemed a harmless creature despite his loathsome manner of ingratiating himself to one. And besides, he had been wounded at the Battle of Trafalgar. So you must see that I *could* not turn him away."

"Oh, I quite understand, Lady Grey," agreed the duke magnanimously. "However, might I suggest that you allow Connings or myself to see to the hiring of the stablehands henceforth? Were there any other witnesses to what happened?"

"I don't really know," Georgina answered shortly, her mood having undergone a sudden alteration at what she viewed as Rathbourne's condescending manner. How dared he treat her like a brainless idiot! Nor did it help one whit to know that she *had* acted stupidly when she took Fenton on despite her aversion to him. "I don't even know for sure what did happen. But I think perhaps it's time I questioned Anson Fenton more closely."

"No, I don't want you to do anything," Rathbourne interjected in accents of deep cogitation. "You will leave that to me."

"Indeed? Why should I?" she retorted, taking instant exception to his arrogant assumption of command.

"Because, little hornet, if there has been foul play of some sort, it would be extremely unwise to let it be known you are in any way suspicious. Not only would you invite peril to yourself—perhaps even to Davey—but you would very likely scare the villain away ere we have caught him."

"And you, I suppose, would not?" she queried in patent

disbelief.

"Since I shall rely on someone less conspicuous than either of us to make inquiries, it is highly unlikely," he agreed maddeningly, and a slight flush crept into Georgina's cheeks at his tone of patient tolerance. As if he were humoring a precocious child, she thought testily and wondered how she could ever have allowed herself to moon over his absence. At the moment it would seem a circumstance for which to be devoutly grateful. "Meantime, perhaps it were best to keep Denby where he is. It may be that he has incurred the enmity of someone in the area. In which case, he will be safer here."

"Of course he will stay here," she said, her momentary crossness receding before the greater worry of Denby's mysterious mishap. "There was never any doubt of it. However, I find it difficult to believe Denby could have so implacable an enemy. He is very well liked. It simply doesn't make any sense that someone would deliberately try to harm him."

"Very likely you are right," Rathbourne smoothly agreed. "And since we must wait till Denby regains consciousness to learn what he meant precisely, if anything, by his odd remark, I suggest there is very little need for you to worry yourself over it any further. Indeed, it occurs to me that you are not in your best looks. You are as lacking in color as the unfortunate Denby."

"How kind in you to point it out, Your Grace," Georgina observed acerbically. "But I assure you I have seldom been in better health."

"You cannot pull the wool over my eyes, madam," he rejoined coolly. "In point of fact, no sooner is my back turned than what must you do but wear yourself to the nub. It is obvious you have been taking too much upon yourself again. Nor, if Bolton is to be believed, have you ceased to deny yourself to your neighbors. When was the last time you spoke to anyone other than a member of the household? Indeed, when was the last time you even allowed yourself the luxury of strolling in the garden?"

"I am quite sure I cannot recall when I last dallied in the garden," returned the countess dangerously and tilted her chin at the duke. Really, the man was impossible. Did he dare to think he could so easily distract her from the matter of Denby's assailant? She was blind, but she was not a child or an idiot. "However, if it is a matter of such great interest to you, no doubt I can ascertain the date from Miss Kingsley. As for my lack of social intercourse, I believe I have already made my view on the subject quite clear. Furthermore, I cannot see why my health, appearance, or social well-being should be any concern of yours."

"No, I am ruefully aware that you do not," Rathbourne murmured provocatively. "However, I have every expectation of remedying that situation in time. Meanwhile, I have taken it upon myself to make sure you do not jeopardize my ward's future standing in the county by your determination to gain the reputation of an eccentric and a recluse."

"I beg your pardon," Georgina gasped, unable to believe her ears. "I do not for a moment consider that my preference for privacy can be so detrimental to Davey's position in the community. It is no secret that I am blind, and doubtless anyone with any sensibility must certainly understand how inconvenient it would be for me to make social calls."

"I see," he returned, and Georgina had little difficulty in imagining from his tone the imperious lift of an odiously arrogant eyebrow. "Then it is their pity which you desire. I fear I must beg your forgiveness for what can only be considered a natural misunderstanding in the circumstances. I had thought you above such puerile motivations, ma'am."

Georgina, who understandably took exception to what could only have been the duke's intentional misinterpretation of her meaning, bit her tongue to keep from delivering a stinging retort. She knew Rathbourne well enough by now to know when he was deliberately trying to get a rise from her, and, though she could not possibly guess in this instance at his purpose, she had no intention of succumbing to a fit of the vapors merely to satisfy his peculiar whimsies.

"I do not pretend to understand your motives in trying to bait me, Your Grace," she answered quite reasonably after a time and favored him with a faintly quizzing aspect which only imperfectly concealed the hurt his words had caused. "I desire no one's pity. It is my independence which I most treasure and which I cannot have anywhere but here. Surely you can understand that."

A brief silence greeted her earnest entreaty, followed by the duke's rueful bark of laughter. Georgina cocked her head, her expression intent, as Rathbourne rose abruptly from the couch and took two long strides across the room before coming to a halt and turning once again to face her. She could feel the sudden tension in him as surely as she sensed his eyes on her—those blue, stormy eyes of the black Celt—and wondered at it.

"I understand, madam," he said oddly, "better than you. But understanding changes nothing. You see, I have determined that you will assume your obligations as the Countess of Emberly, or I shall see to it that David's son and heir is removed entirely from your influence."

"No. I don't believe you," she uttered in stunned accents. "You couldn't take my son from me. I could not be so mistaken in you."

"I could and indeed I shall," he answered, seeming to freeze her soul with his sudden, cold indifference. "It is my legal right and my moral obligation to the well-being of my ward. After all, it was you who pointed out that the boy had need of a whole and healthy parent, but you, madam, have failed to live up to that noble ambition. Indeed, you have allowed yourself to become little more than an invalid, a

222

poor creature too craven to leave the sickroom."

"How dare you!" Georgina cried, swept by a sudden anger which was nearly equal to her sense of hurt bewilderment. "Why are you doing this?"

"I believe I have made my motives quite clear, ma'am," observed the hateful voice, which, though it retained the familiar tonal qualities of the man she had come to consider dearer than a friend, was yet somehow that of a stranger.

"Then you are mistaken, Your Grace," she said, rising from the couch with unconscious grace and drawing herself up to her full height, her hands clasped tightly before her and her face held uncompromisingly to the fore. "For none of this is at all clear. I am not bound to any sickroom, nor am I in the habit of languishing on sofas, smelling salts close to hand. I have simply learned to function within the admittedly close confines of my limitations."

She had spoken with her usual seemingly unshakable composure, but suddenly, as the enormity of Rathbourne's harsh judgment began to dawn on her, her brittle self-restraint appeared to suffer a sudden fissure.

"Do you think for one moment it has been easy?" she demanded passionately. "Do you think I have not awakened in the night and wished with all my heart that I could see some end to this terrible nightmare?"

"Have you?" queried Rathbourne, drawing suddenly so near to her that she had to will herself not to retreat before the unsettling warmth of his body close to hers, the muscles tense with some powerful inner emotion held rigidly in check. "And have you asked yourself *why* you are blind? What happened to you in Elvas, Lady Grey, which caused you to be so stricken? Have you once had the courage to ponder that? Or have you been too busy hiding behind what has become a convenient excuse not to delve too deeply into the past? What is it that you fear so greatly that you would bury yourself at Greystone, too afraid to show yourself to others, too afraid to put your vaunted independence to the touch beyond the security of this damned impregnable haven you have created for yourself?"

"Oh, how sure you are of yourself," she said in unspeakable loathing. "What do you know of what I have had to face day after day? Yes, I have found a safe haven here at Greystone. I am not ashamed of that. Why should I be? I have made a home for myself and for my son in my husband's house, the one place in which his memory lingers. The one place in which I need not feel alone because David is still with me."

"Enough, madam," Rathbourne uttered in bored contempt. "Such maudlin sentiment little becomes you. It is not David's memory which binds you to this house. Rather it is the fear of his memory which keeps you here like some poor, pitiful creature. Tell me, Georgina, what is it that you have refused to remember?"

"That's not true!" she said in bitter anguish. "I-I have tried to remember those lost weeks. But I can't. I can't!" She closed her eyes and clutched her suddenly throbbing forehead with a trembling hand. What did Rathbourne want from her? Why could he not leave her be? But he was to prove inexorable as he continued heartlessly to provoke her.

"Are you not in truth, madam, a hypocrite and a coward? Are you not too craven even to admit that you have been lying to yourself all along? Yes, and lying to your son as well?"

"Stop it!" she cried, her hands rising to cover her ears against Rathbourne's harsh accusations. "I have never lied to Davey. Never!" Her head was pounding now so that she thought she could not bear it. She tried to wheel away from him, wanting desperately to flee, but he grasped her wrists and held her, dragging her hands down so that she must listen.

"Have you not?" he demanded implacably. "Does Lord Emberly know there is no physiological reason for his mama's blindness? Think, Georgina. How will he feel when he learns how you have cheated him?" he ended harshly and, abruptly releasing her, turned his back on her as if he could no longer stand the sight of her.

Georgina swayed and caught herself. No! It wasn't true, she tried to tell herself. She had done everything for Davey. She had even survived for him! But she could no longer think rationally. Her head hurt too badly, and she knew she was going to be dreadfully ill. She must lie down soon. She needed to be still till the sickness passed.

Suddenly her only coherent thought was to be free of Rathbourne's loathsome presence, to be alone before she utterly disgraced herself. But Rathbourne stood between her and the door. Desperately she tried to shove the pain to the back of her mind long enough to visualize the room— the sofa behind her running lengthwise with the room, the teak sofa table somewhere before and to one side of her, the pair of caffoy wing chairs, one at either end of the couch and turned inward to partially face one another.

Yes, she had it clearly now. She need take perhaps two steps to the sofa's end nearest her. Then she could work around the scrolled arm to the back and have a clear run to the door.

Thinking a trifle wildly that if nothing else, she should at least have the sofa between her and this loathsome stranger, she turned and made her way around the arm to the back. She must have made some small noise— perhaps he heard or sensed her hand brushing over the crushed velvet of the sofaback—because all of a sudden she was aware that he had turned and was moving quickly toward her.

"Where do you think you are going?" he said harshly, and suddenly she was lunging wildly for the door.

She heard Rathbourne shout her name, then she had stumbled and was falling. She landed hard and lay momentarily stunned, tears of bitter frustration stinging her clenched eyelids. Then Rathbourne was beside her, his hands hard upon her shoulders as he turned her on her back and lifted her against his chest.

"Georgina, you little fool," he rasped as she tried weakly to shove him away. She gasped as he lifted her without warning into his arms and stood.

"No, please. I'm all right," she said, going rigid with embarrassment. "Put me down, I beg you."

Wordlessly he set her on her feet, but her wrist he kept imprisoned in the steely clasp of one lean hand so that she nearly gasped with pain, and in spite of everything, she yet sensed that he, too, was held in the sway of some terrible emotion. She could not understand what had happened. She felt hurt and betrayed. He had deliberately set out to hurt her. Why? Her head reeled with the horrid realization that he meant to take her son from her, and suddenly she was filled with a cold rage.

"Get out of my house," she uttered in a voice which shook with bitter dislike.

"But you forget, madam, that this is your son's house," he replied, and she winced, sensing the cynical twist of his lips in ironic amusement. "And I am his guardian. I say who comes and goes in this house."

"If it is Greystone you want, Your Grace, you may have it. My son and I will remove as soon as ever to my own house in Kent."

"You will do as you wish, I've no doubt," he shrugged. "But Lord Emberly shall remain here."

For a moment she was too stunned to speak as she realized finally and irrevocably that as long as the duke held legal sway over Davey, she, too, was at his mercy. Rathbourne had won before she had even realized she was fighting for her life! With an effort she roused herself from the lethargy which seemed suddenly to weight her limbs.

"What is it that you want from me?" she demanded finally in a voice devoid of all traces of emotion.

For a long moment he did not answer, and she could feel him staring at her until she thought she must scream from the suspence of waiting to hear her sentence pronounced.

"What I want, madam," he drawled at last, hatefully cool, "is to take you as my wife."

Chapter 10

Lady Georgina Grey, caught in the toils of a dream, stirred restlessly in her bed, her head turning from side to side on the pillows as she murmured incoherent phrases.

"Yes, David. Marry you. India? Oh, yes," she sighed rapturously.

A dreamy smile played briefly on her lips then vanished in the wake of an anxious frown.

"Rathbourne? Here. No. *I* cannot see him," she whimpered, growing increasingly more agitated. "He isn't here, David. I swear it. He is gone. You will not find him. David, I *love* you. Don't make him come. Please, don't make him come. Oh, David. Don't go! No. *Please*, don't go!"

"Miss Georgina!" called Nanny Slade softly, her old face puckered in a worried frown as she bent over her mistress and gently shook her. But Georgina refused to emerge from her troubled sleep. Mindlessly she brushed the nurse's hand away.

"*You!*" she breathed in accents of fear and loathing, and Nanny Slade involuntarily recoiled as the young countess bolted upright, her eyes wide-open and staring on the old nurse's face. "*You* killed him. You and—and *I!*" she stated tragically then collapsed with a moan against the rumpled pillows, her white-lipped accusation seeming to

228

hang in the sudden stillness like an omen.

The old nurse mumbled something beneath her breath and made the sign of the cross over her plump bosom. Her pale blue eyes dimmed behind the rimless spectacles perched low on the rounded lump of a nose.

"So they be come back t' haunt ye, have they?" she said softly and pityingly shook her grey head beneath the linen mobcap. "Me poor lass wot never hurt nobody."

"Who's there?" Georgina queried suddenly in a hoarse whisper and, half-rising, drew back against the head of the bed, the bedcovers clasped tightly to her breast.

"Now, now. 'Tis only Nanny come t' wake ye like I promised," soothed the old woman, leaning over the bedside.

"Oh, Nanny!" sighed the countess tremulously and let her muscles go lax in sudden relief. Nanny Slade watched the wild and haunted look slowly fade from the large brown eyes to leave them shadowed and weary-looking and silently clucked her tongue.

"I was dreaming again, wasn't I," Georgina ventured presently in a low, troubled voice and plucked at the counterpane with listless fingers. The lovely face, so wan and withdrawn, brought a lump to Nanny's throat.

"Aye, ye was," the nurse nodded and tried to think of something to say which might lighten her mistress's melancholy mood. For she little liked to see her darling so sore beset with troubles what she couldn't even trust to her old nanny. Ah. Things wasn't like they used to be when she could kiss away th' lass's hurts and mend her troubled heart with a lump of sugar. "But ye be awake now," she added, suddenly brisk to hide her worried thoughts. "So bestir yourself, Missy, for belike 'twill be a fine day fer weddin's an' th' like."

"Weddings?" Georgina queried sharply, the sensitive fingers going suddenly still. "Why do you speak of weddings?"

"An' why shouldn't I when there be one in th' offing?" retorted Nanny, eyeing her mistress oddly. Now wot 'ad got into th' lass? she wondered, that she should look fair ready t' swoon at th' mere mention of a weddin'? " 'Tis my guess ye won't be th' onliest one wot 'as th' look of a sleepless night,' she added significantly. "Nary a man Jack were t' home till th' wee hours, exceptin' only fer Bolton, wot stayed by th' door all th' night through in case there might be someone needin' 'im afore the cock crew. 'Course 'e might o' saved 'imself th' trouble. If ye was t' ask me, there bain't none kin build a cot wot'll keep th' rain off in less time than it takes th' sun t' set an 'rise again."

"The house-raising!" Georgina breathed. Gradually her heart resumed its normal pace as she realized the old servant had been referring to Wilkins and Gilda's impending nuptials and not Rathbourne's and her own. Gratefully she turned her thoughts from her seemingly insurmountable problems to a contemplation of the happy events which must be well under way by now.

"With everything that's happened, I'd nearly forgotten about it," she said, her face brightening a little with curiosity and a sincere interest in those who were the lifeblood of Greystone Manor. "Have you heard anything? Did they do the thing in time?"

"I ain't 'eard nothin' as yet," Nanny admitted with a sniff—miffed, Georgina thought with an inner smile, to have been excluded from the drama being enacted beneath her very nose. "But Gilda were a moment wi' Wilkins, an' now there bain't no livin' wi' 'er. Mum as a mouse wot ate th' cheese, *she* is."

Eight chimes of the clock brought the countess suddenly bolt-upright with the realization that she had overslept despite Nanny's promise to wake her in time to relieve Nobie, who had undertaken the first watch over Denby while Georgina slept.

"Nanny, how could you let me lie abed when I promised

to take Miss Kingsley's place in the sickroom?" she cried, thrusting the bedcovers from her. "The poor child will be worn to the nub for lack of sleep."

" 'Tain't likely, since she were safely tucked in bed hours past," retorted the older woman. "An' belike her rest were better'n yours, Missy. Leastwise it'd not be worry over Denby wot'd rob Miss Nobie of 'er sleep," Nanny muttered pointedly. "An' ye needn't fret yourself over Denby neither. He be well taken care of."

Georgina, who could not fail to detect the innuendo in her servant's tone, abruptly paused in her hurried exit from the bed, her bare feet dangling over the side as she gave Nanny Slade her full attention.

Drat! What could her cousin possibly have done to incur Nanny's misapprobation? she wondered fleetingly, made uncomfortably aware of a sinking feeling in the pit of her stomach. Good Lord, hadn't she troubles enough?

"Nanny," she said sharply, "you know how I feel about gossip. Just what are you insinuating?"

"Ye needn't fly at me, Mistress," Nanny instantly rejoined in a wounded huff. "I may be naught but an old woman wot 'tis only right nobody should pay no nivver-ye-mind. But less'n I miss me guess, 'tis time ye was takin' note o' wot's goin' on around ye. But don't listen to me. Wot does I know? I be good only fer stayin' in th' nursery. Like as not 'twould be best was ye to pension ole Nanny off now 'is lordhisp 'as 'is tutor."

Georgina, overcome instantly with remorse for having vented her ill-humor on the oldest and most faithful of her retainers, caught her bottom lip between her teeth and closed her eyes against the renewed throbbing in her head. Good God. Things were come to a sad pass indeed when she should find herself ripping up at Nanny Slade, she groaned inwardly and exhaled an exasperated sigh, for not only did she stand condemned in her own eyes of a thoughtless breach of conduct, but she had also managed to set the formidable matron on her high-horse. Nanny Slade in a high dudgeon was capable of being as recalcitrant as a Cornish mule. Thus resigned to the inevitable, Georgina quelled the urge to sink back into her bed and set herself instead to smooth the matron's ruffled feathers.

"Oh, Nanny," she said with a rueful smile, one hand going out in supplication. "I am sorry if I hurt you. And if I have been in some way remiss in my responsibilities, I beg you will forgive me. But you know that I have had a great deal on my mind of late what with settling in here at Greystone and having to cope with the decisions concerning Emberly, and—and learning to—*adjust* to—well, to everything. And now this dreadful thing which has happened to Denby—! Please try to understand. I am not trying to make excuses. It is simply that I truly have not the least notion of what you are talking about, and if there is something I should know, I should be best pleased if you would tell me it."

Nanny, however, was not to be so easily appeased.

"Harumph! Ye needn't waste yer fine airs on me, Mistress," she declared sanctimoniously as she briskly gathered up a flowing negligee from the foot of the bed and draped it around Georgina's shoulders. "For ye shan't turn yer old nanny up sweet. Far be it from me t' speak twicet out o' turn." Then easing herself down on stiff knees, she retrieved her mistress's slippers from beneath the bed and placed them firmly on Georgina's feet.

"I bain't nivver no tale-bearer," she grumbled, climbing laboriously to her feet again. "I'm jest tellin' ye t' uncover your 'ead, Missy. There be things 'appenin' wot even th' blind kin see, if'n they wasn't always lookin' so much to their own selves."

Stung by the old woman's implied criticism, Georgina underwent a swift alteration in mood.

"You go too far, Nanny!" she warned in a flinty voice and suddenly, driven beyond the limits of her patience, did

232

not care that in all likelihood she would later despise herself for speaking so. Was it not enough that she had been made to endure Rathbourne's scathing condemnation without having now to suffer the censure of one to whom she had always looked for solace and understanding? "If you have something to say, Nanny, then be pleased to say it without further roundaboutation. What has Miss Kingsley done to earn your disapproval?"

"Why naught, for it bain't my place to judge them wot be me betters," Nanny answered dourly. "Only if ye was t' ask me, I'd say 'tis odd th' way she keeps to 'erself, sort o' broodin'-like, as if she were thinkin' on some terrible, dark secret. An' lately 'ow she's took t' slippin' out o' th' 'ouse when nobody bain't lookin'. An' when she comes back, 'ow of a sudden 'tis rainbows wi' 'er. 'Good-morn t' ye, Mrs. Slade,' she says. And 'Is it not a glorious day, Mrs. Slade?' But 'tain't long ere she 'as th' look o' th' gallows 'bout her again, an' then there bain't no reachin' 'er. She don't eat nor sleep neither, fer I kin 'ear 'er pacin' in 'er room till all hours o' th' night. An' weepin' too. Nay. I'd not judge th' lass, but I remembers when she were a gladsome little missy, an' I say 'tis time *some'un* tried to find out wot's eatin' at 'er so."

"But, Nanny. Surely the explanation is quite obvious," Georgina said in sudden enlightenment. "Indeed, it is what I have hoped for her. Miss Kingsley is in love. And if I know anything, Lord Robert Penwarren is the lucky swain. But why do they not simply bring it out into the open? I had thought better of Robbie, and surely my cousin must know how happy I should be for them both," she ended in sudden perplexity. . . . Unless, whispered a small insidious voice, Rathbourne were against the match.

Instantly Georgina was swept with righteous anger. It would be just like the insufferable duke to stand in the way of the young couple's happiness. Doubtless he had other plans for his brother than marriage to a penniless orphan who must earn her own way in the world, she thought heatedly, apparently having forgotten that once she had suggested something quite different to Miss Kingsley on the very subject of her cousin's penury.

However, it soon transpired that Nanny Slade, who was not yet finished with her tale, was of a different opinion.

" 'Belike it bain't Lord Robert wot'd keep it secret, Missy," she suggested shrewdly. " 'Twere always plain's a pikestaff 'ow 'e felt. But Miss Nobie nivver let 'im close. Kept 'er thoughts 'id, she did, till a body wondert that th' poor lad's 'eart weren't froze solid by 'er standoffish ways. Then, th' night afore 'Is Grace left fer London town, Miss Nobie come in from th' garden all aglowin'. An' less'n I be naught but an old fool, 'tweren't th' roses wot'd brung th' color t' 'er cheeks. After that she were different, always watchin' fer 'is lordship, she was, an' singin' like a lark when she thought none'd 'ear. Miss Nobie seemed almost like th' wee sprite wot I remembered from th' old days in Kent, Missy. It done me 'eart good t' see 'er."

"Then I don't understand." Georgina said impatiently. "Why are you so concerned now?"

" 'Cause n' more'n a se'ennight past, she were changed again. Wilkins 'eard 'er tell Lord Robert she mustn't nivver see 'im no more. Said she were leavin' Greystone an' wouldn't be back. That was when 'is lordship stopped comin' t' th' 'ouse, an' wen Miss Nobie started aslippin' out fer an hour 'ere an hour there. I tell ye, Mistress, things bain't right wi' th' lass. I 'ears 'er, I does, cryin' 'er 'eart out till th' wee hours o' th' night. An' that bain't all. Denby told Wilkins, wot told Bolton, that 'e seen Miss Nobie down by th' bourne talkin' wi' that no-account, shifty-eyed Fenton. I bain't no tale-bearer, mind ye. But seems t' me ye'd ought t' know when a stable lad sees fit t' lay 'is 'ands on a lady born 'n' bred."

"But you must be mistaken, Nanny!" gasped Georgina, going suddenly pale. "Fenton may be a lot of things, but I hardly think he is a fool. He wouldn't dare to insult a member of this house!"

"If ye was t' ask me, I'd say 'e'd dare a lot more'n that, Missy," Nanny prophesied darkly. "An' if it 'adn't o' been fer Denby, wot come on 'em sudden like, belike Miss Nobie'd found it out quick enough."

"Denby? What had Denby to do with it?" Georgina queried sharply, her pulse quickening as she felt herself suddenly on the brink of something portentous. But apparently Nanny had come at last to the end of her confidences.

" 'Tain't fer me t' say," she declared in such a manner that Georgina could sense the old dame draw up, her arms crossed unequivocally over the plump bosom. "I've told ye wot I seen an' 'eard, Missy. Belike Denby could tell ye wot went on 'twixt 'im an' Fenton, but 'e bain't sayin' naught, an' I doesn't know n' more. So ye needn't ask wot I can't answer."

Georgina, who well knew her formidable nursemaid, recognized at once that nuance of tight-lipped obstinacy in Nanny's voice. Clearly, if all to which she had just been made privvy were true, there was something very much amiss at Greystone, but she would learn nothing more of it from Nanny

Poor Nobie, she thought to herself as she allowed Nanny to help her into the steaming bath awaiting her before a low-burning fire in her dressingroom. Nanny was quite right to accuse her. She *was* guilty of having shamefully neglected the child, for she had known from the beginning that all was not as it should be with her cousin, and still she had done nothing to discover the source of Nobie's trouble. Nor was it likely now that she would be given the opportunity to amend the situation, for she had yet to see her way clear of her own impossible coil. Indeed, she expected the treacherous Rathbourne to arrive at any moment, at which time she would have to make her decision known to him.

Rathbourne! she thought with loathing as she eased

down into the water and rested the back of her throbbing head against the edge of the tub. How dared he come into her home to browbeat and torment her and end up by demanding that she become his wife! The man was mad and obviously without scruples to seek to use her son against her. How could she have misjudged him so? she fretted and squeezed her eyes tightly shut against the sudden swift thrust of bitter anguish.

Oh, God! What had changed him toward her? He had betrayed her trust, deliberately destroyed the growing bond of friendship between them. Why? If he loved her and wanted her for his wife, would he not have been better served in remaining her trusted friend? Did he not see that in time she might have learned to accept him as something more? Indeed, whispered a small, insidious voice, had she not already succumbed so far to his devious charm as to fancy herself on the verge of falling in love with him?

In love with Rathbourne! Good God! What an irony that must have been, she thought with unconscious bitterness. Thank heaven he had shown his true colors ere she had been rendered an utter fool. Indeed, to have attempted a rational understanding of the duke's heinous behavior in terms of the heart was patently a waste of time, for not only was Rathbourne clearly devoid of all delicacy of feeling, but *he*, moreover, had never once mentioned love.

And yet, persisted that earlier, perfidious voice, there had been times ere yesterday's horrendous moment of disillusionment when she had thought he liked her well enough, when she had even believed he entertained a certain affection for her. But immediately she squelched those feeble murmurings emanating from her heart and bitterly reminded herself of the fool she had been to believe for one moment the infamous duke could ever have been something other than his notorious reputation had painted him. She was blind indeed not to have seen that he was merely toying with her, feeling out her vulnerabilities that in the end he might humble and humiliate her. What terrible irony that her own David, the man who had loved and trusted Rathbourne, should have provided him with the only weapon to force her to his will against which she had no defense—her son.

"Oh, David," she whispered in anguish to the empty room. "How *could* you have been so misled in him? How *could* you have loved him all those years? And believed that noblest of sentiments returned! He cannot know what it is to love, for he is utterly cold and vile."

But no sooner had she spoken than again she found herself compelled to question *why*. Why was he doing it?

Oh, damn and double damn! she fumed in helpless frustration. None of it made any sense. If he did not love her, why should he go to such lengths to coerce her into matrimony? Why, indeed, make her his wife at all? For if he were motivated only by desire or some insane need to dominate her, he might just as easily have demanded she become his mistress. That at least might have made some sense, since it would surely have been more in keeping with his reputation as a notorious rakeshame.

For what other reasons than love did a man force a woman into wedlock? she fretted. He could not possibly covet her fortune which, next to his staggering wealth, was negligible. Nor could she see him going to such extremes to add Emberly to his already prodigious holdings. Besides, even as his wife she could not bring him what was not hers, and Emberly belonged to Davey. There had to be something she had overlooked, she told herself, her brow furrowing in a frown. She must try to think.

With a feeling that the whole world had been turned suddenly topsy-turvy, Georgina searched her memory for some clue to Rathbourne's bizarre behavior, but the more she thought about it the more bewildered she became. For, though much of what had transpired the day before had been rendered vague by shock and the torment of a migraine which had led her finally to ingest a strong dose of laudanum, she recalled enough to know that he had begun with a tender concern for her, plying her with a restorative measure of brandy and inquiring gently into the cause of her pensiveness. And he had seemed bent on protecting her from whatever peril had struck Denby down. How, then, had they come suddenly to loggerheads and with such disastrous results?

She remembered he had been out of all countenance with her for remaining cloistered in the house during his absence. But to believe *that* had been the underlying cause of all which had subsequently occurred was patently absurd. No, there had to be something else. What was it that he had demanded of her again and again?

Georgina pressed her fingertips to the sides of her head and began to massage her temples as the throbbing pain grew suddenly more intense. As from a distance she seemed to hear the harsh echo of Rathbourne's voice commanding her to remember Elvas and David and accusing her of deliberately blocking the memories from her mind, accusing her of lying to herself and to Davey. And finally he had humiliated her and stripped her of her hard-won independence, destroying any illusion she might have had that she held dominion over her own life and robbing her—Damn his soul!—of Greystone and the fool's paradise she had created for herself within its hallowed walls.

"Oh, the devil fly away with him!" she cried abruptly and slashed a fist through the bathwater in utter frustration. Marry him? She would sooner cut out her own heart than submit to his demands. And yet she could see no way out of it, for she no longer doubted that he was quite capable of taking her son away from her just as ruthlessly as he had deprived her of her illusion of proud independence. Oh, how she loathed him most of all for that!

She must have time, she told herself, time to think and time to discover a flaw in his hateful scheme. How magnanimous of him to grant her the night in which to consider his gracious proposal of marriage, she thought in bitter irony. Doubtless he had known she would wear herself to the nub mulling over the impossibility of her situation, indeed, had probably counted on it to break down her resistance and further debilitate her will.

Damn Rathbourne! He would come this very morning, just as he had said he would, to demand her answer. And so he should have it, she vowed suddenly, and it would be exactly what he expected to hear.

She pictured the whole quite clearly in her mind. She would be calm and rational as ever she was, and she would agree to become his wife because she had no other options. But she would only be buying time. For today was Monday, and even if the banns were read on Sunday next, the soonest he could force her to the altar was four weeks hence. Surely she could devise some escape in four weeks' time, she thought, desperately fighting off the despair which threatened to rob her of her will. It was, perhaps, a very meager plan, but it was at least a beginning, and she certainly had no intention of giving in to the loathsome Duke of Rathbourne ever!

Thus determined at all costs to best the duke at his own game, she summoned Nanny to wash her hair and left her bath feeling a little better than she had upon entering it. Still, it took all her patience to sit quietly while Nanny dried her hair before the fire then methodically brushed it out till it crackled and no doubt shone in the morning sunlight streaming through the window. Nor had her head ceased to trouble her, though the pain had eased to a dull ache which was only just tolerable. But at last the old nurse had swept the luxurious mass back from Georgina's face and, pinning it there, had allowed the rest to fall in soft curls down the back to the countess's slender shoulders.

At Nanny's low grunt of satisfaction, Georgina raised a hand to the wisps of curls left to frame and soften her face and thought ironically that at least she should look her best when she confronted the Duke of Rathbourne, for Nanny had ever a way with hair. Of course, the effect would no doubt be diminished by whichever of the drab gowns Nanny had chosen for her to wear, for she had nothing in her wardrobe which was not long past its original state of beauty, let alone the current mode.

Consequently she was more than a little startled as, bent over at the waist, her arms raised above her head to allow Nanny to help her into her dress, she felt herself suddenly enveloped in an exquisite cloud of feather-light fabric which seemed to float about her slender frame to her trim ankles. Mystified, she ran her hands over the silk-like smoothness. Sarcenet, she thought, and explored with an almost childish delight the delicately puffed sleeves ending in finely embroidered bands about her wrists. With a blush she discovered the V neck plunged in a more daring decolletage than she was used to wearing though she judged that it was not indecently revealing compared to some her cousin had seen and described to her from the pages of *La Belle Assemblée*. Though she knew it would make her dizzy, she could not resist twirling once about that she might feel the generous skirt swirl deliciously about her legs.

"What color is it?" she queried of Nanny, wanting to 'see' the gown in all its loveliness.

" 'Tis like a green field wot's all abloom wi' deep blue cornflowers," Nanny replied in a rapturous voice.

"Deep blue? Not a pastel. You are quite sure," Georgina persisted.

"As sure as I'm standin' 'ere wi' me eyes full open," assured the old nurse as she stepped back to view with misty eyes the countess arrayed stunningly in the first stare of fashion.

"But where . . . ?"

Georgina's utterance died abruptly on her lips.

"Rathbourne!" she breathed in bitter certainty, and it

was a moment before she could summon her voice again. The duke, it seemed, had been as good as his word. "Are there others as well, Nanny?" she queried finally with only a slight quiver in her voice.

"An even dozen in all," Nanny answered with obvious satisfaction. "An' every one as lovely as ye could wish for. 'Ad 'em give straight into me arms, 'e. did."

"Did he," Georgina intoned, her former delight in the new gown quite diminished. "And where was I when His Grace was playing the gallant gentleman?"

Nanny seemed to hesitate the briefest moment.

" 'Twas after 'e carried ye to yer bed," she said with obvious reluctance. "Aswoonin' in 'is arms, ye was, an' 'Is Grace were as white as a sheet, 'e were. 'Let 'er sleep,' says 'e, gazin' down at ye like ye was a spirit come t' haunt 'im. 'She's been through enough for one night.' "

Georgina made her way down the long gallery toward the library in the east wing, the sarcenet gown flowing about her limbs as she walked a constant reminder of the coming interview with the Duke of Rathbourne. She could not dismiss the lowering feeling that in wearing the dress she had already submitted to Rathbourne's subjugation. At least Emberly had provided the funds for the exquisite creation, she comforted herself, for she had been tempted to discard the gown in favor of one of her old ones. Indeed, she had not done so only because she was ruefully aware that she herself had requested Rathbourne to have the new wardrobe made up and delivered to her, thus rendering such a childish gesture foolish in the extreme. She suffered a sudden pang at the memory of Rathbourne as he had been that afternoon a lifetime ago, gently teasing, his deep voice vibrant with what she had believed was an affectionate warmth.

"Drat the man!" she muttered out loud and with an effort dismissed the duke from her thoughts as she came at last to the library and reached for the doorhandle.

The muffled burr of voices drifting to her from beyond the closed door brought a puzzled frown to her brow. The library had ever been considered the countess's private domain, and except for the servants who maintained it in its polished state, no one ever trespassed its boundaries without Lady Grey's invitation.

Georgina drew sharply back at the sound of the latch slipping free. Momentarily she froze as the door swung open and the faint scent of shaving soap and clean linen assailed her nostrils. Then suddenly she sank into a graceful curtsy all the more eloquent for its deliberate irony.

"Your Grace," she murmured in frigid tones and, rising again to her full, willowy height, confronted the duke with steely composure.

If she had surprised him with her uncanny ability to identify those around her ere they spoke, he gave no sign of it. Indeed, his languid drawl revealed nothing of his inner thoughts even to her discerning ear.

"Lady Grey," he said, and she could not quite suppress the involuntary trembling in her limbs as strong, slender fingers clasped and held her hand. In the sudden, disquieting silence which stretched between them, she could feel his eyes intent upon her. No doubt the heavy-lidded orbs were as maddeningly cool and unrevealing as his voice, she thought, her chin going up in quick annoyance. Oh, how she wished that she might just once be able to *see* the deceitful countenance! But then Rathbourne had broken the hateful silence, and she found herself suddenly hardput indeed to maintain her studied air of imperturbability.

"You do not appear to have profited greatly from a night's rest, madam," he observed sardonically. "If you are feeling indisposed, perhaps it were better to have remained in your bed. You are not, I trust, *prone* to fainting spells?"

Georgina, quick to hide the helpless flash of anger in her eyes, inclined her head in a semblance of gracious humility.

"I beg your forgiveness, Your Grace," she rejoined in

sarcastic, even tones, "for having disgraced myself in your presence. I assure you I am not in the habit of swooning and cannot guess what came over me."

"Can you not?" he murmured provocatively. "But possibly the precipitating cause has slipped your mind. Need I remind you, madam, of my purpose in coming here today?"

Oh, the man was despicable! she thought, the blood leaping in her veins. How dared he taunt her with his infamous proposal. But with an effort she mastered once again the swift rush of anger, knowing that to lose control was to put herself at his mercy. Indeed, she must remain calm if she hoped to hold on to the mental image of her surroundings which she had so painstakingly constructed over the weeks spent at Greystone.

Georgina summoned a frosty smile.

"You need remind me of nothing, Your Grace," she said bitterly. "Indeed, your iniquity is indelibly etched upon my memory. I shall never forget it, nor find it in my heart to forgive you for it ever."

"Indeed," he murmured so strangely that for a moment she thought she detected something of pain or bitterness in his tone. But then the moment was gone, as he continued in his former manner, his languid drawl as dispassionately world-weary as before.

"You surprise me, madam," he murmured mockingly, and she flinched involuntarily, her lovely eyes igniting sparks of resentment as he flicked her chin with a careless finger. "Such fiery passion beneath so cool and lovely an exterior. My cousin must have counted himself fortunate to possess such a wife."

"And how *un*fortunate that he never knew the true nature of the man he loved better than a brother," she replied scathingly. "But surely such matters were better left for our ears alone, Your Grace," she continued pointedly after only the briefest pause. "Perhaps I should return later when your—guest—has departed?"

"On the contrary," he demurred without the faintest trace of discomfiture. "Fenton was on the point of leaving."

"Fenton?" Georgina blurted in stunned disbelief, but the familiar, wheedling voice jarring on her nerves immediately confirmed the man's identity.

"*Ais*, milady. I were just leavin'."

Georgina stepped involuntarily back as she heard Anson Fenton come toward her and, mumbling unctuously, shuffle past her to the door. She was aware that the duke stepped briefly into the hall and heard his low voice issuing what sounded like orders though she could not quite make out the gist of what he said. Then she had turned and groped her way across the room to the bay window where she stood drinking in the sweet drafts of fresh air in an attempt to steady her whirling brain.

Discovering Rathbourne closeted with Fenton had unsettled her more than she liked to admit even to herself, though she did not clearly apprehend why it should have done. No doubt Rathbourne was merely keeping to his promise to look into the matter of Denby's mishap. And yet had he not said that he would have someone less liable to arouse suspicion among the stablehands do the questioning? And if he had changed his mind and decided to do the thing himself, then surely there was nothing odd in his having summoned Fenton to the library for a private inquiry, she told herself, but was not convinced. No. There was something else which bothered her even more than Fenton's actual presence with the duke in Greystone's library. There was the matter of the voices she had briefly overheard upon arriving outside the library door.

There had been two masculine voices issuing from behind the closed door, and one of them she now knew of a certainty had belonged to Rathbourne. But the other had not been Fenton's unctuous whine. At least not Fenton's voice as she knew it. For though she had not been able to distinguish the words, she had caught the subtleties of pitch, intonation, and inflectional pattern, and these had not been consistent either with the stablehand's illiterate manner of speech or with his Cornish burr. Indeed, upon hearing the indistinct exchange of words, she had immediately presumed the library's occupants both to be men of education and culture.

Who was Fenton? Georgina fretted. Indeed, *what* was he? A simple Cornish fisherman down on his luck? A dangerous felon capable of trying to murder Denby? Or something quite different, perhaps even more sinister? And what had he to do with Rathbourne, if anything?

She was not to be given time, however, to ponder the bewildering complexity of riddles, for suddenly she was made aware of Rathbourne standing at her shoulder.

"How unfortunate, madam, that you should have arrived before I had finished with Fenton," he observed enigmatically.

"Unfortunate, Your Grace?" Georgina queried, turning her head ever so slightly toward him.

"Obviously you entertain an aversion for the man," he replied easily enough. "I should have preferred to spare you his disturbing presence."

"Whereas, *I* should have preferred to be present for the entire interview, my lord duke. Indeed, I should like very much to know what you have learned from him."

"No doubt, madam, and yet since such matters need no longer concern you, I shan't presume to burden you with what Fenton had to say."

"Not concern me?" Georgina exclaimed incredulously. "And who, pray tell, should they concern if not the Countess of Emberly?"

"As the earl's guardian, madam, the affairs of Emberly are solely within my province, I believe. In point of fact, it remains to be seen whether you shall retain any influence over the earl himself, does it not?"

"And if I were to tell you that I have decided to accept your proposal, should I still be allowed to raise my son as I see fit?" she demanded, turning at last to face him. "What assurance can I have that you shall keep your word, my lord duke, when you have dared already to betray my trust and David's?"

Her bitter accusation seemed to hang in the air as she waited for Rathbourne's answer, her bosom heaving and her lovely countenance white with the intensity of her feeling.

"You can have none, madam," replied the duke dispassionately. "In point of fact, you can be certain of only one thing. That you shall have *no* part in your son's future do you refuse to become my wife."

For a moment Georgina was filled with a sense of bitter defeat. Rathbourne thought to destroy her very soul, she thought, but quickly she rallied the remnants of her will, telling herself that no matter what she might be made to suffer, she must yet be strong for Davey's sake.

"I see. Then I have no choice but to accept the honor of your proposal, Your Grace," she managed without a quiver of emotion and dropped into a deep, formal curtsy. "I shall strive to be a dutiful wife, my lord duke. In return for which I ask only one thing."

"And that is . . . ?" queried His Grace, taking her hand in his and bidding her to rise.

"I do not know why you have chosen to destroy the affection which I once had for you. But since there can never again be any real feeling between us, I ask only for a semblance of a happy marriage and only that for the sake of my son. He must never know that I have entered into this agreement against my will. You must swear to this, my lord duke, on whatever you most hold dear."

Rathbourne's fingers tightened once about her hand then abruptly released her. For a long moment he made no answer, and when at last he spoke, she realized he must have turned away from her, for his voice was oddly muffled.

"So be it madam," he said with utter finality. "Upon my honor as Penwarren and a Duke of the Realm, I swear the boy shall not learn from me how this day was wrought. In all eyes but yours I shall ever appear the doting husband. And may God have mercy on us!"

Later Georgina was to think his last statement singularly odd in the circumstances. But at the moment of her betrothal to Andrew Addison Randall, Earl of Penwarren, Baron Stanhope, Ridgley, and Ives, Viscount Raleigh and Earl of Parnell, Marquis of Saint-Vere, and eleventh Duke of Rathbourne, she was aware of little more than a vague feeling of paralysis accompanied by a certain relief that it was over and done. However, as it soon transpired, her relief was to be short-lived, for Rathbourne had not yet finished with her.

"In anticipation of your immediate removal from Emberly, madam, I have made arrangements for the transportation of your trunks and whatever personal effects you may deem necessary for yourself, Miss Kingsley, and the earl. Anything else can wait until after you have become acquainted with Rathbourne Castle and have a better understanding of your needs."

"But I have no intention of leaving Emberly in such haste!" Georgina exclaimed. "Indeed, I see no need for my removal to Rathbourne until the day of our wedding."

"But I quite agree, madam," Rathbourne replied ironically. "And since that auspicious event shall occur three days hence, I suggest that you make ready."

Georgina could never after remember how she found her way from the scene of her ignominy to the safe haven of her bedroom. Grateful, however, that neither Gilda nor Nanny was waiting in attendance on her return, she bolted the door and flung herself in despair across her bed.

Bitterly she chided herself for an utter fool. Why did she

never consider the possibility that Rathbourne might have thought while in London to acquire a special license, thus enabling him to forego the banns? How well he had laid his plans! All the time she had been living a pipe-dream here at Greystone, even being so naive as to long for his return, and *he* had been cold-bloodedly going about the final preparations for her downfall. It simply did not bear thinking on.

And yet she must think. She must think more clearly than she ever had before. There must be *something* she could do to avert the final tragedy.

Never had she yearned with greater anguish to be able to *see* again! If she were no longer blind, *nothing* should stop her from making her way out of Cornwall to Exeter and her Grandmama. Lady Bellows was not without influence at court, and even Rathbourne would not dare to defy the Prince Regent had she managed somehow to gain *his* support. And even in the event that all else failed, she might still have taken her son and fled Britain to live in exile till Davey should have safely reached his majority. But she could do none of these in her present state. At least not without help. And the one man who might have aided her was lying unconscious in the Rose Room, the victim of a bizarre accident or worse.

"Denby!" she uttered out loud and sat suddenly bolt upright on the bed. Only Denby possessed the resourcefulness to have pulled it off, and only Denby, the tough little Cockney whose loyalty was ever to her and her alone, would have dared to defy the Cornish duke. And doubtless Rathbourne had known it all along. Heaven help them all, she thought, appalled at where her reasoning had led her. For it seemed suddenly quite clear to her that if Denby had in truth been deliberately laid low, she had stumbled inadvertently across the missing motive. Nor was that all. If Rathbourne had indeed been the instigator of Denby's "accident" and if Anson Fenton had been his tool, then might not the mystery surrounding her cousin's odd behavior be likewise understood?

"Good God. I must be going mad!" Georgina exclaimed and rose in a daze from the bed to wander in nervous starts about the room.

He *could* not be so villainous, she told herself, and yet she could not stop the damning chain of circumstance from building feverishly in her brain. For if Rathbourne *had* seen Denby as Georgina's probable ally and, worse, a liability because he was David's former batman and an outsider who not only knew his way about in the larger world but who would not be hindered by the Cornish sense of provincialism, how must he have viewed Zenobia, her kinswoman? Might he not have sent Fenton to threaten and intimidate her in the hopes that she would be driven from Greystone and Georgina? Or upon realizing that Zenobia and Robbie had developed a tendre for one another, would he not have seen the likelihood of their eventual marriage as a further complication and done his best to prevent it?

Georgina froze in her tracks, a hand pressed over her heart hammering painfully within her breast as piece after piece of the damning puzzle seemed to fall into place.

At Rathbourne's instigation, Fenton must have sought out Zenobia to warn her away from Robbie, even going so far as to lay his hands on her, at which time Denby must have happened on them. Zenobia had fled to the house while Denby remained behind to exchange heated words, perhaps even blows, with his underling. What had passed between them? Georgina wondered. Had Denby learned that Fenton was Rathbourne's hireling? Was that when Fenton had decided in his employer's absence to take matters into his own hands?

It all seemed to make such dreadful sense in everything except that she still perceived no reason *why* Rathbourne should have done any of it.

"He must be mad!" she declared to the empty room.

"Or perhaps it is *I* who am losing my mind." For in truth she seemed to be living some terrible nightmare.

"Denby," she whispered stridently. "I must talk to Denby."

She slipped out of her room and made her way along the long gallery with as much outward calm as she could summon. Unaccountably her heart began to pound as she neared the stairs and heard Rathbourne's voice issuing from somewhere below. Telling herself there was no reason why she should feel like a prisoner in her own house, she stepped boldly on to the landing and proceeded across to the east wing and down the hall, till at last she came to the Rose Room.

"Denby?" she called softly as she pushed open the door and stepped over the threshold into the room.

There was a sudden movement and the soft rustling of skirts.

"Was you lookin' fer someone, milady?" said a woman's voice.

"Mrs. Porter?" Georgina queried in surprise.

"*Ais*, milady. I were just changing the linen and tidyin' up a bit. Is anything wrong, milady?"

"No. No, everything's fine, I'm sure. I just came up to look in on Denby."

"But Denby isn't here, milady."

"N-not here?" Georgina repeated in sudden alarm. "But where is he then?"

"I'm sure I couldn't say, milady," replied the housekeeper. "His Grace never mentioned where the poor man was to be taken. Only that since you and Miss Kingsley were leaving soon for Rathbourne, he'd made arrangements for Denby to go where he'd be well taken care of. We're to close up the house, milady, and except for Bolton, myself, and a few others who'll stay to look after things, His Grace has found places for everyone at Rathbourne."

"Oh, yes. Of course," Georgina murmured distractedly

as she sought to assimilate this startling new information.

"Will there be anything else, milady?" the housekeeper asked in such a manner as to leave little doubt that she thought her mistress was behaving strangely.

"What? Oh. No, Mrs. Porter. There's nothing else. Thank you," Georgina managed and, stepping into the hall, closed the door behind her.

For a moment she stood too stunned to move. Then suddenly she was swept by a terrible rage.

How dared Rathbourne remove Denby without telling her! she fumed. Well, he wouldn't get away with it. She'd not take a step beyond Greystone's doors till she had been thoroughly satisfied as to Denby's well-being. And to a lot more, she vowed grimly as she made her way down the hall to the stairs in search of His Grace of Rathbourne.

Chapter 11

"Gina, what more do you want from me? I've *told* you all I can. You must believe me," Miss Kingsley pleaded, but her cousin's stony expression failed to soften. Nor had it done since Zenobia had been summoned to her presence some twenty minutes past. Miss Kingsley drew her bottom lip between her teeth as she noted the dark shadows beneath her cousin's eyes like bruises against the pallor of her skin and thought the countess had not the look of a bride on the eve of her wedding day. Indeed, Georgina resembled more a woman on the edge of a nervous decline, she worried and wished she could somehow relieve her cousin of whatever troubled her.

If only Rathbourne would release her from her word to reveal nothing of Fenton's identity or his purpose here! Georgina should then at least be spared the burden of not knowing. And later, when her cousin knew the truth, would she not hate her for having kept her in the dark?

Miss Kingsley recoiled from such a thought. Long ago she had reconciled herself to losing Robbie's love. Now must she also forfeit Gina's? Oh, why had she not told her cousin the truth from the beginning!

The countess stirred, appearing to rouse herself from the brown study into which she had fallen.

"Tell me again what happened," she said, her forehead

creased as if her head pained her so that she had to force herself to concentrate. "There must me something, some clue in all of this, which has escaped me somehow."

Reluctantly Zenobia drew breath and began for the second time to relate the sequence of events surrounding her confrontation with Anson Fenton.

"He waylaid me in the park just as I've already told you," she said with scant forbearance, then suddenly keenly aware of her cousin sitting stone-still before the blazing fire and of the wind moaning about the walls of Rathbourne Castle, she began to pace nervously about the room as she talked.

"Fenton seemed agitated and kept looking over his shoulder as if he expected someone to come along at any time. And someone did come—Denby. Only it wasn't what Denby thought. Fenton had—said something which upset me, and I—I must have grown faint for a moment. Fenton grabbed me to keep me from falling, and that's when Denby found us. I tried to tell him everything was all right, but he wouldn't listen. He said something about some people not being all they were painted up to be. Then he told me that it would be better if I didn't stay to see what was about to happen. There didn't seem to be anything I could say or do to change his mind, and—and when Fenton said that it *was* best that I do as Denby said, well, I—I ran!"

"And Fenton said he had come to warn you that trouble was afoot and that he had seen a man spying on the house. Is that all he told you?" Georgina queried tonelessly.

"Yes. That's all," Miss Kingsley agreed. "Except that I should watch out for myself because young beauties caught out alone in the woods had been known to suddenly vanish. Oh, Georgina. I was so frightened. I didn't know what to do." Miss Kingsley shuddered and turned suddenly to the window to look out over the restless sea and the breakers pounding against the cliffs on which Rathbourne Castle stood lonely sentinel.

"Nobie, *why* did you never tell me any of this before?" Georgina demanded, torn between hurt and anger. "Have I seemed such an ogre that you dared not come to me for help?"

Zenobia turned swiftly back to her cousin.

"Oh, no, Gina. Of course you have not!" she hastened to reply. "Indeed, you have been everything which is kind."

"Then why did you not come to me?" Georgina persisted in uncompromising tones, for she was somehow certain that her cousin had not told her all the truth. Indeed, she was utterly out of patience with the girl's closeness, that impenetrable wall of uncommunicativeness which lent an aura of secrecy to everything about her.

"I—I don't *know* why," uttered the girl in sudden anguish. "I suppose I didn't want to burden you with my problems. It has seemed of late that you had enough on your mind without my adding to it. Besides, there was nothing you could have done. Indeed. There's nothing anyone can do. Oh, Gina, I have been such a fool!"

A flurried rapping at the door to the sitting room, which was only one in a luxurious suite of rooms to which the countess had been ushered upon her arrival at the castle earlier that morning, prevented whatever Georgina had been about to reply to her cousin's outburst.

For the space of a heartbeat neither cousin moved. Then Georgina inhaled and nodded once toward Miss Kingsley.

"See who it is, Nobie. You and I shall finish talking later," she said coldly and, rising with deliberation from the plush velvet loveseat ranged before the fireplace, turned to face the door, her hands clasped tightly before her and her back held almost rigidly straight as she waited for her cousin to admit their caller.

Zenobia cast a single, eloquent glance at her cousin's frozen countenance. Briefly her slim shoulders seemed to sag, then abruptly she straightened, and her lovely features assumed once more their normally guarded expression as she crossed obediently to the door and opened it to a vaguely familiar woman whose periwinkle blue cambric high gown and Spanish robe of the first stare of fashion proclaimed her a lady of some wealth and position. Zenobia judged her to be in her early thirties.

"Good morning. You are Miss Kingsley, are you not," observed the lady, smiling with friendly interest. "I have looked forward to meeting you, my dear, for I was used to be acquainted with your mother, and I liked her very well. I believe you have more the look of your father, however. Such a fine, handsome man."

"Yes, he was," replied Miss Kingsley hesitantly, a trifle startled by the exquisitely gowned lady who had bustled past her into the room.

There was an instant of pregnant silence as the strange visitor caught sight of Georgina and abruptly paused, an expression of compassion flickering briefly across her face. But almost immediately she appeared to recall herself and, smiling with obviously sincere warmth, hurried toward the countess, her hands extended in joyful greeting.

"Georgina!" she cried, grasping the countess's hands in her own. "How good it is to see you. When my cousin appeared so unexpectedly in Brighton to tell me you were come home again and to ask me to Rathbourne to serve as his hostess, I could not agree quickly enough. But depend on Rathbourne to keep to himself the best news. I am deliriously happy for you both, my dear. And I know it is just what David would have wanted."

Georgina, confused and a trifle overcome at the lady's effulgent greeting, winced involuntarily at the unexpected reference to David and his probable feelings in the matter of her betrothal to his cousin. Then suddenly it came to her who her caller was.

"Kate?" she queried in dawning gladness. "Katey Ingram? Is it really you?"

"But of course it is, gudgeon," replied Lady Ingram with a rather watery chuckle. "Who else would be so foolish as to abandon Brighton at the height of the summer season and brave the desolation of Cornwall just to see you, Georgina Grey? Though why I should have done, when you have not dropped me a single line in all these years just to let me know how you went on, I couldn't begin to say. But here I am. And I couldn't be more pleased to see anyone, even if I do find you looking even more stunning than when you dazzled the *ton* as a green girl and took the town by storm. I, on the other hand, have grown overly plump and quite matronly. But, alas! I fear one who is the fond mother of seven hopefuls can expect little else."

"Oh, Kate. *Seven*?" Georgina queried in mock-dismay, her vibrant laughter bubbling forth as she sank down on the loveseat and pulled Lady Kathryn down beside her.

"I daresay it *is* amusing that I should have excelled in the one area in which I least wished to have done," reflected Lady Kathryn with characteristically dry humor. "For I am sure I remember confiding in you my ambition to be a famous hostess among the *ton*. And one is never at one's best in the latest fashions or cavorting about the dance floor when one is forever breeding. However, I have since discovered that, like it or not, I have been blessed with an incontrovertible aptitude for motherhood, which I have subsequently learned not to allow to interfere overly with my other pursuits. Indeed, I feel quite certain that my darling Ferdie and I shall not be allowed to stop at a mere seven."

"Oh, Kate," Georgina gasped when she could find her voice again. "It *is* good to have you here. It seems a very long time since I have laughed with such abandon. And I have been looking forward with such dread to the next few days. But with you to remind me of life's little absurdities, doubtless I shall contrive to rub along well enough in spite of everything."

"But of course you will," Lady Kathryn hastened to agree, for she had not missed at the end of Georgina's speech the faint note of desperation in the low-pitched voice or the brief flicker of what seemed very like despair in the lovely eyes. "Indeed, how could you not with Drew by your side?" she added, thinking to further banish what she mistakenly had assumed was, especially in Georgina's particular circumstances, a not unnatural nervousness at the prospect not only of becoming a bride, but of being thrust shortly afterward among a sizeable gathering of strangers. "You of all people must know how totally he dotes on you. Indeed, it is truly marvelous the change in him, for I must confess I had come to believe there wasn't a woman alive who could breach Rathbourne's formidable defenses."

"Has His Grace never been in love then?" queried Georgina curiously, having placed little credence in Katey Ingram's evaluation of the duke's regard for his betrothed. Obviously Rathbourne was keeping to his word that none but Georgina and he should know the truth of their feelings for one another, or the lack thereof. And, indeed, he must be a consummate actor, for Kathryn Ingram was no one's fool, no matter how she rattled on at times.

"Heavens no. Drew has never been one to allow any female too close. Not even I, for whom I am reasonably sure he entertains a certain cousinly affection. Actually I don't suppose he has ever trusted anyone with his intimate thoughts, except for David and to a lesser extent David's father and Robbie."

Lady Kathryn paused reflectively, and when she resumed again, it was with a certain bitter sadness which Georgina had never detected in her before.

"Of course, there was Drew's father," she said in a peculiarly metallic voice. "Not that Drew was ever on *intimate* terms with that flint-hearted, unnatural excuse for a human being. But unaccountably Drew loved him, as only a son can love a father who forever looms as some sort of unattainable, lofty ideal. But the duke could never see anything but his heir's supposed imperfections. Drew eventually learned to hide behind a veneer of cynicism and a discerning heart which led him to anonymously provide the funds, among other things, necessary for his poor relation's come-out in London and later the marriage portion to make her an eligible *partie*. Not that the latter mattered all that much to Ferdie, as it turned out, but with someone else it might have done."

"You?" exclaimed Georgina in no little amazement.

"None other," Lady Kathryn affirmed with a knowing smile. "Obviously you didn't know my father had been disowned by his brother the duke for having married beneath his station. He allowed us to live in near penury rather than accept my mother. The duke was a cold, unfeeling man right up to the moment he was laid on his deathbed. A virulent case of influenza was the diagnosis of the attending physician. But I have always believed he perished from penury of the soul. Actually, dying was the greatest kindness he ever did anyone."

"How greatly you must have hated the duke still to speak so of him after all these years," Georgina murmured in a troubled voice. "Surely it were better to forgive and forget?"

"I believed I had," Lady Kathryn replied oddly, as if she had only just realized the truth of her feelings. "Indeed, I had not thought of this place in years, or all the suffering I witnessed here. It was not until I saw Drew again after so very long and realized that he had not yet laid to rest his father's ghost that I began to remember. And then being here in Rathbourne brings everything back again."

She paused abruptly, and Miss Kingsley who had remained a forgotten witness to all which had passed between the two women, saw her fix Georgina with a keenly penetrating stare.

"You don't think I hated my uncle for what he did to me," she queried with such suddenness that Georgina jumped.

"But did you not?" rejoined the countess, wondering at her friend's odd vehemence.

"No. Not because of what he did to me, but because of what he did to Drew! Perhaps if you had known my cousin as I did, indeed, as David did, you would understand what Rathbourne and this castle have wrought in him. The truth be known, Greystone Manor was more a home to Drew Penwarren than ever was this ancient mausoleum. And the old Earl of Emberly more a father."

Lady Kathryn hesitated then, seeming to recollect herself.

"But surely none of this is to the point," she said, leaning forward to warmly grasp Georgina's hands. "This dreadful castle is dreary enough without resurrecting old ghosts which should have been laid to rest long ago. I want to hear all about you and Drew."

"Yes, of course," Georgina murmured, taken off guard, and, lowering her head as though to hide an embarrassed blush, made a frantic effort to gather her wits. Quickly deciding it was best to adhere as closely to the truth as possible without betraying the real state of affairs between Rathbourne and herself, she summoned the semblance of a smile and began what was meant to be a purely factual account of the events leading up to her betrothal. It was not long, however, before Georgina, who had been endowed with a natural wit and a keen sense of the absurd, found herself describing with lively humor her first encounter with the arrogant duke in the rose-garden at Greystone.

"We were practically on the point of coming to blows," she observed, laughing quite unaffectedly, "when Bolton came to the rescue. He had come to the garden to announce my cousin's arrival, you see. How I should have liked to see the duke's face when he discovered the basis of his entire tirade against me was rendered suddenly and irrefutably groundless. Though I very much doubt," she added with a wry grimace, "that one could have read much behind that arrogant facade. I used to wonder often what he was thinking when I would catch him watching me for seemingly hours on end, with those marvelous blue eyes like the Cornish sea. You could quite literally drown in them," she ended whimsically, her voice trailing off and her face assuming a faraway expression as she appeared to lose herself in some distant memory.

"But I was under the impression you met Drew at Greystone," observed Lady Kathryn, exchanging startled glances with Miss Kingsley.

"I beg your pardon?" Georgina murmured, only slowly losing her abstracted air. "What did you say?"

"I thought that you had only just met Rathbourne since your return from Portugal."

"Why, yes," Georgina nodded unself-consciously. "You must recall how disappointed David was when he could not locate his cousin for our wedding. And we were never sure afterward exactly where he had gone. Until that day in the rose-garden, I had never once suspected he, too, had been on the Peninsula."

"But, Gina. You just said . . . ," Miss Kingsley began, then fell abruptly silent at Lady Ingram's meaningful shake of the head.

"I just said what, Nobie?" queried Georgina, cocking her head intently in Miss Kingsley's direction.

"Why, nothing which was not full of wit," Lady Ingram smoothly remarked. "And vastly entertaining. It would seem to me that my cousin has met his match in you, Georgina. Indeed, I suspect he has at last discovered an infallible cure for his chronic state of ennui. And now I think it is time I was going," she said and, rising to her feet, observed with characteristic candor that the bride-to-be would better profit from a long nap than from her wagging tongue. Then suggesting that Miss Kingsley join her for a comfortable coze in her apartments that they might become better acquainted, she departed as brusquely as she had come, taking Zenobia with her.

Georgina, however, was disinclined to heed her friend's advice to indulge in a nap before they were summoned to dinner, which, since Rathbourne had announced they would keep country hours for the time being, would be scarcely four hours hence. She had far too much preying on her mind to allow for sleep. Nor had she any wish to invite a recurrence of the nightmares which had begun to visit her with ever greater frequency. Thus she sat at length before the fire, pondering all that she had learned that day.

What was it that Lady Kathryn saw in her arrogant cousin to inspire such sympathy? she wondered with a sense of unreality, for she could scarce believe her friend had been talking about the same man who had threatened to take a child from its mother lest she agree to marry him. Indeed, she was astounded at the obviously deep affection Kathryn Ingram bore the present Duke of Rathbourne and likened it to the same, unshakable devotion which had characterized David's obsession for his cousin. As for the *former* duke, David had seldom mentioned him except to say that his cousin's father had died when Drew Penwarren was quite young. Even so, she had always sensed her husband's disaffection. Perhaps he had not hated his uncle as Kate did, but nor had he grieved that he was dead.

Georgina shivered as a sudden blast of wind shook the leaded window panes. The chill, damp air which lingered within the thick stone walls seemed to penetrate to her very bones. What a cold and dreary place this was to be sure, she thought and pulled the kerseymere shawl more snugly about her shoulders.

And yet, upon first arriving, she had thought that under different circumstances she might have adjusted quite easily to her new home, might even have come rather quickly to enjoy a keen pleasure in her surroundings, for she had always been fascinated by the sea and, further, had sensed an immediate accord with the untamed aura of the castle set so dramatically on rugged cliffs buffeted by wind and sea. Indeed, Rathbourne Castle had called to something equally wild and restless in herself which had once led her to accept with a greater eagerness than David's the nomadic existence of a soldier and a soldier's wife. It had long since lain dormant within her, banished forever, she had believed, at the death of her beloved and the onset of her blindness.

How odd to have felt it stir once more within her at the sound of the surf pounding against the cliffs and at the feel and, indeed, the smell of the salt air assailing her senses! And how unsettling to know that less than a week past she had come close to picturing herself in her daydreams as proud chatelaine of the castle on the sea and, unbelievably, as Rathbourne's loving wife! It was ironic, Georgina bitterly reflected, that while the duke had made the gist of her daydreams inescapable fact, he had utterly destroyed the fantasy.

A plague on the man! she thought, recalled to an awareness of her plight. She stiffened involuntarily, her head lifting in angry defiance as she called to mind the previous day's disastrous confrontation with the duke in the great hall at Greystone. She would never forgive or forget his arrogant refusal to tell her anything of Denby beyond a brusque assurance that the injured groom was safe and well on the way to recovery. Nor how unmercifully he had humiliated her when she had claimed she would not set foot from Greystone till he had relented. She felt the blood rush to her cheeks as she remembered with helpless fury the duke's cold assertion that he had little patience for vaporish females and that, further, whether or not she chose to accompany him to Rathbourne on the morrow was her own affair. He had no intention of humoring her childish starts.

But the young Earl of Emberly, along with his new tutor, would indeed depart as planned with or without his mama.

She had had no choice but to summon the shattered remnants of her dignity, and to retreat with as much grace as was possible in order to prepare for her immediate removal from Greystone—and her imminent wedding to the Duke of Rathbourne.

They had left her beloved Greystone—Rathbourne, Miss Kingsley, Davey with his tutor, and Georgina—immediately following an early breakfast, which she had left untouched, and had ridden the intervening ten miles without a stop. And though she had been distracted at first by Davey's buoyant chatter, they had not gone many miles before she began to feel the strain of having to appear as usual before him. Thus she had been almost glad when at last they had come to Rathbourne.

The castle had been rife with a bewildering array of scents and sounds as Rathbourne led her mount through the gatehouse and into the flagstone courtyard. When he lifted her from the saddle and set her on her feet, she had not been able to resist testing the fragrant air with keen pleasure.

"We are inside the original walls raised by the first Earl of Rathbourne at the command of William the Conqueror," he had announced. As if he had only just become conscious of her presence, Georgina brooded in unconscious pique, for those had been the first words he had spoken to her since they had embarked on the interminable journey from Greystone.

"Before you is the keep which has been greatly enlarged and modernized by succeeding generations, some of it in the style of Adams," he had further informed her. "There are several enclosed gardens set within the walls. But perhaps you have already gathered as much."

"There is the scent of lilacs in the air," she had responded in spite of herself, "as well as sweet-williams. And

263

wintergreen, I think, mingled with mint. The woods press about. There is the scent of bracken and blackthorn blossoms and probably mulberry."

She had been about to mention horehound and elderflower when a sudden, raucous cry issuing nearly at her feet surprised a startled "Oh!" from her. Yet the unexpected rumble of Rathbourne's chuckle had startled her even more.

"Softly," he said, his voice vibrant with humor so that, her heart lurching painfully, she was reminded of a different duke, the one who had seemed her dear and trusted friend. "It is only a Cornish chough which has been tamed and allowed the freedom of the grounds."

"A Cornish chough?" she had queried, unable to constrain her natural curiosity. He had then favored her with a vivid description of the crow-like birds with their red legs and bill, and feathers of a peculiar violaceous black. They made their nests in the cliffs, he told her, and since they were easily tamed, it was not uncommon to see them contentedly perched on a Cornishman's ironwork garden gate or atop the 'piskey pow,' the decorative roof tile on which the 'little people' were alleged to dance on moonlit nights.

As if inspired by Georgina's rapt attention, he had gone on to describe the wooded hills slashed with deep ravines which formed the backdrop for the castle and were abundant with pheasant, deer, and wood grouse, as well as songbirds, squirrels, and other wild creatures. She could almost see Glangorn Gill hurtling over the cliffs into the sea below, so vividly did he portray it, and the narrow inlets and protected coves as well, in one of which was moored his ketch, *The Swallow*.

"The third Earl of Rathbourne caused a tunnel to be excavated from the castle grounds to the grottos below," he said, "and thus made it possible to reach 'the zawns' undetected by land or sea. As he was something of a pirate, it was naturally to his advantage to keep his comings and goings shrouded in secrecy, an advantage similarly enjoyed by the ninth duke, my grandfather, who was not averse to encouraging what Cornishmen like to think of as 'free' on 'fair trade.' A practice which my father abhorred and for which he expended a deal of time and effort to bring to an end. Fortunately he never went so far as to have the tunnel destroyed, with the result that I became quite adept as a boy at eluding my several tutors by stealing into its depths and beyond to a small catboat and the freedom of the wind and the Cornish sea."

What a puzzling man he was, Georgina thought as she rose from the loveseat and groped her way across the room to the window overlooking the sea upon which a much younger Rathbourne had found moments of release from his oppressive existence. In truth, it was as if he were many men all rolled up into one. To David he had been a hero and to Kathryn Ingram a sensitive and caring benefactor. She herself had in turn considered him a hardened rake-shame, an irresponsible fribble, a dear and thoughtful friend—indeed, someone she might have loved had it not been for David—and finally a blackguard and a villain. And today she had glimpsed yet another Rathbourne, a man with a deep and abiding passion for his native Cornwall, a man who loved his home.

To which of these would she find herself wed at this time tomorrow?

A soft scratching at the door interrupted the countess's troubled thoughts. Turning from the window, she called out, "Who is it?"

Immediately she heard the door open and the quick step of someone coming into the room.

"I tol' Lady Ingram ye'd not be in yer bed," observed a gruff voice. "If'n I'd 'ad me own way I'd 'ave come t'make certain o' ye, Mistress."

"Nanny!" Georgina cried, sinking rather weakly on to

the window seat. "How ever do you come to be here? I thought you would be well on your way to my cousin in Kent by now."

"Harumph! T'ain't likely I'd leave me lass when she 'ad need o' me. Wilkins brung me on one o' th' wagons wot carried yer trunks. 'Tis a wilderness 'Is Grace 'as brung ye to, Missy. There b'ain't no roads t'speak on. Only two ruts wot no respect'ble gennelman's coach'd last more'n it took t' jar a wheel loose. 'Tis th' Lord's own blessin' I be 'ere atall."

"And, indeed, I'm grateful. But you should not have disobeyed my orders, Nanny," Georgina said, torn between joy at having her dearest old Nanny once more with her and concern for the elderly retainer's well-being. She little liked to think of Nanny having to navigate the many narrow stairs and drafty passageways to serve her mistress. And, what was more, she had earned the cozy little cottage at Edgecombe where she would be near her family and her old friends from happier days.

"Me cot'll still be there when I be ready fer it," Nanny declared stolidly. "But if'n ye doesn't bestir yerself, belike ye'll miss yer supper, Mistress."

The countess, however, shook her head, a look of stubbornness about the lovely mouth.

"I shan't be going down to dinner," she said firmly and wrapped her shawl more snugly about her. "You may inform His Grace that I am suffering from a headache and have chosen to keep to my rooms this evening."

Nanny suddenly cleared her throat, and Georgina stiffened at an inexplicable tingling of her nerves.

"I am grieved to hear you are feeling indisposed, madam," observed Rathbourne's acerbic drawl from the doorway. "Indeed, I should be considerably disappointed to be denied the charming presence of my betrothed on the eve of our wedding day. I have been informed that the tray sent up to you at nuncheon was returned untouched. Might

266

I suggest that a hot meal is the surest cure for whatever ails you?"

"You may of course suggest whatever you wish, Your Grace," returned Georgina, coolly inclining her head in the duke's direction. How dared he eavesdrop on her private conversation! "This is, after all, your house. However, I assure you 'tis not sustenance which can cure my ills, but something quite different. Indeed, I find myself with little appetite either for food or company and most humbly beg you will excuse me from attending the evening repast."

If she had thought to appeal to her betrothed's *savoir-faire*, she was soon to be disappointed, for quite to the contrary, the duke's response displayed a total disregard of what was civil.

"I regret, madam, that I cannot oblige you in this instance. Nor am I inclined to humor what I must presume to be a childish disregard for your own well-being. You, madam, will dress as befits my future duchess, after which you will graciously take your place of honor at my table," he commanded, apparently oblivious to Georgina's sharply indrawn breath at his imperious speech.

"Indeed I shall not, Your Grace," she returned witheringly. "Place of honor, sir? It is obvious that despite your noble rank your manners are as doubtful as this supposed honor."

Nanny Slade, observing the dangerous glitter in Georgina's eyes and the sudden tight-lipped whiteness about the duke's firm mouth, was suddenly hard-put to keep from grinning from ear to ear. Egad, but th' lass were on 'er 'igh-'orse, she were, and about time, too, if some'un was to ask Nanny Slade. For the old nurse had long prayed for the re-awakening of her mistress's fighting mettle—and for the man strong enough to match it.

"Quite so, my love," Rathbourne agreed in a voice of finely honed steel. "And since we agree that I am indeed the unprincipled rakeshame the world has named me, I suggest you would do well not to cross swords with me. Rest assured that, should the necessity arise, I should neither hesitate to strip and dress you myself nor restrain from carrying you kicking and screaming down to dinner. Have I made myself quite clear?"

"Oh!" exclaimed Georgina, livid with rage. "I do not doubt that you are capable of anything. How I detest and loathe you! And should you dare at any time to lay a hand on me, I swear I shall kill you!"

"You may very well be the death of me, madam," Rathbourne agreed, the cold, cynical smile which flickered briefly on the handsome lips reflected chillingly in his voice. "And yet I strongly advise you not to try my patience too far. I shall return at the sounding of the bell to escort my lovely bride to meet her guests. I trust you will be ready."

"You needn't bother, Your Grace," Georgina flung back at him, but the click of the latch made it patently clear that her breath had been wasted. The duke had gone, closing the door firmly behind him.

"Oh! He is insufferable!" she cried, wheeling back to the window that Nanny might not see the tears of rage and frustration which stung her eyelids. "Dress as befits the Duchess of Rathbourne, indeed!" she fumed to herself, hardly aware of Nanny's presence in the room. "To dress as one would expect of *his* lady wife, I should have to don the garish feathers of a ladybird and flaunt myself before his guests."

"Miss Georgina!" Nanny ejaculated in the tone she used to employ when her charge had been a headstrong young hoyden in need of correcting. "I nivver thought to 'ear out o' yer mouth language wot don't become a lady born 'n' bred."

But Lady Grey seemed not to have heard, for suddenly she turned to face her old nurse with a dangerous gleam in her lovely eyes and a most peculiar smile upon her lips which Nanny, rolling her eyes ceilingward, doubted not boded ill for *some'un*.

"Nanny," said the countess with sudden, eager interest, "you said Wilkins had brought our trunks. Did he bring all of them? The one from the attic as well?"

Nanny, though tempted to deny the truth of the matter, grunted a wary affirmation.

"'Twere 'Is Grace's orders t' load everythin' wot were rightly yers, Missy. But why should ye want *that* 'un? There bain't naught in it but odds 'n' ends."

"Never mind, Nanny. Just tell me where it is."

"In the dressin' room wi' th' others," the nurse said grudgingly. "I were goin' t' 'ave it stored soon 's ever I—"

But Nanny was not allowed to finish what she had been about to say, as the countess stepped suddenly toward her and demanded she take her to the trunk immediately.

The dinner bell had hardly sounded before a brisk knock at Lady Grey's door announced the arrival of her betrothed to escort her downstairs.

"Quick, Nanny," Georgina said in a low voice which possessed little of her usual calm. "Help me into my shawl. Then kindly admit His Grace to receive his future duchess, if you please."

"Well I don't please," grumbled the nurse but nevertheless draped her mistress in an elegant India shawl which reached well below the knees and all but concealed the gown beneath. "Ye've 'ad some fine starts in yer day, Mistress. But belike ye'll not live this'n down come many a day. It bain't too late t' change yer mind. There be th' blue silk wot 'Is Grace 'ad made up fer ye in London."

"No, Nanny," Georgina sternly silenced her well-meaning retainer. "This dress is everything I could wish for the occasion. Indeed, I am only sorry I did not think of it sooner. Now, go admit His Grace of Rathbourne before he decides to break in the door."

"I'm goin', I'm goin'. But if'n ye've a brain left in yer head, ye'll not take off thet heathenish shawl till ye be safe agin in this room."

"But don't you see?" Georgina laughed. "I have devised a way that I shall not have to *leave* this room tonight."

The old nurse, however, had glimpsed the steely glint in Rathbourne's eyes and was far from convinced that her mistress had correctly judged His Grace's mettle. Muttering ominously beneath her breath, Nanny Slade obediently crossed the room to admit an elegantly attired Rathbourne.

The duke, instantly aware of Mrs. Slade's tight-lipped inscrutability, sharply arched a single, inquisitive eyebrow. Nor did his fiancee's serenely uttered greeting lull him into any false sense of security. He had left the lady in a high dudgeon hardly three quarters of an hour past. Either his angel, he judged sardonically, was truly possessed of a divinely forgiving nature or Lady Georgina Grey was up to something.

Nothing of Rathbourne's thought was revealed, however, as he strolled easily across the room, and, bowing over his finacee's graciously proffered hand, saluted her lightly on the knuckles.

"Madam," he murmured languidly, lifting sleepy blue eyes to scrutinize the lovely countenance. Again the arrogant eyebrow shot upward as he beheld the change in her appearance.

The earlier pallor of her cheeks had obviously succumbed to the ministrations of the rouge pot, as had her lips, stained a dusky red. He had never before seen her with her eyelashes darkened or her marvelous eyes seductively shaded green, nor could he have said that he cared for the effect. Or for her glorious hair piled high atop her head in an over-elaborate coiffure which made her seem older than her years and lent her a rather wanton appearance not at all in keeping with her true nature.

"Your Grace," she returned with a demureness belied by the faint, cool smile hovering about her painted lips. "I beg your forgiveness for my earlier unseemly behavior. Upon reflection, I see that you were quite right to have taken me to task. It was ungracious of me to fly at you like the veriest fishwife. Therefore, I have tried to do as you requested. I have dressed as befits your duchess and would now take my place at your table."

No sooner had she come to the end of her speech than Georgina flung off the Kashmir shawl and dropped into a deep mockery of a curtsy.

"Your Grace. I give you your duchess."

For a moment absolute silence reigned over the room as Rathbourne took in the splendor of Lady Grey's attire. The gown shimmered with a satiny lustre in the candlelight, a rich emerald green. Made in the empire style with a high waist and short puffed sleeves which left her slender arms bare, it clung provocatively to her limbs, leaving little doubt that she wore next to nothing beneath it. Nor did the square neck and the enticing expanse of bosom swelling above the daring decolletage detract from the overall picture of wanton beauty. A magnificent necklace of emeralds interspersed with diamonds graced the lovely column of her throat, and diamonds sparkled at her lobes.

The duke's lips curled in an appreciative smile. She was priceless. She could not have expressed more clearly her contempt for him, and yet she had retained an elegance of style in her artful set-down which he could only admire.

Nanny Slade, looking on with keen interest, shivered a little at the sudden, peculiar gleam in the duke's blue eyes. Lord help us. Her mistress were in fer it now, she thought, and held her breath in anticipation of Rathbourne's response to her lady's gesture of defiance. But, alas! She was doomed to disappointment, for His Grace, lifting a slender hand, elegantly waved her dismissal.

Not daring openly to defy so lofty a personage as a duke

of the realm, yet determined not to abandon her daring mistress if she could possibly avoid it, Nanny dipped a perfunctory curtsy.

"Be there anything else, milady?" she inquired meaningfully.

Georgina, however, for once failed to read between the lines. Which was understandable in the circumstances, since the whole focus of her attention was centered on the gentleman who had as yet to take up the part she had in her fancy devised for him.

"No, Nanny," she said without stopping to consider the consequences of finding herself suddenly and irretrievably alone with a notorious rakeshame. "That will be all for this evening."

Still Nanny hesitated, till an expectant glance from uncompromising blue eyes clearly left her at *point-non-plus*. She muttered direly beneath her breath as she closed the door behind her.

"Well, Your Grace?" Georgina queried, arching an imperious eyebrow at her frustratingly silent finance. "Have you nothing to say?"

"What can I say? I am rendered speechless at such indescribable beauty," declared His Grace with uncommon warmth and, drawing near that he might murmur softly in her ear, smiled as he felt her start. "Indeed, my love, you fair take my breath away."

"Y—you do not think the gown too daring, my lord?" queried Georgina, striving to maintain the charade when she felt herself poised suddenly and inexplicably on the brink of a yawning precipice. Drat the man! He was not reacting at all as he had ought.

"Not at all," Rathbourne demurred and availed himself of the pleasure of twining a lock of her hair about his finger. "On you it is everything which pleases."

"It is naturally my desire to—er—please," she stammered and only just managed to stifle an indignant gasp as

272

she felt his touch trickle down the bare expanse of her arm.

"I am delighted to hear it, my dear," he murmured, lowering his head to nibble maddeningly at her ear. "Indeed, I had not thought you had it in you to inflame a man's desire as you have done mine."

"Not had it in me!" Georgina blurted, jerking her head away. She would have risked stumbling ignominiously over some unseen object in a further attempt to place a more prudent distance between them, but his arm had slipped unnoticed behind her back, and as she made as if to pull away, it tightened firmly about her.

"How thoroughly you duped me with that cool facade," he whispered huskily, and her senses reeled as she found herself pinned against his muscular chest and felt his lips exploring the delicious vulnerability of her neck below her ear. "And all the time you were keeping concealed this tantalizing creature, this warm-blooded woman of passion I had never thought to see in you."

"Release me, this instant!" Georgina cried, pushing with both hands against his hard chest. Good God, what had she done? came fleetingly to her mind as his arms tightened like steel bands about her slender waist. Oh, why had she not listened to Nanny?

But it was too late. She was alone with the infamous Rathbourne, and rendered defenseless by her own traitorous body which was sending wave upon wave of delirious sensations to her reeling brain.

As from a distance she heard him say her name.

"Gina."

Then suddenly she felt his hand at the neck of her gown, baring her shoulder, and she moaned as he bent his head to kiss her above the soft swell of her breast.

"No. You mustn't," Georgina protested weakly, nearly lost to the breathless arousal of passion sweeping through her body. A gusty sigh heaved through her parted lips, and her head lolled heavily to one side. "Your guests—!" she pleaded, trying desperately to remember where and who she was.

"The devil take them!" he said savagely. Forcing her head up with a merciless hand in her hair, he covered her mouth hungrily with his.

The floor seemed suddenly to lurch and fall away from beneath her. "Rathbourne!" she groaned, losing hold of herself, giving way to something, some terrible, unspeakable truth. "David, help me. Help me," she panted, gasping for air, fighting the thing which had hurt her so that she had wanted to die. Oh, God, she couldn't breathe. She was sinking into some dark, terrifying morass. She was drowning, drowning. She gasped and for a time knew nothing more.

Half conscious, Georgina drifted helplessly through a dense shroud of darkness, fleeing desperately a deeper, more terrifying shadow.

A light flickered dimly at the edge of awareness. A face loomed above her then vanished with the light.

"Drew," she fretted. "Oh, God. He mustn't know. Must never know."

"Must never know what, Lady Grey?" demanded a voice out of the darkness.

"Mustn't know I love him," she moaned. "Mustn't know David . . . Oh, God! David," she sobbed, struggling to rise.

Strong arms held her close, and a new voice, a voice she knew, murmured soothingly in her ear.

"It's all right, Gina. He knows. He knows everything."

"No! He can't! He mustn't!" she wailed and began to struggle in mindless desperation against the arms which imprisoned her. "I must go before he wakens. Must run. Hide. Never find me. Let me go! Let me go!"

The voices murmured indistinctly somewhere above her. More hands grasped and held her. A glass was forced to her lips, and the first voice commanded her to drink. Obediently she opened her mouth. Gagging at the familiar, bitter taste of laudanum, she swallowed convulsively. Then, knowing what would come next, she ceased to struggle. Weeping silent tears, she was only vaguely conscious of gentle hands lowering her against the silky coolness of a pillow.

"She will sleep now," someone said.

"When she awakens, will she remember any of this?"

"Perhaps. If she is ready to accept the truth. But I shouldn't count too heavily on it if I were you. Still, it is a beginning. Come away now. And let her sleep."

Yes, she thought, feeling the delicious stupor already stealing over her. Deep and dreamless, blessed sleep. Still, she had not ceased to weep, and the haunting dream of remembered grief was fading more slowly than it used to do in the past.

"He is alive," she mumbled faintly. Delving more deeply into the comforting veil of oblivion, she sighed tumultuously. "Wait for him . . . at Greystone."

Chapter 12

"Oh, Gina! You're beautiful!" Miss Kingsley exclaimed as she stepped back the better to view her cousin in her wedding gown.

"I knew the moment Mme. Beauvais brought out the oyster white satin that it was made for you," Lady Kathryn declared, obviously pleased with her choice of the robe of Alençon-point lace over a satin petticoat. "Of course, I never supposed it would serve as your bridal dress, but it could not be more perfect. Or the cottage bonnet of matching lace more lovely. I do wish you would consider a veil as well. There is nothing more romantic than a beautiful woman's face seen only indistinctly through a lace veil."

"I haven't the least desire to present myself in a romantical vein," snapped Georgina, who viewed her upcoming nuptials with something less than the enthusiasm of her two companions. "His Grace and I have agreed this is to be a marriage of convenience only, and I mean to do nothing to change his mind."

"She was not always like this," Lady Kathryn remarked

276

soulfully to Miss Kingsley. "I remember when she used to quote poetry and weep over wilted flowers. I wonder can she really have changed so much? I could have sworn I saw her blush just moments ago when she heard the bridegroom's voice coming from his rooms next door."

"Katey Ingram, you saw no such thing!" the bride declared crossly. Indeed, she was very close to wishing her well-meaning companions to the devil. And in the circumstances, one could hardly have blamed her.

Georgina, after all, had awakened that morning feeling distinctly out of sorts. In truth, she suspected her nerves to be quite shattered, for never before had she experienced the irrational compulsion one moment to smash any object close to hand against the nearest wall and the next, to burst suddenly and uncontrollably into tears. Nor had the uncertainty of her state of mind been in any way alleviated by the sudden realization that not only had she no very clear recollection of what had transpired the previous evening after Rathbourne's arrival in her room, but that neither, and most disturbingly, did she have the least notion how she had come to be in her bed attired solely in her extremely skimpy chemise. Furthermore, despite the evidence that she had lain the night through in a profound slumber (her mouth was inordinately dry and her senses groggy), she was troubled by the vague remembrance of strange, incoherent dreams.

Or were they dreams? she had asked herself repeatedly, very much afraid that indeed they were not. For she seemed to recall having imbibed at someone's insistence a strong dose of bitter-tasting laudanum. And, worse, having kissed with passionate longing her abominated future husband!

Ye gods! She would rather die a horrid death than accept that she had truly welcomed Rathbourne's embrace, indeed, had yearned for it with a dreadful urgency which, even if it had only been a dream, was none the less appalling. And it must have been a dream, a nightmare, induced, no doubt, by the drug she had taken. And yet, what if Rathbourne had forced the sleeping draught upon her for that very purpose; indeed, to seduce her? Oh, she would die a *thousand* deaths if he had truly had his way with her! And even now she seemed to remember with dismaying vividness the tantalizing warmth of his body pressed to hers. And his lips! His lips which had seemed to draw upon her very soul. Oh, God! In Rathbourne's arms she had seemed to catch for the briefest moment a glimpse of what it might be to know a sense of wholeness once again. Indeed, for just an instant she had penetrated the veil of darkness and *seen* again, beheld a light, and in the midst of the light a face—Rathbourne's face!

But wait. She was being absurd. How could she have dreamt a face she had never seen before? Indeed, the whole fabric of her reasoning was nonsensical. For why should Rathbourne dose her with laudanum in order to seduce her the very night before he was to become her husband and thus have gained the *right* to bed her? She must have taken the draught herself after Rathbourne left her and then, feeling the effects of the drug, she doubtless only just had managed to remove her dress and slip into bed before falling into a drug-induced stupor.

Yes. That must have been the way of it. In which case nothing had happened of which she need be ashamed, and yet, still dissatisfied, she continued to pick over the fragments of haunting memories. For there had been something else as well, something she had had no wish to recall. Yet she *had* remembered it, and no matter how hard she tried, she could not dismiss it from her mind. For in her dream she had been consumed with bitter resentment toward David for having died, for having left her alone and cut adrift in a world devoid of light and bereft of meaning.

But, no! It was only a dream, she tried to tell herself as she slowly pirouetted in her wedding dress before her cousin and Lady Kathryn. She could not hate David. Not then.

Not ever. And after all, she was awake now and blind. And it was only in her dreams that she could see. Oh, God, that was irony for you, she thought, a trifle wildly. To know the difference between sleep and waking reality only because the one was to dream visions which tormented one and the other was to live a perpetual nightmare of blindness!

Good God. She would go mad if she did not soon discover what had really happened. Yet how galling to know that the only one who could tell her was Rathbourne. And if he chose to oblige her with an answer, how could she be certain what he told her was the truth of it? But then there *was* another way, she realized quite suddenly. Indeed, it really was so very simple she could not imagine why she had not thought of it before.

She had only to 'see' his face, trace with her fingertips the contours of cheeks, forehead, nose and jaw. *Then* she would know. For while she could find a rational explanation for having envisioned in a dream strong, arrogant features possessed of astounding manly beauty, hair the color of raven's wing and silvered at the temples, and, yes, even piercing eyes the color of the sea on a clear day—for these had been described to her—yet to have further conjured up a precise image of bone and facial structure from vague descriptions of them would seem to defy every rationality. *Then* to have imagined as well a blemish she had *not* known Rathbourne possessed must surely be to go beyond what was believable. And, indeed, the face she had seen had been marred by the thin line of a scar running along the left cheekbone.

She would have to "see" him for herself. And when better to achieve her goal than tonight, their wedding night?

The very notion of what she meant to do caused her heart suddenly to pound and the blood to surge in her veins with so disturbing a warmth that all at once she came to an awareness once again of Katey Ingram's teasing and the

279

awful reality of her wedding day.

"See. She is blushing again," laughed Lady Kathryn and hugged Georgina playfully about the shoulders.

"Oh, *enough*, Kate!" Georgina blurted before she could stop herself and jerked sharply away from Lady Ingram's fond embrace.

"Gina!" gasped Miss Kingsley in stunned surprise.

Blast! Georgina thought bleakly and took in a deep, steadying breath. What was the matter with her? She would be lashing out at Davey next if she weren't careful.

"No, it's all right, Zenobia," Lady Kathryn said quietly. "I think I understand."

"No, it is not all right! And, no, you do not understand at all, dearest Kate," Georgina interjected with a wry grimace. "But you mean well, and I am an ungrateful wretch to have used you so badly. Promise you will forgive me?"

Lady Ingram moved quickly to take Georgina's proffered hand.

"But of course I forgive you, Georgina! What bride isn't nervous on her wedding day?"

"Certainly there has never been one more apprehensive than I," agreed Georgina with a rueful laugh.

"Yes, that's it of course," Lady Kathryn soothed. "Now you just take a deep breath and try not to worry. I promise I shan't tease you any more. And, Georgina, do try not to judge Rathbourne too harshly. I have seen happy marriages grow from less, and in spite of your insistence that this is to be a marriage of convenience, I *know* my cousin truly loves you. I have seen it in his eyes."

"Yes, well, I fear *I* have not seen it," Georgina answered in undisguised bitterness, "but, of course, I cannot see. And don't you dare come back with the obvious, Katey Ingram. Love is never blind. Indeed, one can only truly love when one sees clearly the shortcomings and faults of the beloved and can forgive and accept them. And while I have been made acutely *aware* of Rathbourne's imperfections and shall soon even be compelled to *accept* them, I am quite certain I shall not *forgive* them for ever so long as I shall live."

Georgina had spoken with such unshakable conviction that by tacit agreement no more was said on the subject. Even Lady Kathryn, who was aching to know what "imperfections" the countess had been referring to in Rathbourne's character, kept her tongue between her teeth, thinking, no doubt, to quiz her friend about the matter when Georgina was feeling rather less pricklish. Indeed, very little was said at all as the two women guided the countess through the bewildering maze of unfamiliar halls and stairs until at last she heard a door open and was startled to feel a shaft of sunlight fall across her face. To her immediate discomfort, the scent of roses triggered poignant memories of her beloved garden at Greystone.

Georgina swallowed hard, fearful for a moment that she might disgrace herself with tears, a circumstance which did nothing to improve her temper. Her lips parted to demand why she had been brought outside when she had expected to find herself in some sort of stone-bound chapel, but then someone quite tall stepped between her and the warm beam of sunlight. Inexplicably her heart began to race. Then she heard Zenobia inhale sharply and felt the small hand tighten the slightest bit upon her arm. Immediately her pulse steadied to a normal pace, as she realized it was not Rathbourne standing over her.

"Robbie," she said warmly, thinking to ease the tension she had sensed between Penwarren and her cousin. She extended her hand. "I have wondered where you were keeping yourself. Indeed, I was quite out of countenance with you when you quit coming to see us. For you must know how used we had become to having you run tame at Greystone. We missed having you forever underfoot. However, now that I am to be your sister, I hope we shall be friends again."

She sensed Nobie turn her face away and Robbie shift his weight uncomfortably. Obviously there was a deal of disaccord between them, but she pretended to ignore it as Robbie took her hand in his.

"I hope I have never ceased to be your friend, Lady Grey," he said with the usual sincerity she had come to expect in him. Yet his next utterance was marked with a certain restraint which was not at all like him. "It is not that I did not wish to call. I have simply been . . ."

"Away," finished Rathbourne for him as, previously undetected by Georgina, he came to stand behind his bride. Once again to Georgina's dismay, her heart began to behave in a most alarming manner. "To the south of Cornwall, wasn't it, halfling?" the duke continued conversationally. "On some sort of scholarly pursuit, I believe."

Immediately Georgina tensed, her head coming up in quick resentment at what sounded very like a fabrication. Why should the duke wish his brother's whereabouts the past week kept from her? she wondered uneasily and immediately thought of the missing Denby. Surely Penwarren had not had a hand in that. After all, Robbie had never seemed the sort to be ruled by anyone. Surely not even his overbearing brother could make him do anything which was underhanded or say what was not true. She waited with keen expectancy for a denial, which she soon discovered was not to be forthcoming.

"Er—yes, it was," Robbie said in what sounded very like embarrassment. "Actually I have only just got back in time to discover my brother had had the good sense to engage the affections of the most beautiful woman in Cornwall," he added with a hearty cheerfulness which did not ring true to an astounded Georgina.

"That's coming it a bit strong, I should think," she retorted baldly, then instantly thought better of it as she felt every eye turned on her in astonishment at what could only be considered a gross incivility. "I'm afraid you have failed to do justice to Miss Kingsley, after all," she amended a trifle lamely. "And to your cousin, Lady Kathryn."

"Kind of you to include me, Gina dear," Lady Kathryn murmured in a soft aside to the countess, who in turn surreptitiously and none to gently shoved an elbow into her friend's ribcage.

Georgina, uncomfortably aware of the low rumble of Rathbourne's sardonic chuckle, grimaced. But it was her cousin who was to put the topping on the cake.

"No, Gina," Miss Kingsley interjected with an uncharacteristic but distinct tremor in her voice. "You must not tease him so. For, indeed, Lord Robert has always been more than just to me."

Georgina nearly winced at the sound of Robbie Penwarren's sharply indrawn breath.

"I am no doubt gratified to know that you think so, Miss Kingsley," he rejoined stiffly. "It is so difficult, after all, to determine the sentiments of certain individuals at any given time. They seem to change with such unexpected suddenness, would you not agree?"

"Do they, my lord?" queried Miss Kingsley hardly above a whisper. "And yet others are not so fortunate. For though circumstances might dictate the aspect of inconstancy, the heart remains oblivious to change, condemned to yearn for what must be denied."

Oh, dear, Georgina thought, wishing she had kept her tongue between her teeth. Poor Nobie. She sounded positively distraught. Apparently things were in a worse case between the two than she had been led to believe. And no wonder if the absurd child had really been so foolish as to reject Robbie's suit simply because of her straitened circumstances, which was what her rather obscure statement would seem to infer.

An embarrassed silence ensued. It was left to Rathbourne to recall them to the purpose of their gathering.

"Quite so, Miss Kingsley," he stated cynically. "Such are indeed the hearts of fools and poor devils in need of pity. Rather than to be considered either, such sentiments were better suited to the pages of a romantic novel or confined at the very least to one's self. As for myself, I should doubtless prefer the latter. Indeed, anything else, I fear, would be to delay unconscionably the reading of the nuptials. And now, madam," he added, taking Georgina's hand and tucking it neatly beneath his arm, "if you are ready, the bishop is waiting."

Georgina, seething with resentment at what she could not but view as another of Rathbourne's callous set-downs, stood rigidly as His Grace instructed the others of the wedding party to proceed ahead. No sooner was she certain Lord Robert and the ladies had succeeded in putting a relatively safe number of paces between them and herself than she committed the supreme folly of voicing her sentiments aloud.

"Must you always be so odiously insensible of the feelings of others, Your Grace?" she demanded in a low voice that the others might not hear.

"You wrong me, madam," he answered quellingly as he guided her down a surprisingly steep flagstone path enveloped in the heady scent of roses. "I am never insensible of them. Merely bored by the unseemly demonstration of them. And since you saw fit to precipitate what anyone with half a brain should have seen was inevitable, there seemed nothing for it but to extricate you from your embarrassment with as little delay as possible."

"Why, how very chivalrous of you, to be sure," uttered Georgina, stung. "And were you equally chivalrous last night, my lord duke, when you dosed me with laudanum and carried me to my bed?"

Instantly Georgina wished she could snatch the words back. For a moment she thought she might be ill as she felt

Rathbourne's arm tense beneath her hand. And, in truth, she was hardly prepared for his chilling response when it came.

"Can you doubt it, my love?" he queried in a voice she hardly recognized. Then, unbelievably, he had reached across with his free hand to cover hers in a gesture strongly suggestive of the sort of intimacy bred of familiarity.

"Doubt it!" she uttered in frozen accents, her heart suddenly leaden within her breast. "I cannot recall it! *Any* of it."

"Odd that you should remember nothing," he drawled at his most maddening. "I, on the other hand, am not like to forget so memorable an evening should I live to be a hundred."

His sudden, sardonic laughter seemed to affirm Georgina's worst suspicions.

"Oh, how I loathe you!" she gasped, halting in her tracks and whirling to confront him with an aspect of white-lipped outrage.

To her utter amazement, Rathbourne grasped both her hands in a steely grip and raised them to his lips, murmuring frostily, "I suggest, my love, that you smile. Lest you would have the whole world know in what affection you hold your bridegroom. We find ourselves upon the threshold of Llan Penrhyn and, more significantly, in clear view of our wedding guests."

"What do you mean?" Georgina asked suspiciously and suddenly ceased trying to pull her hands free. "You said we were to be wed in a chapel."

"You must tell me sometime, my dearest Gina, why you should have chosen to remember anything quite so mundane as that," he commented with biting humor. "Indeed, I confess to a certain curiosity. My kisses, it would seem, have not the same facility for making so lasting an impression on you."

"Oh! You *cannot* be so base!" she said in utter disbelief.

"What have I ever done to earn such contempt from you?"

She heard him draw in a sharp breath and for a single, wild moment believed she had finally penetrated his formidable armor. But then he was himself again, cool, sardonic, and hard.

"Nothing, my love. Nothing at all," he said as casually as if he had not just insulted her in the most despicable manner possible. "Indeed," he added reflectively, "how could you have done? Not even a devil could hold an angel in contempt."

She had only just begun to digest this startling observation, when he seemed suddenly to change tack again.

"Llan Penrhyn is a chapel of sorts," he murmured somewhat vaguely, as if his thoughts were somewhere else. "Roughly translated, it means The Chapel on the Promontory." He laughed, a short, oddly harsh laugh. "It had occurred to me an *alfresco* ceremony might appeal to you."

"Oh," she murmured faintly, taken suddenly off guard. "Yes, I suppose it might."

Botheration! she thought, put out of all countenance with Rathbourne's infuriating inconsistencies. Why must he be forever stepping out of character? How dared he do anything so considerate as to think of holding the ceremony in such congenial surroundings! For, indeed, she must prefer the fresh air and sunlight to the chill dampness of the stone castle. An annoyed frown darkened her brow.

"I suppose I should thank you, Your Grace, for having considered my feelings in the matter," she offered grudgingly. "Unfortunately, I find suddenly that I am rather weary. Indeed, I should be grateful if we could forget everything which has just passed between us until a more propitious time. If you are still determined that I must become your wife, I should appreciate proceeding with as much dispatch as is seemly."

Rathbourne was so long in answering that Georgina thought he might indeed have altered in his resolve to wed her. Inexplicably she experienced an odd sort of queasiness in her stomach.

"Very well, madam," he drawled cynically. "We shall cry pax till the business is done. And afterward, let the farce begin again."

Rathbourne's last, bitter utterance seemed to ring in Georgina's ears as she submitted to being led up a final series of flagstone steps into what seemed to be an open-aired pavilion. The whisper of a breeze and the distant sound of the sea breaking against the rocks far below mingled with the low murmurings of a number of people gathered on either side of her. Rathbourne led her only a few steps more then halted.

A pleasant voice possessed of a certain gentle dignity spoke the words of the ceremony which would bind Georgina irretrievably to the tall nobleman at her side. As if in a dream she made the proper responses, felt her hand lifted and a ring placed on her finger. More words followed and suddenly she felt strong hands lightly grasp and turn her. Cool lips brushed hers in an unexpectedly gentle kiss which left her breathless and oddly bewildered. And then Rathbourne had tucked her hand beneath his arm and turned to lead her, still dazed and feeling caught up in some distant unreality, from the chapel and down the path again toward the great hall.

It was done. She was Rathbourne's wife. And now, he had said, the farce should begin again. What had he meant by that? she wondered, feeling strangely that he had provided her with a key which, if only she knew its true significance, might unlock the mystery which was Rathbourne.

She was not to be given time to ponder the matter, however, as she was set upon by a host of people wishing to congratulate the happy couple. Rathbourne's hand upon her arm somehow steadied her, as did his calm presence as one by one he received their well-wishers then introduced each to her in turn. She had dipped and curtsied to perhaps a dozen who would remain in her memory little more than a formless jumble of unfamiliar names and voices, when she was startled to hear her cousin speak urgently to Rathbourne.

"Please! I must talk to you. He's here. Vail. He spoke to me. I must tell you . . ."

"Not *now*, Miss Kingsley. Calm yourself."

But her cousin was not to be dissuaded.

"You don't understand," she said so low that Georgina had to strain to hear above the inane chatter of a Mrs. Butterfly or Flutterby or something or other who seemed to have planted herself in front of the duchess. The rest of Nobie's words were lost save for one poignant utterance.

"It's *Robbie!*" Miss Kingsley pleaded in a voice which seemed fraught with terrible foreboding. Whereupon Rathbourne stiffened and murmured something too softly for Georgina to hear.

Her lips fixed in a vacant smile, Georgina nodded mindlessly and mumbled a monosyllable or two for the benefit of the indefatigable gadfly still spouting an endless stream of vapidities in her face. All the time she was wishing the woman to perdition, her every faculty strained to make out what was going on next to her.

At last His Grace suddenly and summarily dismissed the long-winded Flutterby as only he knew how. Hardly had the offended hen-wit finished ruffling her feathers, stalking off in high dudgeon, than Rathbourne coolly turned to murmur in her ear.

"Forgive me, madam, for inflicting that insufferable woman upon you. And because I fear I must leave you for a short time."

"If you leave me here alone for so much as a moment, Your Grace," she replied sweetly. "I am quite sure the last thing I shall do is forgive you."

"My love," drawled the duke infuriatingly. "You mustn't

be greedy. After all, you shall soon have me all to yourself, not only this night, but a lifetime of nights to come."

"Oh! You insufferable coxcomb, I should sooner . . . " Georgina began furiously, but the duke abruptly pulled her close and silenced her with a long, lingering kiss.

"I say, Rathbourne," remarked a voice familiar to Georgina and which was remarkable for its dandified lisp. "You seem to be making something of a spectacle of yourself. I quite understand how you feel, old man, but wouldn't it be better to postpone all this for later? Bad *ton*, you know."

Georgina, who was experiencing a myriad of bewildering sensations, was torn between relief and an inexplicable disappointment at Lord Ingram's interruption. Nor could she stifle the slight, bemused sigh which escaped her lips as Rathbourne lifted his head at last.

"I shan't be long, I promise you," he murmured, still holding her so close that she was acutely aware of his heartbeat against her breast. Then he set her from him, and she felt oddly bereft as his hands dropped away so that she had only the sound of his voice to which to cling. "You stay with her, Ferdie. And see that no one imposes on her good nature, will you?" he said, and then she had lost even that tenuous link as she sensed that he had turned and was leaving her.

"No, wait," she called out, taking an uncertain step forward. "Take me with you." It had been on her tongue to demand that he tell her if her cousin was in some sort of trouble, when Lord Ingram stopped her.

"I am sorry, Your Grace," lisped the dandy apologetically. "I'm afraid he didn't hear you."

"No, I don't suppose he did," she replied, rigid with resentment and not believing it for an instant. How dared he desert her! Indeed, she was anxious about Nobie and angry enough with Rathbourne to order Lord Ingram to take her to the duke at once, but then Lady Kathryn, with the young Earl of Emberly and his tutor in tow, had materialized out of the bewildering muddle of noise, and she knew she could do nothing but wait for Rathbourne to return.

"Davey!" Georgina murmured at the sound of her son's voice and the tug of an insistent hand on her skirt. She knelt and hugged him suddenly close, grateful to have him in her arms again. It seemed an eternity since she had held him last, though it had only been the previous day that they had ridden together to the castle. Still, as she listened to him describe his room which overlooked the sea and was ever so much more exciting than his old nursery at Greystone, for it had been the duke's, too, and was full of toy soldiers and model ships and even a telescope and things, she wished suddenly that she might hold on to him forever. But then Kate was saying something about Rathbourne and more people waiting to meet the bride. And Fairfax had come forward to take charge of Davey so that there seemed nothing for it but to give her son one last squeeze and let him go.

"Georgina," said Lady Kathryn in low-voiced concern. "You needn't look as if he's going away forever."

Georgina blinked and seemed to shake herself.

"No, I've made sure of that at least," she murmured, then assayed to smile as she realized what she had said. "You mustn't mind me, dearest Kate," she added, laughing shortly. "Weddings always affect me strangely. Oh, I do wish Rathbourne hadn't slipped away. Can you see him? He hasn't left me here, has he?"

"Of course he hasn't, gudgeon. He's just a few paces away, speaking with Miss Kingsley."

"Zenobia?" Georgina queried distractedly, wishing everyone would go away and leave her alone as Lady Kathryn nudged her and presented her to a local squire and his wife whose names she made no attempt to commit to memory.

"Why, yes," Lady Kathryn replied when the couple had moved on. "Odd. The poor child seems quite distraught. But then one can never tell about people in love. You must tell me sometime, Gina, why your cousin has apparently refused poor Robbie when it is obvious that they have a *tendre* for one another. Though I can't but be grateful to her for giving my Philippa another chance at him, I confess I find it most peculiar of her."

"I'm sure I couldn't speak for either one of them," Georgina retorted shortly, irritated with Rathbourne for having abandoned her at such a time and with Zenobia for having been the cause of it. And then someone else had come up to her to be presented and to offer felicitations and she must smile and mouth the appropriate phrases.

"I heard my cousin say someone was here—a man," Georgina said to Lady Kathryn as soon as they were alone again. "Oh, botheration! I can't recall his name now. She seemed very upset about it. Who could it have been, Kate? Did you see her talking to anyone before Rathbourne?"

"No one in particular," Kathryn Ingram shrugged, then paused as her glance fell on a tall, elegantly attired young man whose striking blond good looks had already begun to display the marked effects of a dissolute style of living. She frowned slightly, as he worked his way across the lawn in their direction. "Except, of course, for Vail," she added reflectively. "But then he used to know Miss Kingsley, I believe, when she made her come-out in London."

"Vail?" Georgina breathed. "But that's it. The name Nobie said to Rathbourne. Where is he, Kate? Indeed, who is he?"

"No one you would care to know, I am quite sure," remarked Lady Kathryn dryly. "However, I'm afraid it cannot be helped. By all appearances, you are very soon to meet him for yourself."

"Do you not think it odd, my dear," commented Lord Ingram, taking a pinch of snuff and leisurely inhaling it, "that Vail should have found his way from Brighton to Cornwall. Especially when he seemed to have the inside track with the heiress from York. Beastly place York. Shouldn't wonder that the chit would accept anyone rather than have to live there, what?"

"Very true, my darling Ferdie," agreed his spouse. "But I should think even York preferable to a man wed but a year then widowed under somewhat mysterious circumstances."

"Whatever are you saying, Kate?" Georgina queried in sudden alarm, her cousin's unusual agitation as she had uttered the man's name to Rathbourne suddenly very much on her mind.

"Nothing which should not wait till later, my dearest Georgina," murmured Lord Ingram meaningfully. Georgina, who during her season in London had become quite well acquainted with the viscount's idiosyncrasies, knew that he had raised his quizzing glass with an elegant flourish of lace to scrutinize with careless insouciance the man they had been discussing. His peculiarly nasal affectation suddenly quite pronounced, he observed in mild astonishment to his wife, "Odds tooth, my love. I believe 'tis Vail come to pay his respects to your cousin."

"Why, so it is," acknowledged Lady Kathryn artlessly. "How kind in you to have come all the way from Brighton, my Lord. Indeed, I was not aware you were acquainted with the duke or his bride."

"I fear you are quite right, Lady Ingram," replied a silky voice which sent cold shivers down Georgina's back. "I have not the pleasure of their acquaintance. However, since I was in the neighborhood visiting friends, I could not resist dropping by to rectify the error. And to renew my acquaintance with a dear friend who I had heard was in residence at Rathbourne. A Miss Kingsley, who is, I believe, Your Grace's cousin."

"Indeed, Lord Vail, Miss Kingsley is my cousin,"

Georgina said, politely extending two fingers. "However, I do not recall that she has ever mentioned you." And no wonder! It would be unlikely in the extreme that any young woman of quality should acknowledge an intimacy with what was, if Georgina's instincts were at all to be trusted, a scapegrace and a bounder.

"Has she not? But then I suppose that shouldn't surprise me," he rejoined smoothly. "I fear that our last parting was precipitated by an unfortunate misunderstanding. Indeed, I came here today in the hopes that I might in some way make it up with her. But she has unfortunately refused to allow me time enough in her presence to explain myself."

"Indeed, you amaze me, my lord," Georgina sympathized. "And to think that you have come all the way to the Cornish wilds in search of your long-lost love. I declare I have never heard of anything so romantic!'"

"Romantic, perhaps," Vail murmured soulfully. "but a source of unending pain to me. However, if you were to intervene on my behalf, Your Grace, you should have the satisfaction of knowing you helped to bring together two who were fated by the gods to be together."

"But I should never do anything so patently ill-advised, my lord," observed Her Grace of Rathbourne as though surprised at his absurdity. "Alas! Not even for the gods, I fear. Indeed, I suggest you save your Spanish pound for someone either of greater vanity or lesser perspicacity."

There was an instant of taut silence. When the earl spoke again, Georgina shivered at the undisguised venom in his voice.

"Oh, bravo, Your Grace. I must congratulate you on your superb performance. You had me convinced you were as big a fool as your hen-witted cousin. But instead I find you are a cunning little piece. Indeed, I no longer wonder that the Duke of Rathbourne should have been brought to marry a blind freak. Doubtless in the dark you can be as entertaining as any other woman."

"I should think that will be enough, my lord," observed Ferdie Ingram, the soft lisping drawl oddly chilling. "In truth, it has occurred to me that you exceed the bounds of what is pleasing, which, upon reflection, should hardly be surprising when one considers such abominable lack of sartorial discrimination. Tsk, tsk. Really, Vail, I cannot imagine that you would wish to be observed in such a beastly coat. Doubtless you should retire immediately before the whole world has had the misfortune to remark it."

Vail's low laughter was an insult.

"How very amusing," he sneered, "that one oddity in nature should see fit to defend another. Take care, my pretty little peacock, that you do not find your lovely feathers plucked."

"Obviously you are unaware, my lord," Georgina interjected icily, "that in India the peacock is greatly feared. Indeed, it is thought unlucky to in any way offend it. So perhaps it were best that you removed yourself at once to a place better suited to you. The bagnios and gaming-hells of London, I presume."

"You surprise me, my love," a soft voice drawled thrillingly at Georgina's shoulder. "Remind me sometime to ask how you could possibly know language so ill-suited to a lady's ears. In the meantime, I feel sure you are quite right in supposing his lordship has someplace better to take himself. Indeed, I advise you leave immediately, my lord, as the Plymouth ferry departs for Brighton on the evening tide. I shouldn't wish for you to miss it, the inns being what they are in Cornwall. Believe me, you shall do much better in your rooms at Brighton."

"It is no doubt kind of you to be concerned, Your Grace," Vail said, having at the duke's rather more compelling presence hastily resumed the smooth facade of a polished gentleman. "But I shan't be leaving Cornwall until I have completed my business here, and so you may inform Miss Kingsley. I'm sure *you* must understand my position, Rathbourne. It is not so far removed from your own, after all."

"Whatever did the creature mean by that?" queried Lady Kathryn in offended tones, her skin still crawling from the insinuating irony of the earl's laughter as he vanished into the crowd.

"Perhaps you should ask him, my dearest Kate," Rathbourne shrugged indifferently. "And now, if you will excuse us, I believe it's time my lovely bride and I mingled with the guests."

"I warn you, you shan't put me off so easily, my lord duke," Georgina murmured in an undertone as Rathbourne led her away from Lord and Lady Ingram. "Who is that odious man and what has he to do with my cousin?"

"Obviously he is the Earl of Vail, my love. A rake and a bounder, just as you have earlier surmised. Apparently he made advances to your cousin, who quite naturally took exception to them. As you have seen, he can become rather less than pleasant. He frightened her, and she came to me for protection, as was proper in the circumstances. Now, is there anything else you would like to know before we proceed to more pertinent matters?"

For a moment Georgina could think of nothing to say in the wake of the duke's surprising revelations. Not that what he had said was so startling, she thought wryly. It was that for once he had chosen to *give* her an explanation which had so effectively silenced her. In exasperation she fell back on the one thing with which she could fault him.

"I am not your 'love'!" she said snippishly. "And I shall thank you not to call me that."

"Are you not?" instantly rejoined His Grace, raising her hand to his lips that he might kiss the slender wrist. "Then certainly I must apologize. Is there anything else?"

"No," she answered a trifle distractedly, for it seemed her arm was all aflame where he had touched her. Hastily she snatched her wrist away.

"Very well, then I suggest we make our escape now before we are detected." And silencing her with a finger placed lightly against her lips, he pulled her unresisting through a doorway.

Whereupon the wedding guests milling about the grounds discovered that the Duke and Duchess of Rathbourne had apparently simply vanished.

Chapter 13

The new Duchess of Rathbourne was acutely aware of the man who held her before him in the saddle, his lean, strong arms about her waist as he guided their mount along a woodland trail. Indeed, she had forced herself to relax to the gait only because she knew it would ease the horse's double burden, for to do so had meant to rest in a most disturbing manner in the cradle of the duke's firm arm and shoulder so conveniently placed for that very purpose. But gradually lulled by the smooth and easy rhythm of the pace, Georgina's guard was eventually lowered. For a time she lost herself to the heady fragrance of trees and flowers and the crisp, clean breeze, and to a vague, delicious feeling that she might have gone on forever thus, nestled cozily in the circle of strong arms and enveloped by a most peculiar feeling of warm security.

How odd, she mused, that one man had the power to arouse such varied and opposing emotions in her. One moment he incited her to a fury and the next, he instilled in her an odd sense of contentment—and the feeling that so long as she remained within his arms, nothing could ever harm or frighten her. Georgina felt the blood rush to her cheeks as she realized where her fancy had led her. She was not some silly sentimental schoolgirl to succumb so easily to the spell of muscular arms and a manly chest. Better to think of something else, she told herself and firmly turned to a contemplation of the festivities still in progress behind them at Rathbourne Castle.

She was still stunned at the number of people who had shown up at such short notice to witness the marriage of His Grace of Rathbourne to his cousin's widow. Not that every one of the nearly hundred persons who had congregated in and about the castle grounds had actually seen the wedding. That had been reserved for family and for selected friends of long-standing. Rather had they waited to receive the newly-weds at the lavishly prepared reception set up on the well-kept lawns within the bailey.

She was not sorry to find herself fleeing the castle and the unexpected multitude of over-inquisitive wedding guests. She had had enough of well-wishers who no sooner offered her their "sincere" congratulations, than they were inquiring with scant subtlety into her lineage and her history. This was inevitably followed by a demand that she relate just how she had managed to snare the biggest prize on the marriage mart.

In fact, she thought suddenly, she probably would have derived a deal of enjoyment in a leisurely ride over the countryside had it not been for the fact that she had not an inkling of where she was going and, further, that she was going there with Rathbourne.

Indeed, she knew nothing at all of what they were about, for Rathbourne had uttered scarcely a word since he had spirited her away in the wake of the unpleasant scene with the Earl of Vail and led her by a back way to her rooms.

To her surprise Nanny had been waiting to help her out of the lovely gown of satin and lace and into a merino riding habit which she declared rapturously was of the same rich mahogany as her mistress's hair. No sooner had Nanny placed on Georgina's head the nearly brimless beaver riding hat adorned with an ostrich feather fastened on the left and made to curl around the front and down over her right shoulder than Rathbourne had entered her boudoir through the door which connected his rooms with those of his duchess.

Silencing her questions with a curt assurance that all should be made clear to her shortly, he had guided her down a seemingly endless passage, which she strongly suspected to be one of the piratical third Earl of Rathbourne's secret tunnels. At last she had found herself outside the castle and lifted despite her protest to the back of the duke's prized Arabian, Xanthus. Mounting behind her, Rathbourne had ridden at a steady clip away from the castle and the sounds of the sea crashing against the rugged cliffs.

They had been traveling steadily for what seemed an eternity to Georgina but which had probably been no more than twenty minutes or so, and still she knew nothing of where they were going or why they had fled with such stealth.

"Will you not at least tell me where you are taking me?" she queried, unable to stand the silence any longer.

"To a wedding feast, if we are not too late," he answered without the least hesitation.

Georgina stiffened in quick resentment. Good heavens! Did he think she was possessed of more hair than wit?

"Then I wish you will take me back to Rathbourne at once," she said unequivocally. "I may not be all that well acquainted with the customs of Cornwall, but it seems patently odd to me that the newlyweds should leave the wedding guests to attend a feast elsewhere. Besides which," she added pointedly, "it occurs to me that a riding habit is hardly what Rathbourne would consider attire proper for his duchess on such an occasion."

"In short, you don't believe me," laconically observed His Grace.

"Let us rather say that in light of past experiences I have come to hold anything you might do or say as highly suspect, Your Grace," she corrected in dulcet tones.

"Hornet," he commented feelingly, but without noticeable rancor, she thought in some surprise.

Indeed, she was suddenly struck by the notion that the duke seemed to have undergone a certain softening of his mood. Upon which she determined to chance an appeal to his doubtful better nature.

"I truly do not wish to appear uncivil, but surely any further introduction to the gentry can wait for the presentation ball. I cannot imagine that there should be anyone left in the whole of the Tamar Valley to whom I have not been already introduced. Can we not simply cry off from this affair?" she ended reasonably.

"It would seem, madam, that you have yet to comprehend the esteem in which my duchess is held," he drawled infuriatingly. "To cry off now would be to place us both beneath reproach. I fear, on the contrary, you shall just have to make the best of things."

As there appeared to be little point in pursuing the subject further, Georgina lapsed into stormy silence, determined to ignore the insufferable duke for the rest of the interminable journey. And, indeed, they had ridden fully another thirty minutes before the distinct sounds of merriment and a voice excitedly announcing the arrival of the duke and his lady wife startled her into speech.

"But I know that voice," she said, scarcely willing to believe her ears. "It's Wilkins', isn't it?"

But Rathbourne had dismounted and was lifting her down from the saddle, and then someone else had come forward to greet her with such marvelous warmth in the otherwise staid and proper tones that Georgina became acutely conscious of a peculiar lump in her throat.

"Bolton!" she exclaimed a trifle huskily. "How good to hear your voice. But what are you doing here? Indeed," she suddenly laughed, "where *is* here?"

"It is my honor," Bolton announced, "to welcome the

Duke of Rathbourne and his duchess to the gala of Mr. and Mrs. Bromley Wilkins, who celebrate their wedding day. And may I add my sincere wish for happiness to both Your Graces without being thought presumptuous?"

"You who have always been a friend to us could never be thought presumptuous in such a sentiment," Georgina smiled and extended her hand in sincere affection. "Thank you, Bolton," she added softly when, after only the briefest hesitation, the elderly butler had accepted her warm gesture of friendship. "For all your many kindnesses."

"It has ever been my wish to serve Your Grace," intoned Bolton with a revealing quiver of emotion in his normally well-modulated tones.

"I believe our hosts wish us to join them, madam," Rathbourne quietly interjected in the small silence which ensued.

Georgina nodded absently, a sudden, perplexing thought having just occurred to her.

"Yes, of course. We mustn't keep Gilda and Wilkins waiting," she murmured, feeling as if she had stumbled on to something of immense importance and yet uncertain what to make of it.

In all that had happened, she had not forgotten her promise to attend the exchanging of vows between Gilda and Bromley Wilkins, nor had she been able to banish the feeling of guilt at having failed to keep her word. The question was, how had Rathbourne known? And, perhaps more importantly, why should he have been concerned enough to rectify the omission by having brought her here? Such consideration not only for her sensibilities but for the feelings of those far beneath his exalted station was hardly in keeping with his character. If, that is, he was the unfeeling blackguard he had led her to believe him. But he *had* cared. He had unwittingly made that clear, for, as she had listened to Bolton and experienced for the first time a glimmering of the depth of his regard for her, it had suddenly come to her that Rathbourne had not been referring earlier to the "esteem" due a Duchess of Rathbourne but to the affection in which she, who was his duchess, was held by those who had served her faithfully at Greystone.

And, in truth, that feeling abounded in the warm welcome accorded the duke and duchess on every hand as they made their way through the not inconsiderable number of people gathered for Mr. and Mrs. Bromley Wilkins' wedding feast. None, however, exceeded those of the broadly beaming groom himself and his bashful bride, who succumbed to tears at the honor done her. Georgina felt close to tears herself as one after another, the men, women, and children came forward to pay homage to her, and among them Mrs. Dickson, who, blessing her ladyship for her kindness and generosity, placed in Georgina's arms the newest of her several offspring, an infant of some two weeks and three days.

More than one of those gazing with a sense of awe at the beautiful young duchess made more lovely still in her unconscious pose of tender womanhood as she cooed and smiled upon the tiny baby in her arms noted the duke's cool eyes ignite with a strange blue flame as he, too, watched his wife. But it was Mrs. Porter, the housekeeper at Greystone, who made Georgina blushingly aware of it as the elderly woman remarked that doubtless old Mrs. Slade would not soon step foot in her ivy-bound cot awaiting her in Kent, for from the looks of his lordship the duke, belike 'twould be his own babe snuggling in Her Grace's arms ere many a month had passed.

Georgina suddenly relinquished the child once more to its mother. Heavens, what a dunce she was! For she had never once gone so far as to consider the possibility of bearing Rathbourne's children till then. It was perhaps inevitable that the one disconcerting thought should lead to another, or that it should not be long before Georgina had recalled the appalling uncertainties of the previous night, the horrifying implications which had arisen from their heated exchange as Rathbourne escorted her to the altar, and, indeed, everything which they had agreed to forget until after the reading of the vows.

Well, the vows had certainly been read, she thought and wondered vaguely why it was not anger she felt, but rather a strange sort of leaden sensation, as if she did not know what to feel or did not dare to feel anything at all. But then Wilkins was trying awkwardly to thank her for having commissioned Bolton before her departure from Greystone to provide what stores would be necessary for a sumptuous repast. And no sooner had she assured him it was the very least she could do for all those who had made her feel at home at Greystone than someone was urging her to try a bite of saffron cake, gingerbread, or the never to be forgotten figgy pudding sprinkled liberally with sugar.

For some time Georgina was given little opportunity to worry about Rathbourne or her wedding night as she was introduced to Cornish bacon rinds, or 'scallops,' barley bread, and 'gurty' meat pies made from the pudding skin of the butchered pig, potato cakes and boiled rump of beef with turnips, carrots, and potatoes. Though she suspected from the boisterous sounds of merriment all around her that the marriage feast was something of a *success fou*, the ultimate proof of the pudding was a young urchin's awed observation that never in all his life had he seen at one time no less than half a dozen roasted fowl, five rabbit pies, and enough tarts to satisfy even the vicar for a month of Sundays. To wash it all down, there was an abundance of home-brewed mead, which Wilkins and the others called 'metheglin,' blackberry, gilliflower, cowslip, and elder wines, along with the usual cider, sloe gin, and 'mahogany,' which was two parts of gin and one of treacle.

Consequently, Georgina was not overly surprised that the atmosphere of festivity, which had suffered a momentary check at the arrival of their Graces of Rathbourne, was returned to its former high-spirited hilarity. But nor was she sorry to be offered an opportunity to escape it for awhile in the form of Gilda's faltering invitation to a tour of her cottage, which, she assured the duchess was only a little way from the glen in which the tables and games had been set up to accommodate the guests. Since Rathbourne had been induced, much to Georgina's surprise, in accepting Wilkins' challenge to a game of skittles, Georgina readily agreed to go with Gilda.

Shyly warning her former mistress to duck her head, Gilda guided Georgina under the low, granite lintel and down the two steps into the 'hale,' which Georgina soon came to understand was equivalent to the English parlor. Here Georgina was led in turn to three straight-backed wooden chairs, painted smooth to the touch and polished, she doubted not, to a high sheen, a large, well-scrubbed wooden table, a single easy chair, and finally the glassed buffette in the corner which contained the bride's greatest treasures—on the top shelves her best glasses, the tumblers carefully arranged with the top-side down and the two grog glasses right-side up with the best tea-spoons, the bowls spread out like a fan, between them; and on the bottom shelves, with the plates standing up behind the cups, bowls, and saucers to show the design, her grandmother's china.

The opposite side of the one-room house made up the kitchen, which was remarkable for a huge stone hearth large enough to contain a chimney seat on one side and the 'cloam,' or Cornish oven, on the other, a circumstance which caused Georgina to question how it had been possible to construct anything quite so impressive in the length of a single night.

"It couldn't 've been, Your Grace," Gilda admitted nervously. "The chimley an' doorsill was left after th' fire taken th' rest o' th' cot that'd stood here before. An' a good thing they was, 'cause there wouldn't like to 've been nary a soul that'd cross the threshold otherwise. 'Tis bad luck, 'ee know, to go into a new house, but it's like His Grace told Bromley. The heart of a house be the hearth an' the doorsill the remembrance of all who've entered in. So it ain't like it were a new house, rightly speakin'."

"No, I shouldn't think it is," Georgina agreed, smiling strangely. Would Rathbourne never cease to amaze her? she wondered, perplexed at the subtlety of feeling which must have engendered so discerning a kindness. But then everyone from Gilda to Lady Kathryn seemed to entertain a rather different impression of Rathbourne from her own. Perhaps she must assume only *she* incited his darker self, the devil who could render his intended insensible that he might work his way with her and then have the gall to boast to her about it. What had she done to earn his enmity? she wondered, feeling strangely disconsolate.

As Gilda described the cupboards containing her everyday dishes, the settle with the high back which could be lowered to make a table, and the hutch for the flour and pitchers of drinking water, Georgina savored the mixed aromas of mugwort, elderflower, horehound, and camomile hanging in bags from the rafters to dry and experience a sharp stab of envy for the young Cornish bride and her cozy cottage.

How different were their expectations—the simple Cornish girl in her white-washed cob cottage and the duchess in her castle of weathered stone! And yet Gilda's life, which promised little of comfort and a deal of hardship, seemed at that moment far preferable to that of a duchess who might have had anything for the asking, anything, that is, except a real home and her husband's love.

Realizing suddenly the implications of that disturbing notion, Georgina blushed hotly and felt suddenly weak. Her husband's love she thought wildly, her hands rising as if of their own accord to cover her cheeks. Good God, was that what she wanted?

A myriad of memories seemed suddenly to press upon her—memories of Rathbourne as he had been in the beginning—his keen wit and well-informed mind which had teased and challenged her, reminded her that there was a world beyond the boundaries of Greystone and Emberly. The way he had of discerning her every change of mood, of seeming able to know her thoughts even before she did. The sound of his laughter, rich and vibrant with an ever appreciative sense of the ridiculous, which, indeed, he shared with her. His unobtrusive strength and thoughtfulness, his subtle kindness. And the gentleness within him, the depth of sensitivity, which others might not see behind the aloof facade of the cynical Corinthian but which she had sensed from the first touch of his strong, slender hands. Oh, God, his touch, which had always the power to thrill and unnerve her!

Oh, yes, she wanted Rathbourne's love, wanted it because she was shamefully, agonizingly in love with him. Indeed, it seemed, looking back, that she could not remember a time when she did not love him. For her heart had seemed lost to him from the first moment she had heard his voice in the garden at Greystone and felt the touch of his lips against her hand. Doubtless she had already been a little in love with him even before he had ever come to Greystone—been enamored of the reckless, sensitive youth whom David had so fondly described.

Nor had she ever ceased to love him, for even as he had destroyed her trust and humiliated her so that she thought she had never despised anyone so thoroughly as she despised him, still had she gone on loving him. And loved him still, God help her!

"Your Grace? Please, Your Grace. Are thee ill?"

"Wha-at?" Georgina murmured, coming slowly to an awareness of Gilda hovering anxiously about her. "Oh, Gilda. Forgive me. I must have drifted off for a moment."

"You was so pale, Your Grace. I were afeard t' see 'ee

fall into a swoon. Wouldst 'ee take a dram of metheglin, milady, or mayhap a spot of cider to chase away the megrims?"

"Oh. No, Gilda. Thank you. Doubtless I shall be myself again directly. Perhaps if I could just sit quietly for a moment. Alone. So much has happened. So many people. I fear I'm a trifle overcome by it all."

"There's Bromley's chair, milady," the girl suggested doubtfully and helped Georgina to the easy chair beneath the only window in the small cottage. "Does 'ee wish, I'll leave the sash up to give 'ee air to breathe whilst I fetch His Grace, milady."

"No. I mean, yes," Georgina said distractedly, "leave the sash as it is, but say nothing to the duke. I shouldn't want to worry him heedlessly. I shall be fine, Gilda. I promise you. Now you go and enjoy the festivities. I'm sure I can find my way back along the path by myself after I have rested a bit."

For a moment Gilda hesitated, little liking to leave her ladyship with no one to look after her, but at Georgina's repeated insistence that she should do very well by herself, the girl curtsied reluctantly and slipped quietly out the door.

For a long moment Georgina sat with her head back and her eyes closed as she struggled with her stunning revelation. How blind she truly was not to have seen it before! And how dreadful it was, for she could not understand how she could have fallen in love with a man of such questionable character. Could it be that her heart perceived something her mind had not? Yes, she thought, her pulse quickening with sudden hope. That must be it. Rathbourne could not be evil. Deep and odiously obscure, perhaps, but not evil, surely.

There had to be some explanation for everything he had done. After all, it was true that with no one but Bolton and Mrs. Porter in residence at Greystone, it would not have been feasible to keep Denby there. And perhaps for the injured groom's safety it was best that no one but Rathbourne should know where he had been taken. As for Fenton, no doubt she was mistaken in thinking she had heard him speak with the cultured accent of a gentleman. She had not really been able to hear all that clearly when one thought about it, and in her overwrought state she might easily have imagined Rathbourne and the odious Fenton to be conspirators in what most probably had been nothing more than an unfortunate accident after all.

Yes, it all made perfect sense when one considered the evidence or lack thereof quite rationally. And yet even so, she had still to discover a reasonable explanation for the duke's reprehensible treatment of herself. Or had she? she pondered, recalling with a leap of her pulse Rathbourne's cryptic remark that the farce should begin again, for did not the key to all of this lie in the word *farce*?

She was quite sure that it did, since she suddenly knew why his utterance had struck her with particular significance earlier. For she remembered now that he had used the word before in reference to the affair which had culminated in the duel and his lengthy exile from England in disrepute. He had been in love and upon discovering his amour to be a Jezebel unworthy of the sacrifice of name and honor, how great must have been his distrust of all women! Then, too, if all that Kathryn Ingram had said of Rathbourne's father were true as well, was it any wonder that he should have erected an impregnable barrier of cynicism and arrogance to hold the world at bay?

Oh, God, she thought, her heart beginning to pound with painful certainty. What if she had *not* been wrong in thinking he once had entertained a certain fondness for her, an affection which had seemed put to the lie by his subsequently infamous treatment of her? And if he had cared for her, but dared not trust her or his own feelings, might he not have decided in his arrogance simply to make her his and then, playing out the farce, let come what may?

It all seemed so wonderfully plausible. What a fool she was not to have put it all together sooner, she thought and, feeling suddenly as if a weight had been lifted from her shoulders, got up from her chair to inhale a deep breath of fresh air flowing in through the open window.

The sound of a low hiss from beyond the window followed by a harsh whisper seemed suddenly to paralyze her.

"Hist! Over here!"

There was the crunch of approaching footsteps on the gravel outside. Without really knowing why she should have done so, Georgina found herself suddenly with her back pressed against the wall to one side of the window and her pulse throbbing at her temples as she listened to the slow, ever so slight and yet unmistakably uneven footfall of a man who favors one leg and seeks not to show it.

"You took your deuced time getting here," grumbled a voice vaguely familiar to her. "Any longer and I might have been tempted to have done with this tiresome charade and approached you out in the open, your new duchess be damned."

"I suggest, my lord, that in such an event it should not be my wife who was damned but the fool who had succumbed so very unwisely to temptation," observed the Duke of Rathbourne chillingly. "I should warn you, Fenton, that while I have never been particularly enamored of your rather less than engaging manner, you now find yourself in grave peril of becoming a complete and utter bore."

Georgina only just managed to stifle a small gasp as the identity of Rathbourne's companion was made known to her. Fenton! she thought in bitter dismay and beheld the whole fabric of her earlier rationalizations irrevocably flawed. Then the creature's voice, hot with resentment, obtruded once more on her stunned consciousness.

"If I were you, my lord duke," he said venomously, "I should take care not to antagonize the one man in possession of all the scandalous facts in the matter. Personally I don't care a damn what happens to the chit so long as I achieve what I came after. You owe me, Rathbourne. Remember that."

"I must presume," Rathbourne rejoined in deceptively mild tones, "that since you have risked exposure in such a foolhardy manner, you have something of import to convey to me. I do hope for your sake I am not to be disappointed."

"As to that, I couldn't say, Your Grace. However, I thought you might be interested to know that our man has come out in the open at last. Doubtless that business with the groom shook him up a bit. Too bad about Denby. I tried to warn him, but he just couldn't keep his nose out of things. I took care of that little matter for you, Rathbourne, but you might as well know that there's been someone else asking a lot of questions, and I'll not hold myself responsible for him."

"I am well aware of my brother's activities," drawled the duke without a trace of emotion. "You may rest assured that he will not interfere. Was there anything else?"

"You're a cool one all right," Fenton observed, as if forced to reluctant admiration. "I shouldn't be surprised if everything I've heard about you is true. But how, I wonder, shall you keep your precious brother in line when he discovers his bloody lordship, the earl, has abducted Lady Grantham for the purpose of at last deflowering his virgin wife? Which is what is going to happen very soon, my lord duke. And then you had best be ready to move, or I might forget our little bargain. After all, it's possible I should find a settlement with Vail more profitable in the long run."

"I should think twice before deciding anything so extremely foolhardy," drawled His Grace dangerously. "You seem quite certain the earl is ready to make his move.

Why?''

"Because I've watched him and because I know him so well. In truth, there's little I don't know of what's going on around me, as you should have guessed by now. I've learned to fade into the background and keep my eyes and ears open. It's part of the trade of a thief, and I was one of the best till Vail doublecrossed me.''

"Ah, yes. You mentioned before that you and Vail were partners," Rathbourne remarked carelessly.

"Partners? We were never anything like. I did it all. I picked the mark, laid the plans, and took all the risks. All Vail had to do was move about in the right company. Make himself agreeable to the ladies and let me know who would be where on a certain night. It was easy for him. He had the title, the looks, and the reputation of a charming, if impoverished, young man about town—a welcome addition to any social gathering. I, on the other hand, had only the title. Clarence Anson Peregrine Fenton, Viscount Cheseldine," he sneered. "It bought me nothing but m'father's gambling debts, an encumbered estate which had in the end to go to the auction block, and the reputation of a card sharp.''

"Thus you determined to replenish your fortunes through thievery, I presume. Clever of you to employ a front. But Vail became greedy, did he not? Indeed, he saw a chance to marry into money and took it. Only the lady in question was to have been your mark. I don't suppose the earl cared for the notion of sharing his future bride's fortune with you, his erstwhile partner, did he, Fenton?''

"Hardly. He set me up, the bloody little cock. Had the Bow Street runners waiting for me. I got away with a hole in my shoulder, which the Runners fortunately believed was a deal more serious than it was. Indeed, I heard sometime later that Viscount Cheseldine, whose greatly decomposed body had been fished from the Thames, had been mortally wounded in an attempted burglary. A signet ring with

311

which I had parted company several weeks previous was used to positively identify the miscreant. In a sense I was free, so long as I remained in the guise of a beggar. No one ever thought to see Cheseldine in Anson Fenton's rags. Meantime, I kept an ear out for my old friend Vail. Less than a year later I heard he had lost his wife under peculiar circumstances."

"It was reported that Lady Grantham perished of food poisoning," said the duke in apparent boredom.

"Oh, the food she ate that night was poisoned all right, and when I heard rumors Vail had managed to gamble his wife's fortune away, I knew how it got that way."

"And that was when you decided to get even with Vail for betraying you."

"No, not then. With Vail's fortune down the River Tick, it would have availed me little but satisfaction in exposing him. It was a year later, when his name began to be linked with that of another wealthy young heiress who had just made her come-out that I made my move. I thought if I went to her father with what I knew about Vail, he'd not only see fit to make it worth my while but he would make sure Vail was utterly ruined as well. Only Lynton, the girl's father, was no fool."

Georgina's hand flew to her mouth to stifle an involuntary gasp at her uncle's name. Oh, God, Zenobia! she thought in sudden horrified understanding. Then she froze at Fenton's sharp exclamation.

"What was that? Did you hear something?"

"I beg your pardon?" queried Rathbourne, and with a sense of impending hysteria, Georgina visualized the duke's imperious arch of an aristocratic eyebrow.

"I heard something, I tell you," Fenton rasped.

"I shouldn't be at all surprised. It is something of a festive occasion. However, I suggest that we terminate what has doubtless been a scintillating conversation. You will, of course, continue to keep me informed of Vail's activities.

312

Otherwise, I feel reasonably certain that the Bow Street Runners would not be disinterested to learn a certain notorious jewel thief did not, as they had been led to believe, perish three years ago."

"You make yourself patently clear, my lord duke," observed Fenton with something of ironic humor. "And may I wish you greater fortune with your bride than that enjoyed by Vail, who, thanks to my timely intervention, has yet to consummate his marriage vows."

Georgina, her hands still pressed over her mouth to keep from making any inadvertent sound, listened with no little relief to Fenton's stealthy departure. Her limbs were trembling with the inevitable reaction to all she had overheard, and it was all she could do to remain standing till Rathbourne, too, should decide to leave.

Oh, God! What *had* she heard? she wondered, struggling to make sense of the bits and pieces tumbling about in her brain. Was she to understand that her cousin had married the Earl of Vail and then run away before he could bed her? And somehow Rathbourne had found out about it and about Fenton, a thief and a scoundrel, who had in turn stricken Denby down because he knew too much. Too much about what? About Rathbourne and Fenton? About Zenobia and Vail? Fenton said he had handled the Denby business for Rathbourne but would not be responsible for Robbie's silence. So, she had been right to think Robbie had been lying about his whereabouts the past week. He had been nosing about, trying to find out what? About Denby? No. About Zenobia. Why her sentiments toward him had changed. And he had learned something which had made Fenton uneasy enough to risk speaking to Rathbourne here today. Good God! Had he found out about Denby? Was Denby dead and Rathbourne at the very least inadvertently responsible for his death? But then why should Rathbourne go out of his way to protect Zenobia only to turn around and order Denby's murder?

What could Rathbourne possibly wish kept silent badly enough to warrant a man's life? None of it made any sense! Somehow she had to find the courage to confront Rathbourne and make him tell her the whole truth of it. But not now. Not when she felt sick and weak. Not before she had had time to think.

Thus, distraught and plagued by uncertainties, perhaps it was little wonder that she did not detect the slight sounds of someone stepping over the doorsill and down the two steps into the cottage. Indeed, her first awareness that she was not alone was the terrifying touch of a hand upon her shoulder and the sudden murmur of her name.

She screamed and struck mindlessly out at the unknown intruder, only to have her wrists imprisoned in a steely grip.

"Georgina no! No matter what you think you heard just now, I'm not your enemy."

It was Rathbourne! Suddenly Georgina froze.

"Are you not?" she whispered passionately, her sightless eyes huge in the pale oval of her face. "Then take me now to Denby. Prove to me that he is still alive."

"I cannot!" he answered in a hard voice. "It would be too dangerous."

"Dangerous for whom?"

"For Christ's sake, Georgina! Whom do you think?" exclaimed the duke, nearly flinging her from him as he turned abruptly away to stand with his back to her.

Georgina stumbled backward and came up hard against the wall.

"Good God! I don't know what to think!" she cried, wanting him to deny her terrible suspicions. Wanting to trust her heart and not her brain.

She heard Rathbourne draw in a long, shuddering breath. Her own breath was ragged and her throat raw as she struggled not to lose hold of her senses.

"I suppose it is too much to ask that you simply accept on faith that Denby is alive and safe," she heard him say

314

sardonically. "Indeed, why should you? Murder, after all, is not that far removed form rendering a woman senseless with drugs and then raping her." His sudden, bitter laughter flayed her soul. "God! There must be some irony in all of this. If only I could see it."

His voice stopped, and Georgina became suddenly aware that she was weeping silently, the tears streaming down her cheeks to trickle unheeded off her chin. He must have seen it, too, because she heard him curse sharply under his breath, and then he had come back to her. She felt the back of his hand, gentle against her face, as he tried to brush the tears away, and suddenly she sniffed self-consciously and attempted to turn her head to one side.

"Botheration!" she exclaimed on a shuddering gust of air. "I never cry. It's so . . . so blasted *feminine*!"

His surprised laughter rumbled over and through her so that she chuckled a little, too, but uncertainly, as if afraid that once she let go she might never stop. Then he had ceased to laugh. Her heart skipped a beat as his hands closed about her arms in a steely grip. She could feel his eyes intent upon her face. Why did he not say something? Why couldn't she?

Then he was speaking, and she felt herself mesmerized by something irrevocable in his voice.

"Gina, come away with me. Now," he whispered in a husky voice. "To Greystone, where we can be alone. I want you, Gina. All of you. Without questions, uncertainties, or regrets. You're my wife, my duchess. Trust me, Gina. I could never hurt you. Never!"

Georgina closed her eyes against the veil of darkness and swayed slightly. Greystone, she thought, suddenly afraid. But then something deeper, more compelling than her fear roused itself within her. Slowly she opened her eyes.

Rathbourne's breath whistled in his throat at something he saw in her face.

"Yes. I will go," she said. "But hurry. Go and bring the

horse to the cottage. I'll wait for you here. And tell Gilda that . . . Tell her thank-you and God bless. Well? Go," she laughed when he made no move to leave. "I'll be waiting. No questions. No regrets, I promise. Now will you go?"

But it was a lie, she thought as she listened to him turn and stride quickly for the door. She had already one regret. For he had said he wanted her, all of her, without questions or doubts. But those were words of desire only, and he had said nothing of love.

Chapter 14

It seemed exceedingly strange to Georgina to stand before the threshold of Greystone Manor and have once more the evening breeze sweet with honeysuckle and lilacs wafting familiarly about her. For as they had left the horse in the stable and made their way up the gravel drive, she had been visited with the oddest sensation of having been away for a very long time. Indeed, she thought, it was the feeling one had of returning to a place long held in loving memory only to find that while everything seems unchanged, somehow nothing is the same.

Her head lifted at the click of the bolt being released as Rathbourne turned the key. The familiar creak of the old oaken door swinging open brought a small, whimsical smile to her lips.

Poor Bolton, she thought as she stepped past Rathbourne into the spacious entryhall. No matter how often he oiled the hinges, he could never quite rid them of that small complaint. Nor, though she had tried, could Georgina ever convince him that she would not have had it any other way. The creak, after all, she remembered teasing him, was part of the essence of the house, like the rattle of the leaded windowpanes when the wind blew or the scent of old wood and lemon oil on cleaning day. And, indeed, the scents and sounds peculiar to Greystone had all seemed somehow dear and familiar to her, the way a time-faded portrait or the pattern of the wallpaper of a favorite room might have been to someone else, someone who could see them.

And yet tonight she felt differently, distant somehow, as if she had only lived those moments in a dream.

Rathbourne's voice obtruding on her thoughts brought her back to the present and to an uncomfortable awareness of him and why they had come to Greystone. She shivered a little as a chill draught, like the fleeting touch of a hand, brushed against her cheek, and inexplicably, absurdly, she felt suddenly like an intruder there.

"I—I'm sorry," she said, closing her eyes and shaking her head a little, as though to throw off the strange mood which had come over her since arriving at Greystone. "What did you say?"

"I had merely observed, my love, that you appeared a trifle distracted. Is something troubling you?"

"No, of course not. Indeed, why should there be?" she rejoined a trifle sharply and bit her lip in sudden vexation at herself. Really, she was behaving like a veritable schoolroom miss left alone with a man for the first time in her life. If only she did not feel the house so strangely, she mused then, frowning ever so slightly, and wished that Rathbourne would say something. Anything. For it had suddenly occurred to her that it was the unnatural quiet of the manor with all the servants gone which set her nerves on end.

But the duke said nothing, and with a growing unease, she sensed his eyes intent upon her. Indeed, his silence seemed somehow to accuse her of having lied to him.

Feeling compelled, she went on with a false brightness.

"It was nothing really. I was just thinking that if I had not been blind, I would never have come to feel about Greystone what I have felt. It's not a house to me, you know, the way houses usually are to sighted people."

"No, I don't suppose it is," he said then. Gently and without the drawl, she thought. Feeling his eyes upon her, she felt suddenly ridiculously shy.

"I am always acutely aware of Greystone in a way they are not."

She paused, realizing how silly that must have sounded to him.

"But then I have to be, of course, or I should be forever lost or stumbling over things, shouldn't I? Which would be idiotish in the extreme," she said, laughing a little, and nervously reached up to jerk the hat pin out of the brimless beaver set at a rather jaunty angle atop her curls. As she made as if to remove the hat as well, however, her hands stilled for the briefest moment and a pensive frown passed fleetingly across her lovely features.

"It's almost as if I can actually feel the house all around me," she said quite soberly and slowly lifted the hat off her head then laid it carefully on the giltwood console table directly before her. "Rather as if it were alive . . ."

She fell abruptly silent. Her head tilted in the unconscious way she had of trying to sense what was going on about her.

"You must think me an utter gudgeon for rambling on so," she said abruptly, then nearly jumped as Rathbourne deigned at last to make his presence known.

"No, why should I?" he commented easily, having come up behind her. She drew in a quick breath as the strong, slender hands lightly clasped her shoulders. "I should think it extremely odd did you *not* feel a certain affinity for this house."

"Should you?" she murmured hardly above a whisper

319

and shivered at the tingling warmth of his breath against her neck below her ear.

"Mm-hmm," affirmed the duke, apparently intent upon driving her to distraction as slowly he nibbled his way up the slender column of her neck to linger tantalizingly at her earlobe.

For an endless moment she lost herself to the exquisite torment of his lips, titillating and teasing her, rousing her with practiced ease. Till at last she uttered a long, shuddering sigh and lifted her hand to cover his resting still with disturbing warmth upon her shoulder.

"Your Grace," she whispered, drawing her head back and to one side, and smiled a little as she heard him inhale a deep, somewhat shaky breath. "Why are we standing in the hall?"

For a moment he seemed to ponder her question as he turned his face into the delightful contour of her neck and inhaled her sweet scent. She sensed his slow smile even before he spoke.

"Because, my love, unlike you I suffer most regrettably from a debilitating dependence on candlelight. Indeed, I find I am peculiarly intimidated at the thought of groping my way ignominiously in the dark and yet I find myself reluctant to leave you long enough to search for a flint and candle."

"Oh, dear. You are something at a disadvantage," agreed Georgina, surprised into sudden laughter. She had not considered that with Bolton and Mrs. Porter gone from the house, there would have been no one to light the candles or the lamps.

"I am, in fact, completely at your mercy," observed His Grace and kissed her most disturbingly at the base of her throat where the pulse throbbed to his touch.

"I doubt not, my lord duke, that you have never found yourself at anyone's mercy. Least of all at mine," she retorted just a trifle bitterly. Slipping firmly from beneath his hands, she kindly requested that he point her in the direction leading from the door.

How odd it was that she should be leading him through the dark, silent halls of the old manor, she thought, keenly aware of the duke's long fingers curled snugly about her own and of the sound of their footsteps echoing hollowly through the empty house. For once she was glad she could not see. It was bad enough just to imagine without having actually to behold the furniture draped in holland covers, as it must be, for with the house closed up, Bolton and Mrs. Porter were like to remain in the servants' quarters for the most part, there being little point to maintaining the manor in polished condition with the young earl and his mama no longer in residence. Indeed, it suddenly occurred to her that her old rooms would hardly be in order for the mistress's unexpected arrival. Well, they should just have to make do, she thought, remembering the numerous times a bivouac tent had seemed like a palace.

"Here we are," she said as at last she found the door to her sitting room. The duke's hand reached out suddenly to cover hers on the latch.

"That shall be my pleasure, Your Grace," he said and, flinging open the door, bent down to lift her high in his arms. "It is after all traditional," he murmured, as he carried her over the threshold.

For a long moment he held her in the cradle of his arms, until her heart began to pound and her nerves to tingle with suspense.

"You may set me down if you will," she said, trying to speak in a normal voice. "I know where Nanny keeps the candles and flint, though I myself seldom make use of them. I have a dreadful fear of fire."

"Hush," he commanded in a low voice which seemed oddly to caress her. "The room is filled with moonlight, and I am well able to see all that I would wish to see."

Upon which Rathbourne covered her mouth with his,

effectively silencing whatever reply she might have made, and kissed her lingeringly, his lips moving over hers with sensuous tenderness, until at last her lips parted on a sigh and his tongue discovered the tantalizing sweetness of her mouth.

She hardly knew when at last he carried her into the other room and laid her gently on the bed. She felt lost in some sort of dream, a dream which she had dreamt often before, and always in terror. And yet this time she knew with a kind of wonder that she was not afraid. Indeed, this time she seemed to be waiting, but for what, she did not know.

Thus she lay quiescent as Rathbourne undressed first her, with tender deliberation, and then himself.

She heard the sharp intake of breath as he gazed upon her loveliness, and then he was beside her on the bed, his lean length warm against her. Her pulse quickened at the touch of his hand, first gentle upon her body, then demanding, as he began slowly to rouse her, stroking her, teasing her, tantalizing her, till her breath came in long, shuddering sighs and the dream began to give way to reality. And all the time he was kissing her. First her eyes and then her lips, maddeningly, passionately.

Georgina shuddered uncontrollably. She had never known love such as this, the feverish ache, a tormented seeking of release. Nor had she known she could burn with desire, her blood leaping in her veins like liquid flame— consuming her, awakening in her something she sensed but could not define. It was more than the need to touch and be touched. Greater than the hunger for his lips upon hers. She sighed deliriously at the inflaming touch of his hands moving over her, exploring the secret vulnerabilities of her body, teasing and tormenting her, weakening her defenses, until at last she was swept with some terrible urgency which was more than need, greater than desire. Desperately she clung to him, eyes closed, her head turning aimlessly back and forth against the pillow as he sought the moist warmth of her deepest need. She uttered a sharp gasp of rising ecstasy and arched against him, wanting him, needing him to come into her.

His hands spread wide her thighs, and she felt his hard manhood turgid with need press against her.

"Drew," she groaned and opened to his thrust, moved with him in the feverish rhythm of culminating passion, until at last a pulsating explosion of pleasure rippled through her in wave after wave of exquisite release.

She was left trembling and weak, and filled with a terrible, aching tenderness for the man in whose arms she lay.

At last she knew she loved him totally, without reservation. Rathbourne, illusive and sinister, yet fascinating, too, who had lurked always in the background during her marriage to David, a figure of recklessness and daring. Rathbourne, cynical and overbearing, who had strolled unannounced into her garden at Greystone and forever changed her. And, indeed, Rathbourne, ambiguous, unassailable, and obscure, who had forced her into marriage and conquered her heart.

How different he was from the tall, gentle soldier who had wooed her with an endearing sweetness and won her. His had been an enduring, quiet sort of strength built on compassion, patience, and understanding. At three and twenty David was already a man, mature, steady, sure of himself, while at seventeen, she had been a child, willful and impetuous, a girl groping her way toward womanhood, and when he had made love to her with passionate tenderness, she had felt imbued with blissful warmth, a love so wondrously sweet and satisfying that even now she could have wept for its loss.

What had Rathbourne been at twenty-eight? she wondered suddenly.

By the time David and she had married, the duke had

long had the reputation of an inveterate gambler, a womanizer, and a rakeshame. He had been a law unto himself, cold, reckless, and dangerous, and very much a man. A man driven by something she did not understand. How different would her life have been had she met Rathbourne before David! And how tragic. For it was impossible that she should not have loved him, been fascinated, frightened, and even repelled, but still hopelessly in love with him. And had he even noticed her, which was unlikely, and, *more* improbable, had he somehow fallen in love with her, theirs would have been a turbulent relationship, unrestrainedly passionate, thrillingly unpredictable, and yet tempestuous, violent, and doomed in the end to disillusionment and failure. For while David's love had sustained and nurtured her, given her strength and self-assurance, Rathbourne's would have consumed her as surely as the flame consumes a moth.

Her lips curved suddenly into a smile. She had not been ready seven years ago to endure a love such as Rathbourne's. But she was a child no longer. She was a woman, a woman who had been molded by love and strengthened by grief. And a woman with as great a fire and passion as her beloved.

She felt him stir next to her and was swept anew with tenderness. His fingers woven between hers curled over her hand. She tingled as she felt his lips against her hair, then, made inexplicably aware of the cool night air, she shivered.

He hugged her close to his lean strength and murmured in her ear.

"Are you awake, my love?"

"M-m-m," she nodded and stretched luxuriously. Upon which her stomach rumbled ominously. Silently she blushed.

"And hungry, 'twould seem."

Her heart lurched at the marvelous sound of his laughter. Then his lips had found hers and she felt her blood begin to stir all over again. She sighed when at last he pulled away, and tenderly raised her hand to caress his cheek.

Suddenly her mind reeled as her fingers found and traced the distinct line of a scar along the cheekbone. She jerked her hand away as if she had been burned.

Oh God! It had not been a dream! She *had* seen Rathbourne's face as he had carried her to her bed the night before. Then neither had she dreamt the passion which had flared between them leaving her swooning in his arms, nor the resentment she had felt against David. It was all true!

In the wake of this stunning realization, she was swept with an agonizing wave of shame. Not because she suddenly knew that she had wanted Rathbourne to make love to her then, but because she had believed him capable of anything so vile as to drug her that he might have his way with her. Nothing had happened! She knew that of a certainty. Indeed, she remembered that night quite clearly. And something else. Something which hovered at the edge of consciousness, dark and still indistinct like a spectre come to haunt her. A terrible, rending pain pierced her brain. She gasped, feeling sick and weak.

Vaguely she heard Rathbourne say her name, felt his hand grasp and shake her. She wanted desperately to tell him she knew the truth of it and beg his forgiveness, but the thunderous crash of a gunshot resounded through the house. And then a woman's shrill scream.

"Robbie! Oh God no!"

Georgina froze, her breath coming in swift shallow gasps as she fought against the stabbing pain inside her head.

"Nobie!" she breathed and abruptly began to struggle in Rathbourne's grasp.

"Listen!" he rasped, his fingers digging into her flesh as he jerked her back and held her.

For an eternity neither of them moved as they strained to hear. The muffled but unmistakable sounds of a scuffle sounded from somewhere below. Then a man's harsh shout came clearly to them.

"Drop the knife, Vail, and let her go!"

Georgina thought she heard her cousin's quickly stifled scream, then Rathbourne was shaking her.

"Georgina, listen to me!" he whispered fiercely. "I'm going downstairs. I want you to get dressed. Then wait for me here. Do you understand? Wait here!"

Georgina swayed and cried out as Rathbourne left her to hurriedly don his riding breeches and boots. It was the dream again, the nightmare. Rathbourne supplanting David in her heart and leaving her alone in the darkness. She heard his quick, light step and then he was shaking her again, forcing her to take the bundle of her clothes.

"Wait for me, Gina," he said. "I'll be back for you."

Then he had crossed to the door, pausing only long enough to shrug on his shirt before he was gone.

With a groan Georgina sagged to the bed and waited for the tears to come. But she felt oddly empty. The pain had even receded to a dull ache. As if it, too, were only waiting for the dream to begin again, she thought wearily, then dragged herself from the bed and began to dress.

Robbie Penwarren pulled his mount up sharply before the darkened stables at Greystone and leaped noiselessly from the saddle. Quickly he tethered the horse to a fence rail. Then darting a wary look around him, he stole swiftly toward the manor along the narrow drive bordered by chestnuts. Pausing periodically to search the shadows before him, he came at last to the broad sweeping lawns and halted, his face grim, as he caught sight of the cloaked figure of a woman, her hair silvery in the moonlight, stealing furtively across the open to the front door of the house.

The leaden pressure in his chest gave way to a sudden

wrenching pain as he saw the door open and beheld the silhouette of a man framed against a yellow shaft of lamplight. The woman appeared to draw back as if she had had second thoughts about entering, but then she straightened and, slipping sideways past the man, went inside. The door closed, and suddenly a look of agony swept the youthful countenance.

Damn the deceitful little wretch! he thought, wheeling in agony from the sight of the manor bathed in moonlight. He had been so sure that she loved him. He had forced himself to be patient, told himself that she had been badly hurt by someone before him but eventually she would see that he was not like that earlier love who had proven to be false. He had found excuses for her sudden change toward him so soon after that unforgettable evening in the rose-garden when he had broken through the barrier of her reserve at last. Indeed, he had even persuaded himself that she had refused his proposal of marriage out of some misguided notion of self-sacrifice. As if it had mattered one whit to him that she was a penniless orphan! But this! This he could not explain.

It had been Denby who had told him about the "flash cove" he had seen spying on Greystone. And Denby, too, who had only a day or two later reported running into Fenton and Miss Kingsley in suspicious circumstances. Nor had the shrewd little Cockney believed Fenton's story for a moment that the stablehand had come upon the lady shortly after she had twisted her ankle and was only trying to help her. "She were as white as a sheet, milord," Denby said, "and 'scairt." He couldn't have been mistaken about that. Then he had gone on to intimate that there was something "havey-cavey" about "a bloke wot claimed to've been a jack-tar in the King's Navy" but had hands "as soft and white as a lord's doxy," beggin' his lordship's pardon. Nor would he have troubled Lord Robert with the matter excepting that His Grace had asked him to keep an eye on the ladies while the duke was in London.

At first he had not given much thought to Denby's dour speculations. He had been too much in alt over what he had mistakenly believed was his successful breaching of Miss Kingsley's formidable defenses. But then the woman whom he had expected to make his wife had the next day rejected him, going so far as to disallow him any hope than she would ever change her mind and requesting that he never again annoy her with his unwelcome attentions. All of which in turn had been followed immediately by Denby's "unfortunate accident," the duke's return to Rathbourne in a black, most damned peculiar mood and accompanied by Julian Bradford, who spent most of his time in the old castle dungeons talking to human skulls brought with him from London (His Grace apparently having informed him that any such grisly remains of the torture rack and wheel had long since been properly disposed of, speculated Robbie sourly). Nor was that all, for no sooner was the duke installed once more at Rathbourne than Denby suddenly mysteriously vanished. It was simply too much to swallow, especially as his brother refused to discuss the matter with him beyond advising him that he had placed Denby where he could be satisfactorily looked after.

Robbie knew the duke well enough, however, to suspect that Rathbourne was keeping something from him, probably for what he believed were Robbie's "own best interests." Thus Robbie, who was long past needing to be shielded from anything, could not but wonder what had caused his elder brother suddenly to resume his long-abandoned role of paterfamilias. He concluded that anything quite so eccentric must have been precipitated by concern over Robbie's apparent tendre for someone the duke considered an ineligible *partie*, to wit Miss Zenobia Kingsley. Not that Rathbourne had ever before shown the remotest interest in his brother's various affairs of the heart. But then Robbie had never before demonstrated so determined a partiality for any one female as he had done for Miss Kingsley. All of which had led him unavoidably to inquire more deeply into Denby's supposed accident, which seemed suddenly most damned coincidental with the appearance of the man Denby had reported seeing lurking suspiciously about Greystone, the groom's encounter with Miss Kingsley in Fenton's arms, and Miss Kingsley's sudden, swift change of heart.

Taking into account what Denby had told him, he had required no more than a single, unobtrusive scrutiny of Fenton to confirm in his own mind that the man had indeed never seen service on a King's ship. For although strictly speaking his hands were not as white as those of a "lord's doxy," they bore little evidence of having ever belonged to a sailor. A sailor's hands would be scarred and calloused from fighting the canvas in all kinds of weather. Fenton's were not. Other than that, however, he had been able to learn very little. Rathbourne had seen to that.

The duke had not ordered him to cease nosing about. He had not needed to, Robbie had later realized, for Rathbourne could be very persuasive when he chose to be. Instead he had laid his cards on the table. Or at least at the time he had appeared to have done, saying man to man that to arouse anyone's suspicions by asking too many questions at this time could only put a certain lady in grave peril of her life. Since it was impossible that he could have been referring to any lady other than Lady Grey or Miss Kingsley, Robbie had had little choice but to agree to do no more in the matter. As to what the matter was, the duke was bound by his word to say nothing.

Blast his brother and his word of honor! He might have at least given some hint that Miss Kingsley was involved with the Earl of Vail rather than to let him discover it like *this*.

It had not taken him long to come to the conclusion that the strikingly handsome but obviously dissipated gentleman who had accosted Zenobia Kingsley shortly after the wedding party descended from Llan Penrhyn had to be Denby's mysterious "flash cove." It had, after all, been painfully obvious from the lady's startled reaction to his sudden appearance and low-uttered words that they were not strangers to one another. Egad, she had turned suddenly as white as a sheet and had given every indication that she was on the verge of a swoon.

What a fool he had been to think she required his intervention! Indeed, she had laughed in his face. The memory of her eyes glittering with defiance as she turned and clung to the earl seemed forever burned into his mind.

Robbie clenched his fists, his heart bitter with gall as he recalled the slight curl of the earl's lip in contemptuous amusement. Vail could not be more than two or three years his senior, and yet he had made Robbie feel like some brash and foolish boy meddling in the affairs of grown men as he coolly turned his back on him and, murmuring something provocative to the slender girl on his arm, led her away to a secluded corner.

For a moment his mind had seemed to go blank with white-hot rage. Had it not been that suddenly Lord Ingram had appeared out of nowhere, casually linking an arm through his and lisping a steady stream of what had at first seemed inanities, doubtless he would have called the earl out at once. As it was, some shred of awareness that he was a gentleman and owed his brother's guest at least the semblance of civility had kept him from delivering the insipid fop a blistering set-down. Gradually then his blood had cooled, and he had suddenly perceived the gleam of understanding humor in the heavily drooping eyes.

"Ah, yes. That is better," observed Lord Ingram, drawing an exquisite porcelain snuffbox from his pocket and, with a flair of lace cuffs, inhaling a pinch. "I could not help but witness your rather less than pleasant encounter with his lordship, the earl. Something of a rogue, that one. I shouldn't think it would be at all the thing to antagonize him when one has rather less than all his wits about. But then I shouldn't dream of telling you how to go on, dear boy. It simply has occurred to me that Miss Kingsley does not really appear all that enamored of Lord Vail's rather dubious charm. She would seem to me to have more the aspect of a female in trouble. But then I could be wrong. One can never tell about a woman."

Damn! What the devil was she doing stealing out alone at night to meet a man like Vail? If she were indeed in some sort of trouble, why had she not come to him? he thought, wheeling once more to gaze in perplexity at the great bay window lit from within by lamplight.

Then suddenly he straightened, his breath whistling in his throat as he saw framed in the lighted window Zenobia, her arms extended before her as with both hands she raised a gun and with deadly deliberation aimed it.

"Good God!" he uttered in a low voice. He stole swiftly across the lawn to the house and, thrusting open the door, burst into the foyer. He heard Vail in the next room, his back turned toward the door, say something indistinguishable and laugh. Then Zenobia's voice came chillingly distinct.

"I have given you the paper you came for. You have everything you need to make your claims stand up in court. I don't care about the money. It's yours. But you shan't have me, my lord. I shall kill you first. And then myself."

"But I'm afraid I can't allow that, my dear," Vail rejoined easily, moving deliberately toward the girl, his eyes never leaving hers as the gunbarrel wavered ever so much. "Oh, you will kill yourself, I'm quite sure, since I have other plans which don't include a wife who would be something of an embarrassment, after all. But I have no desire to die so untimely a death. Now give me the gun. You know you don't intend using it."

"Stop! Don't come any closer. I warn you. I will use it."

But Vail lunged at her, his hands reaching for the weapon. The gun went off, the bullet sailing past Vail's head to strike a burning oil lamp set on an occasional table near the bay window. Suddenly oil and flames spread along the carpet toward the drapes. Then Robbie had reached Vail and the girl struggling in his grasp.

Robbie's hand closed over Vail's shoulder, and the earl turned, a look of hideous surprise on the handsome face. Smiling in grim enjoyment, Robbie swung and connected a bone-crunching right to Vail's unprotected jaw. The earl's head snapped to one side. He staggered, arms flailing, then, stumbling over a rosewood sofa table, sprawled full length on the floor.

For an instant Robbie froze as he caught sight of the drapes going up in flames. Then he heard Zenobia scream and turned to see Vail coming at him with a knife and Zenobia throwing herself between them. He uttered a bitter oath as Vail clasped the girl to his chest and held her, one arm around her throat and the point of the knife pressed against her side.

"Drop the knife, Vail, and let her go!"

"Oh, I think not," the earl sneered, his face suddenly ugly. "The lady is, after all, my wife."

For a moment Robbie stared without comprehension at the dissipated face, then at Zenobia, weeping softly, her eyes ashamed and desolate as she stood helpless in the earl's cruel embrace.

It was true. He could see it in her face. All the time he had loved her, made a fool of himself over her, she had been Vail's wife. And suddenly everything which had seemed so perplexing, so mysterious about her made sense. Everything but how she could ever have married the Earl of Vail.

"Robbie?" Zenobia whispered hoarsely, seeing his disgust and the hurt disbelief in his eyes. Then she bit back a cry as Vail tightened his hold and pressed the point of the knife significantly against her side.

"I am sorry we cannot stay to exchange further pleasantries, Penwarren," he shouted above the steadily crescendoing roar of the fire. His lips curled in a thin, chillingly ironic smile. "Things are becoming rather too warm, I should think. If you would be so kind as to move out of the doorway, Lady Grantham and I shall be going."

Suddenly Robbie's gaze narrowed to hard, glittering points.

"I don't know what you did to force her to marry you, Vail," he said dangerously. "But I can guess. And I won't stand by and let you take her against her will. Now drop the knife and get out of here while you still can."

The earl darted a nervous glance at the rapidly spreading fire. The drapes were nearly consumed in flames which licked greedily at the ceiling and already smouldering walls, and the air was thickening with smoke which burned the eyes and throat. In a matter of minutes none of them might be alive.

Zenobia shrank, a rending gasp torn from her lips, as the knife suddenly drew blood.

"All right!" Robbie uttered harshly and began cautiously moving away from the door in a half-circle around the other two. "All right. But if you hurt her, I swear I'll not rest till I've hunted you down."

"I doubt that you will be in a position to do anything, you fool," Vail laughed as he dragged the girl to the door. "But since you obviously desire her company so greatly, you shall have her."

Abruptly he thrust the weeping girl into the burning room and backed quickly through the doorway. Then the door slammed shut, and as Robbie caught Zenobia in his arms, the key sounded ominously in the lock.

"Zenobia!" Robbie uttered hoarsely and dragged the slender form fiercely against him. He felt her sag against him, her body racked with weeping.

"I . . . love . . . you," she gasped between sobs, her

fingers clenching the fabric of his coat. "He was dreadful . . . A beast! He abducted me. Took me to Gretna Green. Fenton told my father, then followed us expecting Papa to reward him. He burst in on us in that vile room at the inn before Vail could . . . could have his way with me. Knocked him out. But Papa didn't wait for word from Fenton. He came after me. My mother . . . insisted on going with him, and the carriage . . . Oh, God! I killed them! And now I've killed you!"

"Hush! You haven't killed anyone, my dearest Nobie. I'll get us out of this somehow. I promise. But you must buck up," he said, shaking her a little. Then he had put her from him, and crossing quickly to the door, threw his weight against it. The door shuddered and held. He drew back to try again. Then he stiffened, a grin crossing his face, as he heard someone shout his name from the other side.

"Drew! We're in here!" he shouted back and pounded against the door with his fist.

He heard Rathbourne curse.

"The key's missing. Stand back! I'll have to break it down."

Coughing and nearly overcome with smoke, Robbie backed hastily to Zenobia and dragged her to one side away from the door. The door shuddered with the force of a heavy weight thrust against it. Then Rathbourne was through dragging them both out of the burning room.

Robbie nearly stumbled over Vail's inert form lying ominously still in the foyer. His stomach heaved at sight of the bloody shirtfront and the dagger buried to the hilt in the earl's chest. He felt Zenobia gasp and sag against him, then Rathbourne, his eyes like blue, piercing flames, was shouting at him to get the girl out and go for help.

"Drew, wait! Where are you going?" he choked as he saw his brother turn away and start up the stairs two at a time.

Rathbourne either did not hear or ignored him as he continued his wild dash up the curving staircase. Behind him the great hall in which the first Earls of Grey had held court was consumed in flame and directly above, Georgina waited for him.

Smoke curled in wispy trails through the hall as at last the duke came to the room in which he had left Georgina. His heart pounding in dread of what he might find, he thrust open the door. He heard Georgina scream.

"Rathbourne, no!"

Instinctively he threw himself, twisting, to one side as he caught a glimpse of Georgina standing in a shaft of moonlight, her eyes dark with fear, and Anson Fenton, Viscount Cheseldine, a gun pointed toward the door, waiting.

A blinding flash followed by the nerve-splitting crack of a shot filled the room. Rathbourne staggered at the sudden heavy blow. He landed hard and rolled. For an instant he lay stunned, his breath coming in painful gasps. He had been a fool not to realize Cheseldine must be somewhere in the house the moment he had seen Vail's body in the foyer below. Then he heard Georgina utter a strangled sound and looked up to see her, her face white and convulsed with grief.

"You've killed him!" she cried brokenly, and reached one hand out blindly in front of her. Rathbourne's breath caught painfully in his throat as he saw the pale gleam of a candle stick clutched in the other hand partially concealed in the folds of her dress and guessed what she meant to do. Then Cheseldine's low laughter brought her head around, and Rathbourne knew that she had what she had been waiting for. He tried to push himself up to stop her and gasped at the sudden rending pain in his shoulder. It seemed that he looked through a red filmy mist as helplessly he saw Georgina fling herself at Cheseldine.

In surprise the viscount fell back, one arm rising instinctively to ward off the unexpected attack. Cheseldine cursed and clutched his forearm where Georgina's blow had struck him, then, raising the gun, he brought it down hard against Georgina's temple. In agony Rathbourne saw the slender form crumple to the floor and with a small groan go deathly still. Swept with cold fury, he lurched to his feet, his breath coming in painful gasps, and lunged across the room.

"Cheseldine!" he uttered chillingly.

The viscount wheeled and lashed out at Rathbourne with the barrel of the gun. Rathbourne ducked beneath the blow and rammed his shoulder hard into Cheseldine's belly, his right arm grasping the other man around the waist as his momentum carried them both backward to the floor. The duke gasped, one hand clutching at the wound, as the fall wrenched his injured shoulder. Then Cheseldine was up. In a daze Rathbourne saw him coming and rolled heavily to one side as the other man sent a savage kick into his ribs. Rathbourne groaned and, pushing himself up on his good hand, launched himself at Cheseldine's legs.

With a sense of unreality Rathbourne watched Cheseldine, caught off balance, his face contorted with sudden horrid realization, crash through the window at his back.

The duke staggered beneath a wave of dizziness, one hand going blindly to the throbbing wound in his shoulder to come away wet with blood. Shaking his head to clear it, he stumbled to Georgina's side.

A low groan breathed through her lips as he tried to lift her. Her eyelashes fluttered, and then her eyes were open wide and staring blindly.

"Rathbourne?" she whispered, stealing a hand up to touch his face where the scar throbbed along his cheek. Then she was in his arms and hugging him desperately close. "Thank God," she breathed. "You're alive!"

She felt him shrink from beneath her touch, the breath sharp between his teeth, and she pulled away in sudden alarm.

"You're hurt!" she cried, but already he was climbing unsteadily to his feet and suddenly she became aware of the crackle of flames and the smoke stinging her throat and Rathbourne swaying drunkenly, one hand pulling her, dragging her up.

She could feel the fear welling up inside her as Rathbourne knelt and, grabbing her around the knees, took her across his shoulder. Suddenly she was living the nightmare of Talavera with the flames terrifying all around her as she searched among the dead and wounded for David. She remembered the horrifying sound of cannon fire and men and horses screaming everywhere. And suddenly a man, his face pale and bloodied from a cruel gash across his cheek, riding out of the thick pall of smoke straight at her.

She had been too terrified to do anything but stand stone-still, a silent scream raw in her throat as she waited to be ridden down. But he had seen her, and dragged the horse rearing to one side. She had heard the sudden loud report of a musket and the sickening thud of a bullet striking flesh, and then he was down, and she was kneeling beside him, trying to get him to stand, trying to drag him out of the path of the raging fire. The sergeant-major had appeared like the answer to a prayer, and, torn between the need to find David and the dreadful knowledge that it was because of her the soldier had been hit, she had followed as he carried the wounded officer off the field to safety.

Then it had all come back to her—everything— Rathbourne and Elvas and the night she had given in at last to the love which had been growing steadily within her. She remembered awakening in his arms to the imperative knock at the door and flinging on her dressing gown. And then the message that a new batch of wounded had been brought to the convent and that Rathbourne's brother had come looking for him. Oh, God! She remembered David!

It seemed that the flames leaped out of the darkness at

her and she couldn't breathe. And then she was being carried outside into the blessed air, cool against her skin, and hands were clutching her, lifting her tenderly to the ground. In a daze she saw Greystone engulfed in flames. Then a beloved face hovered briefly over her, and she tried to say his name before the darkness closed once more around her.

Chapter 15

Georgina became aware of voices somewhere close by and then of the red glare of light against her closed eyelids. For a moment she lay still, feeling weak and enveloped in a strange sort of lassitude. The way one feels when awakening from a deep, restful sleep after a lengthy illness, she thought somewhat vaguely and let her attention settle on what sounded very like a low-voiced argument of some kind.

"Damn it, Drew. Look at you! You're as white as one of my bleached skulls and twice as bone-headed. Good God, man! Surely you must be aware that you've lost more blood than most men live to tell about. You should be flat on your back in bed, I tell you, as would any other man who had a hole in his shoulder."

"I feel sure I must be gratified at your concern, Julian," replied a voice, which, though unmistakably weak and strained, yet could not fail to thrill her with its familiar drawling arrogance. "However, do you not wish to find yourself stretched flat on your back, you will kindly remove yourself from that door immediately and allow me to pass."

"I tell you she is out of danger and sleeping comfortably. There is no need for you to see her. Egad, man, you have only just recovered from a fever yourself."

"Nevertheless, I shall see for myself that all is well with her."

"Oh, very well then," Julian conceded with a deal of reluctance. "Obviously you are as mad as were those poor souls whose remains await me in your dungeons. And belike you shall end up as empty-headed as they if you don't have a better care for yourself."

"In that case, my dear friend, I shall will my skull to you, which shall greatly please you, shall it not. Now will you let me pass?"

Georgina felt her pulse quicken at the muffled sound of footsteps approaching the bedside. With all her heart she longed to hold Rathbourne near, and yet some compulsion she did not fully understand persuaded her to remain yet awhile longer with her eyes closed.

She sensed him standing over her and in her mind saw his eyes, blue like the Cornish sea, gazing down at her. She thrilled to the touch of his fingers, cool against her wrist. Then her heart nearly stopped as she felt his weight lurch against the side of the bed and Julian's sudden cry of alarm.

"Easy, old man. Now, what did I tell you. You should be in bed. Here. Sit down. Yes, that's better."

"Her pulse is erratic," the duke ground out between clenched teeth. "By God, Julian, if you have lied to me . . ."

"Drew!" Georgina uttered, surprised that her voice should sound hoarse and hardly louder than a whisper.

She heard him draw in a sharp breath and let it out again. Then her hand was clutched tightly in his.

"Gina?" he said with such anguish in his voice that she knew she could not wait another moment to know the truth. Her eyes fluttered open, then closed again, blinded by the sunlight streaming through the window.

"The curtains," she whispered. "Please. The light hurts

my eyes."

She heard his breath catch in his throat and felt his hand tighten thrillingly on hers. Then Julian had closed the drapes and hurried back to his patient's bedside.

"Now, Your Grace, if you would try and open your eyes once more."

She let her eyelids drift slowly open. The muted light was blurred as was the face hovering anxiously above her. She blinked and suddenly everything began slowly to draw into focus. A tremulous smile quivered on her lips as she looked finally into blue eyes gazing down at her with such anxious concern, such tender love, that immediately they began to blur once more in her vision as tears sprang to her eyes.

"Oh, my love," she whispered, reaching up to trail gentle fingers over the white line of the scar along his cheek bone. "How drawn and pale you are. Have you been so very ill?"

A beautiful light shone suddenly in his gaze. Then, as if he could not find the words, he raised her hand to his lips and, closing his eyes, bowed his head almost convulsively over it.

"I remembered everything. The fire brought it all back again. Seeing you fall from your horse at Talavera as the bullet struck you and knowing that if you had not pulled up to keep from trampling me, the shot would have missed you. I was obsessed with the need to find David, and there you were, grievously wounded because of me. Oh, Drew, I was so torn. I did not know what to do."

"So you stayed to care for me," observed the duke quietly, his hand continuing to move over her hair in long, steady strokes. "And thus missed finding David among all those other poor devils."

Julian Bradford having at last been persuaded that they should rub along very well without his continued presence, the Duke and Duchess of Rathbourne were lying in

Georgina's bed. Georgina's cheek rested against Rathbourne's hard chest, one arm clasped around him, as she told him about Elvas and David and everything which had happened after she had vanished from his life a year before. There had been so much to talk over, so much to fill in before all the pain and grief should at last be forever laid to rest. Nor was it easy for either of them. So very much had happened.

Swallowing to relieve the sudden pressure in her throat, Georgina nodded.

"I stayed. And later, when I learned who you were, that you were David's cousin, I could not leave you. I had to keep you alive because David loved you and I knew it was what he would have wanted. But then I found myself falling in love with you, and I could not bear it. How could I love you and David too? And yet I knew I did, though I tried so very hard not to. That last night as you cried out over and over in your sleep, and I tried to keep you quiet that you would not break open the wound again, I was so filled with despair. I paid a woman to sit with you whenever I received word new wounded had been brought to the convent. And then I would go and search among them for David or someone who could tell me something about him. I had been there that day, and as always there was no word, nothing of David. And suddenly it came to me that he was dead. He had to be.

"Oh, God. I could not bear it. I wanted to die, too. And then you cried out, tried to rise from your bed so that I had to hold you down. Suddenly you stilled and looked at me with such terrible need, and though I knew it was not really I but that other woman, your 'angel' to whom you had called repeatedly in your delerium and to whom you would make such desperate love, I lay with you. I loved you, shamelessly, and I told myself it was all right because David would have understood. David would have wanted it that way. But it was all a dreadful lie. It was not for David that I gave myself into your arms. It was for myself, because I loved you even though you loved that other woman. Your angel."

"But, my foolish little dove, did you not know *you* were my angel?" he whispered softly. "I have loved you from the moment I opened my eyes to behold your face. A beautiful angel of mercy."

"You l-loved me even then!" she queried tremulously.

"Then and always, my sweet angel," he said, his Celtic eyes alight with love for her.

Suddenly she could not go on though she had not yet told everything. Oh, God. How could she put the rest of it into words?

She felt his hand go suddenly still in her hair and with a dreadful sense of stunned unreality heard him say it for her.

"And then the messenger came with news of new wounded at the convent," he murmured. "So you dressed and went there as you always had, only this time believing David was dead. My poor angel, how terrible it must have been for you. To find David alive at last and then to have him die."

"You knew?" she whispered harshly. "But how . . .?"

"I received word when I was in London. From a fellow officer in intelligence. We had worked together aiding the Spanish guerrillas. Months before, when I first started trying to find you again, I wrote to him asking him to find out what he could."

"Did he tell you all of it? What else do you know of what happened that dreadful day?"

Rathbourne's arm tightened with a convulsive leap of muscle.

"I know that you must have been in shock. That you walked mindlessly out of the hospital and wandered aimlessly through the streets, until finally you were set upon by two ruffians. In the scuffle you received a blow to the head, which may or may not have contributed to your amnesia.

Luckily the officers from the Bomb Proof Barracks came along and chased the villains off. Then, realizing you were ill, they carried you to the convent."

Georgina raised up to stare accusingly into his face.

"Why did you not tell me? Why did you let me go on living in blind forgetfulness?"

A fleeting shadow like pain flickered briefly in his eyes.

"Because, my love, Julian believed it was imperative for you to discover the truth for yourself. You must understand that the blindness and the loss of memory were a haven into which you withdrew to heal yourself. You blotted out everything which had hurt you, everything which you were not strong enough to face. If I had told you what you were not ready yet to hear, you might have remained forever blind. As you seemed determined to do at any rate," he added bitterly. "Indeed, I could not understand at first why you clung so tenaciously to Greystone, refusing to go beyond the grounds even on brief visits to neighboring houses. It was Julian who suggested that so long as you had Greystone in which to hide, there was never any need for you to remember or any reason for you to see again."

Georgina stiffened in sudden dawning suspicion.

"So that was why you determined out of the blue that I must marry you!" she said, her lovely eyes flashing in mortified anger. "I suppose that was Julian's idea too. And did he suggest as well that you take me to Greystone in order to seduce me? Did you intend, Your Grace, to jar my memory by making love to me?"

She blushed hotly and tried to push away as she saw his eyes dance with sudden humor and something even more disturbing. But then his arm tightened and drew her irrevocably to him.

"You are a green girl indeed do you think for one moment I should require Julian to advise me in such matters," he murmured, one arrogant eyebrow rising incorrigibly toward his hairline. "I doubt there is much he could tell me that I hadn't learned long ago," he added, lowering his head to nibble most unfairly at her tender earlobe. "Or had you forgotten, my love, that you married an infamous womanizer and a rake?"

If she had forgotten, he soon recalled it most vividly to her mind, as he proceeded with maddening deliberation to rouse her as only he knew how.

Thus it was some time later that inexplicably a last troubling question popped unbidden into her whirling brain.

"Your Grace," she said, drawing away with sudden firmness. "There's just one thing more."

"Indeed?" sighed His Grace when it soon became apparent that his love was quite determined to resist any further proof that his reputation had been justifiably earned. "And I am to assume, it would appear, that it is something which cannot wait for a later time."

"You are, indeed," she said unequivocally. "For though I understand that Vail was desirous of proving that he had married my cousin since her fortune was bound in trust till she should be legally wed. And it seems clear that he had intended doing away with her as soon as he could in order that he might be free to marry the nabob's daughter. And I understand that Fenton determined to kill you that there would be no one left to inform Bow Street that he had not as they believed perished three years ago. And perhaps I can even see that it was necessary to keep all of this under wraps until such time as Vail exposed himself for what he was so that Nobie could in the end be free of him and thus wed Robbie. I suppose I can even forgive you for keeping me in the dark, since you appeared to have been motivated out of concern for my well-being. You thought, I have assumed, that it would be best not to distract me from trying to regain my memory. But that still leaves unresolved the one thing which drove me nearly mad. Where, my love, is Denby?"

"But surely it is obvious," he drawled, a devil of laughter in his eyes. "Julian, you know, is not really so mad as he has been made out to be. Indeed, I rather strongly doubt that he makes it a practice to carry on conversations with the dead as has been rumored. Actually, it was convenient for all concerned that he should pursue in the castle dungeons his study of the skulls of those rumored to have died in a state of insanity. Such a morbid preoccupation was bound to discourage the intrusion of any inquisitive servants. Cornishmen, you see, are peculiarly superstitious about the dead. Which meant that Julian should be left to tend his patient undisturbed."

"You cannot mean that you have been keeping Denby locked in the dungeon all this time?" Georgina demanded incredulously. "I cannot believe you could be so inhuman."

"Well, it did seem advisable at the time to keep his whereabouts hidden," observed His Grace in apparent innocence. "He had, after all, only just prevented the earl from abducting Miss Kingsley as she wandered unattended along the bourne berry-picking. Had it not been that Fenton came along in time to frighten him off, I suspect Denby would not have lived to tell me what had happened. Nor do I believe Denby has found his quarters all that unsatisfactory, since the dungeon was converted several generations ago to a very fine and well-stocked wine cellar. I fear, however, that you shall just have to take my word for it," he ended in such a manner as gave little doubt that he was fast losing all interest in the wholly irrelevant topic of the heretofore missing Denby. "Unless, of course, you intend that we should conduct an immediate tour of the castle dungeons."

"Oh, dear," she said, apparently much struck at the idea. "Upon serious consideration, I cannot think that would be at all feasible, Your Grace. Julian, after all, has positively forbidden either of us to leave this bed till such time as we are quite recovered."

"But how very insightful of him, to be sure," murmured Rathbourne, pulling her close with every intention of insuring that what seemed certain to be a rather lengthy recuperation should be made as painless as was possible. "Indeed, I am quite certain he is in the right of it."

Georgina smiled secretly, thinking of all that had happened, thinking for a moment of David and Greystone. She felt only sadness now where before there had been such a terrible burden of grief and guilt. That was gone as was the manor which had seen him grow to manhood. David could never have blamed her for loving Rathbourne. Indeed, he had made sure that she should. Just as she would make sure that one day Greystone Manor should stand again.

REGENCIES BY JANICE BENNETT

TANGLED WEB   (2281, $3.95)

Miss Celia Marcombe's dark eyes flashed with righteous indignation. She was not a commodity to be traded or bartered to a man
as insufferably arrogant as Trevor Ryde, despite what her high-
handed grandfather decreed! If Lord Ryde thought she would let
herself be married for any reason other than true love, he was
sadly mistaken. He'd never get his hands on her fortune—let
alone her person—no matter how disturbingly handsome he
was . . .

MIDNIGHT MASQUE   (2512, $3.95)

It was nothing unusual for Lady Ashton to transport government
documents to her father from the Home Office. But on this particular afternoon a gust of wind scattered the papers, and suddenly an important page was lost. A document desperately
wanted by more than one determined gentleman—one of whom
would murder to get his way . . .

AN INTRIGUING DESIRE   (2579, $3.95)

The British secret agent, Charles Marcombe, had done his bit
against that blasted Bonaparte. Now it was time to nurse his
wounds and come to terms with the fact that that part of his life
was over. He certainly did not need the likes of Mademoiselle
Therese de Bourgerre darkening his door, warning of dire emer-
gencies and dread consequences, forcing him to remember things
best forgotten. She was a delightful minx, to be sure, but it would
take more than a pair of pleading emerald eyes and a woebegone
smile to drag him back into the fray!

*Available wherever paperbacks are sold, or order direct from the
Publisher. Send cover price plus 50¢ per copy for mailing and
handling to Zebra Books, Dept. 2851, 475 Park Avenue South,
New York, N.Y. 10016. Residents of New York, New Jersey and
Pennsylvania must include sales tax. DO NOT SEND CASH.*

GOTHICS A LA MOOR — FROM ZEBRA

ISLAND OF LOST RUBIES
by Patricia Werner
(2603, $3.95)

Heartbroken by her father's death and the loss of her great love, Eileen returns to her island home to claim her inheritance. But eerie things begin happening the minute she steps off the boat, and it isn't long before Eileen realizes that there's no escape from *THE ISLAND OF LOST RUBIES*.

DARK CRIES OF GRAY OAKS
by Lee Karr
(2736, $3.95)

When orphaned Brianna Anderson was offered a job as companion to the mentally ill seventeen-year-old girl, Cassie, she was grateful for the non-troublesome employment. Soon she began to wonder why the girl's family insisted that Cassie be given hydro-electrical therapy and increased doses of laudanum. What was the shocking secret that Cassie held in her dark tormented mind? And was she herself in danger?

CRYSTAL SHADOWS
by Michele Y. Thomas
(2819, $3.95)

When Teresa Hawthorne accepted a post as tutor to the wealthy Curtis family, she didn't believe the scandal surrounding them would be any concern of hers. However, it soon began to seem as if someone was trying to ruin the Curtises and Theresa was becoming the unwitting target of a deadly conspiracy . . .

CASTLE OF CRUSHED SHAMROCKS
by Lee Carr
(2843, $3.95)

Penniless and alone, eighteen-year-old Aileen O'Conner traveled to the coast of Ireland to be recognized as daughter and heir to Lord Edwin Lynhurst. Upon her arrival, she was horrified to find her long lost father had been murdered. And slowly, the extent of the danger dawned upon her: her father's killer was still at large. And her name was next on the list.

BRIDE OF HATFIELD CASTLE
by Beverly G. Warren
(2517, $3.95)

Left a widow on her wedding night and the sole inheritor of Hatfield's fortune, Eden Lane was convinced that someone wanted her out of the castle, preferably dead. Her failing health, the whispering voices of death, and the phantoms who roamed the keep were driving her mad. And although she came to the castle as a bride, she needed to discover who was trying to kill her, or leave as a corpse!

Available wherever paperbacks are sold, or order direct from the Publisher. Send cover price plus 50¢ per copy for mailing and handling to Zebra Books, Dept. 2851, 475 Park Avenue South, New York, N.Y. 10016. Residents of New York, New Jersey and Pennsylvania must include sales tax. DO NOT SEND CASH.

THE BEST IN HISTORICAL ROMANCES

TIME-KEPT PROMISES   (2422, $3.95)
by Constance O'Day Flannery

Sean O'Mara froze when he saw his wife Christina standing before him. She had vanished and the news had been written about in all of the papers—he had even been charged with her murder! But now he had living proof of his innocence, and Sean was not about to let her get away. No matter that the woman was claiming to be someone named Kristine; she still caused his blood to boil.

PASSION'S PRISONER   (2573, $3.95)
by Casey Stewart

When Cassandra Lansing put on men's clothing and entered the Rawlings saloon she didn't expect to lose anything—in fact she was sure that she would win back her prized horse Rapscallion that her grandfather lost in a card game. She almost got a smug satisfaction at the thought of fooling the gamblers into believing that she was a man. But once she caught a glimpse of the virile Josh Rawlings, Cassandra wanted to be the woman in his embrace!

ANGEL HEART   (2426, $3.95)
by Victoria Thompson

Ever since Angelica's father died, Harlan Snyder had been angling to get his hands on her ranch, the Diamond R. And now, just when she had an important government contract to fulfill, she couldn't find a single cowhand to hire—all because of Snyder's threats. It was only a matter of time before the legendary gunfighter Kid Collins turned up on her doorstep, badly wounded. Angelica assessed his firmly muscled physique and stared into his startling blue eyes. Beneath all that blood and dirt he was the handsomest man she had ever seen, and the one person who could help beat Snyder at his own game.

Available wherever paperbacks are sold, or order direct from the Publisher. Send cover price plus 50¢ per copy for mailing and handling to Zebra Books, Dept. 2851, 475 Park Avenue South, New York, N.Y. 10016. Residents of New York, New Jersey and Pennsylvania must include sales tax. DO NOT SEND CASH.

CATCH UP ON THE BEST IN CONTEMPORARY FICTION
FROM ZEBRA BOOKS!

LOVE AFFAIR (2181, $4.50)
by Syrell Rogovin Leahy

A poignant, supremely romantic story of an innocent young woman with a tragic past on her own in New York, and the seasoned newspaper reporter who vows to protect her from the harsh truths of the big city with his experience—and his love.

ROOMMATES (2156, $4.50)
by Katherine Stone

No one could have prepared Carrie for the monumental changes she would face when she met her new circle of friends at Stanford University. For once their lives intertwined and became woven into the tapestry of the times, they would never be the same.

MARITAL AFFAIRS (2033, $4.50)
by Sharleen Cooper Cohen

Everything the golden couple Liza and Jason Greene touched was charmed—except their marriage. And when Jason's thirst for glory led him to infidelity, Liza struck back in the only way possible.

RICH IS BEST (1924, $4.50)
by Julie Ellis

From Palm Springs to Paris, from Monte Carlo to New York City, wealthy and powerful Diane Carstairs plays a ruthless game, living a life on the edge between danger and decadence. But when caught in a battle for the unobtainable, she gambles with the only thing she owns that she cannot control—her heart.

THE FLOWER GARDEN (1396, $3.95)
by Margaret Pemberton

Born and bred in the opulent world of political high society, Nancy Leigh flees from her politician husband to the exotic island of Madeira. Irresistibly drawn to the arms of Ramon Sanford, the son of her father's deadliest enemy, Nancy is forced to make a dangerous choice between her family's honor and her heart's most fervent desire!

Available wherever paperbacks are sold, or order direct from the Publisher. Send cover price plus 50¢ per copy for mailing and handling to Zebra Books, Dept. 2851, 475 Park Avenue South, New York, N.Y. 10016. Residents of New York, New Jersey and Pennsylvania must include sales tax. DO NOT SEND CASH.